SPECIAL MESSAGE TO

THE ULVERSCROFT FO

(registered UK charity n
established in 1972 to provide fun...s for
research, diagnosis and treatment of eye diseases.
Examples of major projects funded by the
Ulverscroft Foundation are:

- The Children's Eye Unit at Moorfields Eye
  Hospital, London
- The Ulverscroft Children's Eye Unit at Great
  Ormond Street Hospital for Sick Children
- Funding research into eye diseases and treatment
  at the Department of Ophthalmology, University
  of Leicester
- The Ulverscroft Vision Research Group, Institute
  of Child Health
- Twin operating theatres at the Western Ophthalmic
  Hospital, London
- The Chair of Ophthalmology at the Royal
  Australian College of Ophthalmologists

You can help further the work of the Foundation
by making a donation or leaving a legacy. Every
contribution is gratefully received. If you would like
to help support the Foundation or require further
information, please contact:

THE ULVERSCROFT FOUNDATION
The Green, Bradgate Road, Anstey
Leicester LE7 7FU, England
Tel: (0116) 236 4325

website: www.ulverscroft-foundation.org.uk

FIRST STRIKE

MI5 officer David White was always a good father, so when his daughters want to go to a music festival in Israel, he agrees to take them. But his daughters are killed in the Hamas massacre that left 1,400 innocent civilians dead.

White is taken hostage down in the tunnels under Gaza and Dan 'Spider' Shepherd and a crack SAS team are sent in to rescue him.

Back in London, White is a changed man. He wants revenge for what happened to his family and wants to kill the men who planned and financed the Hamas attacks.

And as White embarks on a killing spree, Shepherd is the only man who can stop him.

STEPHEN LEATHER

FIRST STRIKE

Complete and Unabridged

LARGE
PRINT

ISIS
Leicester

First published in Great Britain in 2024

First Isis Edition
published 2024
by arrangement with
the author

*A catalogue record for this book is available
from the British Library.*

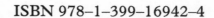

ISBN 978–1–399–16942–4

Published by
Ulverscroft Limited
Anstey, Leicestershire

Printed and bound in Great Britain by
TJ Books Ltd., Padstow, Cornwall

This book is printed on acid-free paper

1

The speedboat was cutting through the waves, leaving a white trail behind it that made it easy enough to spot from the air, even with the naked eye. It was heading north-west, towards the British coast. There were eight passengers, all wearing bright orange life jackets. Dan 'Spider' Shepherd was sitting in the cabin of an AgustaWestland AW109S Grand twin-engine, eight-seat multi-purpose helicopter. It was in civilian livery and had been chartered from a British company that often did work for MI5. The 109S had a top speed of close to two hundred miles an hour and it had no problems keeping the speedboat in sight as it left the Belgian coast.

The pilot was a former US Navy pilot, Steve Lepper, grey haired with a close cropped beard, who was looking over to his left as he kept the helicopter at two thousand feet, half a mile off the starboard side of the speedboat. 'How's this, Dan?' asked Lepper. He had lived in the UK for more than ten years but still had his Nebraskan accent. He was totally relaxed at the controls as if keeping the two ton helicopter in the air was no big thing. Shepherd knew enough about helicopters to appreciate just how much skill was involved just to make them fly straight and level. 'Perfect,' said Shepherd.

Sitting next to Shepherd was Jimmy 'Razor' Sharpe, a former Glaswegian cop who now worked for the National Crime Agency. Sharpe was peering at the boat through a pair of high powered binoculars. 'How fast are they going?' he growled. They were both wearing pale green noise cancelling headsets and spoke over the radio.

'Thirty knots, give or take,' said Shepherd.

'What's a knot?'

'It's that thing that stops your tie falling off your neck,' said Shepherd.

Sharpe took the binoculars away from his eyes. 'I've missed your sense of humour.'

'I do my best,' said Shepherd. 'So a knot is a unit of speed equal to one nautical mile per hour, which is pretty much 1.15 miles per hour.'

'So in real money, our guys are travelling at about thirty-three miles per hour?'

'Give or take. They should reach the UK in about an hour, depending on where they're aiming for.'

'Probably Broadstairs, right?'

'That's what Tuk says. But he's not sure. Which is why we're up here and not waiting for them in the UK.'

Sitting opposite them was Petrit Ajazi, an officer with Albania's State Intelligence Service, the equivalent of MI5. It went by the acronym SHISH, from the Albanian *Shërbimi Informativ I Shtetit*. Sharpe took great delight in referring to Ajazi and his colleagues as kebabs, and when Ajazi had asked what he meant, he had taken even more delight in explaining what a shish kebab was. Luckily Ajazi had seen the joke. It was Ajazi's man who was on the boat below, a police officer and former soldier by the name of Tuk Marku who had spent the last two years undercover penetrating the Italian arm of a gang that now controlled the drugs market in the south of England. Ajazi was short and stocky, his head shaved to reveal a rope-like

2

scar above his left ear that was now hidden behind his noise-cancelling earphones. He was wearing a distressed leather bomber jacket and tight jeans.

'Are you okay?' Shepherd asked Ajazi. The Albanian forced a smile and gave Shepherd a thumbs up. He had made it clear he wasn't a fan of helicopters, but it was the only way of keeping the speedboat under surveillance.

The boat had left a small Belgian coastal town called Blankenberge, which had a promenade facing a long sandy beach and a busy marina. The eight passengers had boarded on the Belgium Pier which stretched 350 metres out into the North Sea. The skipper was Albanian and he had made the trip to the UK more than a hundred times, getting passengers illegally into the country for ten thousand Euros a trip. He charged slightly more for the return journey, and there were plenty of people willing to pay to get out of the country without being clocked by Border Force.

The hundreds of illegal immigrants who cross the Channel every day in inflatable boats wanted to be intercepted by a Border Force vessel or an RNLI lifeboat, because it meant they would be safely taken to a UK port where they would be given a hot meal, a mobile phone and a four star hotel room. It was the culmination of a journey that would hopefully end with them being given a British passport. The passengers on the speedboat below didn't care for free phones, they simply needed to get into the country without anybody knowing. Usually the boat was filled with a mixture of nationalities, wealthy Pakistanis, Libyans, Syrians and Iranians happy to pay for the VIP service, but this trip was Albanian-only. All eight passengers belonged to the gang that Tuk Marku had infiltrated, the gang that operated the speedboat service. They had gathered at a hotel in Bruges early that morning and breakfasted together. The man in charge of the group had removed their mobile phones and used a portable metal detector to check for keys and wallets before the passengers were loaded into a windowless van and driven to Blankenberge. Only the man in charge knew where the speedboat would depart from, but only the skipper knew where it would arrive in the UK. The secrecy was the reason that the speedboat had never been intercepted, that and the fact that it could outrun all the Border Force vessels. Border Force operated a fleet of coastal patrol vessels — they had a range of just under three hundred miles when travelling at twenty knots with a crew of six, but their maximum speed was thirty two knots. Even fully loaded, the speedboat the Albanians used could hit forty-five knots.

The eight passengers were on their way to join the Albanian Hellbanianz gang, who had emerged from the council estates of East London to control the drugs market across South East England. Anyone buying heroin, cocaine or cannabis from Maidstone to Southampton was almost certainly buying from the gang. The gang was controlled by Fisnik Haziri, a forty-something giant of a man who went by the nickname 'Qofte', which meant meatball in Albanian. Haziri was six feet six inches tall and weighed close to three hundred pounds and had shoulder length jet black curly hair and a straggly beard. Despite his striking appearance, the NCA had never come close to arresting Haziri and his present whereabouts were unknown. He only ever dealt with other Albanians,

4

preferably those that he was related to, and rarely slept in the same place twice. The plan was for Marku to infiltrate Haziri's gang and to ultimately betray him.

Over the last decade, drug traffickers had turned Albania into a narcotics transit hub, bringing heroin into the country hidden in clothing and shoe imports brought in from Turkey and concealing cocaine from Colombia in shipments of bananas and palm oil. Gangs then loaded the drugs onto high-speed zodiac inflatable boats and took them to the Italian coast. And every day a dozen or so small planes flew drugs over the Adriatic to Italy, landing on small runways hidden in mountain valleys. Once in Italy, the Albanian Mafia could move their drugs around the EU with impunity, and it was a simple matter to get it across the Channel and into the United Kingdom. Under Haziri's leadership, the Hellbanianz gang now controlled almost half of the United Kingdom's £5 billion cocaine market. Putting him behind bars would be a major coup for MI5 and the NCA, though Shepherd was enough of a realist to know that within hours of Haziri being arrested, his place would be taken by someone else. The so-called war against drugs was a war that could never be won, no matter how many battles were fought.

The speedboat had kept in a straight line pretty much, and its heading would take it to Broadstairs, but Shepherd had a gut feeling that the vessel would at some point make a turn to starboard and head for Southend-on-Sea or one of the small ports nearby on the Essex coast. It was a much longer journey but there were far fewer checks and most of the Border Force vessels were concentrated around the Strait of Dover.

'Something's happening,' said Sharpe.

Shepherd picked up his binoculars and tried to focus on the speedboat. A man in a dark blue windbreaker had stood up and was facing the stern. 'Is that a gun?' asked Shepherd. The man was holding something in his right hand.

'I think so,' said Sharpe.

'Steve, can you get the camera on it?' asked Shepherd. The helicopter had two nose-mounted cameras, one with a powerful zoom lens, the other equipped for thermal imaging.

'Roger that,' said Lepper.

One of the passengers was standing up now. Shepherd couldn't see the man's face. 'Is that Tuk?' asked Shepherd. 'Petrit, are you seeing this?'

Ajazi had his binoculars to his eyes but was having trouble focussing on the boat. 'I can't see anything,' he grunted.

As Shepherd watched, the passenger removed his life jacket and dropped it onto the floor. Then the gun jerked in the man's hand and the passenger fell over the railing and into the sea.

'What the fuck?' shouted Sharpe. 'Did you see that? He just shot him.'

'Was it Tuk?' said Ajazi.

'I'm not sure,' said Sharpe. I think so. The guy with the gun made him take off his life jacket and then I'm not sure if the guy shot him and he fell, or if he jumped and the guy shot him as he jumped. It all happened so fast.'

'He's in the water,' said Lepper over the radio. 'I can see him.'

'We need to go down,' said Shepherd.

'We don't have a winch capability,' said the pilot.

6

'We're not equipped for a rescue.'

'Just get down there, Steve,' said Shepherd. 'Let me worry about that. Jimmy, keep eyes on him.'

'I didn't see anything,' said Ajazi. 'What's happening?'

'He's shot and in the water,' said Shepherd.

The helicopter tilted to the left and Shepherd's stomach lurched as it went into a steep descent. The manoeuvre caught Ajazi by surprise and he yelped and threw his hands in the air.

'I've got him,' said Sharpe.

'Is he alive?'

'I can't see, but he's there.'

The helicopter was in a steep dive now, but the turbines had throttled back. Shepherd saw the waves rushing towards them and he gritted his teeth. The pilot knew what he was doing, he was just taking the quickest route down, but it was still an unsettling experience. The dive continued until they were about a hundred feet above the waves at which point Lepper pulled up the nose and increased power to the turbines. Shepherd's stomach lurched again.

The Albanian grabbed a sick bag and threw up into it, the cabin was filled with the stench of vomit.

The helicopter steadied in a hover about ten feet above the waves. Shepherd grabbed the handle of the door and pulled it back. The downdraft from the rotor tugged at his hair and the salt water stung his eyes. He narrowed his eyes as he peered out and saw the man in the water, rising and falling with the waves. The swell was moving the body but Shepherd couldn't see if the man was alive or not.

He looked over at Ajazi but the Albanian had already ripped off his headset and unbuckled his seat

7

belt. Shepherd opened his mouth to shout a warning but before he could say anything, the Albanian had launched himself through the doorway. Shepherd stared in amazement as Ajazi disappeared under the water and then reappeared a second later, arms flailing.

Shepherd looked over at Sharpe and held out his hand but Sharpe shook his head. 'No way,' he said. 'I can't swim.'

'Your life vest is under your seat, give it to me.'

Sharpe bent down and pulled out a yellow pouch. Shepherd unbuckled his seat belt, pulled out the life vest from under his seat, then took off his headset. He stripped off his jacket and kicked off his boots.

'You have got to be joking!' shouted Sharpe but Shepherd couldn't hear him over the noise of the turbines.

Shepherd grabbed the pouch from Sharpe, pulled out the vest and hooked his arm through it. He did the same with his own life vest, then he took a deep breath and jumped out.

He hit the water feet first and immediately started kicking. The water was ice cold and he gasped, but he immediately clamped his mouth shut and squeezed his nostrils together as he went under. He kicked harder and his head burst through the surface. He gasped for air, and kicked again to keep his head up. He saw Ajazi and swam towards him. The downdraft from the helicopter was flattening the water around him and the roar of the turbines was deafening.

His wet clothes were dragging him down and he had to kick hard to stay up. He flailed his arms, dragging his way through the waves until he reached Ajazi. Ajazi had grabbed the injured man but was having

8

trouble staying afloat and waves were breaking over his bald head.

Shepherd grabbed the collar of Ajazi's jacket and pulled him around so that he could see the Albanian's face, then he pulled off one of the lifejackets and showed it to him. Ajazi nodded as he gasped for breath and he reached for it. Shepherd grabbed the other man and pulled his left arm through the second life jacket, then did the same with the right arm. He clipped the nylon strap across the man's chest and then he pulled the red cord to inflate the jacket. The man bobbed in the water. His eyes were closed but his lips were moving.

A wave washed over Shepherd's head and he gasped. His legs were burning now but he carried on kicking, it was the only thing that was stopping him from going under.

Ajazi was struggling with his life jacket so Shepherd helped him get it on before pulling the cord. The life jacket inflated and Ajazi bobbed up in the water.

Shepherd held Ajazi's lifejacket with his left hand and gripped the other man's vest with his right. He looked up, gasping for breath, and shook his wet hair from his eyes. The helicopter was about ten feet above his head, but it might as well have been a mile away, there was no way of reaching it. He roared in frustration.

A head appeared in the doorway. Jimmy Sharpe was shouting something but there was no way of hearing him above the roar of the turbines. Sharpe disappeared then the helicopter started to descend. Shepherd shook his head, trying to clear his eyes. The helicopter was moving slowly but it was definitely getting closer. The problem was there was nothing to grab onto except the wheels and they were a couple of feet below the hatch which is where Shepherd needed to be.

Ajazi was reaching up but he was wasting his energy. Even if he managed to grab a wheel he wouldn't be able to hold on to it.

The helicopter was just a few feet above the waves now. Ajazi kicked his legs and rose up out of the water. His fingers touched the wheel but then he fell back, screaming in frustration. Shepherd looked up, gasping for breath. He was exhausted and had lost the feeling in his legs. His chest was heaving and every breath was an effort. He looked over at Ajazi and he saw the look of helplessness in the Albanian's eyes. He was close to giving up.

Shepherd looked up again, blinking the saltwater from his eyes. Sharpe's head appeared again. He had taken off his headset. Sharpe held out something. Shepherd realised it was Sharpe's nylon holdall, the black nylon bag that had contained his clothes, wash-bag and a bottle of Glenfiddich Scotch whisky. The bag was empty now and Sharpe had extended the carrying strap so that it was fully out. Shepherd grinned. 'Nice one, Razor,' he thought, but he was too tired to say it out loud. He looked over at Ajazi and pointed at the helicopter. The Albanian looked up and saw the bag. He snarled and reached for it, kicking with legs and stretching his fingers out. He caught the bag and grabbed it with both hands. The helicopter dipped another couple of feet and Sharpe began pulling. Ajazi pulled himself out of the water, still kicking his legs. The helicopter dropped another foot, its wheels almost touching the water, and Sharpe pulled harder. Ajazi managed to get a foot up onto one of the wheels and he pushed himself up. Sharpe grabbed his life jacket and hauled him in. Shepherd saw Ajazi's boots disappear through the hatch as the helicopter rose up into the air again.

Shepherd had both hands on the injured man's lifejacket now. The man's eyes were still closed and Shepherd couldn't tell if he was breathing or not.

Sharpe appeared again, holding out the bag. The helicopter descended and the turbines roared. The bag dropped lower and Shepherd reached up with his right hand to grab it. Sharpe leaned further out of the helicopter. Presumably Ajazi was holding on to his legs. A team effort.

Shepherd managed to get the bag over the injured man's head and he pulled the straps under his arms. Sharpe heaved on the strap, then Ajazi appeared next to him and together they pulled the man up. As Shepherd released his grip on the man, he realised he was now on his own with no lifejacket and reaching the end of his energy reserves. He was exhausted and every breath was an effort. He watched as the man was hauled in and the helicopter rose into the air again.

He had lost all feeling in his legs now and he was shivering from the cold. His brain was telling him that he was still kicking but there was no sensation, just numbness. He was using his arms to keep his head out of the water but waves kept washing over his head. His eyes and nose were burning from the saltwater and he was coughing and spluttering. It would be the easiest thing just to close his eyes and sink beneath the waves, but he gritted his teeth and forced himself to keep moving, even though he had almost no energy left.

The helicopter was about thirty feet above him now and he wondered if they were going to leave him, but then it started to descend again and the down-wash flattened the waves around him. Sharpe's head appeared, then Ajazi joined him, and together they lowered the bag towards him. The helicopter seemed to be moving in slow motion, It was taking forever and the bag was still out of reach. Then the helicopter turbines increased in pitch roared louder and the helicopter dropped so close that one of the wheels almost clipped his head. Then the bag was in front of him and he grabbed it with both hands. A massive wave washed over him and he choked as the saltwater filled his mouth. He was still coughing and retching as Sharpe and Ajazi pulled together, dragging him out of the freezing water and into the cabin of the helicopter.

As soon as Shepherd's feet were inside, Sharpe pulled the door shut and the helicopter began to climb into the air.

The injured man was lying on the floor, face down, and watery blood was pooling around his chest. Ajazi was sitting next to him, exhausted.

Shepherd climbed onto one of the seats, gasping for breath. Sharpe patted him on the shoulder and grinned. 'You're welcome,' he said.

Shepherd couldn't help but laugh.

Sharpe looked down at Ajazi and nodded at the injured man. 'We need to roll him over,' he said.

Ajazi nodded and got up on to his knees. Sharpe leaned forward and together they rolled the injured man on to his back. There was a bullet wound in the man's left shoulder.

Shepherd stood up to get a better look. 'There's

no exit wound so the round is still in there,' he said. 'We need to put something over the wound and apply pressure.'

The contents of Sharpe's holdall were strewn across one of the seats. Shepherd picked up a pair of boxer shorts and held them up. 'Are they clean?'

'Of course they're clean? What do you think I am?'

'They'll be fine.'

Shepherd gave the shorts to Ajazi. Ajazi was still gasping for breath as he stared at the man on the floor of the helicopter, his chest rising and falling. 'That's . . . not . . . Tuk,' he said.

2

Steve Lepper flew the helicopter to the William Harvey Hospital in Ashford, Kent. The hospital had close to six hundred beds and a 24-hour Accident and Emergency Department, and it had the added advantage of a helicopter landing pad.

Ajazi kept the boxers pressed against the wound of the injured man, who was still breathing, but shallowly, and his eyes remained closed. He was in his late twenties, with a thick moustache and eyebrows that almost met above a hooked nose. Ajazi had no idea who the man was, but he knew it wasn't Tuk Marku.

Lepper had radioed ahead and as they touched down on the landing pad, two paramedics ran forward with a trolley. 'Gunshot wound, left shoulder, no exit wound,' said Shepherd. 'He was in the sea for fifteen minutes.'

'What's his name?' asked one of the paramedics as they pulled him out of the helicopter.

'Sorry, we don't know,' said Shepherd.

The paramedics laid him on the trolley and rushed him away.

They had trollies for Shepherd and Ajazi, but they both insisted on walking into the Accident and Emergency Department. Sharpe carried the bags. His own holdall was soaking wet so he'd put his clothes, washbag and whisky into Shepherd's bag.

A nurse took blood pressure and pulse readings from Shepherd and Ajazi, but other than the fact they were still shivering from the exposure to the freezing water she pronounced them fit and well. She found towels for them and pointed them towards the bath-room where they stripped off their wet clothes, showered, then dried themselves off and changed into clean clothes.

Sharpe was waiting for them when they came out of the bathroom. 'The guy's out of danger, they took out the bullet and stitched him up. He'd lost a lot of blood so they've given him plasma or whatever they give them, and he's as well as can be expected.'

'No ID, obviously?' said Shepherd.

'No, and he hasn't given them a name. Claims he can't speak English. I explained that we have an Alba-nian speaker and they're happy enough for us to go in and speak to him. The pilot wants to know what we want to do with the chopper.'

'He's on the clock and we have him for the rest of the day,' said Shepherd. 'Let's see what the story is with his guy before we decide what to do.'

Sharpe took them up to the third floor and along to a single room. 'I explained this is an NCA case and he's a suspect in a major crime, so we've got him in a room on his own.'

He opened the door. The man was lying in bed, connected to a machine measuring his heart rate and blood pressure. A line from a plasma bag wound its way to the man's right arm. The man's left wrist was handcuffed to the bed frame. 'They weren't happy about the handcuffs, but I insisted,' said Sharpe.

'Probably best,' said Shepherd. 'He'll probably run the first chance he gets.'

The man opened his eyes. He frowned when he saw the three of them standing by the door.

Ajazi spoke to the man in Albanian and the man

15

replied. 'I was just telling him not to worry, that we're the ones who saved him,' Ajazi said to Shepherd. 'Let me have a chat with him, see where we stand.'

'Sure. Do you want us to wait outside?'

'It might make him feel less under pressure,' said Ajazi. 'I don't think we'll need to play Good Cop, Bad Cop with him, not after what happened.'

'There's a food court on the ground floor, we'll wait for you there,' said Sharpe.

Shepherd and Sharpe took the lift down to the ground floor and walked to a table. Sharpe was carrying the bags. Shepherd's body temperature was back to normal but he was still dog tired. He dropped down at a table while Sharpe put the bags on a chair and went to get their food. He returned after a few minutes with two mugs of coffee, two bacon rolls and two plates of chips. Shepherd grinned. 'I see you went for the healthy option.'

'After what you did out there in the Channel, I don't think you need to worry about your cholesterol levels,' laughed Sharpe as he sat down. He unzipped Shepherd's bag, looked around and then took out the bottle of Glenfiddich. He unscrewed the top and poured a slug of whisky into his coffee mug, then he held the bottle over Shepherd's mug. 'It's medicinal,' he said.

Shepherd chuckled. 'What the hell, I've earned it.'

Sharpe poured whisky into Shepherd's mug, then screwed the top back on the bottle and put it into the holdall

Shepherd sipped his fortified coffee and felt the warmth of the alcohol spread across his chest.

'So what do we do about Tuk?' asked Sharpe, picking up his bacon roll.

'There's nothing we can do, other than to wait for him to contact Petrit. The plan was to see where the passengers went, but that's obviously dead in the water — no pun intended. They took all means of communication off the passengers before they boarded and the metal detector meant we couldn't use any sort of tracking device, so the ball is now in Tuk's court.'

They were just finishing their chips when Ajazi appeared. He hurried over to their table and sat down. 'His name is Redjon Plauku, he's worked for the Hell-banianz gang in Italy but they wanted to move him to London. He has a criminal record in Italy so he can't pass through a UK airport, so they got him a seat on the boat. But then they accused him of being a police informer.'

'Had they seen the helicopter?' asked Shepherd.

'No, it was nothing to do with the helicopter,' said Ajazi. 'A consignment entering Italy was intercepted last night, and for some reason they blamed him.'

'Why?'

'Very few people knew about the plane that was bringing the drugs in. The Hellbanianz gang work in small cells, information isn't widely shared.' Ajazi lowered his voice as if he feared being overheard. 'Tuk also knew of the consignment, he told me about it a few days ago, the last time I spoke to him. I owed a contact in the Central Directorate for Anti-Drug Services a favour so I passed the intel to him.' He grimaced. 'So this is my fault, I'm sorry.'

'You weren't to know,' said Shepherd. 'But if anything it works in our favour. They think that Plauku is the informer which hopefully means that the pressure is now off Tuk. The fact that we pulled him from

17

the sea will convince them that we were rescuing our man. And if Plauku has any sense, he'll turn informer now.'

'I've told him that, and if we can guarantee the safety of his family, he'll cooperate. He wants to know if he and his family can move to England.'

'I can ask,' said Shepherd. 'A lot will depend on how helpful he can be and how much hard evidence he can provide. I can definitely talk to my bosses. But in terms of putting Haziri behind bars, Tuk is still our best bet. When do you expect to hear from him again?'

Ajazi took out his mobile phone. 'He'll call me on this, but it's not working after it went in the sea.'

'I'll get you a new one. The SIM card should be okay. Is he supposed to check in every day?'

'Only when it's safe,' said Ajazi. 'His safety is paramount.'

'So what are your plans until then?'

'I'll check into a hotel close to the hospital. I'll stay here as long as they'll let me. In view of the fact that Plauku says he'll cooperate, can you arrange security?'

'Jimmy can do that through the NCA.'

He looked over at Sharpe and Sharpe nodded. 'Yeah, I'll get right on it. And I'll stay here for the duration. What about you?'

'I'll head back to London with the heli. Not much else I can do until Tuk makes contact.' He looked at Ajazi. 'Were they trying to kill him on the boat or did they just want him in the water?'

'He says they were going to shoot him but he jumped. If he'd stayed on the boat he'd have been dead for sure.' Ajazi held out his hand. 'Thank you for this. For everything.'

Shepherd smiled and shook his hand. 'We just want

18

to put Hazri where he belongs, and shut down as much of the Hellbanianz gang as we can.'

'You saved my life, Dan. I jumped into the water without thinking. If you hadn't come in after me, I would have drowned.'

'No, you were thinking you had to save a man's life, that's why you jumped in. Admittedly you thought you were trying to save Tuk, but that's not the point. Not many men would have done what you did.'

Ajazi grinned. 'Right back at you.' He stood up and motioned for Shepherd to do the same.

Shepherd got to his feet, unsure of what was happening.

Ajazi walked around the table, pulled Shepherd close to him, and hugged him tight. Then he released his grip and patted him on the back, hard. 'We are brothers now.'

'I guess we are,' said Shepherd.

3

David White woke to the sound of air raid sirens. He opened his eyes and frowned as he struggled to get his bearings. There was blue nylon above his head, rippling in a breeze, and not the bedroom ceiling that he had been expecting. He looked at his watch, blinking to get it into focus. It was just before six-thirty. He smiled as he remembered where he was. Camping. With his daughters in the next tent. White never really enjoyed camping but Hannah and Ella had nagged him to take them to the open air music festival, begged, pleaded and cajoled until he'd agreed. Their mother hadn't been so easy to persuade and she had stayed behind in Tel Aviv with her parents.

He sat up, rubbing his eyes and looked at his watch again. Was it a drill? He'd heard the air raid sirens go off twice while he'd been in Tel Aviv, and both times they had been drills. He stood up. He was wearing a blue Cambridge University sweatshirt and baggy grey jogging pants. He padded barefoot to the tent opening and peered out. He saw azure blue sky and wisps of white cloud. And dozens of young people standing around, most of them holding their phones. He walked the four steps to his daughters' tent and patted on it. 'Hannah? Ella? Are you awake?'

'Of course we're awake,' said Hannah from inside. 'Can't you hear those sirens?'

'Get dressed, just in case it isn't a drill.'

'Where are we going to go, dad? We're in the middle of the desert.'

White smiled. She had a point. By law, all homes, residential buildings and industrial buildings had to have bomb shelters. But they were at the Supernova Sukkot Gathering and bomb shelters hadn't been on the list of facilities available. The music festival had been thrown together at short notice. It had originally been planned for a venue in the south of Israel but had been switched to the grounds of the Re-im kibbutz, just three miles from the Gaza Strip, the narrow strip of land between Israel and Egypt that was home to more than two million Palestinians. It was basically a rave, packed with DJs that White had never heard of, but Hannah and Ella had known most of them and it became a matter of life and death for them to go. White was still at the stage of wanting to build memories with his daughters so had agreed to take them. They had arrived the previous day and pitched their tents in the camp ground, a hundred yards from a line of portable toilets that stretched across a field. There were three stages for the bands and DJs to perform on, and a food and beverage area with a large bar. There were almost four thousand people there, most of them aged between twenty and thirty, though there were a lot of teenagers around. The police were there in force, along with a large contingent of security guards, but everyone White had met had been good humoured and friendly.

The music wasn't anything that White would listen to by choice, so he had spent much of the time in the bar, sipping beer and sharing parenting stories with other fathers on memory-building duty.

'Just get out here while we work out what we're going to do,' said White.

A group of teenagers began shouting excitedly and

began pointing their phones up at the sky. White shielded his eyes and looked up. High above something metallic was streaking through the sky leaving a white trail in its wake. A missile. White was never good at judging distances but it looked to be several thousand feet in the air. It looked as if it had been fired from the Gaza Strip, which was just three miles to the west. So far as White could tell, it was heading north, towards Tel Aviv. White scanned across the sky. He saw another white trail. And another. As he slowly turned he realised that there were dozens of missiles, all heading north. Tel Aviv was just a hundred kilometres away and the Israeli capital, Jerusalem, was even closer.

Missile attacks were an ever present risk in Israel, a country that was surrounded by enemies. Protection came in the form of the Iron Dome, a network of anti-missile batteries that used radar to detect incoming rockets and intercept them. Manufactured by the US Raytheon company, the systems were able to detect if an incoming rocket was going to attack a populated area. If it wasn't, if it was headed towards the open sea or an open area, then it would be allowed on its way. If there was the possibility of casualties then the system fired a missile to intercept and destroy the rocket. Iron Dome was supported by the David's Sling system, also manufactured by Raytheon, which was designed to intercept and destroy enemy planes, drones, tactical ballistic missiles and cruise missiles but with three times the range of Iron Dome. The systems were so effective that fewer than five per cent of Hamas missiles fired at Israel ever reached their target. That didn't stop the terror group from trying, though.

'Hannah, Ella! Come on, get out here!' he called. He had lost count of how many trails there were. Certainly dozens.

'Don't burst a blood vessel, dad,' said Hannah scornfully. The tent flap opened and she stepped out, blonde hair unkempt, wearing a black hoodie and black cargo pants. She was going through a black phase, not quite Goth yet but heading that way. She saw that everyone around her was looking up at the sky and she followed suit, using both hands to shade her eyes. 'What are they, dad, planes?' Hannah, like her sister, had been born and bred in London. This was their first trip to Israel and White and his wife had played down the terrorism risk, and he certainly hadn't told them that from time to time the Hamas terror group fired missiles across the border.

'No, they're missiles. You've heard of Hamas, right?'

'The spread they make from chickpeas? Of course.' White opened his mouth to reply but she laughed and shook her head. 'Of course I've heard of Hamas, dad.' Her face turned serious. 'Oh my God. Missiles? Like rockets? Bombs?'

White nodded. 'I'm afraid so,'

She pulled her phone from a pocket on her thigh. 'I've got to get this on Insta and SnapChat,' she said.

White looked up at the sky again. There were maybe a hundred trails now, all heading north.

Hannah held her phone up, trying to catch a shot of her face with missiles in the background. She moved the phone around, then pouted as she took picture after picture. 'Are you serious?' he said.

'What's happening, dad?' asked Ella, emerging from the tent, wearing just a t-shirt and cut-off jeans.

She had just turned thirteen but still dressed carelessly and for comfort, not realising that men were starting to look at her. She was pretty, with a cute snub nose and mischievous eyes, still a child but all the signs were that she was going to be a stunner, like her mum.

'Sweatshirt and jeans,' he said to her, pointing inside the tent.

'These are jeans,' she pouted.

'Don't argue, jeans with legs. Now.'

Ella sighed theatrically and ducked back into the tent.

The sirens were still wailing but nobody seemed in a hurry to leave the campsite. There would be air raid shelters in the nearby kibbutz but from the height of the missiles it didn't look as if there was any immediate danger.

Hannah had switched to video mode, presumably taking the view that a Hamas missile attack was a Tik-Tok moment. White looked around. Thousands of people were now out of the tents, looking at the sky, most of them holding cellphones. Security guards were waving their arms and pointing towards the kibbutz, but nobody seemed to be following their instructions.

'Ella, get the binoculars for me, will you?'

'The what?'

'The binoculars. Quick.'

There was another sigh from Ella. 'What did your last servant die of?'

'Just do it,' snapped White. 'And get dressed, quickly.'

The flap opened again. Ella was wearing a Harry Styles sweatshirt and baggy jeans and holding a pair of binoculars.

White took them from her and scanned the sky.

'What's happening?' she said.

'Rockets,' said Hannah, pointing upwards.

Ella squinted at the sky. 'Like fireworks?'

'Missiles,' said Hannah.

'Wow, cool,' said Ella as she saw the white streaks. She pulled out her phone.

'Guys, this is serious,' said White. 'Those rockets are Ayyash long range surface-to-surface missiles, they can take out targets 250 kilometres away. They're not selfie opportunities.'

Hannah frowned. 'When did you become an expert on Hamas missiles?' she said.

'I read the papers,' he said. In fact he knew that the Ayyash warhead weighed close to six hundred kilograms and contained prefabricated shrapnel that created a six hundred metre killing zone on detonation. It was based on Iran's Zelzai 3B rocket and had the capability of striking any target in Israel if fired from Gaza. He also knew that it was named after Yahya Ayyash, a notorious Hamas Bombmaker who was responsible for the deaths of dozens of Israelis before he was assassinated in 1996, but he wasn't going to share that information with his daughters.

He scrutinised the sky. There were maybe more than a hundred missiles in the sky now. But they were all high and streaking north, away from where they were. But this was big. Very big.

'Grab your gear, girls,' he said. 'Leave the tents and the beds, just take your bags.'

'Dad, we're not leaving,' said Ella. 'There's a whole day of concerts. Astral Projection are on later. We're not . . .'

White put up a warning finger. 'Stop talking and don't argue. This isn't a joke, Ella. Do as you're told. Grab your stuff and we'll head over to the kibbutz and use one of their shelters.'

'Fine,' said Ella, and she ducked back into the tent.

'Dad, are we in danger?' asked Hannah quietly.

'Just better safe than sorry,' said White. 'Those missiles are heading far away, but that many is very unusual. I'd just be happier if we were in a shelter.' He forced a smile. 'Don't worry, the Israelis have a very efficient system to deal with missile attacks.'

'Shall I call mum?'

White shook his head. 'There's no need to worry her,' he said. 'We'll be fine. Just grab your things and we'll go to the kibbutz.'

He put the binoculars back to his eyes and scanned the sky again. More missiles. A lot more. Hundreds now. Definitely hundreds. The sky was covered with white trails. He turned slowly towards Gaza, where the missiles were coming from. Something flashed into view and was gone. Like a large bird. He searched for it again with his binoculars but could't find it. He took the binoculars away and shaded his eyes with his right hand. There was something flying lower than the missiles, a lot lower, like a huge soaring bird. It was moving slowly but purposefully, towards the kibbutz. He spotted a second shape, and a third. He blinked his eyes, trying to focus, and when he looked again he could make out half a dozen of the shapes, less than a thousand feet in the air. He put the binoculars back to his eyes and pointed them in the direction of the shapes. One came into focus and his breath caught in his throat. It was a motorised paraglider, with two men sitting on a tricycle below a black chute,

26

powered by a large propellor behind them. The man in front was holding a Kalashnikov assault rifle.

He swung the binoculars to the right. Another paraglider. Two more men. With Kalashnikovs.

'Hannah, Ella, change of plan! In the car, now!'

'I'm still packing!' shouted Ella.

White ripped back the tent flap. Both girls were kneeling on the ground, shoving clothes into their rucksacks. 'In the car, now! No arguing. Now.'

Hannah opened her mouth to argue but when she saw the look of concern on his face she just nodded and stood up. She put her hand on her sister's shoulder. 'Come on,' she said.

White held the tent flap open for them as they hurried out clutching their rucksacks. Their rented Kia EV6 SUV was behind White's tent. He opened the rear door and helped them push in their rucksacks. White heard the crack-crack-crack of an assault rifle being fired off in the distance.

'What's happening, dad?' asked Hannah, looking over her shoulder, her voice trembling.

'Just get in the car honey,' said White, his mind racing. His first thought had been to seek sanctuary in the kibbutz, but it might make more sense to get on the road and put as much distance as they could between themselves and the attackers. There was no way of knowing how many of them there were, but the fact that they were using motorised paragliders suggested that a lot of planning had gone into the attack.

Hannah ran around to the front passenger door and pulled it open. Ella got into the back. Off in the distance there were more shots, and screams. People were running now. Some were frantically getting into their cars and others were running towards the orchards that bordered the campground.

White flinched at the sound of louder shots, a machine gun being fired on fully automatic.

He looked up and saw a paraglider, just a few hundred feet away. The front passenger was firing his Kalashnikov at the crowds below. He had a black and white keffiyeh scarf wrapped around the lower part of his face.

'Dad!' shouted Hannah. 'Come on!'

White flinched as if he had been slapped. He rushed to the driver's side, pulled open the door and climbed in.

'Hurry!' shouted Hannah, looking over her shoulder. 'They're coming!'

White started the engine and put the SUV in gear.

'Dad, go! Please go!'

White's eyes flashed to the rear view mirror. Two men with black and white scarves over their faces had driven onto the campsite on a trail bike. The pillion passenger was holding a Kalashnikov and firing it into the crowds. White saw a teenage girl's face implode, and another scream as a bullet hit her in the shoulder.

Hannah scrambled back into her seat and grabbed for her seatbelt as White stamped on the accelerator but as the SUV leapt forward a red Honda appeared ahead of them, driven by a panic-stricken woman, White had to brake hard to avoid hitting her. Hannah wasn't wearing her seatbelt and she yelped as she fell against the dashboard and slid down into the footwell. Ella also hadn't been wearing her seat belt and she crashed against the back of White's seat.

White looked at the rear view mirror. He couldn't see the terrorists on the motorbike but he could hear the crack-crack-crack of the Kalashnikov. There was more gunfire off to the right, and more screams. Hundreds of people were now running away from the campsite, many of them heading for the orchards.

The Honda went by and White accelerated and followed it. There was gunfire all around them now.

Then a shadow passed over the SUV and there was the deafening crack of a Kalashnikov being fired from above. A paraglider passed over them like a giant hawk swooping in for the kill. The front passenger was spraying bullets, firing on fully automatic. Blood splattered teenagers were falling to the ground, some clearly dead, others screaming in pain.

Hannah was staring at the carnage through the side window. White patted her on the leg. 'Keep looking straight ahead, honey,' he said.

Dozens of cars were now trying to leave the camp ground. Off to the left was the main parking area where there were hundreds of vehicles, cars, trucks, coaches and minibuses. Panicked festival goers were running to their vehicles but there were already queues on the two tracks leading to the highway.

Another motorcycle roared by, the passenger waving his Kalashnikov in the air and screaming 'Allahu Akbar!'

Two pick-up trucks approached from the right, running through tents and scattering festival goers. There were masked terrorists on the back of each truck, armed with Kalashnikovs, handguns and machetes.

A uniformed policeman was firing at one of the trucks but he only managed to get off a few rounds before he was mown down by a hail of Kalashnikov fire.

29

'Daddy . . .' wailed Ella from the back seat.

'It's okay honey, don't worry,' said White, but he knew his words meant nothing. There was a lot to worry about, and as he looked around at the carnage he had a sick feeling in the pit of his stomach that he was locked into a situation with no means of escape.

Panicking drivers were pounding on their horns. They were moving forward at walking pace. Cars were driving across the sandy ground and trying to force their way in the queue. White peered at the highway. It was relatively clear and dozens of cars were speeding both ways, north and south. He bent forward and peered upwards. There were now hundreds of vapour trails criss-crossing the sky, most streaking north but there did appear to be others heading east. The rockets that Hamas were using could reach any city or town in Israel. The Iron Dome and the David's Sling system would neutralise the vast majority of the attacks, but there was a chance that some would get through. It was the scale of the attack that was so worrying. Hamas fired missiles all year round, but White had never heard of an attack on this scale. And the trucks meant that the defences around the Gaza Strip must have been breached. That and the paragliders meant this wasn't just a terrorist attack, this was the start of a war.

The army — the Israel Defence Forces — would respond but it would take time and until they arrived the festival goers were at the mercy of the terrorists. All they could do was run and hide, though the terrain was flat and other than the orchards there was nowhere that offered concealment. As he looked over at the orchard to the left, he could see some festival goers climbing trees, as if that would keep them from harm.

There was firing going on all around them now. A paraglider landed in the car park, the chute deflating behind it as it came to a halt. The passenger jumped off and began firing. He shot three teenagers in the back and they pitched forward, their shirts a bloody mess. The man who had been flying the paraglider got to his feet and unslung a rifle on his back. He put it to his shoulder and began shooting. He was aiming at a small boy who couldn't have been more than eight or nine years old, who was running with a woman, her long brown hair trailing behind her. The shots missed, kicking up puffs of sand around the boy's bare feet. The woman bent down and scooped the boy up. She began running with the boy in her arms, but the shooter took aim and shot her in the back, right between the shoulder blades. She fell and the boy tumbled from her arms. His shirt was wet with blood and White realised that the bullet had gone through the woman and into the boy, killing them both.

'Dad!' screamed Hannah, her hands over her face.

'It's okay honey,' said White, but again he realised his words were meaningless. It was far from okay.

Another motorcycle appeared to their left, bucking up and down on the uneven ground. For a moment White locked eyes with the passenger, who had a black and white scarf shielding his nose and mouth. The brown eyes were glaring with anger and hatred and the man swung up his Kalashnikov but by then the bike had wizzed by.

The bike came to a halt about fifty yards away, then it toppled over and both men fell to the ground. The passenger was up first. 'Allahu Akbar!' he screamed and began firing at a white SUV. The windows shattered and there were screams that were almost immediately cut short. White could see four or five figures slumped in the vehicle. The man kept firing. Clouds of steam began to billow from under the bonnet.

The man was on his feet now and he pulled a handgun from a holster on his waist. He moved to the car behind the white SUV. The driver's side door opened and a woman in a denim dress got out, screaming. The man fired at her. The first shot missed but he fired again and this time the top of her head blew away and she fell to the ground. The rear door opened and three teenage boys climbed out. The man shot one of them in the chest and the man with the Kalashnikov mowed down the other two.

None of the cars were moving now and White knew that if they stayed where they were they would be sitting ducks.

'Girls, listen to me,' said White, trying to keep his voice calm. 'We're going to have to get out of the car and run to the orchard. Stay in front of me and no matter what you see or hear, you keep running.'

'We can't go out there, dad,' said Hannah fearfully. 'They're shooting people.'

The man with the handgun had moved down the queue of cars towards them. He stopped, held the gun with both hands and began firing at a silver Toyota.

'We can't use the car, we have to go,' said White. 'Hannah get out and I'll climb over. Ella, get out of Hannah's side, okay? As soon as you get out, crouch down low and wait for me.'

The girls were sobbing now.

'Girls, come on! Now! Do it!'

Hannah fumbled for the door handle and pushed the door open. She immediately went down on all fours. White straddled the centre console and wiggled over into the passenger seat. Ella opened her door and joined Hannah on the ground. The sound of shooting was much louder now that the doors were open, and White could smell the gunsmoke in the air.

'Okay, girls, listen to me.' He waited until the girls were looking at him before pointing back down the line of cars. 'We need to go that way. See that minibus, we're going to go behind that and then we run as fast as we can towards the wall around the campground. There's an orchard on the other side of the wall.' He flinched as a Kalashnikov fired on fully automatic. It sounded as if it was only a few yards away, so close that when the firing stopped his ears were buzzing.

'Right, go,' he said.

The two girls shuffled along the line of cars, bent at the waist, Ella in front and Hannah sticking close to her. They reached the minibus. There were half a dozen teenagers in the back, most of them filming on their phones. The driver, a man in his fifties, was shouting at them but White couldn't hear what he was saying over the sound of the sirens and shooting. They went around the back of the minivan. Hannah put a hand on Ella's shoulder. 'Wait,' she said, peering to the right. White joined her. The men who had been on the motorcycle were still shooting at the cars in the queue.

'We have to run,' said White.'

'They'll shoot us,' said Hannah tearfully.

'They're looking at the cars, they won't see you,' said White. 'Just run to the orchard, I'll be right behind you. Don't stop and don't look around, just keep your eyes on the wall and run until you get there. Okay?'

Ella was shaking and her eyes had gone blank. White put his hands on either side of her face. 'Ella, honey, we have to do this,' he said. 'I know it's scary but we can get through this. Okay?'

'Okay,' she said, her voice trembling.

White kissed her on the forehead. He looked at Hannah, who had covered her ears with her hands. 'Hannah, honey, we have to go.' The firing was getting closer now. A shadow passed over them. Another paraglider.

White stood up, though he kept his head down. He took an arm each and pulled them to their feet. 'Go,' he said, turning them towards the orchard. They didn't move. 'Go!' he shouted and pushed them forward.

The girls began to run, their arms pumping furiously, their hair whipping behind them. White followed, keeping close, trying to shield them from the men shooting at the cars.

Hannah looked around to see where White was and she tripped and fell. White picked her up. Her face was streaked with tears. Ella had stopped and White shouted at her to keep running. He put his arm around Hannah's shoulders. 'Come on, you can do this,' he said. 'Imagine you're at the school sports day. Just run as fast as you can and don't look back.' She nodded tearfully but didn't move. White turned her around and pushed her after Ella. 'Run!' he shouted. Hannah finally did as she was told.

The paraglider flared and landed off to their left, then pitched forward sending the pilot and the passenger sprawling. The passenger rolled out from under the canopy and put his Kalashnikov to his shoulder. He began firing at the line of cars, screaming 'Allahu Akbar!' at the top of his voice.

White ran after his daughters, putting his body between them and the shooter. A second Kalashnikov began firing, probably the paraglider pilot. He heard screams of terror which were cut short by a burst of automatic fire. White took a quick look over his shoulder. A family had climbed out of a people carrier and the shooters had mown them down.

In the distance a group of Hamas fighters, their faces hidden behind scarves, were dragging two young girls towards a pick-up truck. One of the girls was screaming and two of the fighters lifted her off the ground and threw her into the back of the vehicle.

Ella screamed and White turned to look at her. A motorcycle with two Hamas fighters was roaring towards her, bucking and rocking over the rough ground. The passenger was firing his Kalashnikov into the sky and brass cartridges spewed from the weapon and spun through the air. The rider was bent over the handlebars, his lips twisted into a savage sneer. White bent down, picked up a tennis ball sized rock and threw it with all his might at the bike. The rider saw the rock coming and twisted the handlebars to the right. The rock hit him on the shoulder and the handlebars started swinging from side to side as he fought to get the bike under control.

Ella had stopped running so White put his arm around her. 'Come on!' he shouted.

The bike stopped and the rider and passenger climbed off. The passenger already had his Kalashnikov in his hands and he swung it towards White. White stared at the man in horror but he continued to run. Just as the man pulled the trigger a teenage girl ran in front of him and the bullets ripped through her chest. Her arms flailed and her dress turned red and she whirled around as she fell to the ground.

'Run, Ella!' shouted White. He moved so that he was behind her and matched her speed. 'Good girl, you're doing fine,' he gasped. His lungs and throat were burning now and his legs felt like lead. Hannah was ahead of them, her arms pumping as she ran. Ahead of them was the stone wall that ran around the orchard of orange trees. There was a gate off to their left but it was being guarded by a red pick-up truck. There were three scarf-wearing Hamas fighters in the back, firing single shots from their Kalashnikovs. The campground was littered with dozens of bodies, now. Hundreds maybe. It was a massacre, White realised, a coordinated attack that had obviously been well planned and executed.

Hannah slowed as she reached the wall, not sure which way to go. The wall was just over six feet tall, but they had no choice other than to go over it. White linked his fingers together and bent down so that Hannah could use him to clamber up the wall. He pushed her up and she grabbed at the top and then went over.

'Right, Ella, your turn,' he said, linking his hands again and bending down. Ella's cheeks were wet with tears and her lower lip was trembling. He forced a smile. 'Up and over, honey,' he said. 'You can do it.'

There was the rat-tat-tat of automatic fire off to their left and Ella flinched.

'Over you go, Ella. Don't worry, Hannah's on the other side.'

Ella wiped her eyes with the back of her hand,

nodded, and placed her left foot into his hands. He grunted and pushed her up and she reached out to grab the top of the wall.

White heard the crack of a Kalashnikov behind him and Ella jerked. There was a second crack and Ella jerked again. She fell back on top of White and they both crashed to the ground. White pushed himself up and wailed in anguish when he saw the two massive holes in Ella's chest, filling with blood. She was still alive, but only just, and as he reached for her hand her eyes went blank and her chest stopped moving.

The Kalashnikov fired again and a bullet smacked into the wall above White's head. He stared in dismay at his daughter, his breath caught in his throat. He wanted to help her, to save her, but it was too late, there was nothing he could do.

'Dad, what's happening?' shouted Hannah from the other side of the wall. White looked around, panic gripping his heart. The man who had shot Ella was grinning in triumph. 'Allahu Akbar!' he screamed, and pointed the Kalashnikov at White.

White reacted instinctively, twisting around and throwing himself up the wall. His hands grabbed the top and as he pulled himself up he heard the crack-crack-crack of the Kalashnikov and bullets smacked into the wall to his left. The adrenaline coursing through his system gave him a strength he never realised he had and he hauled himself up and over the wall. The Kalashnikov fired again as he fell to the ground and smashed into the dirt.

'Where's Ella?' screamed Hannah. 'Dad, where is she?'

White got to his feet and put his hands on her

shoulders and put his face close to hers. 'Ella's not coming with us, Hannah. I'm sorry.'

'What?' Her eyes stared at him in disbelief. 'What do you mean?'

Tears were stinging White's eyes and he blinked them away. 'She's . . . she's dead.'

'Noooo!' Hannah wailed. 'Noooo!'

'We have to run, Hannah. We have to get out of here.'

'What happened?' she screamed. 'What the fuck happened?'

'I'm so sorry, she was shot. They shot her.'

'We have to help her, Dad! We can't leave her.' Tears were running down her cheeks.

'It's too late to do anything for her. I'm sorry.'

There were shots all around them now, assault rifles and small arms fire. People were clawing their way over the wall, but often they would scream and fall back. Those that did make it over scrambled to their feet and ran towards the trees.

The strength went from Hannah's legs and she collapsed. White grabbed and held her. 'Hannah!' he shouted. 'You have to be strong. 'You can do this!'

She shook her head. 'I can't,' she whispered.

He put an arm around her and under her right arm, then supported her as he dragged her over the wall. 'Come on, Hannah, you can do this! Do it for Ella!'

Hannah was sobbing but her legs began to move. He continued to support her as he increased the pace and headed into the trees.

A women screamed off to their right. Hannah turned to look but White pulled her away. He heard the roar of an engine and he looked left. A black pick-up truck was heading towards them with three

38

Hamas fighters in the back. They began firing into the air, screaming 'Allahu Akbar!'

The pick up screeched to a halt and the fighters jumped down.

'Hannah, come on, faster!' shouted White.

'I can't,' she sobbed. 'I'm sorry, I can't.'

Two of the men ran towards them. They were wearing camouflage pattern t-shirts, tight jeans and plastic flip-flops. White turned to face them, pushing Hannah behind him. He held up his hands. 'Please, please don't do this,' he said, hating himself for begging but knowing that he had no choice.

One of the men laughed and cursed him in Arabic. He put his Kalashnikov to his shoulder, pointed the barrel at White's chest and pulled the trigger. There was a click but no shot. The magazine was empty. The man held his gun up and laughed.

The second man stepped forward and smashed the butt of his weapon into White's stomach. White doubled over, then fell to his knees, barely able to breathe. The two men grabbed Hannah and dragged her over to the pick-up truck. They ripped off her hoodie. One of the men put it on and held his arms out, nodding his appreciation.

Another pick-up truck arrived and four more fighters jumped down. Two of them raced over to White and began pounding him with the stocks of their weapons. He rolled over, trying to protect his head.

He saw the fighter in the hoodie rip off Hannah's t-shirt. She wasn't wearing a bra and her breasts sprang free. They threw her on to the bed of the truck and began pulling off her cargo pants. Her screams of terror chilled White to the bone. He struggled to his knees, calling out her name.

She was naked now and one of the fighters was climbing on top of her, screaming obscenities in Arabic. More fighters were running over to the truck. One slapped her across the face but she continued to scream. The man pulled a machete from his belt and raised it above his head. He screamed 'Allahu Akbar!' as he slashed down with the massive blade.

'Hannah!' shouted White, but then the stock of a Kalashnikov hit the back of his head and everything went black.

4

Shepherd's phone rang, dragging him from a dreamless sleep. He rolled over and picked up the phone from the bedside table. He peered at the screen. 020 7930 9000. The MI5 switchboard. It was just before seven o'clock. He took the call and rolled onto his back.

'Mr Shepherd, I am so sorry to bother you this early,' said a female voice. It was Amy Miller, MI5 director Giles Pritchard's secretary. 'Mr Pritchard would like to see you in his office right away. And he said it would be helpful if you had your passport with you.'

Shepherd sat up. It was Saturday and strictly speaking it was his day off, but MI5 officers couldn't afford to be clock watchers, the shit tended to hit the fan twenty-four-seven. He had arrived back in London just before dusk, courtesy of Steve Lepper and the AgustaWestland helicopter. They had landed at London Heliport in Battersea, not far from where Shepherd lived. As soon as they had landed, Shepherd had called Pritchard, and once Pritchard had heard about Shepherd's unexpected dip in the English Channel had told him that he should go home and get a good night's sleep. Shepherd had done as he was told and he had been asleep the second his head had hit the pillow.

'Not a problem, Amy,' said Shepherd, running a hand through his unkempt hair. 'I was just getting up anyway. I don't suppose you could give me a clue as

41

to what it's about.'

'If you switch on your TV, you'll see it,' said Amy, and she ended the call.

Shepherd got out of bed and padded into his sitting room. He picked up the remote, switched on the TV and clicked through to BBC rolling news. There was a banner across the bottom of the screen. 'DOZENS DEAD IN HAMAS ATTACK'. A truck full of men with black and white scarves across their faces were standing in the back of a pick-up truck, firing Kalashnikovs. The footage had been shot on a phone and it was jerking around. Whoever was filming was running, Shepherd realised. Another clip started to play, showing bodies lying on grass, though the bodies had been blurred. A reporter was describing the scenes, mentioning Hamas several times. The attack had taken place at seven o'clock in the morning at a music festival, dozens of men with guns attacking festival goers, killing men, women and children. The attack on the music festival had coincided with a mass missile firing with more than three thousand rockets fired at towns and cities around the country.

'Shit,' Shepherd muttered under his breath. It was clearly bad, but he wasn't sure how it could involve him. Israel wasn't his area of expertise.

He went through to the kitchen and slotted a coffee pod into his Nespresso machine, pressed the button to start it, then went through to the bathroom to shave and shower. He changed into a grey polo shirt, black jeans and grabbed a black leather jacket.

He poured milk into his coffee and used his mobile to call for an Uber. The Uber was shown as close by just as he was finishing his coffee, so he took the lift down and climbed in the back of a white Prius.

The driver's name was Mo, presumably short for Mohammed, and he was pleasant enough, asking if the temperature was to his liking and what type of music Shepherd would like to listen to. Mo didn't speak for the rest of the ride, which suited Shepherd just fine. He had ordered the Uber to take him to Burberry's headquarters building in Thorney Street. It was no secret that MI5, the country's domestic counter-intelligence and security agency, was based at Thames House in Millbank, overlooking the River Thames, so taxi drivers would know that anyone they dropped there was probably a spy. It wasn't really a security issue, it was just that Shepherd was fed up with the James Bond jokes. Better to be dropped at the Burberry offices and walk around to Thames House.

He went into the building and took the lift up to Pritchard's office. Amy Miller was at her desk. She was in her sixties wearing a pale green suit over a starched white shirt, and with her grey hair tied back in a tight bun she had the look of a stern headmistress. She smiled brightly and told him he could go straight in. As she waved at Pritchard's door, half a dozen brightly-coloured bracelets rattled on her wrist.

Giles Pritchard was standing at his window, looking out over the river. He was casually dressed which was unusual because he almost always wore a suit and his White's tie when he was in the office. Today he was wearing a dark blue V-neck sweater with the sleeves pulled up to his elbows and well worn brown corduroy trousers. He turned to look at Shepherd and smiled apologetically. 'Sorry to drag you in at the weekend, Dan, especially after everything you went through yesterday. But things are moving very quickly.'

'Not a problem,' said Shepherd.

Sky News was showing on a screen on the wall facing Pritchard's desk, with the sound off. Pritchard peered over the top of his metal-framed spectacles and gestured at the screen. 'This is a nightmare. God knows where this will lead. They're saying hundreds dead, now.'

Sitting on the sofa by the window was Ken Reid, MI5's head of Technical Operations, Analysis and Surveillance. He nodded at Shepherd. 'It's a shit show, that's what it is.' His dour Aberdeen accent always made him sound depressed, but today he sounded practically suicidal.

'Grab a chair, Dan,' said Pritchard. He went behind his desk and sat down behind his two large monitors. His eyes flicked between the screens as Shepherd sat down next to Reid. 'Ken, why don't you do the honours? David is your man, after all.'

Reid nodded. There was a manila file on the coffee table in front of him and he flipped it open to reveal a five by seven inch photograph of a man in his forties, with close cropped dark brown curly hair, deep set brown eyes and thin lips, and an MI5 human resources print out detailing the man's employment and personal details. Reid gestured for Shepherd to pick it up.

'David White, he's an analyst on our Middle East/North Africa desk. Almost fifteen years with Five, mainly in analysis but we have used him on a number of operations and he has always conducted himself well. But he's very much cerebral rather than physical.' He forced a smile. 'Unlike your good self.'

'I hope you're not suggesting I'm brawn and not brains,' said Shepherd.

'I'm just pointing out that David isn't a fighter and

44

isn't much use with a gun,' said Reid. 'That's relevant to his current predicament because he was at the music festival that Hamas attacked this morning and we believe that he might have been taken hostage, along with his two teenage daughters.'

Shepherd scanned the printout. Date of birth. Address in St John's Wood. Attended Highgate School in North London. First class degree in Computer Science from Cambridge University. Chairman of the Cambridge University Jewish Society in his final year. Married to Rachel, a doctor at St Mary's Hospital in Paddington. Yearly career assessments, always exceptional or very good. Shepherd's trick memory kicked in and all the facts were locked away to be recalled whenever he needed them. He had never had any contact with the man, but that wasn't unusual, more than five thousand people worked for MI5.

'We don't have official confirmation that David has been kidnapped, but he was definitely at the music festival and his phone, and the phones of his daughters, have gone dark. It was his wife who contacted us two hours ago. She saw the news and tried phoning her husband and daughters. They didn't answer. She's frantic, obviously. We've sent someone from human resources to keep her company until this is resolved.'

'They could be dead,' said Shepherd quietly.

'We considered that,' said Reid. 'So we've had a team combing through social media and news footage.' He scowled. 'It never ceases to amaze me how people in life-threatening situations find the time to video what's happening and post it on Instagram or Tik-Tok or wherever.'

'Take a look at this, Dan,' said Pritchard.

Shepherd stood up and went over to the desk.

45

Pritchard turned one of the screens so that Shepherd could get a better look. A YouTube video was playing, shaky footage of people running across a field, many of them teenagers. To the left of the screen was a motorcycle, two masked men on it, the passenger shooting a Kalashnikov. A man went down, the top of his skull a bloody mess. 'This was shortly after the attack started,' said Pritchard. 'This was a live Facebook feed that someone loaded onto YouTube. There are literally hundreds of videos across social media as we speak, though the various companies are taking them down as quickly as they can.' He clicked his mouse and the picture froze. Off to the left of the screen was a man in a blue sweatshirt, with two teenage girls in front of him. They were running between parked cars.

'This is David. The girl on the left is his daughter Hannah and on the right is Ella.' He clicked the mouse again and the family ran around the back of a minibus, flinching at the sound of gunfire. The camera jerked to the right and Shepherd lost sight of the Whites. Pritchard clicked the mouse several times and another video appeared, this one showing terrified festival goers running through an apple orchard. The video was shaky, whoever was holding the phone was clearly running for their life. In the distance was the thud-thud-thud of a heavy machine gun followed by terrified screams. Pritchard clicked the mouse and the picture froze. He pointed at the middle of the screen. There were two figures running between the trees, bent double as if trying to avoid incoming fire. Shepherd couldn't make out their faces but he recognised the clothes. It was definitely White and the older of his two daughters.

'So here they were running away from the camp-site, through an orchard. On the other side of the orchard is some agricultural land and then the Re-im kibbutz. The kibbutz has more secure buildings including bomb shelters so he was presumably hoping they'd be safe there.'

'Plus the residents of the kibbutz would be armed, right?'

'Well, sadly not,' said Pritchard. 'If they had been, there might not have been so many deaths. It was a bloody cock-up, from start to finish. According to the Israeli Army, the erection of a border fence around the Gaza Strip means there was zero chance of a Hamas ground attack. Well, 'close to nil' is what they said, along with 'Gaza is no longer a threat'. They removed their forces from the area leaving local security as the only line of defence. But to make it worse, the Israel Defence Forces took away most of the weapons belonging to the local security details. During the attack today, the local security people did what they could, but all they had was a few pistols and they were up against Kalashnikovs and heavy machine guns.' He smiled ruefully. 'The IDF is probably going to rethink that policy, obviously.'

'Is there any more video of the Whites?' asked Shepherd.

'We're still looking, and there's new footage going up all the time,' said Pritchard. 'But he was very much alive in those two videos. The fact that he and his daughters haven't used their phones suggests that they have been prevented from using them so while at the moment we don't know for sure that David White is a hostage, we are going to proceed on the assumption that he is. I need you and an SAS team

47

out there ASAP. I had thought about using E Squadron but at the moment I'd prefer to keep MI6 out of the loop.'

Shepherd nodded. E Squadron, which in the past had been called the Increment, was an elite unit that carried out covert operations for the government, often in close contact with MI6, the Secret Intelligence Service. E Squadron could draw on the Special Air Service and the Special Boat Service for manpower, but Pritchard was right, using E Squadron would mean involving MI6 and if White really was a hostage, the fewer people who knew, the better.

'There's a plane waiting for you at Brize Norton, and we've arranged a car.'

'Who do I liaise with in Israel?'

'We've already spoken to the IDF and they're happy to brief you on arrival. We need their intel, obviously. I'm not sure how involved they'll allow you to be but they know how well trained the SAS is, so I'm sure they'd want to make use of the team's expertise.'

'And if they don't?'

'Well there's no use crossing bridges before we get to them. Let's see what they say when you're there.'

'Do we have anyone local?'

'Six obviously have people in Jerusalem and Tel Aviv but again I'm holding back from informing them at this stage. The fewer people who knew who David is and what he does, the better. It's bad enough that he's been kidnapped, but if Hamas find out that he works for MI5's MENAD well . . .' He shuddered.

Shepherd turned to look at Reid. 'What sort of access does he have?'

'Total access. He was DVd, obviously, but he is also approved for SCI and SAPs.'

48

Developed Vetting was the UK's highest level of security clearance, and it was applied to most workers at MI5, MI6 and GCHQ. It involved lengthy interviews and had investigators digging into their private and personal lives, leaving no stone unturned. SCI — Sensitive Compartmented Information — required a higher level of clearance, as did Special Access Programs, usually involving special operations or new technology.

'David is an analyst, primarily, but he was dealing with a lot of human intel, most of it domestic but a lot coming out of the Middle East, including Israel and the Palestinian territories. None of what he saw would be redacted so he would be aware of agents and officers throughout the region, operations underway, financing details. The works. Plus he's seen a lot of stuff that the Israelis have given us. Plus there's a danger if they find out who he is they might use him as a bargaining chip against the UK. There are plenty of Palestinians in UK prisons.'

'I'm assuming that David will keep quiet. Would his kids know he worked for MI5?'

'Almost certainly not,' said Reid. 'His wife knows, but he'd have told his daughters and other family members that he had a desk job with the civil service. But you know kids, they can be as devious as the KGB.'

'There'd be no ID on him that would show he worked for MI5. So provided he keeps his mouth shut, he should be okay.'

'The problem is, we don't know how Hamas is treating the hostages,' said Pritchard. 'Unlike you, he's never been trained to resist interrogation. We've no idea how he'll perform under pressure. We need to get him out of there as soon as possible.'

'And his daughters,' said Shepherd.

'Yes, absolutely,' said Pritchard, though it was clear to Shepherd that the analyst was the man's primary concern. Pritchard looked at his watch. 'I think you'd best be on the way, it's a two hour drive to Brize Norton. You'll meet up with the SAS team there.'

'What about the Hellbanianz investigation?'

'I'll talk to the NCA and give them any support they need,' said Pritchard. 'But from what you told me yesterday, we're waiting for the Albanian undercover guy to make contact, and that could take some time. David White is your priority and will remain so until we have him back in the UK.'

5

Shepherd climbed into the back of the black Vauxhall Corsa and pulled the door shut. The driver waited until he had fastened his seat belt before pulling away from the kerb. The man was clearly a pro and wasn't using GPS. As the car headed south, following the river, Shepherd took out his phone and called Jimmy Sharpe. 'Razor, hey, how are they hanging?'

'Straight and level, Spider. I had a few drinks with Petrit last night. He can knock back the shots like there's no tomorrow.'

'I thought he was a Muslim.'

'He is, but he's one of the good ones. I can't get him to try a bacon sandwich, he says he draws the line at that. I did take him for a shish kebab, though. But seriously, he's one hell of a cop. The way that he jumped into the sea to save that guy, that was something.'

'Speaking of which, did you fix up security at the hospital?'

'There's an armed officer outside Plauku's door as we speak. The hospital says they can discharge him later today and we're arranging a safe house. I tell you, it was a real bonus Plauku getting shot. Takes the pressure off Tuk and opens up a whole new line of investigation. Plauku knows all about the gang's Italian connection and he says he'll give us everything he has.'

'It doesn't help us so much with Fisnik Hazari, though,' said Shepherd. 'Anything Plauku has will be

51

hearsay, we're going to need Tuk for that.'

'I know, but Interpol are going to be jumping up and down with glee now that we have Plauku. It's going to earn us a lot of brownie points. So where are you?'

'About that,' said Shepherd. 'I've got to love you and leave you, for a few days, anyway.'

'Going anywhere nice?'

'Israel.'

'Fuck me, I've just seen that on the news. How are you involved?'

'Need to know, mate, sorry. But I shouldn't be away too long. In the meantime, Thames House will send someone to hold your hand.'

Sharpe chuckled. 'Yes, because I need my hand held, don't I? You stay safe, Spider. Don't do anything I wouldn't do.'

'Like jump out of a helicopter into the sea?' Shepherd laughed and ended the call, then phoned Chris Thatcher. Thatcher was an old friend, a former London detective. They had met when Thatcher was working as a security consultant for a shipping company, but now he worked for an international security firm that included kidnapping insurance in its portfolio. Thatcher was a skilled hostage negotiator who had worked in trouble spots around the world. He answered almost immediately. 'Chris, hey, sorry to bother you but I need to pick your brains.'

'Pick away,' said Thatcher.

'Have you been following what's happening in Gaza?'

'Very closely. We have client involvement, unfortunately.'

'Does your firm have someone out there?'

'We have offices in Tel Aviv and Jerusalem so our staff out there are handling it.'

'Kidnap insurance?'

'Two young men, Jews from New York, both named on family Kidnap And Ransom policies. They were staying at the Re-im kibbutz and were at the music festival when it all kicked off.'

'Are you negotiating yet?'

'So far there's been no contact. We don't even know if the boys are alive. They will both have a phone number to give to their kidnappers that will start the ball rolling, but this isn't a regular kidnapping, as you know. Hamas have more than two hundred hostages and the Gaza Strip is pretty much a no-go area at the moment.'

'It's a nightmare.'

'You can say that again,' said Thatcher. 'You know the background, right, and the significance of the October Seven date?'

'I am literally just hours into this,' said Shepherd. 'Any intel gratefully received.'

'This attack started on the fiftieth anniversary of the Yom Kippur War, when Egyptian and Syrian forces launched a surprise attack on Israel. October Seven was also Simchat Torah, which concludes the Jewish holiday of Sukkot. It's a holy day so Israelis don't go to work or school, and most of the IDF are off duty and with their families. The Israelis came close to losing that war, and it was only with American help that they managed to push the invaders back. More than two and half thousand Israeli soldiers died and more than eighteen thousand Arabs perished. If it wasn't for Operation Nickel Grass, a US airlift which delivered twenty two thousand tons

53

of weapons and ammunition, then Israel would have been wiped from the map. Following the Israeli victory, Palestinians were confined to the West Bank of the River Jordan, and to the Gaza Strip. Close to five million Palestinians became refugees, flooding into Jordan, Lebanon and Syria. Three million or so stayed in the West Bank, and about two million are in Gaza. For obvious reasons, most have a vociferous hatred towards Israel. This attack had obviously been a long time in the planning.'

'So how do you think this will play out, Chris?'

'My gut feeling is that the Israelis will negotiate. And pay a heavy price. There is a precedent. Back in 2011 Netanyahu agreed to swap a thousand Hamas prisoners in exchange for the release of a single Israeli soldier — Gilad Shalit — who had been held hostage for going on five years.'

'That was one hell of an exchange.'

'I suppose it gave the Israelis bragging rights. One of ours is worth a thousand of yours, sort of thing. The problem is, the exchange did backfire. One of the Hamas prisoners that Israel released was Yaha Sinwah who went on to become the head of Hamas in Gaza. He's almost certainly one of the planners of this attack and I'm sure the Israelis are hunting him down as we speak. Because of that, the Israeli public is generally against prisoner swaps.'

'And what do the Israelis have that Hamas want?'

'Well a ceasefire, obviously. The IDF will be ruthlessly thorough at tracking down the Hamas fighters and planners, it'll definitely be a shoot to kill operation. Hamas will want that to stop. Also Israel has close to seven thousand Palestinians behind bars on security charges, and more than five hundred are serving life sentences for the killing of Israeli soldiers and civilians. My gut feeling is that Hamas will demand that all seven thousand are released in exchange for the hostages they have.'

'And if Hamas don't get the exchange they want?'

'Will they kill the hostages, do you mean? One or two, perhaps, to show that they mean business. But they're not stupid, they know that the hostages only have bargaining power if they're alive. If it was ISIS, they'd just chop the heads off the hostages, just for spite. But Hamas are more pragmatic. They would just wait. They waited five years to hand back Shalit, so they have the patience. They've played the long game before. And it's not about money with Hamas. Money is pouring in from Iran, Syria, Saudi Arabia and the Gulf States. The three top leaders of Hamas are collectively worth eleven billion dollars and live a life of luxury in Qatar, so they're not short of cash. Hamas is a terrorist group, but more pragmatic than ISIS and al Qaeda. They've more in common with the Provisional Irish Republican Army, killing civilians, soldiers and police officers while negotiating with the government through Sinn Fein. Hamas has its own political wing but the entire organisation has been declared a terrorist organisation by the United States, the United Kingdom and the European Union. But most other countries only define the military wing as a terrorist organisation, while countries such as Russia, China and Turkey consider that Hamas are waging a legitimate struggle. How are you involved in this, Dan, if you don't mind me asking?'

'We have a particular interest in one of the hostages, that's all I can say.'

'Are you heading out there?'

'I am, yes. The plan is to talk to the Israelis and see if we can help.'

'Good luck with that, Dan. I hope there's a successful outcome.'

'Thanks, Chris. Me too.'

Shepherd ended the call and sat back in his seat. He stared out of the window with unseeing eyes. Luck was all well and good, but he was going to need more than luck if he was going to rescue David White and his family.

6

The car arrived at Brize Norton just after eleven o'clock. The airport security staff had been briefed and as the Corsa approached the main entrance the barrier lifted up and two armed Military Provost guards waved them through. They drove past the main terminal towards a parking area where a Gulfstream jet was waiting with its steps down. Shepherd frowned when he saw the executive jet, he'd been expecting to see a C17 Globemaster, the SAS's aviation workhorse.

He climbed out, thanked the driver, and walked towards the jet as the car drove away. There was a man standing at the bottom of the stairs, his back to Shepherd, wearing a black fabric bomber jacket, blue jeans and what looked like black Alt-Berg boots, the footwear favoured by the SAS. The man was on the phone, but as Shepherd walked over he realised who it was, Matt 'Lastman' Standing. He and Standing had never served together — Standing was almost twenty years his junior but their paths had crossed on several occasions, more than enough times to build a mutual respect. Standing was about the same height as Shepherd but probably twenty pounds lighter, hardly surprising as Standing was an SAS sergeant on active service with one of the world's top special forces units while Shepherd spent most of his time behind a desk or playing undercover roles, often in bars or restaurants.

As Standing turned, slipping his phone into his jacket, he saw Shepherd and his face broke into a wide grin. 'I was hoping it would be you, Spider,' said Standing. 'They said a secret squirrel would be joining us but they didn't give us a name.'

The two men hugged. 'Good to see you, Matt. Ditto, they didn't say who I'd be working with.'

The two men broke apart and Shepherd looked up at the jet. 'So what's the story with the Gulfstream?' he asked.

'Powers that be don't want us arriving in a military plane,' said Standing.

'Their powers that be or ours?'

'I think both,' said Standing. 'So it's a civilian plane and we're to go in wearing civvie clothes.'

'Gear?'

Standing grinned. 'Plenty of gear but it's all locked away in the hold. Apparently we have to wait for a green light from the Israelis. Are you ready to go?'

'Sure.'

'No kit?'

'Three hours ago I was tucked up in bed looking forward to a day off,' said Shepherd.

'Yeah, this has all happened quickly. What the hell are Hamas thinking? You poke the tiger and you end up getting bit.'

'Is that a proverb?'

'It's a fact of life, Spider, especially when the tiger is Israel. This doesn't end well for Hamas.' He patted Shepherd on the back. 'Right, let's get you strapped in and the wheels off the ground.' He pointed up the stairs. 'There's a few familiar faces up there.'

Shepherd went up the steps with Standing following close behind. A pilot in a white shirt, black tie and black pants emerged from the cockpit. She was in her thirties with close-cropped black hair and eye lashes so long that Shepherd assumed they had to be false. 'You're the last, sir, so we'll start the engines and be on our way.'

'Which airport?' asked Shepherd.

'Be'er Sheva Airfield, IATA code BEV, close to Beersheba. It's forty kilometres from the festival showground that was attacked. It's a small airfield used mainly for flight training and general aviation. We're looking at a flight time of approximately four hours, but I'll update you en route.'

Shepherd thanked her and she went back into the cockpit.

'She's fit,' said Standing.

'Fit or not, it's her piloting skills I care about.'

'Got her licence twelve years ago, close to ten thousand hours as pilot in command, more than a thousand in the Gulfstream.'

Shepherd raised his eyebrows. 'Now how would you know that?'

'We had a chat while we were waiting for you to turn up.' He winked. 'And yes, I got her phone number.'

Shepherd turned to enter the cabin and grinned when he saw who was sprawled across a beige leather sofa on the left. Andy 'Penny' Lane had been with the Regiment for more than twenty five years, joining just six months after Shepherd, and they had served together on several missions in Afghanistan and Iraq. Whereas Shepherd had left the Regiment to join the police and eventually MI5, Lane had stayed where he was and had served with distinction in Afghanistan, Iraq, Libya and half a dozen other war zones. Lane stood up and fist-bumped Shepherd. 'They're still letting you out from behind that desk?' asked Lane. He was wearing a black North Face fleece over a denim shirt, and like Standing was wearing Alt-Berg boots.

'Can't keep a good man down,' laughed Shepherd.

'I'll be handling comms, and I have two SatPhones, do you want one?'

'You keep them,' said Shepherd. 'I'll shout if I need one.'

Sitting in a single seat opposite Lane was Ricky 'Mustard' Coleman. He was a decade or so younger than Shepherd and Lane, and had been with the SAS for six years or so after ten years with the Paras. He was wearing wraparound Oakley sunglasses. His hair had started receding when he was a teenager and he usually kept it cut short. He stood up and hugged Shepherd. 'Still running around with a rucksack full of house bricks, Spider?' he asked.

Shepherd laughed. 'Not as much as I used to.'

There was a younger guy sitting in the seat behind Coleman, not long out of his twenties and growing a moustache to try to make himself look older. Coleman gestured at him. 'This is Virgin,' he said. 'Still wet behind the ears but we have high hopes for him.'

The man stood up. He was an inch or two taller than Shepherd and probably twenty kilos heavier. Most SAS troopers were whippet thin but Virgin was heavily built with wide shoulders and forearms that stretched the fabric of his Fred Perry polo shirt. 'Pleasure to meet you, Spider. I've heard a lot about you. Obviously.' He stuck out his hand. He had a firm handshake but Shepherd sensed that he was holding back deliberately. He had piercing blue eyes and a strong chin that looked as if it could take a punch or two. He smiled, showing gleaming white slab-like teeth. 'And I'm not a Virgin, before you ask.'

'The thought hadn't crossed my mind,' said Shepherd.

'The name's Jordan Branson. My middle name is Richard. It was one of the directing staff who called me Virgin and it stuck.'

'Yeah, we don't get to choose our nicknames,' said Shepherd.

'You got yours by eating a tarantula on the jungle phase of selection, right?'

Shepherd grinned. 'Yeah, that was me.'

'So what did it taste like?'

'Like a big hairy spider,' said Shepherd. 'I wouldn't recommend it.' He caught sight of the last member of the team, who was standing at the back of the plane. 'Well you're a sight for sore eyes, Clint,' he said. The last time he had seen Brian 'Clint' Heron was at Kabul Airport in Afghanistan, where he had been helping to arrange a mass evacuation which turned into a rout. Heron's nickname came from the fact that he was a dead ringer for the actor Clint Eastwood, back when he was playing the role of vigilante cop Dirty Harry. Heron was tall and thin, wearing a black Adidas tracksuit top over a white sweatshirt, and blue jogging pants. From the look of the gear and the Reebok trainers on his feet, Shepherd figured that Heron had been in the gym when the call came.

Heron grinned and stuck out his hand. 'Good to see you again, Spider.'

'Glad you managed to get out of Kabul.'

The two men shook hands. 'Right shit storm that was,' said Heron. 'But the top brass said that I did such a good job I could start specialising in hostage rescue situations, so here I am.'

'I'm glad you're on board.'

61

A second pilot, this one a man in his late twenties, came out of the cockpit and retracted the steps.

Shepherd sat down in the seat opposite Standing and buckled his belt. The engines kicked into life as the rest of the team fastened their seat belts, and two minutes later they were taxiing to the runway.

'This definitely beats a Globemaster,' said Shepherd.

'Wait until you've seen the toilet,' said Standing. 'Luxury.'

'Quilted toilet paper?'

'Gold leaf,' said Standing. 'The only downside is they didn't trust us with a stewardess.'

The engines roared and the jet leapt forward. It sped along the runway and Shepherd was forced back into his seat as the nose went up and the jet headed towards the clouds. It was a far cry from the lumbering Globemaster, which like the Hercules it replaced always seemed unwilling to actually leave the ground. 'We grabbed some sandwiches and soft drinks from the Mess and I'm pretty sure Penny has tucked away a couple of bottles of Scotch,' said Standing.

'Good thinking,' said Shepherd.

'The sandwiches, or the whisky?'

'Both, but I don't think I can arrive in Israel smelling of booze. How much have you been told?'

Standing chuckled. 'How much are we usually told?' he said. 'Just that we needed to get to Brize Norton and that we'd be briefed on the plane. Though I did hear the words Hamas and massacre.'

'Yeah, that's about it.'

'I know that Islamic terrorists generally aren't the sharpest knives in the block, but you have to ask what the hell the thinking was. Breaking through the border

62

and attacking civilians will get you so far, but before long you'll be facing one of the best equipped armies in the free world.'

'I'm far from being an expert, but yeah, it seems that you'd have to have a death wish.'

'One of the guys was saying that maybe Hamas wanted Iran and Hezbollah to join the fight. A combined attack on several fronts.'

'That would make more sense, but it doesn't seem to be happening,' said Shepherd. 'Hamas went in, grabbed a shed load of hostages and then retreated.'

'And then what? They think that the Israelis will just stand at the border and wag their fingers. There'll be retribution, on a major scale.'

'That's how I read it, too.'

'So what's our role?' said Standing. 'As Clint is on board, I'm guessing hostage rescue.'

Shepherd nodded. 'Yeah. They grabbed an MI5 analyst and his family. Said analyst has a lot of information that we can't afford getting into Hamas hands.'

'Do we know his location? Please tell me he took his phone with him.'

'No phone, no GPS, I'm just hoping the IDF has some idea where he might be.'

'And what about Mossad? The Israeli intelligence agency has clearly dropped the ball.'

'Seems so, yes.'

'Have you seen the videos online? The bad guys flew over the fences on paragliders and burst through with bulldozers. Then hundreds of Palestinian gunmen rode in on trucks and bikes. Can you imagine the planning and logistics that went into that? How does that happen without Mossad noticing?'

'It's a good question.'

'I mean, you guys at MI5 are stopping potential terrorist attacks every week, right?'

'We're kept busy, yes.'

'And when a terrorist attack does happen in the UK, it's usually a lone wolf or like the guys who bombed the London Tube, the ones that were off your radar. What do you call them?'

'Cleanskins,' said Shepherd.

'Yeah, cleanskins. Cleanskins and lone wolf nutters, they can escape detection, I get that. But when you have hundreds of fighters, most of whom were presumably known to Mossad, with bucketloads of ammunition and guns, you have to ask yourself why they weren't spotted. And did no one wonder why Hamas were lining bulldozers up at the border?'

'There might well have been a failure of intelligence, as they say.'

'Yeah, well the rumour mill is in full swing at Stirling Lines.'

'I'd have thought you'd have better things to do with your time,' said Shepherd.

'Hey, I'm just telling you what I heard, that's all. Mossad is generally on top of Hamas, right? Spy planes, drones, satellites, agents in the field. If a sparrow farts in Gaza, they know about it. MI5 had the drop on the IRA for years before the Paddies packed it in, they were so riddled with informers, but Mossad operates at a level way above even you guys.'

'They have their strengths, true.'

'So where were those strengths before the attack? Seriously, they didn't see it coming? There was no hint? Not a sniff? Even just a suggestion that maybe they should increase security at the border? There was a music festival just three klicks from the fence.'

Shepherd shrugged. 'You're asking me questions I can't answer, Matt.'

'Well, suppose Mossad did know what was being planned, and suppose they told the government and the government thought, what the hell, here's a chance for us to crush Hamas once and for all. There were lots of foreigners at the music festival, including Brits and Yanks, and they knew casualties would be high. But after the attack, the government would have carte blanche to do whatever they wanted in retaliation. Remember George W. Bush after Nine Eleven — you're either with us or against us. That's the position the Israelis are in now. Hundreds dead, many of them women and children, who's going to argue if now they level Gaza to the ground?'

'That would be cold, Matt. Letting Hamas murder civilians so that they could then counter-attack? If that was true and if it ever came out . . .'

'By the time the truth gets out, Israel will have achieved its objective. Hamas will be a spent force. The government will find someone to blame and say that lessons have been learned blah blah blah. It's a sick world, Spider, and you know it is.'

'I'm just a small cog in a very big machine, Matt. My job is to get the analyst back in one piece, the rest of it, the politics, is way above my pay grade.'

'Yeah, but what if we can't get him out. Hypothetically speaking. What then?'

Shepherd frowned. 'What do you mean?'

'Well, this guy has all that damaging intel in his head, intel that Hamas could make good use of, in a bad way. Presumably your bosses would prefer that him giving them that intel wouldn't be an option.'

Shepherd's frown deepened. 'You think they've told

65

me to slot him?'

'Have they?'

'No, of course not. We don't do that.'

'Yes we do. We've been out in Iraq and Syria with hit lists and you know we have. And there'd be British names on that list. British born. So let's not pretend that the government doesn't order the execution of its own citizens from time to time.'

Shepherd wrinkled his nose. 'This is different. This guy isn't a homegrown jihadist, he's an MI5 analyst, one of ours.'

'Let me put it this way, Spider. If you had been given orders to slot the guy, would you tell me?'

Shepherd's smile widened. 'Probably not,' he said.

7

The Gulfstream jet touched down at Be'er Sheva Airfield at just before 5pm local time. Shepherd was wearing a Breitling Emergency watch which allowed him to input the Israel time into a digital display while the hands continued to show UK time. A similar watch had helped save the life of his son Liam in Mali, it had a satellite beacon that identified the GPS position of the wearer in case of an emergency. Shepherd had been so impressed with the watch that he'd bought one for himself and wore it every time he was out of the country.

The jet taxied off the runway and headed towards a large hangar around which were gathered a number of military vehicles. Beyond them was a line of more than two dozen private jets, and beyond them a parking area for many more smaller propellor aircraft, mainly with single engines. The sun had already gone down and the hangar and tarmac were illuminated by bright white floodlights.

The jet came to a halt alongside the hangar and the engines powered down. The female pilot came out of the cockpit and lowered the steps. 'Thank you for flying with us, please don't forget to post a five star review on Tripadvisor,' she said.

Shepherd grinned. 'Definitely,' he said. 'Are you tasked with taking us back to London?'

'We are,' she said. 'We're to stay put until you're ready to return.'

'So we can grab a drink when we get back to the

UK?' said Standing.

The pilot laughed. 'I can't make any promises,' she said. 'Besides, from my experience you guys are always busy, busy, busy. Anyway, I hope you achieve your objectives, whatever they are.' She flashed Standing a smile and went back into the cockpit.

Standing winked at Shepherd. 'Told you, I've cracked it.'

'Whatever you say, Matt.'

'Putty in my hands.'

Shepherd chuckled as he headed down the steps to the tarmac. He looked over at a line of grey hangars. A man in his late forties with steel grey hair was standing by a beige SandCat composite armoured vehicle, wearing olive fatigues and with a black leather holster on his hip. Shepherd knew that the vehicle was designed and built by the Israelis, based on a commercial Ford F-Series chassis. It could carry up to eleven people and was used for patrol and security missions, and for ferrying officers around. It weighed eight and a half tons fully loaded and could be equipped with missiles and grenade launchers if necessary. The grey haired man had his arms folded and clearly had been waiting for the jet to arrive. With him were half a dozen IDF soldiers.

Shepherd's team gathered at the foot of the steps. 'Let me talk to them first,' he said, and he walked across the tarmac to the SandCat. The grey haired man had dark green epaulettes each with a black oak leaf pinned to it, designating him as a Rav Seren, equivalent to the rank of major in the British Army. He didn't offer to shake hands, which was fine with Shepherd, and the man had his game face on, tight lipped, eyes slightly narrowed, chin up. Shepherd smiled and nodded. 'I'm Dan Shepherd, sir,' he said. 'I'm guessing you're waiting for me.'

The major nodded. 'I am Rav Seren Amos Kasher and I have been told to welcome you to Israel.' He pulled a face. 'So, welcome to Israel. Now would you do me a great service, get back on your plane, and fly back to wherever you have come from.'

'I'm afraid I can't do that, sir,' said Shepherd. 'My orders are to assist you in the rescue of a number of British citizens currently being held hostage by Hamas.'

'We don't need your assistance, the matter is in hand,' said the major.

'I'm sure it is, sir,' said Shepherd. 'But we do have specialist skills that might be useful.'

'We have our own specialists,' said the major. 'This isn't my military action, Mr Shepherd.' The emphasis was on the word 'mister', letting Shepherd know that the major didn't have a high opinion of civilians. 'I don't want amateurs getting in the way.'

'My colleagues are serving members of the Special Air Service and have served with distinction in Iraq, Afghanistan and Libya.'

'You are not in Iraq, Afghanistan or Libya, Mr Shepherd,' said the major, again with the emphasis on the civilian title. 'Have any of you ever served in Israel?'

'No, sir.'

'Or Gaza?'

'No sir, but . . .' The major silenced him with the wave of a hand. 'Then you will only get in the way. Hamas are like no enemy you have ever faced, and you have never been in an environment like Gaza. Your participation would put my men at risk, and I

69

am not prepared to allow that to happen.'

'We've been trained for situations exactly like this,' said Shepherd. 'We can . . .'

'Enough,' said the major, raising his hand, palm outwards. 'If you were one of my men you would be up on an insubordination charge by now. I am telling you that you are not welcome in Israel, that you are most definitely not entering Gaza and that unless you get back on your plane I will have you clapped in irons.'

Shepherd smiled thinly, and nodded at the major. 'Please give me a minute, sir,' he said, and walked back to his team.

'Problem?' said Standing as Shepherd walked back to his group.

'The major's getting territorial,' said Shepherd.

'Want me to go over and give him an attitude adjustment?'

Shepherd chuckled. 'We're not here to fight the Israelis, Matt, but thanks for the offer.' He nodded at Lane. 'I'll take a SatPhone now, Penny,' he said.

Lane handed a SatPhone to Shepherd. He walked away and called Giles Pritchard's mobile. He answered on the third ring. 'I've got a problem,' said Shepherd. 'We've just arrived in Israel and a major here is playing hardass. He says he's not prepared to allow us to get involved and wants us back on the plane and out of here.'

'What's this major's name?'

'Rav Seren Amos Kasher. The Rav Seren is the major rank. So his name is Amos Kasher.'

'Give me a few minutes,' said Pritchard. 'I'll get this sorted.'

Shepherd went over to Lane and gave him back

the SatPhone. The major was standing by his vehicle, glaring at Shepherd. Shepherd smiled and nodded at him.

'We good?' asked Standing.

'Not yet,' said Shepherd. 'But I have a feeling that's going to change.'

They heard heavy machine gun fire off to the west. 'I guess Hamas are still out there,' said Heron.

'That could be across the border,' said Shepherd. 'The Israelis will be wanting their payback. It might have already started.'

'They don't fuck around, do they?' said Coleman.

'They can't afford to,' said Standing. 'There are fewer than ten million in the country and they're surrounded by enemies, most of whom would like to see every one of them erased from the face of the earth.'

The major took his mobile from a pocket of his fatigues and put it to his ear. He visibly straightened and thrust his shoulders back as he listened, then began to talk. As Shepherd watched, the major nodded as he listened, before speaking again. Eventually he put the phone away and looked over at Shepherd. It was impossible to tell what the officer was thinking as he strode over the tarmac to where Shepherd was standing.

'You didn't tell me that you know the prime minister,' said the major.

'I don't,' said Shepherd. 'But I guess my boss does. And if he doesn't he has the ear of our PM and I'm sure your PM takes his calls.'

The major nodded. 'Well, Mr Netanyahu tells me that I have to offer you every facility, up to and including taking you into Gaza.'

'I'm sorry if I've caused you any problems,' said

71

Shepherd. 'But I was told that this operation is very, very important and nothing must stand in our way.'

'No need to apologise. Mr Netanyahu says the same. And while he's a great one for using the stick to get what he wants, with me he proffered a decent carrot so there is a tangible benefit to my helping you. So what do you need, Mr Shepherd?'

'If you're sure that the hostages from the festival were taken down the tunnels, then that's where we'd like to go.'

'I can't be certain, obviously. But that's what I would do. We've been told we'll be going across the border later this evening so you're welcome to come with us.' He looked at his watch. 'There's a canteen in the terminal building, you and your men can eat while I get a room here ready for a briefing. Let's say we get together in an hour.'

'Thank you for that, sir. It's much appreciated.'

'So long as Mr Netanyahu shows his appreciation, I'll be happy. Now, what do you need in the way of kit?'

Shepherd gestured at the Gulfstream. 'Everything we need is in the hold. We just need your permission to unload it.'

The major nodded. 'You have it,' he said.

'And we all have our passports, if you need to see them.'

'That won't be necessary,' said the major. 'I am told you are the personal guests of the prime minister.' He smiled sarcastically. 'Though I am also told that you were never here.'

8

Shepherd and the team ate in the airport canteen, tucking into burgers, chips and onion rings, washed down with mugs of strong tea. They had changed into desert fatigues and had sidearms strapped to their hips. Their weapons were on a neighbouring table. Everyone had a Heckler & Koch 417 assault rifle, except for Lane who had brought along his regular weapon of choice, a Mossberg 590M pump-action shotgun with a magazine holding twenty shells. They had stacked their body armour and helmets on chairs.

'Anyone been in Gaza before?' asked Shepherd. The four men shook their heads. It was hardly surprising, the Israelis tended to keep a tight grip on the territory and weren't in the habit of seeking help from outsiders.

'How much intel is in your trick memory, Spider?' asked Standing.

'Just the basics,' said Shepherd. 'Some twenty miles long, between three and seven miles wide, on the eastern coast of the Med, bordered by Egypt on the southwest and by Israel on the north and east. It started life as a refugee zone for Palestinians who were forced to leave when Israel was formed in 1948. After the Six-Day War of 1967 Israel occupied the strip, then in 2005 they withdrew their forces but the UN says that the area is still under military occupation. Israel denies that but they enforce a land, sea and air blockade that pretty much prevents people and goods from freely entering and leaving.'

'I've heard it described as the biggest open air prison in the world,' said Lane.

'The Palestinians can move around within the strip but yes, they probably do feel like they're in a prison,' said Shepherd. 'There's about two million of them on 141 square miles.' As always the number and statistics came easily to Shepherd, tucked away in his trick memory and available for almost instant recall. He never forgot anything that he had seen, heard or read. 'It's one of the densest population areas in the world, with an unemployment rate of more than fifty per cent, seventy per cent for teenagers. There are eight refugee camps in Gaza, most of then Sunni Muslims.'

'And what about Hamas?' asked Lane.

'Hamas likes to play the Sinn Fein card. Remember how Sinn Fein always claimed that they were a purely political organisation and that they were in no way connected to the actions carried out by the IRA?'

'Yeah, and if you believe that I've got a bridge I can sell you,' laughed Heron.

'Yeah, well certainly most of the world believes that Hamas is purely a terrorist organisation, except for the Russians and the Chinese,' said Shepherd.

'And the Arab world,' added Standing.

'Yeah, they have their supporters,' said Shepherd. 'Which is why they have access to so much finance and weaponry.' He took a bite out of his burger and chewed before continuing. 'The military wing is called the Izz ad-Din al-Qassam Brigades — al-Qassam for short — which has a core of a few hundred members who have been trained in Syria and Iran, but with a back up of maybe twenty thousand civilians who would be prepared to pick up a Kalashnikov if asked, or told, to do so. Now, if you were to ask the al-Qassam, they would see that their aim is the liberation of Palestine and to repel the Zionist invaders, and that their military operations are restricted to attacking the Israeli Army and exercising self defence against armed settlers. They'd say that, but they have a history of firing rockets at Israeli targets and as we've seen today . . .' He shrugged and left the sentence unfinished and tucked into some French fries before continuing. 'The al-Qassam leadership has been consistently targeted for assassination over the years, something the Israelis have always been good at.'

Lane looked up from his plate. 'That *Munich* film, about what the Israelis did after their athletes were murdered at the German Olympics, I really liked that.'

'It was a Spielberg movie,' said Heron.

'I'm told it was pretty accurate,' said Shepherd. 'And they apply the same thoroughness to dealing with the Hamas top brass. The al-Qassam Brigades are split into four and five man cells, like the IRA used to do. Then the cells are grouped together into companies and battalions. It makes penetrating the organisation really tough.'

'Wasn't that tough with the Paddies,' said Lane. 'They were riddled with informers throughout the Eighties and Nineties.'

'The Palestines are maybe more religiously committed,' said Shepherd. 'Mossad do use informers, I'm sure, but I think their intel is more down to surveillance and telephone tapping.'

'Well they certainly slipped up over this,' said Standing. 'How could they not have seen this coming?'

'I'm sure they're asking exactly that question in Jerusalem as we speak,' said Shepherd.

75

He was just finishing his meal when the doors to the canteen opened and the major appeared, flanked by two Israeli soldiers. 'How's the refreshment?' he asked.

'Not bad, for airport food,' said Shepherd.

'Well it's on the IDF, so there's no charge,' said the major.

'Thank you for that, sir.'

'Well you'll need a full stomach for what lies ahead of you,' said the major. He looked at his watch, a stainless steel Rolex. 'I have a room ready, so I can start the briefing with your team now. And there's a Saveret Matkal team on the way. You will be going in with them.'

Savaeret Matkal was Israel's special forces unit, also known as The General Staff Reconnaissance Unit. It was based on the SAS and had even taken the regiment's motto, Who Dares Wins. It was primarily a field intelligence gathering unit, but its men were also trained in black ops, combat search and rescue, and long-range penetration.

'I think we'll be okay without babysitters, sir,' said Shepherd.

The major flashed him a cold smile. 'I'm sure you would be, but the PM insists.'

'Then all I can do is thank you,' said Shepherd, knowing that there was nothing to be gained by arguing with the officer. He put down his knife and fork and stood up. The team bolted down the rest of their meal and then followed the major out of the canteen. There was a lift but the major ignored it and he and the two IDF soldiers took the stairs. He led them back to the terminal's reception area, then along a corridor towards a door which was being guarded by a young

76

IDF soldier. The soldier saluted and opened the door.

Shepherd and the SAS team followed the major into a large room overlooking the hangars that faced the terminal. There were two whiteboards on easels and a square table around which were half a dozen white plastic chairs.

The two IDF soldiers took up position either side of the door while the major went to stand between the two whiteboards. On the whiteboard to his right was a large satellite photograph of the area, to his left were a dozen photographs of Hamas fighters, some on trucks, some on motorcycles and others on foot, most of them with black and white scarves hiding their faces.

Shepherd stayed on his feet but the SAS team sprawled on the chairs. Branson was still munching on a piece of toast and Lane was holding a mug of coffee. The major looked around to make sure that he had their attention before starting to speak. 'We are in the midst of a very fluid situation at the moment, so what intel we have is in some cases vague, and evolving as we speak. What we know for sure is that at oh-six-thirty-hours this morning, hundreds of Hamas fighters launched an unprovoked surprise attack on more than twenty communities across Israel, utilising rockets, boats, paragliders, trucks and motorcycles, leaving at least a thousand dead, several thousands injured and a number of hostages have been taken into Gaza. As we are only twelve hours into this, we don't even have an accurate number of deaths yet, and only a small fraction of the dead have been identified. A lot were burned, they were using bombs and grenades to attack the kibbutzes. They're going to need dental records, DNA, the works. And a lot of the dead are foreigners which makes it that much harder. The unidentified remains are being taken to the Shura military base. There are already hundreds being stored there in refrigerated containers.'

'The hostages were all taken to Gaza?' asked Shepherd.

The major nodded. 'The hostage-taking was clearly part of the plan,' he said. 'It was all very well organised. They used explosives and bulldozers to break through the fence. And paragliders to fly over it. They used trucks and motorbikes to reach the festival and the kibbutzes, killed as many as they could before kidnapping another two hundred or so. They were put on the bikes and trucks and taken back into Gaza.'

'Held together, or separately, do you think?'

'They'd be crazy to keep them together. They'll have split them up and be holding them across Gaza.'

'And then what? They start negotiating with the Government?'

Kasher sneered. 'There'll be no negotiation, not after what they've done. Gaza will be raised to the ground for this.'

'Revenge?'

'You say that as if it's a bad thing. They have to learn that you don't fuck with Israel because if you do, Israel will fuck with you.'

'What will they do, the Government?'

'They'll bomb the shit out of Gaza, then they'll send us in to root out the terrorists. I doubt we'll stop until every one of them is dead or behind bars, hopefully the former.'

'And when will that be?' asked Standing.

The major's jaw tightened a fraction at the question,

but he answered almost immediately. 'There are logistics involved, so I would assume weeks rather than days,' he said. 'It will be a fully-fledged military operation rather than just a few sporadic attacks, I'm sure.'

'What about the civilians?' said Lane. 'What about the Palestinians who aren't connected to Hamas?'

'I've no doubt they'll be given the chance to evacuate.' The major shrugged. 'But if not . . .' He left the sentence unfinished.

'Surely it would make sense to wait until the hostages are returned before attacking Hamas,' said Lane.

There was another momentary tightening of the jaw before the major answered. 'Then they win,' he said. 'And they cannot be allowed to win. They need to be smashed.'

There was a fierce intensity in his eyes now and his cheeks were flushed. Shepherd frowned. Soldiers, especially officers, generally kept their emotions in check but something was clearly upsetting the major. 'This is obviously none of our business, sir, but did you lose someone in this attack?' asked Shepherd quietly.

For a second or two Shepherd thought he might have overstepped the mark. The major glared at Shepherd with undisguised anger and he took a deep breath as if he was about to let loose a torrent of abuse. Then he seemed to regain control of himself.

Kasher nodded. 'My sister. And her family. Her husband was shot dead, so were their three sons. My sister was raped. Gang raped. Half a dozen of the animals raped her and the last one shot her in the head. They were at the Holit Kibbutz, just two kilometres from Gaza. It's a small kibbutz, just two hundred people. Thirteen were killed, a lot more injured.'

'I'm sorry for your loss,' said Shepherd.

Kasher shook his head. 'I don't need your sympathy, but I do want you to understand what has happened to my people and why we have to strike back. This is not like the IRA terrorists you fought in the Eighties and Nineties. They committed terrorist atrocities because they wanted to achieve a political objective. But the Palestinians, they have only one objective — to kill all Jews and to wipe Israel from the face of the map. We have to defend ourselves.'

The major's eyes were still burning so Shepherd tried to get the briefing back on track. 'Do you have any idea where the hostages might be?' he asked.

'At this stage we can only make suppositions,' said the major. 'There are satellites scanning the area as we speak, and there are already four drones over Gaza with more on the way. My gut feeling is that they will go underground and stay there. Hamas has a network of tunnels far below ground that allows them to move around without being observed. They use them to smuggle goods in from Egypt and to attack our cities. They store rockets and ammunition there and have command and control centres that we can't see from our aircraft and surveillance drones. They'll be sitting ducks above ground, we might not attack them but we will certainly be able to track them. But once they're in the tunnel system we have no way of tracking them.'

'And you think they will keep the hostages underground?' asked Shepherd.

'Again that would be supposition at this point,' said the major. 'In theory, it would be perfectly possible to bring them up almost anywhere, there are shafts leading to and from the tunnels all over Gaza.

And there are Hamas sympathisers everywhere, and even if they're not sympathisers, they are unlikely to resist if Hamas thugs demand to use their premises. Hamas are not above torturing and killing their own people. They force their own children to be suicide bombers, human life means nothing to them. Most of them believe that if they die in jihad, they get to live in Heaven with Allah and have seventy two virgins at their beck and call. But if they do bring them above ground, there is the possibility that the extra surveillance will spot them. Plus they have no way of knowing when the IDF will attack them. It will be easier to defend themselves in the tunnels.' He shrugged. 'So if I was a betting man, which I am not, I would be putting money on them being in the tunnels.'

'The attackers would probably have taken the shortest route back to Gaza, right?'

'Of course. They are cowards and they would know that we would respond quickly.'

'And once inside Gaza, wouldn't they be more likely to hide the hostages close by?'

'Possibly.'

'So the place to start looking for the hostages from the music festival is just across the border, right?'

'Again, possibly. But . . .' They heard the beating rotor of a helicopter outside. 'That could be the Matkal now,' said the major, clearly grateful for the interruption.

He and Shepherd went outside and peered up at the night sky. Shepherd could make out the shape of the helicopter heading to the airfield from the north but it wasn't until it came within the range of the floodlights that he could see what it was. It was a Eurocopter Israeli Army AS565 Panther, in dark blue and light blue livery. In the commando-transport configuration the Panther could ferry ten fully armed soldiers.

The helicopter flared, kicking up a cloud of dust, and it landed rear wheels first, then settled down onto its nose wheel. The side door opened and a short, stocky man in desert fatigues climbed out. He bent double as he jogged away from the helicopter and its still turning rotors, revealing a bulky desert-patterned backpack. Two more soldiers in fatigues followed him.

The three men jogged over to the major. There was no saluting, these were special forces soldiers and not regular Army. The first soldier spoke to the major in Hebrew and the major replied and then looked at Shepherd. 'This is Staff Sergeant Ariel Friedman,' said the major. 'He has been with the Savaeret Matkal for almost ten years.'

Friedman grinned at Shepherd and offered his hand. He was in his mid thirties with curly black hair. There was no name tag on his fatigues and nothing to identify his unit, standard operating procedure for special forces. 'Pleasure to meet you,' said Friedman. He gestured at his two companions. 'Shalev Eshel and Danit Blai,' he said. Eshel was the taller of the two, with a close-cropped beard and round glasses, Blai was as tall as Shepherd but probably twenty pounds lighter and with a receding hairline. All three men were tanned. They had handguns holstered on the hips and Tavor X95 assault rifles slung over their shoulders.

The Tavor had been the weapon of choice for the IDF for more than twenty years. It was referred to as a bullpup rifle, where the firing grip was located in front of the weapon's breech instead of behind it, making

82

it shorter than traditional assault rifles but without compromising on barrel length, muzzle velocity and range. Compact rifles like the Tavor were perfect for clearing rooms and working in tight environments, and useful when there was a lot of entering and exiting of armoured vehicles.

Shepherd shook hands with Eshel and Blai.

'I have started a general briefing with Mr Shepherd and his SAS team,' said the major. 'Now you're here we can get down to details. This way.'

The major led the way back to the briefing room.

Friedman fell into step beside Shepherd as they followed the major across the tarmac towards the terminal. 'Have you been into Gaza before?'

'Unfortunately yes,' said Friedman. 'Many times.'

'Not pleasant?'

Friedman scowled. 'It's an environment where pretty much everyone hates you and wants you dead. At least in places like Iraq and Afghanistan you have friendlies, locals who want to help you or at least wish you no harm. It's not like that in Gaza or the West Bank.'

'Hopefully by going in at night we won't run into any locals,' said Shepherd.

'I wouldn't bank on that,' said Friedman.

'You can run through any reservations you have at the briefing,' said Shepherd 'Before we go into any operational situation we have what we call a Chinese Parliament where we discuss what's going to happen and everyone gives their view. Once we're all in agreement, there can be no 'I told you so' moments afterwards.'

Friedman grinned. 'Snap,' he said.

They reached the terminal building and they followed the major inside and along to the briefing room.

83

The SAS team were gathered around the satellite photograph and they all looked around as the door opened. 'Bloody hell, Lastman Standing,' said Friedman as he spotted the sergeant standing by the window.

Standing's face broke into a grin. 'Fuck me, is that you Daz? Small world, innit?'

The two men hugged enthusiastically and slapped each other on the back.

The major was frowning in confusion, and he looked at Shepherd. 'Daz?'

'It's a washing powder,' said Shepherd.

The major's frown deepened.

Shepherd couldn't help but smile. 'Daz and Ariel are detergents in the UK. The SAS has a habit of giving its people nicknames, so it looks as if Ariel got stuck with Daz.'

The major nodded. 'Okay,' he said, though he still appeared confused.

The two sergeants broke apart. Standing grinned over at Shepherd. 'Daz here was at Stirling Lines about four years ago. We did a personnel swap with the Savaeret Matkal. They sent two guys over and we sent them two of ours. Daz was with us for three months in all.'

'That should make liaison between the two groups easier,' said the major. He nodded at Friedman. 'I have briefed the team on the general situation following this morning's attack, I think it best that Mr Shepherd now briefs us on what he hopes to achieve with this operation.' He smiled at Friedman. 'I'm as interested as you are to hear what he has to say.'

Friedman sat down next to Standing while Eshel and Blai took seats at the front. The major stood by the door with his arms folded. Shepherd went over to the whiteboard dotted with the photographs of Hamas fighters. He pulled three photographs from the top pocket of his fatigues. There was a pack of Blu Tack on a ledge at the bottom of the whiteboard and he used some to fix the photographs to the surface. He stepped back when he had finished and pointed at the photograph of White. 'David White is an MI5 officer, a high value target that Hamas could make good use of if they knew who he was. He was at the music festival with his two daughters, Hannah and Ella. They were last seen running towards the orchard next to the festival grounds. So far as we know, they are not among the dead so we are assuming that they have been taken hostage. We have been tasked with locating Mr White and his family and returning them to the UK. After talking to Major Kasher, my feeling is that the most likely place for Hamas to be holding the Whites is in the tunnels that run under Gaza.'

'You know how many tunnels there are?' asked Friedman. 'Hundreds of miles.'

'It's likely that they wouldn't move them too far, but even if they did we could question intel sources underground and get a location from them.'

'Question?' said Friedman. 'You mean interrogate?'

'Whatever it takes,' said Shepherd.

'I have to say, Mr Shepherd, it doesn't sound much of a plan,' said Friedman. 'There are a lot of ifs and maybes.'

'If you have a better idea, I'm all ears,' said Shepherd.

'We could wait until we have decent intel.'

'The longer Hamas have him, the more likely it is that they'll find out who he is,' said Shepherd. 'He isn't

85

trained in interrogation resistance and his daughters will be leverage. My feeling is that we go down into the tunnels and either find them or find someone who knows where they are.'

'And how do you plan to get down into the tunnel network?' asked Friedman. 'The entrances are usually well disguised.'

'I was hoping you might have some thoughts on that,' said Shepherd.

There was a knock on the door and one of the IDF soldiers opened it. A female soldier in fatigues stood on the threshold holding a laptop. She spoke to the major in Hebrew and he nodded and beckoned her inside. She was in her late twenties with black hair tied back in a ponytail and matching bright red lipstick and nail varnish. Standing made a clicking noise with his tongue and when Shepherd looked over he grinned unashamedly. 'What?' he said. 'I'm young, free and single.'

'Gentlemen we are in receipt of some intel which might be of use,' said the major. He gestured for the soldier to take the laptop over to the table. She flipped the laptop open and bent over the keyboard as the men gathered around her. She had no name or unit tags on her fatigues, but Shepherd guessed she was with Israeli Military Intelligence, usually abbreviated to Aman, which was the Israeli Army's main intelligence gathering unit

'We always have drones above Gaza, pretty much twenty four-seven,' she said. 'Once we became aware of the attacks, more drones were sent up, but by then the attack was nearing its end. So we don't actually have much footage of the attacks, but we do have this.' She pressed a key and stood back.

The drone was positioned over Gaza and was moving slowly. 'To the left of the screen we are seeing Israeli farmland, in the centre of the screen is the border — you can see where it was breached — and to the right are orchards and farmland inside Gaza.'

Two pick-up trucks were racing across the Israeli farmland to the border, kicking up clouds of dust behind them. They were accompanied by half a dozen motorcycles. There were men waving Kalashnikovs in the back of the trucks, squatting over hooded hostages.

'We think more than two hundred Israelis have been taken across the border, mainly women and children,' said the woman.

'Can we get in closer on the trucks?' asked Shepherd. There was no way of identifying the hostages with the footage they had.

'Not at the moment, but we are working on it and hope to have clearer images over the next few hours.'

The trucks and motorcycles crossed the border. There were two massive bulldozers either side of a gaping hole in the fence.

There were fields and orchards on the Gaza side of the border and the trucks raced along a narrow track. The bikes overtook the trucks, presumably to get away from the swirling dust clouds kicked up behind them. The drone moved to keep the trucks in the centre of the screen.

The date and time was shown in a strip along the bottom of the screen, along with the latitude, longitude and height of the drone. 'Why didn't the operator go lower?' asked Shepherd.

'They're told not to go below a thousand feet without authorisation,' said the woman. 'And this was all happening very quickly.'

The bikes reached a built up area, mainly concrete blocks with flat roofs, interspersed with mosques. The trucks had to slow down as the roads were narrow. The drone kept pace with the vehicles and soon the screen was filled with square buildings separated by narrow lanes giving it the feel of a video game.

'This is the Palestinian town of Maghazi, also referred to as the Al-Maghazi refugee camp, located in the Deir al-Balah Governorate,' said the woman. 'It's relatively small, just over half a square kilometre, with a population of close to thirty-three thousand people. As you can see, the houses are packed close together and it is one of the most crowded places on earth.'

The three trucks slowed as they drove down a narrow alley. People flattened themselves against walls as the trucks went by. The trucks slowed even further to make a right turn, then they drove through a crowded market, carving their way through the shoppers like sharks ripping through a shoal of fish. They entered a small alley barely wide enough to accommodate them, then drove into a small courtyard in front of a five storey building. The motorbikes had already stopped and the riders dismounted. Shepherd realised that there had been hostages on some of the bikes and they had been thrown to the ground. One of the Hamas fighters was kicking a hostage in the stomach. The hostage curled up into a foetal ball. Shepherd couldn't tell if it was a man or a woman.

'This is the Al-Maghazi Secondary School, which has close to two thousand pupils,' said the woman.

The trucks stopped and the Hamas fighters jumped down from the back of the trucks and began dragging their hostages into the building. Half of them seemed to be children.

'So the hostages are being held in the school?' asked Shepherd.

'That's possible,' said the woman. 'But Hamas often conceal their tunnel entrances in schools, hospitals and mosques, and build their command centres under such buildings.'

'It means that when we launch attacks against what are valid military targets, we are accused of killing innocent civilians,' said the major. 'In fact it is Hamas that is responsible for their deaths by using them as human shields.'

'So you think the hostages were taken through the school and down into the tunnels?' Shepherd asked the woman.

'I would say that is the most likely scenario,' said the woman. 'But they could be being held in the school building itself. There's no way of knowing for sure.'

The video came to an end. The major spoke to the woman in Hebrew and she closed the laptop, picked it up, and left the room.

Shepherd looked over at Friedman. 'So we get to the school and get down into the tunnels?'

Friedman nodded. 'We can do that. But it won't be easy.'

'Have you been down the tunnels before?'

'A couple of times. Not in Al-Maghazi, but further north in Jabalia. It's a hostile environment, no question. Tight spaces, booby traps, not much room to duck and dive.' He looked over at Standing. 'Have you guys had tunnel experience?'

'Not really. Lots of close quarter battle training obviously, but corridors rather than tunnels.'

89

'We'd best go in first,' said Friedman.

'What about getting there?' asked Shepherd. 'Can we use the heli?'

'We can, but I wouldn't recommend it for infil,' said Friedman. 'There'll hear us coming and we know there are hundreds of armed Hamas over there who would love the opportunity to blow an Army chopper out of the sky.'

'So we go in on foot?' asked Standing.

Friedman nodded. 'It's dark, we've got night vision equipment and the border has already been breached.' The sergeant looked over at the major. 'Sir, could we get the lights killed at the border while we cross?'

'I don't think that would be a problem. For how long?'

Friedman went over to the map and ran his finger from the border fence to the school. 'Just until we're in Al-Maghazi. Including cutting across the farmland on this side of the border, fifteen minutes max. We can have the helicopter drop us a kilometre from the border. That should be far enough.'

'What about your exfil?' asked the major.

'We can use the helicopter for that,' said Friedman. 'It can wait where it drops us and we can call it in when we're ready.' He peered at the map, then tapped on it. 'Here's the school. Easy enough to get to on foot. We go in, locate the tunnels, and hopefully retrieve the hostages. Once we have them we call in the helicopter and it can land in the yard in front of the school.'

'You're not worried about the heli being compromised?' asked Shepherd.

'Hopefully it will be in and out before Hamas realise what's happening,' said Friedman. 'But if the area does go hot, we can exfil on foot. We'd need IDF forces on standby close to the border to provide covering fire if needed.'

The major nodded. 'I can arrange that.'

Friedman looked over at Shepherd. 'How does that sound?'

Shepherd nodded. 'Works for me.' He looked at his team and was faced with a line of nodding heads. Shepherd looked back at Friedman. 'Yes. Sounds like a plan. When can we can go in?'

'Within the hour,' said Friedman. 'I'll need to brief the pilots and we'll have to check our gear, but other than that we're good to go.'

'How confident are you that you'll be able to find the tunnel entrance in the school?' asked Shepherd.

'They do a good job of hiding their entrances but we have experience in that area.' Friedman went over to the table and gestured at the weapons lying there. 'You might want to rethink your kit,' he said. 'There are large rooms and command centres down there but the shafts are usually quite tight and the tunnels can be even tighter. You won't have room to swing the HKs around, especially if you have suppressors fitted, and you will need them.' He pointed at the shotgun. 'And you really won't want to be firing one of those underground.'

'They're good for clearing rooms,' said Lane defensively.

'I suppose they are, but the noise will be deafening in a confined space. To be honest, handguns with suppressors is always the best way to go.'

Shepherd looked over at Standing who shook his head. 'Sorry, it was kick, bollock scramble and we didn't bring suppressors.'

'What do you have, Glocks?' asked Friedman.

Standing took his gun from its holster and held it up. It was a Glock 17.

'We've got plenty of Glock suppressors,' said Friedman.

'But we can take the HKs with us, right?' said Standing.

'I think you'll find them unwieldy down the tunnels, but sure, just keep them on your backs. Or if you're up for it, I can get you Tavors.'

'Appreciate the offer, but an unfamiliar weapon might slow me down.' He looked at the other SAS men. 'What about you guys?'

'I'm OK,' said Branson. 'Like you say, better the devil you know. Especially if we're going to be in the dark.'

Heron nodded in agreement. 'I'm fine with my HK,' he said.

'I'll take a Tavor,' said Lane. 'Seeing as how my Mossberg has been ruled out.'

Friedman grinned. 'I'll get one for you.'

'And what about night vision gear?' asked Shepherd.

'There are two schools of thought,' said Friedman. 'Back in the Vietnam War, the American tunnel rats went down with just a gun and a flashlight and some of our guys prefer doing it that way. Me, I'm happier with night vision goggles. But you'll want armour and helmets during the infil in case we're unlucky enough to cross paths with a sniper or a Hamas patrol.'

Shepherd looked over at Standing who winked. 'We've got night vision goggles,' said Standing.

'What about body armour and helmets?' asked Shepherd.

'Swings and roundabouts,' said Friedman. 'Protection is always good but body armour slows you down and makes it harder to move through the tunnels. Ditto helmets, plus you need your ears uncovered. Me, I just wear a vest.'

'And I'm guessing you're not in favour of flashbangs?'

'They're never a good idea in confined spaces, but I usually take a couple in case you emerge into a room packed with hostiles.'

'What if there are Hamas fighters down there?' said Standing. 'Do they stay in darkness or do they have a lighting system?'

'It varies,' said Friedman. 'Parts of the tunnel system have generators and power, with proper lighting systems. In other parts they have portable battery operated lanterns. You're thinking about the night vision goggles?'

Standing nodded. 'It can ruin your night vision if someone shines a torch at you.'

'At this time of night most of the hostiles will probably be sleeping,' said Friedman.

'Except they'll all be fired up at what happened today,' said Shepherd. 'They'll probably be sitting around telling war stories.'

'Or gearing up for an Israeli counter-attack,' said Heron.

'Yeah, I can't see that they'll all be tucked up for the night,' said Standing.

'I think we're better off assuming that they're awake and waiting for us,' said Shepherd.

'Which is why we'll need night vision goggles,' said Friedman. 'They'll see flashlights coming.'

'I'm happy to take point,' said Shepherd.

'No, Spider, that's down to me,' said Standing.

'I appreciate the enthusiasm guys,' said Friedman, 'but I'll be going point. This is our turf, it's what we train for.'

Shepherd knew that the sergeant was right and that there was no point in arguing. 'Agreed,' he said.

'What about comms?' said Lane. 'Can our systems talk to each other? Our system is digital now.'

'Our's too,' said Friedman. He gestured at Eshel. 'Shalev is our comms guy, you two can work it out. If necessary we can fit you out with our kit.' He looked around the group. 'Any questions?' He was faced with only shaking heads and he grinned. 'Okay, let's do this.'

9

The Panther flew low over the farmland. Shepherd already had his night vision goggles flipped down and the fields below had the look of a dark green sea. The side doors were open. Friedman and Eshel were on the port side, looking down, Standing and Branson were on the other.

Lane was sitting next to Shepherd, cradling his newly acquired Tavor assault rifle. They all had comms earpieces in with transceivers clipped to the belts. The night vision goggles were attached to their Kevlar helmets and could be flipped down when needed.

Friedman was looking forward, the wind rippling his cheeks. He turned and flashed Shepherd an OK sign. Shepherd grinned and returned the gesture.

The helicopter began to turn to the right and descend. Shepherd caught a glimpse of Gaza in the distance, and beyond it the black nothingness that was the Mediterranean, then he was looking at an orchard and then a ploughed field. The helicopter levelled off, then smoothly descended as the turbines quietened.

The touchdown was as gentle as any that Shepherd had experienced. The turbines powered down and the rotors began to slow. Friedman and Eshel climbed out. Shepherd followed them, cradling his HK. There was a tiny sliver of moon high above them. The men filed off the helicopter and walked over the ploughed earth, away from the still turning rotors.

They gathered around Friedman, who waited until he had their attention before pointing to the north. 'It's clear ground, but you need to watch yourself, a sprained or broken ankle will put you out of commission, so let's aim for twelve minutes to get to the border. The fence is still down and there are troops in the area keeping watch. Those troops will be able to lay down covering fire if we have to beat a hasty retreat, but they are under orders not to cross into Gaza.'

The helicopter's turbines were quiet now. It would remain where it was until it got the call to assist with the exfil.

'Right, let's do it,' said Friedman. He started walking towards the border. Eshel and Blai followed him, spreading apart. Lane and Branson moved to the side as they followed, making an arrowhead formation. Coleman and Heron were next, cradling their HKs, and Standing and Shepherd brought up the rear.

Normally Shepherd could cover a kilometre in less than four minutes, but crossing farmland while wearing night vision goggles was far from normal. The goggles worked just fine, the problem was that the wearer couldn't see his own feet, visibility was restricted to about a yard in front, which means there was no way of seeing obstacles close by. Moving forward at speed could be dangerous, so unless they were under fire, slowly and surely was the way to go.

They reached a grove of olive trees and moved through it like ghosts. It was a warm night with a soft breeze ruffling through the trees. The men moved apart as they passed through the grove. Shepherd saw a curved root emerging from the soil ahead of him. He moved to the side as it passed from view, then moved again to avoid a cricket ball-sized stone. He and Standing kept checking the rear, more from force of habit than because they expected an attack.

Eventually Shepherd could see a group of IDF vehicles ahead of them. There were two SandCats, four M113 variant armoured personnel carriers and a Namer armoured personnel carrier with a Trophy radar system and projectile launcher on the roof. Shepherd knew that Namer meant leopard in Hebrew and that the vehicle was based on a Merkava Mark IV tank chassis. The Trophy active protection system was an Israeli-made system designed to protect vehicles from rocket propelled grenades and high explosive anti-tank rounds by firing what were called Explosively Formed Projectiles at incoming threats. A computer calculated the nature of the threat, the time to impact and the angle of approach, and then the EFPs were fired from two rotating launchers on either side of the vehicle.

There was a group of soldiers standing at the rear of the Namer, and more standing in a line facing the breached fence.

Friedman held his carbine above his head, and Eshel and Blai followed his example. Friedman called out to the soldiers in Hebrew and as they turned they brought their rifles up to the shoulders. Friedman shouted in Hebrew again and the soldiers lowered their weapons.

Shepherd and the SAS team had their weapons above their heads but the IDF soldiers were clearly expecting them and they were waved over.

Friedman had a brief conversation with an IDF lieutenant and then went over to Shepherd. 'We can go now,' he said. 'They've seen no activity since they got here, which is good news. They'll cover us as we cross over but as I said before, they are not authorised to cross the border.'

'But we are?' said Standing with a sly smile.

'Good point,' said Friedman. 'We're in a very grey area.' He looked around the group. 'So, are we all good?'

The SAS team nodded.

'Hopefully we'll get to the school without incident, but if we do encounter hostiles they are to be treated as such. We've got suppressors on our weapons so if possible let us return fire.'

'What if we come across civilians?' asked Shepherd.

'At this time of night, civilians will be tucked up in bed,' said Friedman. 'There shouldn't be any women or children out, and if they are they'll be up to no good. Okay, let's do it. Again we'll maintain a slow pace as we cross the farmland, but once we're in the built up area we'll be able to move faster.'

Friedman walked across the border, flanked by Eshel and Blai. The SAS team spread out behind them, with Shepherd and Standing bringing up the rear. They cut across a ploughed field which was hard going as every step was a potential twisted ankle. After a hundred yards or so they reached a field that had been planted with carrots and that was easier. They reached a road but there was no traffic and they jogged across to a patch of wasteland that appeared to be used as a rubbish dump, it was dotted with abandoned fridges and washing machines, and littered with used plastic bottles and carrier bags. Behind the wasteland were low rise concrete houses with flat roofs. There were washing lines swinging in the night breeze and satellite dishes pointing up towards the sky.

The men spent a few minutes scanning the buildings ahead of them, especially the roofs and the windows, perfect places for a sniper to hide. When they were satisfied that there were no threats, they moved across the road. Friedman led the way to a narrow street with no pavements or lights, barely twelve feet across. Eshel and Blai followed him, their carbines constantly in motion.

Lane, Heron and Coleman moved after them, in single file. Shepherd and Standing scanned the wasteland and the border. All was quiet. Standing gestured with his carbine for Shepherd to start down the street. 'Age before beauty,' he said with a grin.

'Pearls before swine,' Shepherd replied, before heading down the street, keeping close to the wall on his left.

Friedman began to jog and they all increased their pace. He slowed as he reached a junction, then moved to the left to get a better view of the street to his right. It was clear and he began to jog again. The team followed him.

The streets were deserted and most of the buildings they passed were in darkness. Friedman had a small tablet strapped on his left arm and he was following a GPS route to the target. Shepherd didn't need any electronic help, one look at the map in the briefing room and he had committed it to memory. The school was only minutes away.

Friedman slowed to make another turn, then quickened his pace. The school was at the end of the alley and the team slowed, their guns at the ready. Shepherd and Standing looked behind them. The alley was clear and there were no lights on in any of the windows overlooking it.

The Israelis moved slowly towards the low concrete block wall that surrounded the school courtyard. The motorcycles had gone but two of the pick-up trucks were still there, parked close to the building. Shepherd froze when he saw a man emerge from behind the truck on the right, smoking a cigarette and holding a mobile phone to his ear. They all crouched down behind the wall. They had a clear view of the man through their night vision goggles but he probably wouldn't be able to see them in the darkness.

'I'll take care of this,' said Friedman over the radio. He slung his carbine on his back and pulled a commando knife from a scabbard on his right leg. He moved to the left, bent in a low crouch, keeping below the wall.

The man with the phone had his back to them and was leaning against the truck. If he was there as a lookout, he was doing a lousy job, thought Shepherd. He looked around the courtyard. There was more than enough room for the helicopter to land, and the buildings facing the school were just two stories tall with flat roofs. The noise would be an issue, obviously, but with any luck the helicopter would be able to get in and out before Hamas realised what had happened.

A second man had appeared from behind the trucks and Shepherd's breath caught in his throat. Unlike the man on the phone, the second man was armed, though his Kalashnikov was hanging from its sling. Shepherd looked at Standing. This was a problem. Standing nodded. 'Daz, we've got two hostiles at the trucks,' he said over the radio. 'I'm coming over.'

Standing moved on tiptoe, skirting the courtyard and heading to where Friedman was crouched by the wall. Eshel and Blai had their suppressed Tavors targeted on the two Hamas fighters. Even with suppressors fitted, there would still be a loud pop if the guns were fired, one of the reasons that professionals hated it when they were described as silencers. Nothing could truly silence the sound of a gun being fired, suppression was the best you could hope for.

Standing reached Friedman and the two men rolled over the wall and slipped into the courtyard. They moved like shadows towards the school building and then Shepherd lost sight of them.

The man on the phone was waving his left hand around now, clearly agitated, and the other man was watching him. Shepherd's heart was racing now. If there were two lookouts, there could well be more, and they needed to get inside the school without being seen. If the guards spotted them, the mission could well be over there and then.

The man ended the call and put his phone away. Then he went around the pick-up truck and reappeared holding a Kalashnikov. He began talking to the second man. The seconds ticked by. Shepherd couldn't see Friedman or Standing, but knew that they would be stealthily approaching the Hamas fighters, knives at the ready. They would only get the one chance, knives only ever worked against guns when you had the element of surprise.

A pale green shape emerged from behind the truck. Shepherd couldn't tell if it was Friedman or Standing, but whoever it was pulled a knife across the throat of the man who had been using the phone. The second Hamas fighter grabbed for his Kalashnikov but a second pale green shape appeared and grabbed him in a choke hold. After several seconds the man collapsed.

'All done,' said Standing over the radio. 'Move in.'

Eshel and Blai straightened up, looked around, and entered the courtyard. The SAS team followed them. They jogged over to the pick-up trucks. Friedman was wiping his knife on the trousers of the man he had killed. Standing was bending over the Hamas fighter that he had strangled. The man was still breathing but his eyes were closed. Standing grinned up at Shepherd. 'Thought he'd probably know where the tunnel entrance is,' he said.

'Nice one,' said Shepherd. 'You okay to carry him inside?'

'Light as a feather,' said Standing.

Friedman slid his knife back into its scabbard. 'We need to check that the inside is clear,' he said. 'We should leave one man out here to keep watch. We don't want any nasty surprises.'

Standing looked over at Branson. 'Sorry, Virgin, you get the short straw.'

Shepherd could see from the look on Branson's face that the trooper wasn't happy about being left outside, but he just nodded. 'Roger that.'

Shepherd knew it made sense to choose Branson as he was the biggest of the men and size would be a disadvantage down in the tunnels.

'You see anything, you let us know,' said Standing. He picked up the unconscious fighter and threw him over his shoulder, then looked over at Friedman. 'Ready when you are, Daz.'

Friedman had his carbine in his hands now, and he and Eshel and Blai followed him to the school entrance. The wooden double doors weren't locked and Eshel held the right hand door open as the other two men slipped through. Heron and Lane followed.

Then Coleman.

Shepherd took the door from Eshel and the Israeli slipped through. Standing carried the unconscious fighter inside and Shepherd followed him. Branson moved to guard the entrance as Shepherd let the door close behind him.

They was a counter facing the door, and a corridor that ran right and left. The floor was tiled and there were large bladed fans set into the ceiling. To the left of the counter was a flight of concrete steps leading up. Standing dropped the unconscious fighter on to the floor.

'Lastman, can you get your guys to clear the ground floor rooms?' asked Friedman. 'I don't think we need to clear the whole building, Shalev and Danit can wait at the stairs to catch anyone who comes down.'

Standing nodded. 'Penny, can you and Clint go left? Mustard can you take Spider with you and go right? Make sure there are no hostiles around, but also keep an eye out for tunnel entrances.' He grinned at Shepherd. 'I'll have a chat with Mr Hamas here while you're gone.'

'Probably best I'm not around to see that.'

Standing winked. 'That's what I thought.'

Eshel and Blai walked up the stairs and stopped just before the upper floor. Lane and Heron headed down the corridor to the left.

Coleman nodded at Shepherd and they both moved down the corridor to the right. The first room they came to had a glass window set into the door through which they could see lines of wooden desks facing a blackboard. Coleman opened the door and went in, his HK at his shoulder. Shepherd followed him. The floor was tiled with no obvious breaks in the grouting.

The walls were painted concrete and other than the desks there was no furniture in the room.

Coleman and Shepherd went back into the corridor. The next three rooms were almost identical classrooms, the only difference being the number of desks and the size of the blackboards.

At the end of the corridor was a double door that opened into a gymnasium with high ceilings and fluorescent lights hanging by chains from a concrete ceiling. There were horizontal wooden bars running along one wall, basketball hoops on two walls, a trampoline, a vaulting horse and a stack of plastic mats in one corner. There was another door at the far side of the gymnasium and Shepherd headed towards it.

'All clear here,' said Lane over the radio.

'We're in a gymnasium,' said Shepherd. 'Just checking it out.'

He pulled the door open. It was a storage room packed with rolled-up yoga mats, basketballs, skipping ropes and other gym equipment. It was hard to make out details with the night vision goggles so he flipped them up and pulled out a small Maglite torch from a holder on his belt. He switched it on and played the beam around the walls of the cupboard.

Lane appeared at his shoulder. 'Are you okay there, Spider?' he asked.

'Just give me a second, Penny.' He shone the beam down on the tiled floor and frowned when he saw scratches there. The wall facing him was lined with shelves filled with cardboard boxes containing weights and yoga bands. He gripped one of the shelves and pulled. The shelf moved and the back wall moved with it. It was hinged on the right and opened easily. Shepherd pulled it half open and shone the torch inside.

Behind the false wall was a steel ladder leading down a concrete tube. 'Bingo,' he said. He slowly closed the wall and stepped out of the cupboard.

'Daz, we've found a tunnel shaft in the gymnasium.'

'Roger that,' said Friedman. 'Heading your way now.'

10

Friedman peered down the shaft and nodded. 'Well spotted,' he said. 'This is obviously well used, you can see the marks on the ladder. There's fresh dirt on the rungs, and there's blood. Looks like someone who went down there was injured.'

'Hostages?' said Standing.

Friedman nodded. 'Almost certainly.' He switched off his torch.

'So we go down, right?' said Shepherd. 'Strike while the iron is hot.'

'Definitely,' said Friedman. 'That's why we're here.'

'Someone is going to have to stay behind, to watch over the prisoner and keep an eye on our guns,' said Shepherd.

'We could get Virgin in,' said Standing.

'I'd feel happier if he stayed outside,' said Shepherd. 'If any Hamas fighters arrive we need to know straight away. If they get inside, it'll be too late.'

'Truth be told, Spider, you'd be the obvious choice,' said Standing.

'Because?'

'Because we're all match fit and, no offence, you're probably the heaviest of us and size is a disadvantage down there.'

'How much do you weigh, Matt?'

'That's not the point.'

'I doubt that there's more than a few pounds between us.'

Standing patted his stomach. 'Yeah, but mine's

all muscle.'

Shepherd ignored the jibe. 'You need me down there if we go any distance in the tunnels,' said Shepherd. 'Easy to get lost down in there in the dark. We don't have a map and the GPS probably won't work underground.' He tapped his forehead. 'My memory will get us in and out.'

Standing nodded as he considered what Shepherd had said. 'Yeah, fair point,' he said. He turned to look at Lane. 'Penny, are you okay to mind the shop?'

'I was hoping to try out my Tavor,' he said.

'I'll stay,' said Coleman. 'I've got to be honest, I've never liked confined spaces.'

'Mustard it is,' said Standing. 'Right, I suggest I go down first to check that all's clear and you can follow me.'

Friedman held up his hand. 'It's not as simple as that, Lastman,' he said. 'First of all, we need to decide whether we use flashlights or night vision gear. The problem is that the goggles are attached to our helmets, and helmets can get in the way down in the tunnels.'

'Torches are fine with me,' said Standing. He pulled a Maglite from a holster on his belt.

'And we talked about guns before. You can see how tight that shaft is, you're not going to be able to use an HK on the way down. It's too tight even for a Tavor.'

'So handguns it is,' said Standing. 'Handguns and torches. Old school.'

'Yeah, but here's the thing,' said Friedman. 'You can see how narrow that shaft is. Barely enough room to turn around. We've no way of knowing if that shaft goes down twenty feet or a hundred. If you go down feet first, you might well end up with a Kalashnikov round up your backside and that would ruin your day.' He knelt down and shrugged off his backpack. The two other Israelis did the same.

Standing winced at the thought. 'Hopefully you've got a workaround?'

Friedman grinned as he pulled a coil of climbing rope from his backpack. 'Headfirst is the way to go,' he said. 'And I doubt that's something that even the SAS train for.'

Shepherd stared at the sergeant in disbelief, but the man was serious. 'You've done this before?'

'Several times. Piece of cake.'

Eshel and Blai had pulled similar coils of rope from their backpacks and Friedman deftly tied them together. He placed his carbine on the floor by the wall and took off his helmet. He sat down and tied one end of the rope around his ankles. 'I'll be using the radio, but if I make contact with hostiles I'll probably start shooting straight away.' He grinned. 'So unless I tell you otherwise, pull me up at the first sound of gunfire. Assuming I get to the bottom without bumping into hostiles, you can join me. Obviously you can come down in the traditional manner, feet first.'

Friedman crawled over to the shaft. Eshel and Blai picked up the rope and let it play through their hands. Shepherd and Standing both bent down and grabbed the rope. 'The more the merrier,' said Standing.

Friedman pulled his Glock from its holster and slid a small flashlight from a pocket on his fatigues. He pulled a suppressor from his pocket and screwed it into the barrel of the Glock. 'See you down there, hopefully,' he said. He reached out to grab the ladder and eased himself head first through the hatch. The four men kept a tight grip on the rope as Friedman disappeared. There was no light in the shaft so Shepherd assumed he was going down in darkness.

Shepherd kept an eye on the rope as it played through his hands, counting off the feet. After twelve feet of rope had gone down the shaft there was a quick flash of light. Shepherd tensed but almost immediately there was a soft whisper over the radio. 'Twenty feet or so to go,' said Friedman. 'All clear so far.'

They continued to play out the rope. After another ten feet, Friedman told them to hold. They gripped the rope tightly and waited. 'Okay, I heard movement, but it's a rat,' said Friedman over the radio. 'A big one. But it's gone now, lower me again.'

They let the rope slip through their hands, a foot every second or two, slowly but surely. Ten seconds passed and then Friedman told them to stop. 'I'm at the bottom,' he said quietly. 'Give me a few seconds.'

The seconds ticked by. 'All clear down here,' he said. 'It's quite a big tunnel, looks like it might be one of their main thoroughfares.'

'Do you think we can use our night vision gear?' asked Shepherd. 'Helmets and all.'

'Yeah, I think so. I can stand up and there's still headroom. Might as well bring your gear down. My guys can come down first. You and your people can follow.'

'Roger that,' said Shepherd.

'I'm releasing the rope now,' said Friedman.

The rope went slack and they pulled it back up. Blai coiled it up and put it into Friedman's backpack.

Eshel slung his rifle over his back, and stepped on to the ladder. 'Coming down,' he said.

Once he had disappeared down the shaft, Blai followed him.

'Do you wanna go first, Spider?' asked Standing. 'Or tail end Charlie?'

'I'll go first if that's okay,' said Shepherd.

Standing waved at the shaft. 'Be my guest,' he said.

Shepherd slung his carbine over his shoulder, grabbed the ladder and stepped on it. He moved slowly down. The shaft was lined with rough concrete, pretty much circular with the ladder fixed to the wall with steel bolts. He looked up and saw Standing step onto the ladder. Shepherd concentrated on the climb. Left foot. Left hand. Right foot. Right hand. It was surprisingly tiring and his calves were soon burning.

He counted off thirty rungs and then leaned back and peered through his legs. He saw Blai below him, still on the ladder. Left foot. Left hand. Right foot. Right hand.

He looked up again. Standing was on the ladder now, following him down.

Shepherd counted off another ten rungs and then looked down. Blai was off the ladder now. Shepherd continued to climb down. He reached the bottom and stepped off the ladder. He was in a concrete-lined tunnel, just over six feet tall and about three feet wide. Blai was ahead of him, and beyond him was Fried-man. They were both looking down the tunnel.

Shepherd turned. Eshel was facing the other direction, his carbine at the ready.

'There are recent marks on the floor here,' said Friedman over the radio. 'They went this way. North.'

Shepherd moved away from the ladder to make way for Standing. 'I didn't think the tunnels would be as big as this,' said Standing, looking around. 'This is a professional job, all right. Must have cost a fortune.'

'They've been working on them for years,' said

Eshel. 'They run all over Gaza. They're not all as big as this one, but most of them are lined with concrete. They're pretty much bomb proof.'

Shepherd eased past Blai and went over to Friedman. The Israeli pointed at marks in the dust. 'A lot of people have been down here, and the tracks are going north.'

Shepherd looked down the tunnel. It ran for about fifty feet and then branched left and right. There was just about enough space for two men to squeeze by each other but they would need to move in single file. He wanted to ask if he could lead the way but it made sense for Friedman to take point.

'We need to stay three or four metres apart, just in case we hit a booby trap,' said Friedman.

'Got you,' said Shepherd. The Israeli didn't have to state the obvious — that the spacing meant that any booby trap would only kill the man who triggered it.

Standing joined them and looked down the tunnel. 'Not much room for manoeuvre,' he said. 'One guy with a Kalashnikov could put us all down.'

'Not if we stay spaced out,' said Friedman. 'Plus we'll see their lights.'

'Unless they've got night vision equipment as well,' said Standing.

'Let's try and look on the bright side,' said Shepherd.

Lane arrived at the bottom of the ladder, closely followed by Heron.

'Okay, let's do this,' said Friedman. He began moving slowly down the tunnel, looking up and down, left and right.

Booby traps could come in many forms. A wire linked to a grenade, a photosensitive cell linked to an

111

IED, even a simple hole in the floor filled with spikes. Friedman had to check for all possibilities. Shepherd followed him, keeping his distance. Friedman slowed as he approached a junction with tunnels leading left and right. He peered around the corner, checking that the left branch was clear, then looked right. 'All clear,' he said. He looked down at the tunnel floor. 'Looks as if they went right,' he said. He headed down the right branch. This tunnel was a little smaller than the one leading from the shaft, a little over five and a half feet high and three feet wide. Shepherd had to bend down to stop his helmet from clipping the roof. He kept his carbine close to his chest. The weapon was virtually useless in the tunnel, any shot he fired would only hit Friedman.

The tunnel ran straight for almost a hundred feet. Friedman continued to move slowly, looking all around. At the end of the section was a large room, twenty feet square, with two tunnels leading off it. There were half a dozen rough wooden stools and a low wooden table in the room. 'Hold while I check it's safe,' said Friedman over the radio. He methodically checked all the furniture and the entrances to the two tunnels before confirming that he was satisfied. Shepherd stepped into the room. Standing followed.

Friedman pointed at the floor of the tunnel to the right. 'This way,' he said.

Blai entered the room, followed by Heron and Lane.

'Comms check,' said Standing over the radio. 'Can you hear us, Mustard?'

'Loud and clear,' said Coleman. 'What's it like down there?'

'Not as bad as you'd expect,' said Standing. 'Not exactly all mod cons, but you can imagine people living down here, if they had to.'

Friedman headed down the right hand tunnel. It was slightly bigger than the tunnel they had left, and he was able to stand upright. Shepherd followed. They moved down the tunnel in single file for two minutes, then Friedman stopped and raised his right hand, fist clenched. At first Shepherd thought he had spotted a booby trap, but then he turned, pointed at his ear and then pointed down the tunnel. He'd heard something. Shepherd swung his carbine down so that the barrel was pointing at the tunnel floor. His finger was off the trigger, there was still no way he could fire. It would all be down to Friedman, who began to move forward in a low crouch, his carbine at the ready.

The tunnel began to curve to the right. Shepherd could hear voices now. At least two men. Maybe more. They were talking in Arabic. Shepherd's heart was pounding now. They weren't down in the tunnels to take prisoners so the encounter would have only one of two outcomes. Hopefully the element of surprise would mean that they had the upper hand, but even if it went bad there was nothing that Shepherd could do. His life was in Friedman's hands.

Friedman had his carbine up to his shoulder now. Ahead of them was the glow of an electric light, a torch or maybe a lantern. Friedman stopped and flicked up his night vision goggles. Shepherd did the same. He looked over his shoulder. Standing and the rest of the team had all stopped using their night vision.

Friedman was moving forward again, placing his feet carefully, making no sound. Shepherd moved his head to the side to get a better look, but all he could see was a patch of orange light reflecting off the tunnel wall. The voices were louder now.

Suddenly Friedman sprang forward. He pulled the trigger. Even with the suppressor, the sound of the shot was loud enough to make Shepherd flinch. He had to fight the urge to slip his finger on the trigger of his HK but he still wasn't in a position to shoot.

Friedman stepped to the left and fired again, this time two quick shots.

There was a burst of fire from down the tunnel and rounds ripped into the tunnel wall, splattering Friedman with concrete dust. Friedman dropped to the ground and fired two more shots. Shepherd rushed forward. With the Israeli on the floor, Shepherd now had room to fire.

A second burst of fire sent rounds smashing into the tunnel wall again. One ricocheted by Shepherd's left foot, missing it by inches. Friedman fired again. Shepherd came up behind him and saw the shooter, a Palestinian man in his twenties standing in the middle of a circular room wielding a Kalashnikov. Behind him were two men on the floor, their chests bloody. The gunsmoke was stinging Shepherd's eyes but he ignored the discomfort and aimed at the man's chest. Both rounds hit home and the man fell back and slumped to the floor.

Shepherd kept moving, stepping to the side of Friedman, gun at the ready. There were two camp beds in the room and a small table on which were plates of food — cheese, flat bread and olives.

There was just one tunnel leading off the room and Shepherd went over to it. It was in darkness. Shepherd turned his head from side to side, listening intently. Friedman's Tavor and Shepherd's HK had both been suppressed, but the Kalashnikov had been

114

firing flat out and the sound was sure to carry. Standing joined him, looking down the tunnel. 'They must have heard that,' he said.

'Maybe, maybe not,' said Shepherd. 'Bends in the tunnel might keep the noise down.'

'If they know we're coming, we need to move fast.'

'I hear you,' said Shepherd.

Friedman got to his feet. 'Is everybody okay?' he asked over the radio.

One by one, the team checked in.

'What do you think?' Shepherd asked Friedman. 'Do we move on or wait?'

'The worry is that they hear the shots and move on,' said Friedman. 'If that happens, we risk losing the hostages for ever.'

'So we move?'

'I think we have to,' said Friedman.

'If they did hear the gunfire, they'll be waiting for us,' said Standing. 'And that won't be pleasant.'

'We need to get the hostages,' said Shepherd.

'The hostage, the one that your bosses want,' said Standing.

'We'll rescue as many as we can,' said Shepherd. 'But we have to move quickly.'

Standing nodded. 'I hear you, Spider. But if we're the ones doing the pushing, I should be leading the way. It's not fair to put the Israelis in the firing line.'

'This is our op,' said Friedman quickly. 'Our turf. And we train for this.'

'I get that. But these tunnels mean that the guy in front takes any fire heading our way.'

'I'm fine with that, Lastman.'

'I know you are. And fair play to you. But I don't want you putting your life on the line for one of our assets.'

'Rock, paper, scissors?' said Friedman.

Standing frowned. 'What?'

'Rock, paper, scissors. We don't have time to keep discussing this, every second counts. So we'll rock, paper, scissors it.'

'You're mad.'

'He's right, Matt, we need to be moving,' said Shepherd.

'Fine,' said Standing. He held out his clenched right hand. Friedman did the same.

Standing nodded and the two men raised and lowered their fists three times. On three Standing's fist stayed clenched while Friedman's palm was open. Friedman grinned. 'Paper beats rock,' he said.

'Best of three,' said Standing.

'No,' said the Israeli. 'We're done. If it makes you feel better, you can be number two.' He looked over at Blai. 'Danit, you stick behind Lastman. Okay, let's do this.' He headed down the tunnel, his carbine up against his shoulder. Standing followed, leaving a ten feet gap. Blai went next and Shepherd followed him.

The tunnel widened as they walked along it. It went straight for almost a hundred metres and then curved to the left. Friedman was moving cautiously, on the lookout for booby traps. They reached a fork and Friedman spent a few seconds examining the ground before pointing down the tunnel on the right. They moved into it. This tunnel ran straight, and Shepherd knew they were heading north. He thought back to the map they had studied on the table and his trick memory clicked in. They had moved away from the school and were now passing under streets of small houses. Ahead of them was a hospital.

116

The tunnel opened into another chamber. There were two wooden benches and a stack of bottled water, and next to it was a garbage bag filled with empty plastic bottles. There were two tunnels leading off the chamber, one to the left and one straight ahead. Friedman moved forward. This tunnel was a long one, more than two hundred metres, running true north. It opened into a square chamber lined with shelves filled with boxes of canned food. There was a toilet in an alcove to the left and Shepherd wrinkled his nose at the foul stench that was coming off it. He followed Friedman. To the right was another room, this one filled with metal bunk beds, and beyond it a third chamber with two metal desks and a map on one wall showing what appeared to be a section of the tunnel system. There was an air-conditioning unit on the wall close to the ceiling and a fluorescent light operated by a switch by the doorway.

Shepherd and Friedman flipped up their night vision goggles and Friedman switched on the light.

'All mod cons,' said Standing, as he raised his goggles and looked around the room.

'They take electricity and water from the hospital overhead,' said Friedman.

'Do the authorities know?' asked Shepherd.

'The hospital authorities?' Friedman shrugged. 'Maybe. Maybe not. But even if they objected, what can they do? No one says no to Hamas. Not if they want to stay healthy. That's what they do. They build their command centres underneath hospitals, schools and mosques. They emerge to fire rockets and missiles and then they run back to the tunnels to hide. What can we do? If we attack them then we risk hurting civilians and then we're the bad guys. They're cowards, they hide behind women and children every chance that they get.'

'Is it possible they've taken the hostages up into the hospital?' asked Shepherd.

'The tracks suggest they took the hostages north in the tunnels,' said Friedman. He pointed at the map. 'This way.' He reached up and ripped the map off the wall.

'Can I have a look?' asked Shepherd.

'Sure,' said Friedman. He gave it to Shepherd, who ran his eyes over it, effortlessly committing it to memory.

'Our intelligence guys will make good use of this,' said Friedman, taking the map back from Shepherd and shoving it into his backpack. He switched off the light, flicked his goggles down and headed back to the tunnel. Shepherd and Standing followed him.

The tunnel widened as they went north, and before long they could walk upright. The roof of the tunnel was festooned with power and communication cables. This section of the tunnel network was made from prefabricated panels which curved above their heads, clearly built by experts who knew what they were doing.

Friedman was still checking for booby traps, but he had picked up the pace. Shepherd cross referenced the tunnel map with the map he'd seen in the airport terminal. They were moving under a market now, heading towards one of Gaza's largest mosques. Shepherd could understand that the willingness of Hamas to use human shields made them a formidable opponent. It was a similar technique to that used by the Viet Cong during the Vietnam War, where fighters blended into the population before and after their attacks. It became impossible to tell the difference between the enemy and civilians, and any retaliation risked killing and injuring innocents. America had lost its war against the North Vietnamese and all the signs were that Israel wasn't going to find its war against Hamas any easier.

There were more rooms and chambers under the mosque, all empty. They were as well equipped as the rooms under the hospital, with air conditioning, water, and toilets. The Israeli soldiers did a quick recce, grabbing anything that might be of interest to their intelligence people, then carried on north.

After another hundred yards they reached a t-junction. Friedman raised his right hand in a fist and they all stopped. He moved his head from side to side, clearly listening intently, then slowly walked backwards until he was next to Standing. Shepherd and Blai moved closer.

'I can hear voices to the right,' whispered Friedman. 'And there's a woman, sobbing.'

'Is it the hostages?' asked Standing.

'No way of knowing,' said Friedman. 'But Hamas wouldn't usually have women down in the tunnels.'

'How do you want to play it?' asked Shepherd.

'I can see light ahead, so we go in without night vision. You can see how narrow the tunnel is, we have to go in single file.' Friedman saw Standing open his mouth but he held up his hand to silence. 'We're not rock, paper, scissoring this,' he said. 'I'm going in first.'

Standing grinned. 'You read my mind.'

'You can come in behind me, if you want.'

Standing's grin widened. 'That's what she said.'

Friedman chuckled and shook his head. 'You haven't changed.' He looked over at Blai. 'You go third.

Spider can go fourth. But the tunnel the size it is, I'll be the only one shooting until we're in the chamber.'

'There are four chambers at the end of the tunnel,' said Shepherd. 'The first one has a room to the left, and there are two to the right. There are two tunnels leading off the room on the left so if there are hostages being held they'll most likely be to the right.'

Friedman frowned. 'How do you know that?'

'Spider has a trick memory,' said Standing. 'He remembers everything he sees and hears. One look at that map and he'll remember it for ever.'

'That's a good skill to have,' he said. 'Okay, so we'll assume the hostages are to the right. I'll go right, Lastman you go left. Danit, right with me. From then on, play it by ear, you'll know where the action is. We've no idea how many Hamas fighters there are so watch yourselves.' Friedman looked around, checking that everyone was in agreement, then turned and headed back to the t-junction. The rest of the team followed him.

Standing followed just behind Friedman. If there were fighters to the left, Standing would have to move quickly to cover the Israeli's back.

Friedman reached the t-junction and stopped. Shepherd listened intently. He couldn't hear a woman crying but he could hear men talking in Arabic. Two men. Maybe three.

Friedman looked over his shoulder and nodded at Standing. Standing nodded back. Friedman took a deep breath and then stepped into the junction, his carbine up on his shoulder. He took two quick steps to the right, making space for Standing who moved left. Blai went right.

Shepherd heard the suppressed pops of Friedman's

weapon. Then a second weapon started firing. It was also suppressed, which was a good sign.

Shepherd stepped into the t-junction. He was about to follow Blai when he heard Standing's HK firing a quick double tap followed by the deafening crack-crack-crack of a Kalashnikov. Shepherd turned and went left. The tunnel ran for about twenty feet and opened into a room filled with a soft yellow light. Standing was crouched at the entrance to the room, firing again. As Shepherd came up behind him, Standing went left, still firing. As he moved, Shepherd saw two men getting to their feet. They had been lying on camp beds and were reaching for their Kalashnikovs. Shepherd kept moving forward, aimed at the man on the left and squeezed the trigger twice. Both rounds hit the man in the chest and he fell back, sprawling over his bed, his weapon clattering to the floor.

The second man had his Kalashnikov in his hands now. He was young, barely out of his teens, tall and gangly, his cheeks pockmarked with acne scars. His eyes were wide and staring and his mouth was open, showing brilliant white teeth. He was wearing a Blondie t-shirt and without any hesitation Shepherd shot Debbie Harry in the face, twice. The man fell back as the shirt turned red. He slammed against the wall and slid down it, smearing it with blood.

Standing was still firing. Shepherd took a quick look to the left. Standing was down in a crouch, aiming at an elderly fighter, grey haired and wearing a baggy tunic, who was holding a pistol with both hands. The old man pulled the trigger but his grip was too loose, the gun jerked up and the bullet went high. Standing fired once and the round hit the man between his eyes, spraying blood and brains over a younger fighter standing behind him. The younger fighter was holding a Kalashnikov but he took his right hand off it and wiped away the blood across his face with his sleeve. As the old man crumpled to the floor, Standing put two rounds in the younger man's chest.

Shepherd saw something moving in the shadows, then a glint of metal. He took two quick steps forward, down in a crouch, A teenager in t-shirt and baggy shorts rushed out of the darkness, a machete in his hands. He lunged at Standing, screaming in Arabic. Standing started to turn but he still had his back to the attacker when Shepherd shot the man in the face. The man went down and the machete clattered to the floor.

'I owe you one,' said Standing.

'I'll add it to the list,' said Shepherd with a grin.

'Is there a list?'

Shepherd's grin widened. 'Yeah, there's a list.'

They went back along the tunnel to rejoin the rest of the team. Heron and Lane were standing in the outer chamber. Two Hamas fighters were dead on the floor, blood pooling around their chests. A doorway led to another chamber. Blai and Eshel were standing in the doorway so Shepherd couldn't see inside. Someone was talking in Arabic.

Shepherd came up behind Blai. Blai heard him and looked over his shoulder, putting his finger up to his lips to tell him to keep quiet. Shepherd nodded. Blai moved to the left and Shepherd took his place in the doorway.

Friedman was standing in the middle of the chamber, his Tavor hanging on its sling. His hands were up in the air, fingers splayed, and he was talking in a low, hushed voice to a young man who had a gun pressed to the temple of a tearful young boy. The man with the gun was in his teens, with round lensed glasses and a black and white scarf around his neck. The gun was a Berretta M9, black and streaked with dirt. It was a 9mm semi automatic with a range of close to a hundred metres, but range obviously wasn't an issue down in the tunnels. It was a heavy gun with a steel frame, weighing just over two and half pounds, and it was shaking in the teenager's hand. He screamed something at Friedman. Shepherd knew only a few words of Arabic but the message was clear — go away or he'd pull the trigger. The M9 had a fifteen round staggered box magazine with a reversible magazine release button that could be positioned for either right or left-handed shooting. The Hamas fighter was right handed. His left arm was around the neck of the boy, who was between ten and twelve years old.

Friedman replied, his voice soft and non-threatening. The man shook his head and screamed in Arabic again. Standing appeared behind Shepherd and Shepherd moved to the side to allow him in. The man screamed again and pointed his gun at Standing.

'He wants you to lower your weapon,' said Friedman. 'I'd suggest you do what he wants.'

Standing glared at the man as he slowly lowered his HK, but he kept his finger on the trigger.

At the far end of the chamber, a group of men, women and children were huddled against the wall. Shepherd recognised White immediately, he was in the middle of the group, his arms around a young girl. The girl wasn't one of White's daughters, she was too young. Tears were running down her face and she was gripping one of White's arms with both hands. Shepherd scanned the anxious faces. White's daughters weren't there. All the hostages had chains around their waists which were padlocked to metal rings set into the wall.

Friedman spoke again, his hands still up.

'That's an M9, right?' Standing whispered.

'It is,' said Shepherd.

'And it's not cocked?'

'Apparently not.'

The teenager interrupted Friedman, screaming at him in Arabic and pressed the gun so hard against the hostage that the boy yelped in pain.

'Double action trigger pull is what, nine pounds?' said Standing.

'It's variable. Between seven and a half pounds and sixteen and a half pounds.'

With the hammer down, the gun needed a double action to fire. The trigger pull first had to bring the hammer back and then it needed further pressure to fire. It took a lot of effort, even for a trained shooter. The teenager had probably just forgotten to cock the gun and now he would have to use up to sixteen and a half pounds of pressure to fire it. The gun was shaking which meant that his hand was already weak.

'Yeah, that's what I thought,' said Standing. 'And that kid doesn't look as if he works out.'

'Be careful, Matt. The hostages are all in your field of fire.'

'The Israelis aren't going to let him go, so this only ends one way,' said Standing.

Shepherd nodded. Standing was right. Friedman was still talking, but the teenager wasn't going to be walking away from this. Friedman's only concern was the hostage.

Standing eased by Blai. The teenager pointed the gun at Standing and screamed at the top of his voice.

'He says you're to stop moving, Lastman,' said Friedman.

'So long as he's pointing that gun at me, the hostage is safe,' said Standing quietly. 'And Spider and I have decided that the trigger pull of an uncocked M9 is probably more than the kid can handle.'

Friedman looked over at Standing, frowning. Then realisation dawned and he looked back at the teenager. He spoke to him in Arabic. Standing took a step to the left. The teenager's head moved from side to side, trying to watch them both. Standing raised his HK. 'Time to put up or shut up,' he said.

The teenager wailed like a banshee and pointed the gun at Standing. His hand was shaking and Shepherd could see he was struggling to hold the gun up. Even if he did manage to pull the trigger, the recoil would probably twist the gun from his hand.

Standing put his HK to his shoulder. It was an easy enough shot for a marksman like Standing, but Shepherd was worried that at such close range the round would pass through the teenager and injure one of the hostages.

The teenager gritted his teeth as his finger tightened on the trigger. He was clearly struggling and he let go of the boy so that he could use both hands. The boy fell to the floor, sobbing. The teenager opened his mouth to scream but then a round smacked into his chest and he staggered back. Friedman fired again and a second round hit the teenager in the neck. Blood spurted from between his lips and the gun clattered to the floor. Eshel dashed forward and kicked the gun away, then grabbed the boy and lifted him up.

125

'Nice shooting, Daz,' said Standing, lowering his HK.

'You were right, the trigger pull was going to be a problem for him,' said Friedman. 'But you were taking one hell of a risk there.'

'Nah, I knew you could handle it. And the hostages were out of your field of fire.'

Shepherd went over to the hostages. There were two men — David White and a grey haired man with a bandaged right hand — three women, and three children. White was still holding the girl, and she turned away and buried her face in White's stomach as Shepherd approached her. White bent down and spoke to the girl in Hebrew as he stroked her hair. 'I'm just telling her that you're here to help us,' he said to Shepherd.

'David, we're here from London,' he said. 'We've come to take you back. Where are your daughters?'

David's lips tightened and he shook his head. 'They didn't make it,' he said.

'I'm sorry,' said Shepherd. He gestured at the young girl. 'What about her? Where are her parents?'

'Her name is Naomi.' He lowered his voice and leaned forward to whisper to Shepherd. 'They were killed in front of her. She has a sister but they took her away yesterday. We don't know where she is.'

'We'll take you all back to Israel,' said Shepherd. 'And we have a plane waiting to fly you to London.'

White forced a smile. 'Thank you.'

Shepherd grabbed the chain that was padlocked around White's waist. 'Who has the keys?' he asked.

'Him,' said White, pointing at one of the dead Hamas fighters.

Shepherd went over to the body and went through

126

the pockets. He found a metal ring with more than twenty keys on it attached by a chain to the man's belt. He unclipped the chain and went back to White. It took him several tries to get the right key, but once he had opened the padlock and released White he gave him the keys. 'Can you undo the rest of the locks?'

White nodded and started work on the padlock at Naomi's waist.

Shepherd took a step back. 'Right, everybody, if you could please listen to me. We'll be taking you back through the tunnels to the school where we will have a helicopter to fly us back to Israel. I know this is stressful but please follow any instructions we give you.'

Friedman walked over. 'Is everyone okay? Anyone hurt?'

All the hostages shook their heads. Friedman knelt down and smiled at two young boys who looked like brothers. 'And you boys? Are you okay to go for a walk?'

'They'll be be fine,' said the man standing behind them. 'I'm their father.'

'What's your name, Sir?' asked Friedman.

'Tamar,' said the man.

'I'm Ariel,' said Friedman. He smiled at the boys. 'What are your names?'

'Ari,' said the bigger of the two. He had his head up and his fists were clenched as if he was ready to fight.

The smaller of the two boys was more nervous, and he stared at the ground as he mumbled 'Shimon'.

Friedman patted him on the shoulder. 'Everything's going to be fine, Shimon. You just stay close to your brother.'

He stood up. 'Right, everybody, listen to me, please. We're going to have to move along the tunnel back to the school where you were brought in. We have flash-lights so we'll be able to see where we're going, but it will be a little dark. We'll have soldiers at the front and at the rear so you'll be safe, but you'll need to keep together. We'll be moving quickly because we don't want to stay down here any longer than we have to. Does anybody have any questions?'

Ari raised his hand.

'You don't have to raise your hand, Ari,' said Fried-man. 'What is your question?'

'I'm hungry,' he said.

Friedman laughed. He reached into a pocket inside his flak jacket and pulled out an energy bar. He gave it to the boy.

White had dealt with all the padlocks and the chains were lying on the floor.

'Right, form a line, please,' said Friedman. 'If the adults could keep an eye on the children, that would be great.' He looked over at Standing. 'Lastman, are you and your guys okay to bring up the rear? We'll go point. We'll use flashlights, shouldn't be any hostiles on the way back. Not ahead of us, anyway.'

Standing nodded. 'We should get a move on, they might send guys to see what all the fuss was about.'

All the soldiers had flipped up their night vision goggles. They pulled torches from holders on their belts and switched them on.

Friedman addressed the hostages again. 'Right, off we go. Stay close, and just concentrate on breathing. You'll all be home soon.' He nodded at Blai. 'You follow me, Danit. Then Shalev. Keep an eye on the hostages, if they start to lag, let me know.'

Standing nodded at Shepherd. 'Do you want to stay with White?'

'Good idea,' said Shepherd.

The hostages had formed a line along the edge of the chamber. Shepherd went over to stand next to White, who was still holding Naomi's hand. 'We'll soon be out of here,' he said.

White nodded. His face was smeared with dirt, his lips were cracked and there were bruises around his eyes. 'Thank you,' he said.

'Are you okay?'

'I've been better.' He forced a smile. 'I thought I was going to die down here. They kept beating us, just for the hell of it.'

'It's over now,' said Shepherd, patting him on the shoulder.

Friedman and Blai led the way out of the chamber, using their torches to illuminate the way. The hostages followed them. Shepherd looked over at Standing. Standing flashed him a thumbs up. So far, so good.

11

Shepherd climbed out of the shaft and switched off his torch. He walked through the storeroom and into the gymnasium, where all the hostages were huddling together. White was still holding Naomi's hand.

Eshel was on the radio, calling in the helicopter. Shepherd went over to Friedman, who was standing next to a wooden vaulting horse with Blai.

'We've got a problem,' said Shepherd. 'The Panther has a maximum takeoff weight of 4,300 kilogrammes, and with eight of us and two pilots, plus White, we'll be close to that. We can't take another eight hostages, even if we could fit them in.'

Friedman looked at Blai. 'He's right.'

Standing walked over with Heron, Lane and Branson in tow. 'You're talking about the heli, right? We're well over weight.'

'We can't all get on board,' said Shepherd.

'I'll stay,' said Standing immediately. 'The border is less than half a mile away, I can cover that in less than five minutes.'

Heron nodded. 'I'm up for it,' he said.

'Me too,' said Lane. He looked over at Branson who nodded enthusiastically and flashed Shepherd a thumbs up.

'I can't ask you guys to do that,' said Shepherd. 'I'll stay.'

'You're not asking, Spider,' said Standing. 'We're volunteering. And like I said before, we're combat fit and you're not.'

'Thanks for that,' said Shepherd.

'I'm not saying you're not fit, but you're not match fit and we are.'

'Sorry to interrupt, but if anyone is going back on the ground it'll be us,' said Friedman. 'This is our backyard.' His two troopers nodded enthusiastically.

'Assuming we can take all the hostages, how many of us can get on the heli?' asked Shepherd.

'The three smaller kids can sit on laps, the two teenagers could maybe sit on the floor. The three adults will need seats, so I'm thinking seven of us can get in. That means only two of us have to go overground.'

'You and me then, Daz,' said Standing. 'Rank has its privileges.'

'That works for me,' said Friedman. He looked at Shepherd. 'Is that okay?'

Shepherd grimaced. He wasn't happy at the men being left to make their own way out of Gaza, but there didn't appear to be a choice. Overloading a helicopter could easily lead to a disaster, especially when there was the added risk of being shot at. 'I guess so.'

'Sarge, better we come with you,' said Eshel. 'Two's not enough to lay down covering fire, you need Danit and me with you. Plus it'll lighten the chopper's load.'

'You sure?' asked Friedman.

'The four musketeers,' said Blai.

'Four of us will be safer than two,' Friedman said to Shepherd. 'And Lastman is right, it's a five minute run. We'll be fine.' He nodded at Eshel. 'Tell the pilots what we'll be doing.'

The helicopter was closer now, the pilots doing a quick three-sixty to make sure there were no threats. Eshel was talking to the pilot in Hebrew.

'They're landing,' Eshel said to the group.

131

'We'll stay here to provide covering fire if needed,' said Friedman. 'Once you're in the air we'll start our run. If there are no interruptions, we'll be at the fence in five minutes.' He looked over at Eshel. 'Tell the guys at the border to expect us, running into friendly fire wouldn't be good.'

Eshel nodded and began talking in Hebrew on the radio.

'Okay, let's go,' said Shepherd. 'Everybody keep your heads down.' One of the teenage boys was close to tears. Shepherd patted him on the shoulder. 'You're going to be okay,' he said. 'You all are.' He put his arms around the boy and guided him towards the helicopter. The rotors were still a blur, the pilots clearly wanted to be up and away as quickly as possible.

Heron grabbed one of the small girls and held her close to his chest. 'Have you been in a helicopter before?' he asked.

The little girl shook her head tearfully.

'You're going to love it,' said Heron. He jogged after Shepherd.

Lane nodded at the two women hostages. 'Are you okay, ladies?'

One of them swallowed nervously. 'We're okay.'

'Could you do me favour and take care of the little girls? I think if I pick them up they might think I'm going to hurt them.'

'Of course, of course,' said the other woman. She gathered up the smaller of the two girls and whispered to her in Hebrew.

'Right, stay close to me, and keep your heads down.'

'Is it dangerous?' said the woman with the smaller girl.

132

Lane grinned. 'Not if you keep your head down,' he said.

'Let me help,' said White. He took the girl from the woman. 'Come on.' They jogged towards the helicopter where Branson and Coleman had taken up position either side of the door, guns at the ready as they scanned the surrounding buildings.

Once all the hostages were on board, Shepherd flashed Standing a thumbs up. 'We're ready,' he said over the radio.

'See you on the other side,' said Standing. 'And I mean that in a good way.'

'Try to keep up with the Israelis, they look fit,' said Shepherd. 'Don't let the Regiment down.'

Standing laughed and gave Shepherd the finger. Shepherd turned and heaved himself into the helicopter. He dropped into a rear facing empty seat next to the teenage boy he'd helped in earlier. The boy was trembling and biting down on his lower lip, clearly terrified. Shepherd winked at him. 'I'm Dan, what's your name?' he said.

'Gabe.'

'We'll soon be out of here, Gabe, and we'll get back to your parents.'

Gabe swallowed. 'They're dead,' he said. 'Hamas killed them when they took me.' His eyes teared up and he began to shake. Shepherd was lost for words, he just didn't know what to say. All he could do was pat the lad on the leg.

The helicopter's turbines roared and the rotors began to spin faster. Coleman and Branson swung into the cabin and sat down with their guns pointed through the open door. The helicopter lifted into the air and immediately turned to the south. Its turbines roared as it gained height.

Shepherd looked out through the port side door. There was a line of half a dozen apartment blocks, eight stories tall, festooned with clothing and bedding drying on balconies. Behind them were more featureless blocks, interspersed with factories and mosques.

They were about two hundred feet in the air now, just above the tower blocks. Shepherd's eyes flicked back and forth. Two hundred feet still put them in harm's way and an Israeli Army helicopter would be a prize target. Branson and Coleman were scanning the ground below them, guns at the ready.

The helicopter was still climbing when Shepherd saw a shower of sparks and a long blue flame on the roof of the block furthest to the right. He immediately knew what it was — an RPG, a rocket propelled grenade, probably Russian or Chinese made and more than capable of bringing down a helicopter. It was almost certainly a HEAT — a high-explosive anti-tank round — which would detonate on impact or when the fuse ran out, probably once it had travelled between 800 and 1200 feet.

'RPG, port side, aft!' Shepherd shouted through the radio. 'RPG port side aft!' There was no point in telling the pilots what action to take, it would have to be their call. All he could do was to identify the threat and leave them to work out what to do. Once the RPG had fired it carried on in pretty much a straight line — the rocket couldn't be guided onto its target — so as long as the pilots made the right call it was just a case of getting out of the way.

Coleman and Branson both twisted around to look through the port side windows but the helicopter was already taking evasive action, diving down and twisting to the right. Shepherd's stomach lurched at the sudden change of direction and the children all began to scream. Shepherd gritted his teeth. The sensation wasn't pleasant but it meant that the pilots were doing the right thing.

The diving turn continued for several seconds and then the helicopter levelled off. There was the thud of an explosion somewhere above them, presumably the warhead detonating.

'Nice call, Spider!' said Coleman.

'How close was it?' asked Shepherd.

'Close enough that Virgin is going to need clean underwear.'

'Screw you, Mustard,' said Branson. 'It missed us by a mile.'

'Just so long as it missed us,' said Shepherd. 'That's all that matters.'

The helicopter levelled off and began to climb again. Shepherd kept an anxious eye on the tower blocks but there were no more telltale sparks and once they reached a thousand feet he began to relax. He twisted around in his seat. Ahead of them he could see the border fence, and beyond it the orchards and farmland of Israel.

He tapped Coleman on the knee. 'Any sign of the guys?' he asked.

Coleman shook his head as he stared out through the doorway. 'Too dark,' he said.

12

'What the hell was that?' said Standing, coming to a halt and looking up at the night sky. They had heard the thump of an explosion but the buildings around them had blocked any view of what had happened.

'Sounded like an RPG,' said Friedman over the radio.

Standing turned his head from side to side as he listened intently. He could still make out the turbines of the helicopter so if it had been the target then the warhead had obviously missed.

'We need to keep moving,' said Friedman. 'That will have woken the dead.'

They started jogging again. Standing scanned the buildings, checking windows for light or movement. They were wearing their Kevlar helmets but weren't using their night vision goggles.

Friedman slowed as he reached a junction. He moved to the side to get a better look at the street to the left, then started jogging again. They were in single file, Eshel and Blai staying twenty feet apart with Standing bringing up the rear. They all had their carbines at the ready.

Standing had fallen into a rhythm, two steps then a look over his left shoulder, two more steps and a look over his right. A light went on in a window to his left, casting his shadow across the street. He aimed his carbine at the window as he ran by but it stayed closed.

He heard a buzzing sound behind him. A motorcycle. The buzzing got louder. 'Bike approaching from behind,' he said over the radio.' He stopped and turned, his carbine across his chest.

A motorbike appeared from a side alley, a trail bike with two figures on it, two men, the passenger holding a Kalashnikov. Both figures turned to look in Standing's direction, then the bike accelerated out of view. 'We've been spotted,' said Standing over the radio.

'Roger that,' said Friedman.

Standing turned. The rest of the team had also stopped and were looking back down the street.

'They'll call in reinforcements, we need to up the pace,' said Friedman. He turned and started to run. The rest of the team followed him. Standing took a final look over his shoulder, then sprinted after them.

Friedman reached another junction. He ran wide but barely slowed. Eshel and Blai followed. As Standing reached the junction, a hail of rounds smacked into the concrete above his head, splattering him with fragments that pitter-pattered on his helmet. He ducked and whirled around. He spotted the shooter immediately, crouched on the roof of one of the buildings overlooking the junction. All he could see was the top of the man's head and the barrel of his gun. Standing stopped and aimed, his finger tightening on the trigger. The seconds crawled by slowly and Standing found himself counting to maintain his concentration. On three the man raised his head and Standing squeezed the trigger. The round hit the man between the eyes and the back of his head exploded as he fell back. Standing was already running down the street by the time the man hit the roof.

Standing heard the roar of a vehicle ahead of them and then a pick-up truck appeared, bucking and heaving on the uneven street surface. There were four Hamas fighters in the back, faces covered with keffiyeh scarves, all aiming their Kalashnikovs down the street. They started to fire but the truck was moving so erratically that their rounds all went high and peppered the buildings behind Standing. Several windows shattered and there were screams coming from all around. The three IDF soldiers ducked into doorways.

Standing went down on one knee and brought his HK up to his shoulder. His heart was pumping slowly and steadily and his breathing was even and unhurried, as it always was when he was in combat mode. All his senses were working on overdrive and time seemed to have slowed to a crawl. He aimed at the chest of the fighter at the rear of the truck and squeezed the trigger twice. The man fell back, his Kalashnikov tumbling to the floor. The man to the left's weapon was pointing in the air so Standing ignored him and shot the man next to him, another clean double tap to the chest.

The two surviving men in the rear of the truck were screaming in terror now, one of them banging on the cab, probably begging for the driver to get the hell out of there. Standing sighted on the driver and pulled the trigger. The driver's head exploded and blood and brains splattered across the windscreen. The man must have still had his foot on the accelerator because the engine roared and the truck leapt forward. The steering wheel span and the truck smashed into a doorway with a deafening thud. The front of the truck was immediately obscured in a cloud of steam.

As Standing straightened up the two remaining

fighters in the back of the truck jumped down and started running towards him, screaming and waving their Kalashnikovs. Standing brought his HK up to his shoulder but before he could fire, Friedman and Blai stepped out of their doorways and gunned the two fighters down.

'We need to get out of here,' said Friedman over the radio. 'Shalev, call our guys and let them know we're coming and that we're hot.'

Standing heard the buzzing of motorcycles behind him and he turned to see two more trail bikes heading towards him. He brought his HK up and shot the rider of the bike on the left, two shots to the head. The rider fell back against his passenger and the bike went out of control, slamming into a building and spinning across the street, the rider and his passenger flying through the air, arms and legs flailing.

The second bike braked hard and swung around so that it was side on to Standing. The rider twisted the handlebars to the right but before he could accelerate away Standing put a round in his head and two rounds into the head of the passenger. The bike toppled over, its engine still roaring.

Standing jogged over to the Israelis and they all began running flat out, carbines cradled across their chests.

They reached the outskirts of the town and stopped at the road that divided them from the farmland and the border beyond. Two pick-up trucks appeared to their left, tyres squealing on the tarmac. There were Hamas fighters in the back of both, firing haphazardly. They were too far away to be accurate but they were getting closer by the second.

The three Israelis ducked back into the alley.

Standing stood his ground and took aim at the leading truck, but before he could pull the trigger a missile streaked through the air from the Israeli side of the border and smacked into the side of the vehicle. There was ball of yellow flame accompanied by a gut-wrenching explosion that sent the truck spinning on to its roof, crushing the fighters who had been riding in the back.

The second truck braked hard, so hard that the fighters in the back were knocked off balance. As they struggled to stand up straight, a second missile hit the driver's door and the vehicle was engulfed in flames. The men in the back began screaming as their clothes, scarves and hair caught fire. They dropped their guns and threw themselves on to the ground and began to roll around, trying to extinguish the flames.

Standing walked towards the burning trucks and put his HK to his shoulder. One by one he put the dying men out of their misery and soon there was only the sound of the trucks burning.

The Israelis stepped out into the road.

Standing looked across at Friedman. 'Matadors?' he said.

The Matadaor was a disposable man portable weapon system. The Israelis had developed the weapon with Germany and Singapore and produced a lightweight weapon that could destroy light tanks and thick walls for less than five thousand pounds a pop. It was the first time Standing had seen one fired in anger. Matador was a short form of Man Portable Anti-Tank Anti-Door, because the defence industry, like the SAS, did love its nicknames.

Friedman grinned. 'We call it the Nut Cracker,' he said. 'And those guys certainly got their nuts cracked.

Come on. Home run.'

Friedman ran across the road to the rubbish strewn wasteland. Standing and the two Israelis followed him. Without the night vision goggles to slow them down, they ran at full pelt. Ahead of them were a line of IDF solders standing on the Israeli side of the border. Two of the soldiers had Matadors on their shoulders, awaiting the arrival of more Hamas trucks, but the road behind them stayed clear. Standing figured any Hamas fighters in the area would have heard the explosions and realised that their best bet was to keep well away from the area.

Eshel was talking to the IDF over his radio. Standing took a quick look over his shoulder. There were no vehicles on the road, but there were faces at several of the windows in the buildings behind them. He slowed to a jog, letting the Israelis get ahead of him as they approached the border fence. If the IDF soldiers shouted in Hebrew, best they were answered by their own people. He needn't have worried — the IDF soldiers were cheering them home, whooping and waving their guns in the air. They surrounded their colleagues, patting them on the back and high-fiving them.

13

Shepherd sat next to Standing at the front of the Gulf-stream jet. The rest of the SAS team were behind them, most of them asleep. David White and his wife had refused to get on the plane without the bodies of their daughters. Shepherd had phoned Pritchard and explained the situation and the MI5 director had agreed that the Whites should stay behind. Now that David White was no longer a hostage, the pressure was off and obviously they couldn't be forced on to the plane. Pritchard had spoken to White and assured him that he could stay in Israel as long as he wanted. The Whites had booked into a hotel in a town called Beersheba, about twenty miles from the Gaza Strip, where they would wait until the authorities had identified the bodies of their daughters.

'I can't imagine what they're going through, the Whites,' said Standing. 'Having your kids killed like that.'

'Nightmare,' said Shepherd.

'But you have to wonder what they were doing that close to the Gaza Strip. It's the last place I'd choose for a holiday.'

'I don't think anyone was expecting trouble.'

'Yeah, well that raises a lot of questions, doesn't it? The attacks were well planned, hundreds of fighters, lots of equipment. They used hang gliders, did you hear about that? They flew hang gliders over the fence and used bulldozers to break through parts if it. That takes a lot of planning. How did the Israelis not see it coming?'

'You can't always be ahead of the game,' said Shepherd. 'Look at Nine Eleven. The London Tube bombings. Sometimes things slip through the cracks.'

'And the Whites pay the price,' said Standing. He sighed and stretched out his legs. 'The world sucks sometimes.'

'It does,' agreed Shepherd.

'So what else are you working on at the moment?'

'Trying to bust an Albanian drugs gang.'

'I didn't realise you secret squirrel boys were involved in the drugs trade. I thought it was terrorists you were after.'

'It's all connected these days, Matt. Terrorism, money-laundering, drugs, people smuggling, counterfeit goods, everything feeds into everything else.'

'I don't know how you keep a grip on it all. It's so much easier with the SAS. They point you at the bad guys and off you go. Bang, bang, bang, job done and on to the next.'

'Life's simpler in the Regiment, that's for sure. But I'm told you're stretched thin at the moment.'

Standing nodded. 'Like you wouldn't believe. Stirling Lines feels empty most of the time. And we can't get new blood, either. The pool we can draw from is getting smaller every year. The only way to get more guys in would be to lower our standards, and no one wants to do that.' He scowled. 'Well, the government does. They keep putting pressure on the MoD to drop our standards to get numbers up and increase diversity but it's a slippery slope and the Regiment is resisting. But until they come up with some way of boosting numbers we're running ourselves ragged. I'm supposed to be out in Ukraine now, Clint and

Penny got pulled off a training exercise, and we've had to cut back on our undercover patrols. If something big were to kick off now I don't know what they'd do.' He grinned. 'You could always come back.'

'As you keep telling me, I'm not match fit.'

'It wouldn't take much to get you there,' said Standing. 'A few weeks of running around with your old brick-filled rucksack and you'd be good to go.'

'In your dreams.'

'I'm serious. We've had two guys over fifty rejoin this month. One of them's a grandfather. They waive the fitness tests, so long as they've got two arms and two legs they're in.' He gestured at the back of the plane. 'Penny's about your age, and they're happy for him to stay in as long as he wants.' He grinned. 'I'd be happy to give you a reference.'

'I'll think about it,' said Shepherd.

'Really?'

Shepherd laughed. 'No, of course not. My days of shooting people are over.'

'Well you say that, but you had no problems down in the tunnels, did you? It's like riding a bicycle.'

'Yeah, well I don't do much bike-riding these days either,' said Shepherd. 'Too big a risk of breaking a hip.'

Standing patted him on the leg. 'Call me if you change your mind,' he said. He reclined his seat and closed his eyes. Like soldiers the world over, Standing grabbed food and sleep whenever he could.

Shepherd reclined his seat and closed his eyes, but sleep wouldn't come. Standing was right, killing had come easily to Shepherd down in the tunnels. His muscle memory had kicked in and he had pointed the HK and pulled the trigger, almost without

144

thinking. Maybe killing people was like riding a bicycle and once you had acquired the skill it never went away. He went back through the killings, his memory providing total recall. He could remember every shot, every round hitting home, the way the bodies had fallen. There was no guilt, he realised. No regret. Nothing. He'd had a job to do and he'd done it. Now the job was done, he doubted that he would give it any thought at all.

14

There was a black Vauxhall Corsa car waiting for Shepherd when the Gulfstream jet had landed at Brize Norton, but it wasn't the same driver. Shepherd had hugged the SAS team one by one and left them as they were loading their kit into two black Range Rovers.

Shepherd called Jimmy Sharpe once the Corsa was on the A40 heading to London.

'Are you back already?' asked Sharpe.'

'Yeah, the SAS doesn't mess around.'

'Everything went okay?'

'Yes and no. We got our guy out but his daughters didn't make it.'

'Bugger,' said Sharpe.

'Yeah, bugger is right. So how's it going with Tuk?'

'He's still dark. But Petrit says that's to be expected. It might be a while before Tuk gets a phone, and even then he'll have to be careful.'

'And what about Plauku?'

'Singing like a canary,' said Sharpe. 'We've got him in an NCA safe house in Richmond. Not far from the park. It's got Sky Sports and a well-stocked fridge so I'm a happy bunny.'

'And Petrit is happy with the way things are going?'

'Happy as Larry. Plauku is a mine of information about what's going on in Italy and was involved in half a dozen targeted killings in Rome and Milan.'

'Involved in what way?'

'Planning and logistics. He says he never pulled the

trigger but Petrit doesn't believe him. He's not pressing him, it's kid gloves all the way at the moment.'

'Be careful, Razor. We can promise him immunity in the UK but make sure the Italians don't come after him.'

'Petrit has already spoken to someone at the Guardia di Finanza and they'll arrange full immunity. The Albanians are going to put his family in protective custody today.'

The Guardia di Finanza was a militarised police force that dealt with financial crime and smuggling, as well as battling the country's illegal drug trade. It patrolled Italy's territorial waters with more than six hundred ships and a hundred aircraft, and was in charge of the country's borders and customs. They were an armed equivalent of the UK's Border Force, but Shepherd doubted that the Border Force would ever be trusted with weapons of any kind, most of them seemed to have trouble just tying their own shoelaces.

'Is that why Plauku was brought into the UK, to work as a hitman for Haziri?'

'Reading between the lines, I'd say so,' said Sharpe. 'So, when are you coming over? I'll text you the address.'

'I'm a couple of hours outside London and I'm dog tired,' said Shepherd. 'I'll see you first thing tomorrow.'

'Breakfast is on me,' said Sharpe. 'As I said, the fridge is full of goodies.'

15

Shepherd arrived at the Richmond safe house at just after nine o'clock in the morning. The house was a detached stone cottage with a black barred gate set into a high stone wall. Shepherd parked his BMW SUV outside and pressed an intercom set into the wall. A CCTV camera was looking down at him and he smiled at it. The gate rattled back and Shepherd walked across a gravelled driveway where two cars were parked, a blue Honda CRV and a grey Skoda Octavia that Shepherd recognised as an NCA vehicle. The front door opened as Shepherd approached it. He was planning to head to the office later so he was suited and booted. Jimmy Sharpe was casually dressed in jeans and a grey pullover. 'The early bird,' said Sharpe, ushering Shepherd into the hall.

'Everything okay?' asked Shepherd.

Sharpe closed the door. 'All good.'

'Has Tuk checked in yet?'

'Not yet, no.' Sharpe nodded at a closed door. 'Petrit is in there with Plauku,' he said.

'Plauku is still talking?'

'Nineteen to the dozen,' said Sharpe, leading Shepherd down the hall to a small kitchen that overlooked the back garden. There was a frying pan on the stove and a packet of bacon and a box of eggs next to it. 'Petrit is recording everything. They're talking in Albanian and he'll provide us with a transcript. Look, I know I promised you breakfast, but could I have a word first?'

'Sure,' said Shepherd.

Sharpe gestured at the kitchen door. 'Outside, yeah?'

Sharpe opened the door and took Shepherd out into the back garden, which was surrounded by a thick hedge, almost ten feet tall, and not overlooked. 'There's a problem, in Albania,' said Sharpe once they were well away from the house. 'The cops went to pick up Plauku's family, but they'd gone. According to neighbours his wife and three kids were taken away in a van by half a dozen heavies.'

'When did this happen?'

'The cops went around last night, apparently they missed them by less than an hour.'

'So the cops have got a leak?'

'According to Petrit the Albanian Police Force leaks like a sieve. He spoke to a guy he trusts about Plauku, but he has no way of knowing who else got the information.'

'And there's no ransom demand or anything like that?'

'They don't need one, do they? The message is clear. Shut up or your family dies.'

'How's Plauku taking it?'

Sharpe looked pained. 'That's what I need to talk to you about. Petrit hasn't told Plauku what happened.'

'What?'

Sharpe held up his hands. 'I know, I know. But he says that the minute Plauku knows, he'll clam up.'

'Well, yes, because he doesn't want his family killed.'

'The intel coming out of Plauku is gold, Spider. Names, dates, bank accounts. His memory is almost as good as yours. He's given Petrit a dozen phone numbers that could well blow the organisation apart.'

'And if Haziri knows that Plauku is still talking, what's to stop him having the family killed?'

'Well, yes, but if he's still talking, there's nothing to be gained by killing them, is there? The damage is done.'

'Razor, listen to yourself. These are Albanians we're talking about. They'll kill his wife and kids just to teach him a lesson. And they'll be a long time dying, too.'

Sharpe shuddered. 'I know. You're right. Of course you're right. But Petrit wants to get more out of Plauku before he gives him the bad news.'

'That's just so wrong, Razor. He's cooperating because he thinks we'll get his family out. But we know that's not going to happen. And the longer we lie to him, the more likely it is that his family are going to be tortured and killed.'

'The Albanian cops are looking for the family.'

'I'm sure they are. But do you seriously think they'll find them?' Shepherd shook his head. 'This is a nightmare.'

'I know. If it was my call, I'd have told Plauku already. As it is, I'm just keeping out of his way. You should do the same.'

'The guy has a right to know that his family are in danger.'

'But if we tell him, he'll stop talking. And even if he does stop talking to us, what guarantee does he have that they'll let his family go?'

Shepherd sighed. 'I don't know what to say. I can't be a part of this.'

'That's why I'm telling you now. You can just walk away and let Petrit get on with it.'

'You can't unring the bell, Razor. You've told me

that we're lying to Plauku so that makes me part of it.'

'Not if you don't talk to Plauku. Just get back in your car. Forget you were ever here.'

Shepherd smiled thinly. 'I never forget anything, Razor. You know that.'

'I'm sorry, Spider. But this is down to Petrit. It's his investigation.'

Shepherd shook his head and held up his hands. 'No, it's an NCA and MI5 investigation. This isn't his country, he's a guest here. If there's flak over this, we'll be the ones catching it.'

'All the conversations have been in Albanian.'

'That's your defence? That he can't speak English?'

'He can speak English. Some English anyway.'

'Has he specifically asked you about his family?'

'He did in the hospital, and I said there shouldn't be a problem getting them to the UK. I haven't spoken to him since Petrit told me about his family being taken. So I haven't lied to him, if that's what you mean.'

Shepherd nodded. 'You're playing with fire. And I think you're right, I should just go. I'm going to pass on breakfast. I've lost my appetite.'

16

Shepherd thought long and hard about what he should say to Giles Pritchard. Saying nothing wasn't an option. If it became known that Plauku was being lied to and that MI5 was a part of that deception, there would be repercussions. Lying was part and parcel of being an MI5 officer, especially one like Shepherd who spent most of his time undercover. But lying to a cooperating witness was a different matter, especially when the lies could well lead to the murder of innocent women and children.

He had to wait outside Pritchard's office for ten minutes before Amy sent him in. Pritchard apologised profusely for keeping him waiting. 'This whole Hamas thing has got everyone on edge,' he said, getting up from his desk. 'The PM wants a full briefing this afternoon so I'm trying to pull everything together. And congratulations on getting David White out. That's one less thing I have to worry the PM with.'

'I'm just sorry about what happened to his daughters.'

'A lot of children were killed,' said Pritchard. 'The true extent of the massacre is only just becoming clear. The Israelis are going to be wanting revenge, and they'll be hoping for support from us, the Americans and the EU. I'm not sure the PM wants to hear that. He doesn't like upsetting the Arab nations.' He waved Shepherd over to the sofa by the window, a sign that he wanted a longer conversation.

Shepherd sat down and Pritchard joined him on

the sofa. 'So how's the Fisnik Haziri investigation going?'

'Slowly but surely. We're still waiting for the Albanian undercover agent to make contact.'

'But you have the guy they tried to kill. What's his name? Plauku?'

Shepherd nodded. 'Redjon Plauku. Looks like he was a Hellbanianz hitman in Italy. But there's a problem I need to run by you.'

'Okay, I'm listening.'

Shepherd explained about what had happened to Plauku's family, and the fact that he hadn't been told that they were in danger. Pritchard listened without interruption. 'So the Albanian police are looking for the wife and children?' he said once Shepherd had finished speaking.

'They are. But there's a good chance that there's a leak there. How else would they know that we had Plauku and that he was alive?'

'They'd have seen the helicopter rescuing him. They could have checked with the local hospitals. Once they realised he was alive, it would make sense to take his family as leverage. It doesn't necessarily mean there's a leak.'

'Okay, but leak or not, they have his family. And I think he has the right to be told.'

'I'll talk to SHISH, but they do things differently in Albania,' said Pritchard. 'They might not consider that their man is doing anything wrong.'

'Petrit says they'll be looking for the wife and kids, but I don't hold out much hope on that score. The only hope of getting them back alive is for Plauku to stop cooperating, but even then . . .' Shepherd shrugged and left the sentence unfinished.

'They'll kill them anyway,' said Pritchard. 'They might well be dead already.'

'That's how I read it,' said Shepherd.

'If they are dead, what do we gain by telling Plauku?'

'We don't gain anything, of course. But we'd be in the wrong if we don't tell him.'

'Let's see what they say at SHISH. For all we know they might be close to rescuing his family.'

Shepherd forced a smile. 'I won't be holding my breath.'

17

Shepherd spent the next day reviewing the transcripts of Ajazi's interviews with Plauku. Sharpe was right, it was gold. The Albanian was providing details of shipments from Turkey into Italy, by ship and by boat. He was able to provide names and sometimes phone numbers of Hellbanianz gang members. There were also details on the assassinations of rival gang members and Italian government officials. Shepherd had the impression that Plauku was being less than honest about his involvement in the killings, but that was to be expected, he had no idea how much he could trust his interrogator.

He had lunch in the canteen on his own, and he was just finishing his chicken salad when his phone rang. It was Amy, summoning him to a meeting with Giles Pritchard. Pritchard was behind his desk, and he waved Shepherd to one of the two wooden chairs, an unspoken directive that the meeting was going to be brief. 'I've spoken to my opposite number at SHISH and off the record they are reasonably sure that Plauku's family are dead. They're quite sanguine about the fact that he hasn't been made aware of the fact that his family have been killed.' Shepherd opened his mouth to protest but Pritchard raised his hand to silence him. 'But Plauku is in the UK and not in Albania so British laws apply. I've spoken to the NCA and they are of the opinion that he should be told, and the Crown Prosecution Service says there's no question that he should be told, and that in fact he should have been informed already. Not telling him could well jeopardise any UK prosecutions down the line. Fruit from the poisoned tree, as they say. Anyway, long story short, Plauku will be told today.'

'Not before time,' said Shepherd.

Pritchard nodded. 'Exactly.' He looked at his watch, another not-so-subtle hint that the meeting was going to be a short one. 'Also, just so you know, David White and his wife will be returning to the UK tomorrow, with the body of their younger daughter. We've arranged a private plane to keep them out of the public eye. They'll bury her at the Jewish cemetery in Willesden. I've told David to take off as much time as he needs.'

'What about the other daughter?'

Pritchard shifted uncomfortably in his seat. 'It's a bit of a mess, frankly. The younger daughter was shot in the chest so it was easy enough to ID her. But the older daughter, Hannah, was raped, along with a lot of other girls at the festival. It looks as though following the rapes most of the girls were shot. Their bodies were piled together and petrol was poured over them and they were set on fire.'

Shepherd winced. 'That's awful.'

'Oh, it gets worse. According to some eye-witness reports, not all the girls were dead when they were set on fire.'

Shepherd shook his head, lost for words.

'The remains, ashes and bone fragments mainly, have been taken to the Shura military base and forensic experts will be working on identification,' said Pritchard. 'But it's not going to be easy and it's going to take weeks if not months.'

'I can't imagine what they're going through,'

said Shepherd.

'We'll arrange counselling, but yes, he must be in hell. Him and his wife.'

18

Jimmy Sharpe looked up from his copy of the Daily Mail and put down his coffee mug as Ajazi came into the kitchen. 'How did he take it?' Sharpe asked.

'How do you think he took it?' scowled the Albanian.

'Not well, obviously.' Ajazi had gone into the bedroom to break the news to Plauku about his family. Ajazi had spent the day questioning Plauku and had close to ten hours of tape to be translated and transcribed. Ajazi had received a phone call from Tirana in the afternoon when he was told that the British were insisting that Plauku was given the bad news, no matter the consequences. Ajazi had blamed Sharpe and the two men had argued for almost half an hour before Sharpe had managed to convince him that he had nothing to do with the decision. In fact Sharpe had agreed with the Albanian that telling Plaauku was probably a very, very bad idea. Sharpe had volunteered to break the bad news, but both men had known that Plauku needed to hear it in his own language. 'What did he say?'

'He said he needed time to think. And he asked what we'd do if he wanted to leave.'

'What did you say?'

'What could I say? We can't let him go, can we?'

Sharpe shrugged. 'This is the UK. Under PACE we'd have to charge him or release him.'

'PACE?'

'The Police and Criminal Evidence Act. It lays

158

down what the cops can and can't do. And we can't detain him without charging him.'

'He's confessed to all sorts of crimes.'

'In Italy. Not here.'

'So we can hold him for the Italians.'

'They'd have to issue a warrant, and since we left the European Union, international arrest warrants have become a lot more problematical.'

Ajazi went over to the fridge and took a can of beer. He popped the tab, drank from the can, then wiped his mouth with the back of his hand. 'So what if he insists on leaving? There's nothing we can do?'

'I'm not saying that. He entered the country illegally, so he can be arrested for that. Of course he could immediately claim asylum, which would complicate things, but then he'd have to be processed by Border Force. That will take time. Plus some of the things he's already given us are terrorism related, and he can be held longer for questioning on terrorism offences. So he can't just up and leave.'

Ajazi took another drink from his can. He drained it, crushed it with one hand, and tossed it into the sink. 'He said he wanted to think about it overnight. I told him that his best option was to continue talking to us.'

'Did he buy it?'

Ajazi sneered at him. 'What do you think? Would you?'

'I guess not. Do you think he might do a runner?'

Ajazi frowned. 'A runner?'

'Try to run away? Escape.'

'Run away to where? He has no money, no phone, and the gang he works for have already tried to kill him. We're his only way out, and he knows that.'

Sharpe nodded. 'Okay, his window's locked and he's probably not ready to go climbing yet with the wound in his shoulder, but one of us needs to be in the hall outside his door at all times, just in case.'

Ajazi took another beer from the fridge. 'Do you want one?'

'Yeah, go on.'

Ajazi tossed him a can and Sharpe caught it one-handed. 'Do you want to do the first shift outside his door?' asked Ajazi. 'I want to start transcribing the last of the tapes.'

Sharpe picked up a chair. 'Sure. Just come and relieve me when you're ready.' He tucked the paper under his arm and carried the chair out of the kitchen.

19

Jimmy Sharpe woke up at dawn, not because he was an early riser but because two birds in the garden decided to have a singing contest. He rolled out of bed and shaved and showered before pulling on a clean shirt and his jeans. He had fallen into bed at midnight after Ajazi had taken over guard duty outside Plauku's room. The Albanian had translated three hours of his final interview with Plauku, and it was full of useful intelligence, useful to the Italians anyway. The man really did have an amazing memory.

He opened the bedroom door. Ajazi was sitting with his legs stretched out and his eyes closed, but as Sharpe walked towards him he opened one eye. 'You thought I was asleep, didn't you?' he growled.

'Thought didn't cross my mind,' said Sharpe. 'I'm going to grab myself a bacon sandwich and a coffee and then I'll take over. Do you want a coffee?'

'Sure,' said Ajazi, opening his other eye.

'And a sandwich?'

'You keep trying to get me to eat one of your bacon sandwiches, don't you?'

Sharpe laughed. 'I'll do you an egg sandwich. With tomato sauce. It's an English delicacy.'

'Okay. But no bacon.'

'Understood.' Sharpe gestured at the door. 'Ask your man what he wants.'

Ajazi leaned over, knocked on the door, and shouted something in Albanian. He listened but there was no reply. Ajazi stood up and hammered on the door, and shouted again. When Plauku didn't reply he grabbed the door handle and twisted it. As he pushed the door open, they saw Plauku kneeling by the wardrobe. His belt was twisted around his neck and hooked over the wardrobe doorknob, his face was swollen, his eyes were bulging and his tongue was protruding from between his lips.

Sharpe cursed, pushed Ajazi to the side and rushed into the room. Plauku was naked and he'd soiled himself as he'd died. As Sharpe fumbled to unfasten the belt, his hands touched the Albanian's cold flesh.

Ajazi stood behind Sharpe, muttering in Albanian.

Sharpe eventually managed to undo the belt and Plauku pitched forward, his naked body slapping onto the carpet. Only then did Sharpe become aware of the foul smell in the room and he had to fight the urge to throw up. He took a couple of steps back, muttering 'Shit, shit, shit.'

'This is your fault,' said Ajazi. Sharpe turned and opened his mouth to yell at the Albanian, but then Ajazi put up both his hands. 'Not you personally, I don't mean you, Jimmy. But it's your people that have done this. We should never have told him that they had his family.'

Sharpe nodded. 'I hear you,' he growled.

'This was his only way out. He didn't have a choice. We didn't give him a choice.'

'But it won't save his family, will it?'

Ajazi shook his head. 'No. It won't.'

20

There were several synagogues closer to his home in St John's Wood, but David White much preferred to attend services at the Lauderdale Road Synagogue in neighbouring Maida Vale. He loved the building, built in the Byzantine style in 1896, with its large domed ceiling, magnificent stained glass windows set in arched recesses, and highly polished wood floors with tapestry carpets. In deference to the synagogue's Victorian heritage, the rabbi and wardens — including all former wardens — wore traditional top hats.

He also relished the fact that he was less well known in Maida Vale, which meant fewer probing questions about how he was feeling and why they hadn't seen Rachel for some time. He knew the questions were well intended, but they were unwelcome nevertheless. The death of his two daughters had left a gaping hole in his heart which he suspected would be there on the day he died. Rachel had if anything taken it worse, entering a black depression which kept her confined to her bedroom most days. She hadn't worked since they had got back to the UK, and showed no signs of returning to the hospital. She barely spoke to White and her nighttime tossing and turning meant that he often slept in either Hannah or Ella's bedroom. The last thing White wanted was to talk about what had happened and the Maida Vale synagogue allowed him to maintain a lower profile.

He walked out of the main entrance, past a security

guard wearing a bullet-proof vest who was keeping a watchful eye on the road. There had long been guards assigned to protect the synagogue, but the vest was a new addition, a sign of just how fearful the Jewish community had become, even in leafy Maida Vale.

'David!' He heard his name being called behind him and he turned to see who it was. It was Ben Hoffman, a doctor who worked with Rachel at St Mary's Hospital. He waved and David waved back. Hoffman was tall and thin with curly black hair. He always had problems getting suits that fitted and as a junior doctor he wasn't yet paid enough to get them made to measure. Standing next to Hoffman was a small man with pointed features and thinning black hair that he had combed back to cover a growing bald patch. He wore a baggy blue suit over a rumpled white shirt and a red and black tie. The two men walked over to White. 'Good to see you,' said Hoffman. He looked around. 'Is Rachel not with you?'

'No, she's at home.'

'How is she?'

'She's . . .' White shrugged, not sure how to finish the sentence.

'She must be shattered. You both must be. I can't imagine . . .' He shuddered. 'I'm so sorry. Please do tell her that I was asking after her.'

'I will, Ben. Thank you.'

'I would have been at the funeral, if I'd known. I have so many fond memories of Ella. She was such a bright girl. So full of . . .'. He left the sentence unfinished. White knew that he had been meaning to say life. Full of life.

'We just wanted a private funeral,' said White. 'Just family.' In fact only he and Rachel had been there.

Rachel's parents had wanted to fly over but her father was infirm and her mother had been under sedation ever since she had heard the news about the two girls. White's parents were both dead, his father from a stroke five years earlier, his mother from a broken heart just six months later. The death certificate had said heart failure, but she had early onset dementia and White knew that she had just given up when her husband wasn't able to care for her any more.

'I am so sorry for your loss, David,' said Hoffman, gripping his shoulder tightly. 'If there's anything I can do. Anything.'

'That's appreciated, but there's nothing anyone can do. What's done is done.' White turned to go, but Hoffman spoke again, quickly.

'David, this is Joel. He's a very old friend.'

White turned and nodded at the man. 'Pleased to meet you,' he said.

The man stuck out his hand. 'Ben speaks very highly of you.'

White frowned. 'In what way?'

'In every way. And I just wanted to say how sorry I am for your loss. What happened out there was truly, truly awful.' They shook hands. The man had a soft grip with barely any pressure.

'Thank you. I haven't seen you at the synagogue before, have I?'

'Oh, I've seen you around.'

White was fairly sure he hadn't seen the man before. It was a fair size congregation, catering to more than six hundred families, but he had a good memory for faces.

Ben patted White on the shoulder. 'I'll leave you to it,' he said, and hurried away.

White smiled at the man, not sure why Ben had introduced them.

'Do you have time for a coffee, David?' asked the man.

White looked at his watch. It was just after eleven thirty and he had nothing planned for the rest of the day, though he hoped to persuade Rachel to leave her bedroom and venture out for dinner. It was clear that the man had an agenda, and White was curious to know what it was. 'Sure, why not?'

'Why don't we take a walk along the canal? I'm deskbound most of the time and I look forward to a walk on Saturdays, providing the weather is fine.'

White looked up at the near cloudless blue sky overhead and smiled. 'Why not,' he said.

The man led the way, down Warrington Crescent, then past Warwick Avenue Tube station. 'David White is the name you go by,' said the man. 'Good English name, White. Probably comes from the Old English *hwit*, probably used to describe someone with white hair or a pale complexion. Though *wiht* meant bend in Middle English, so it might have referred to someone who lived near a bend in a river or a road.' He smiled to reveal yellowing teeth. 'Here's a little known fact about the surname White that you might not be aware of. The first child of English descent born in the US of A was one Peregrine White, who was actually born on the *Mayflower*, moored in Cape Cod harbour. His father was William White.'

'I didn't know that,' said White.

'Well why would you, David? Why would you?' They walked through Rembrandt Gardens and on to the canal tow path, heading east towards Paddington. 'It's not as if you're an English White, is it? Weiss is your family name.'

White shrugged but didn't say anything.

'Your grandfather changed it, not long after he and his wife fled Germany. Jacob and Ruth Weiss. Came to the UK with three children. Martha, Esther and Samuel your father. Now Weiss also means white of course, in German and in Yiddish. It comes from the Middle High German word *wiz* which means white or blonde, or the Old High German word *wiz* which means white, or shining or bright.'

White forced a smile. 'Good to know.'

'Oh, I have always been fascinated by the history of names,' said the man. 'But at the end of the day. White and Weiss are the same, a rose by any other name. Same meaning, and they do almost sound the same. Though of course in Germany the W would have a V sound. So it sounds like vice. Weiss. White. Weiss.' He smiled. 'So why do you think your grandfather changed it?'

White sighed. 'You know why.'

'I suppose I do, yes. But I'd like to hear it from you, David.'

'I assume that my grandfather wanted to make it sound less foreign.'

'Less foreign? Or less Jewish?'

'I never discussed it with him. And he died when I was still young.'

'You were ten.'

White noted that the man knew when he was born, and when his grandfather had died. If he knew that, how much more did he know? Probably a lot. A teenager whizzed towards them on an electric scooter and they stood to the side to let him go by.

'What about your father?' asked the man as they

167

started walking again. 'Did you ever talk about it with him?'

'Talk about what, exactly?'

'About why you were disguising your family name.'

'Hardly disguising. Weiss means white. We live in England, it makes sense to have an English name.'

'It does, doesn't it? Weiss becomes White. Schwartz becomes Black, Levi becomes Lewis, Schultz becomes Shaw. It makes life so much easier, doesn't it? It made a lot of sense in Hollywood, especially back in the golden age. Would Betty Persky have been a star if she hadn't become Lauren Bacall? Would Issur Daniclovitch Demsky have been Spartacus if he hadn't renamed himself Kirk Douglas? They flocked to see Tony Curtis on the cinema, but would they have paid their hard-earned money to see Bernard Schwartz?'

'I guess not.'

'Exactly. It pays to blend, to fit in. You ring up The Ivy for a table in the name of David White, and it's a done deal. If it's for David Weiss then it has to be spelled out, doesn't it? More so if it was Uriel Weiss.'

White gritted his teeth. He had been at The Ivy two days earlier. Dinner with an old school friend. Did the man know that, or was the mention a coincidence?

'My family name is Schwartz. That means black, of course, but our family never anglicised it. They did shorten it though, from Schwarzkopf.'

'Blackhead.'

'Exactly. Nobody wants to use the name of a skin condition, do they? So Schwartz we became and Schwartz we remain. A small coincidence that you are Mr White and I am Mr Black.'

'I suppose so.'

'So here's another question for you, David. What is the most popular boy's name in the UK these days?'

White didn't have to think about the answer. 'Mohammed.'

'That's right. Mohammed. The name of the prophet. The most popular boy's name in the UK, by far. And the most popular boy's name in Israel, too. Now that I do find strange, but it just goes to show you how many non-Jews live there now.' He shrugged. 'So what does that say about Muslims, David?'

White frowned. 'What do you mean?'

'Well, we change our surnames to blend in. And we give our kids Anglicised names. I mean when was the last time you heard a Jewish kid in England with the name Reuben, or Melech, or Hershel? Nowadays it's Oliver or Harry or Charlie. But your average Muslim mum and dad are quite happy to send their kids out into the world with the name Mohammed. We hide our religion, and they push theirs in our faces. Every time I get an Uber and the driver's name is Moham-med, I know what his views are. If my Deliveroo takeaway comes courtesy of a guy called Mohammed, well, I know there's a good chance he wants me dead. If I get taken into hospital and the doctor in A&E has Mohammed on his name tag then I really have to wonder if he's going to give me the best possible care.'

'I've got Muslim friends,' said White.

Schwartz smiled. 'Of course you do.'

'And I work with plenty of Muslims.'

'Again, I am sure you do. But you have to admit that the UK is no longer a safe place to be Jewish. It's not the country that your grandfather fled to when the storm clouds were gathering over Western

Europe. How do you think he would have felt if he had seen hundreds of thousands of Muslims demonstrating in cities across the UK, calling for Israel to be wiped from the face of the earth? Shouts of 'Death to Jews' and 'Hitler had the right idea.'? Jews being assaulted for no other reason that they are Jewish. Our schools have to be protected, our women and children are at risk, while the police stand by and do nothing. Write a Facebook criticising Islam and the police will be knocking on your door. But thousands of people can march through the streets shouting 'death to Jews' and the police stand by and watch.' He leaned towards White and lowered his voice to a whisper. 'Are you happy with what is happening to your country?'

'I don't think anyone is,' said White quietly.

21

Shepherd was staring at a whiteboard on which were stuck half a dozen photographs of Albanian gangsters that had been identified by Plauku prior to his suicide. Underneath the photographs he had written their names, and under four of them he had written mobile phone numbers. Shepherd was hoping to get the numbers checked in Italy to see if any of them had been used to phone numbers in the UK, but it had been explained to him several times that having left the EU, the UK lost access to the Schengen Information System and was no longer a member of Europol so all phone enquiries had to go through Interpol, which took time.

Shepherd's mobile rang and he pulled it from his pocket. It was Jimmy Sharpe. Sharpe and Ajazi were staying at the NCA's Richmond safe house. Someone in accounting had decided that it was cheaper than putting the Albanian up in a London hotel.

'Tuk has been in touch,' said Sharpe.

'He's okay?'

'He's fine, but jumpy. Says all of them are being watched like hawks after they shot Plauku. They don't trust anybody.'

'Has he seen Fisnik Haziri yet?'

'No. But they've moved them all to London. Four of them have been moved to an urban cannabis farm, Tuk thinks it's in Brixton but doesn't know exactly where. At the moment they're using Tuk as muscle but they've told him he'll be working on one of their county lines. The good news is that they've given him a phone. A Samsung Galaxy A14 with 128 gigabytes of memory.'

'Colour?'

'Black.'

'If I get a phone fixed up for him, can we arrange a swap?'

'Not a face to face swap, but from what Ajazi says, we could arrange a dead drop. Tuk is out and about most days, but he's never on his own.'

'I'll get something sorted. In the meantime, has he got GPS activated?'

'He has. I'll text you the number.'

'I'll get right on it. And how is Ajazi?'

'He still blames us for Plauku's suicide.'

'He probably has a point,' said Shepherd. 'But we couldn't have kept him in the dark. It would have been morally and legally wrong.'

'I don't think he sees it that way. But he's perked up now that Tuk has been in touch.'

'Leave it with me, Razor. As soon as I've got the phone ready I'll call you to arrange the dead drop.'

Shepherd ended the call and took the lift up to the office of Amar Singh, one of MI5's top technical experts. His office was an Aladdin's cave of equipment, stored on metal racks and in wooden cupboards, and smelled of solder and Singh's favourite Dior Sauvage aftershave.

Singh was sitting in a high-backed executive chair with his gleaming black Bally shoes up on his desk, a keyboard on his lap. He grinned when he saw Shepherd and stood up to shake his hand. He was wearing a black Hugo Boss suit and a crisp white shirt that was open at the neck to reveal a slim gold chain. 'So what do you need, Spider?' asked Singh.

'Rush job, Amar. An undercover guy we're using has just been given a black Samsung Galaxy A14 with 128 gigabytes of memory and I need a ringer rigged up and ready to go ASAP.'

Singh went over to one of his shelving units and pulled out a large plastic box marked SAMSUNG GALAXY. He placed it on the desk and took off the lid to reveal more than a dozen brand new phones, still in their cellophane-wrapped boxes. He rifled through the boxes, then grinned with triumph and held up a box. 'Black?' he said.

'Black,' confirmed Shepherd.

Singh waved the box. 'Black it is.'

'How long?'

'Rush job?'

'Yeah.'

'I mean rush, rush? I've got a backlog as long as my . . .' He grinned. 'Arm,' he said.

'You weren't going to say 'arm', were you?' laughed Shepherd.

'I don't like to boast,' said Singh. 'Okay, give me an hour. What about the SIM card?'

'I figured we'd get our guy to use the SIM card he has. And once we've done the swap, I'll bring in the phone that he has so that you can give it a going over.'

'No problem,' said Singh, replacing the lid on the box and putting it back on the shelf. 'I'll give you a bell when I'm done.'

173

22

There was a coffee truck ahead of White and Schwartz, parked next to a line of trestle tables by the canal. 'The coffee here is excellent, David,' said Schwartz. 'My treat. What can I get you?'

'A cappuccino would be good.'

'A croissant perhaps? Or a muffin?'

'I'm fine, I had breakfast.'

'Grab a seat while I get the coffees.'

Schwartz went over to the coffee truck while White sat down at one of the tables. He watched as Schwartz placed his order with the young woman in the truck. Schwartz hadn't said who he worked for, but White was sure that he was connected to the intelligence community. The introduction at the synagogue had been forced, and Schwartz had obviously been keen for a private chat. Most of the conversation so far had been Schwartz probing White's feelings for his country. Schwartz wanted something, White would have bet money on that. The question was, what did he want?

Schwartz came over with two coffees and a bag. He sat down, opened the bag, and took out a muffin. 'I couldn't resist,' he said. He waved a hand at it. 'Grab a piece, please.'

'Really, I'm fine,' said White. He picked up his coffee and sipped it as Schwartz picked at his muffin. 'The thing is, David, this isn't really your country. Not any more. They treat you as an outsider. An embarrassment. They don't care about your wellbeing, or the

174

wellbeing of any of the three hundred thousand or so Jews who call the UK home. It's a numbers game. There are four million Muslims in the country, with thousands more arriving every week. They already outnumber us by a factor of thirteen or fourteen. And the gap widens every year.'

'I was born here, Joel. I'm British.'

'But you're Israeli, too. What are you saying, that you can be loyal to Britain but not to Israel. What are you? A part-time Jew?'

White's eyes hardened. 'You've no right to say that to me. Not after what I've gone through. Fuck you.'

Schwartz put a hand on his shoulder. 'I apologise, and I take it back. I'm sorry. I had no right to imply that you weren't anything but a committed Jew. And all that stuff I said about changing your name. I was just trying to prove my point that Jews are vulnerable in this country. We have to do what we do to survive.'

'I know what you're saying, Joel. And I know what you want. There's only one reason you'd be saying this to me.'

'And will you help? Will you do what needs to be done?'

White sipped his coffee. Joel broke off a piece of muffin and popped it into his mouth before chewing noisily. 'You're planning another Wrath of God, aren't you?' said White.

'Of course. How could we not? This is the largest massacre of Jews outside of the Holocaust, how can we not respond robustly?'

White sipped his coffee again. Operation Wrath of God had been Israel's response to the kidnapping and murder of eleven Israeli athletes at the September 1972 Munich Olympics. A top secret Israel committee headed by Prime Minister Golda Meir authorised the assassination of every single person who was involved in the planning and execution of the killings. A hit squad — codenamed Bayonet — was set up using resources from Mossad — Israel's foreign intelligence agency — and the Israel Defence Forces. Over a period of twenty years, assassination squads killed dozens of targets, including members of the Black September militant group who carried out the attack and members of the Palestine Liberation Organisation, who helped plan it.

'Does this operation have a name?' White asked eventually.

'It does, but it's need to know.'

'And I don't need to know?'

'No, you don't.' Schwartz popped another chunk of muffin into his mouth.

'And you'll be operating in the UK?'

Schwartz looked around as if he feared being overheard, then looked back at White. 'Two hours before the Hamas attack, three men left on a flight from El Arish Airport in Egypt to Heathrow. They weren't travelling together, they sat separately on the plane and they left the airport independently. But all three were Hamas leaders involved in the planning of the attack. Mohammed Sharif, Ahmed Abu-Rous and Ibrahim Fayyad.'

'And they flew into Heathrow as easily as that? They weren't on a watch list?'

'They used fake passports. And you know what a joke Border Force is these days. Border Farce is one of the kinder terms used to describe it. Heathrow is a sieve, they're understaffed because so many of their people are down on the Dover coast welcoming all the jihadists coming over on rubber dinghies. Anyway, they flew in without a hitch, and so far as we know they're still here.'

'And you're targeting them?'

'We're targeting a lot of people, David.'

'Do you know where there are?' He smiled. 'Of course you don't. That's why we're having this conversation. Why did they come to London?'

'To get as far away from Gaza as they could, because they knew that the retaliation would be devastating. Maybe to help with fundraising. And to meet with the organisers of the pro-Palestine demonstrations that took place in cities across the UK.'

'If three members of Hamas were here in the UK, we'd know about it.'

'Maybe you do. If by 'you' you mean Five.'

'Haven't you asked?'

'You mean officially? Through channels?' Schwartz laughed, and it was the sound of a barking fox. 'They're the ones who should be approaching us, through channels. They're the ones who should be telling us that Mohammed Sharif, Ahmed Abu-Rous and Ibrahim Fayyad were here in the UK. And they're the ones who should be scooping them up. Hamas is a banned terrorist organisation and its proscription was extended on November 2021. Just being a member of Hamas is enough for a fourteen year prison sentence in the UK.'

'So they're here under the radar?'

'That's what we'd like to know, David.'

'And again, why haven't you asked my bosses? It's a valid request. You say that the three of them flew in to Heathrow, show them the evidence and let them track them down.'

'The problem with that is that if anything were to happen to them, it might look as if we were involved.'

White chuckled. 'Perish the thought.'

Schwartz sipped his coffee. 'So we'd like to run some checks on the QT. Are you up for that?'

'You want me to spy against my country?'

'I want you to share intel that should be shared with us anyway. The UK and Israel are supposed to be allies, especially when it comes to the War Against Terrorism. But after what happened in London after the Hamas attacks, we no longer have much confidence in that alliance. Remember what your Prime Minister said about those anti-Semetic protests? That they were disrespectful. Calling for the death of Jews and the destruction of Israel is disrespectful? Well I guess it is. But it's so much more than that, isn't it? Hundreds of thousands of people showing support for Hamas while they're still threatening to kill more than two hundred hostages?' Schwartz shrugged. 'And what do the police do? Hunt down a football supporter because he called them terrorists, that's what they do. They made it perfectly clear where their sympathies lie, and it's not with Israel.' He leaned closer to White. 'You wouldn't be spying, David. We're not a hostile power. And you have an Israeli passport.'

'You think that will be a defence if I get caught?'

'You won't get caught, David. The information we want is just a location. An address. The name of a contact. You read a file, you memorise a name or an address and we meet for coffee and a chat. Or a game, maybe. Do you play badminton?'

'I do, yes.' White laughed. 'Of course you know I play badminton. You know everything.'

178

Schwartz sat back and grinned, showing his yellowing teeth again. "So you and I can start playing badminton. And between games we can chat, the way friends do. No dead drops, no microdots or thumb drives, no tradecraft. Just a game of badminton and a chat.'

White nodded slowly. 'I'll have to put you down as a contact.'

'Of course. I would expect nothing else.' He pulled a brown leather wallet from his pocket and fished out a business card. White studied the card. It was crisp and white with slightly raised black type, with a star of David and the address of the Israeli embassy. Joel Schwartz was in the middle of the card, and below it, Public Affairs Manager. In the right hand bottom corner was an e-mail address, a landline number and a mobile number.

'So you're what, a press officer?'

'For my sins, yes. There's a mobile number on the back of the card. That is solely for you.'

White turned the card over. The number had been scrawled in blue ink. White nodded slowly. 'Okay,' he said. 'And how did we meet? If anyone asks.'

'At the synagogue. We met, we chatted, we realised we both had an interest in badminton. I'm a member of the Paddington Sports Club in Castellain Road. We can play there.'

'I'm a member there too.' He sighed and shook his head ruefully. 'You know that already. But I've never seen you there.'

'I'm a member of a number of clubs. I move around. But we could start having a weekly game. What day is good for you?'

White shrugged. 'Wednesday?'

'Wednesday works for me.'

'So if I have something for you, I arrange a game?'

'No, we should just play every Wednesday. Let's say at seven.' He patted his stomach. 'I could do with the exercise. Middle age spread.'

White smiled. There was barely an ounce of fat on the man. He put the card into his top pocket.

'So we're good?' said Schwartz.

'Yes, we're good.'

Schwartz stood up. 'Any problems, any worries, anything at all, you have my mobile number. Otherwise I'll see you on Wednesday.'

White thought that the man was going to stick out his hand to shake, but he just smiled and nodded and turned away, walking along the towpath towards Paddington Station. White nursed his coffee as he watched him walk away. He doubted that Joel was his real name. He was almost certainly Mossad. Mossad was one of Israel's three intelligence agencies, tasked with foreign intelligence gathering and analysis, and covert operations. It worked alongside Aman — Military Intelligence — and Shin Bet, Internal Security. Its full name was Mossad Merkazi Le Modiin Uletafkidim Meyuhadim, Hebrew for Central Institute For Intelligence and Special Operations. And it was the agency which killed the enemies of Israel.

23

Shepherd brought his BMW SUV to a halt outside the Richmond safe house and pressed the intercom button. The lock clicked and the gate rolled back. He parked next to the grey Skoda Octavia. Jimmy Sharpe was already waiting at the door, wearing the same grey pullover and jeans he'd had on the last time that Shepherd was there. 'How's Petrit?' asked Shepherd.

'About the same. At least now he can focus on Tuk.'

'They've taken the body away?'

'They were here less than two hours after we found him,' said Sharpe. 'I guess you guys are used to clearing up bodies.'

'There is a department for that,' said Shepherd. 'They should have done a full clean up.'

'They did. It's as if he was never there.'

'That's sort of the point,' said Shepherd.

'So what do they do with the body? Bury it in a forest somewhere or ship it back to Albania?'

'I never ask, Razor. And if I did they probably wouldn't tell me.'

'Secret fucking squirrel. It would drive me crazy.'

Shepherd stepped into the hall and Sharpe closed the door. Sharpe waved at the kitchen, 'Petrit's in there. He's had a few beers.'

'Is he okay?'

'He's not off his head. I haven't mentioned it and I wouldn't if I were you.'

Shepherd nodded and followed Sharpe into the kitchen. Ajazi was sitting at a pine table, looking out of the window. He was wearing a tight black vest that showed off his bulging biceps and was holding a can of Budweiser.

'Everything okay, Petrit?' asked Shepherd, sitting down at the table.

The Albanian shrugged. 'Tuk is safe and well, so that's something,' he said, still looking out of the window.

'That's great news. Did you get much chance to talk to him?'

'A minute. He used a payphone, he says they monitor his mobile.'

'So they don't trust him?'

'They don't trust any of the new arrivals, after what happened on the boat. They want them to prove themselves.'

'How will they do that?'

Ajazi drained his can, crumpled it and tossed it into the sink. 'We didn't have time to talk about it, he didn't want to be caught on a payphone, but if it was me, I'd get them involved in a killing.' He stood up and walked over to the fridge to get another beer.

'That makes sense,' said Shepherd. He looked over at Sharpe. 'That's going to be a problem.'

'You're telling me,' said Sharpe.

'Do you think they'll want Tuk to pull the trigger?' Shepherd asked Ajazi.

Ajazi sat down at the table and popped the tab of his can. 'It's the only way they'll trust him.' He drank from the can.

'We can't let him get involved in murder,' said Shepherd.

'The Police And Criminal Evidence Act again?' sneered the Albanian.

'There are rules about what undercover agents can and cannot do,' said Shepherd. 'And murder is at the top of the 'can't do' list.'

'But if he doesn't do what they want, they'll kill him,' said Ajazi.

'Then we'll pull him out before it gets to that stage,' said Shepherd. 'We're not putting him at risk.'

'That ship has sailed,' said Ajazi.

'I know he's at risk, I've worked plenty of under-cover cases myself so I know the dangers, but we're not going to let him commit murder. Besides, if he is told to carry out a killing and we can show that the order came from Haziri then we would have enough to charge Haziri with conspiracy to commit murder which means we can pull him in. And once Haziri is off the streets, we'd probably find more people willing to testify against him.' He reached into his jacket pocket and took out the mobile phone that Amar Singh had given him.

He slid it across the table to Ajazi who picked it up and examined it. 'It looks like a regular phone,' said the Albanian.

'It is,' said Shepherd. 'But it has a few extra features now. It records everything said in the vicinity, and once a day sends a burst transmission to our computers with all audio and texts sent and received. Even if the phone is switched off, the microphone and transmitter continues to function. The GPS is perma-nently on and each time the phone moves location, we get a message. Tuk doesn't have to do anything, it all happens automatically.'

'If they catch him with it, they'll kill him.'

'No, it's identical in appearance to the phone they gave him. You could take it apart and examine everything under a microscope and you wouldn't be able to tell that it had been tampered with. All you need to do is to swap this for his phone.'

'I can't go near him. Neither can you.'

'No, but you can find out where he goes. A restaurant or a shop. A filling station. Anywhere he can use a toilet. You can leave the phone there and he can do the switch himself.'

'A dead drop?'

'Exactly. A dead drop.'

Ajazi nodded. 'Okay, yes that could work.'

'And provided that Tuk always has the phone with him, he can use it to call for help. You can give him a phrase, something innocuous, and he'll know that if he says it, we'll send someone in to rescue him.'

Ajazi flashed him a thin smile. 'You've done this before?'

'Rescued people?' Shepherd grinned. 'Hell, yeah.'

24

White walked to Paddington Sports Club. He was wearing a dark blue Adidas tracksuit over his badminton gear and carrying his racquet in a bag over his shoulder. It was a warm evening and he figured a brisk walk would loosen him up. Rachel had been in bed when he got back from work, and from the look of the room she had been there all day. There was an empty bottle of wine on the bedside table and a half empty glass. She alternated between anti-depressants and wine depending on her mood, and he was forever warning her of the dangers of mixing the two. He'd told her that he was off to play badminton and that he'd be back before nine, but she just stared up at the ceiling and acknowledged him with a quiet 'Okay.' He knew that there was nothing he could do or say that would jolt her out of her depression, she had good days and bad days and today was obviously a bad day.

Schwartz was already on the court when White arrived, briskly running through some warm-up exercises. He was wearing baggy shorts that came down over his knees and an Oxford University sweatshirt. His trainers were a generic brand and were well worn, but his Yonex racquet looked brand new. White wondered if he had bought the racquet specifically for the occasion. His own Carlton racquet was almost ten years old and had been restrung several times.

White stripped off his tracksuit and dropped it at the side of the court and unzipped his bag. He took out the racquet and a fresh tube of shuttlecocks. They

185

hit back and forth as they warmed up. Schwartz was nimble and quick on his feet, darting back and forth like a humming bird, and it soon became clear that he was an experienced player. What he lacked for in height he more than made up for with speed and rat-like cunning.

White won the first game 21-16 but he had the impression that Schwartz was going easy on him. Schwartz kicked into another gear for the second game and won it 21-18. Both men were drenched in sweat and they sat on the floor and drank water as they readied themselves for the final game.

'I'm afraid I don't have anything for you,' said White.

'That's okay, David, I'm enjoying the game.'

'The trouble is, everything we do on line is tracked. They can see everything I do, everywhere I go.'

'The irony of spies being spied upon is not lost on me.'

'You understand the problem? If I get the intel you want and something happens to the guy, first thing they'll do is look to see who accessed their files.'

'David, I understand. We didn't expect to get results immediately. Softly softly, catchee monkey, as they say. Your security has to be paramount. I would not want you to put yourself at risk.'

'Do you have anyone else looking for the three men?'

'We are exploring several avenues. But I will be honest with you, you are our best hope.' He screwed the top back on his water bottle and got to his feet. 'How long have you been playing?'

'Since I was at university.' He chuckled. 'My wife played and it was the only way I could think of to get to talk to her.'

'So it was a ruse?'

'Initially, but I grew to really enjoy it. I was on the university team in my final year and I've played ever since.'

'How is Rachel?'

White's stomach lurched. 'Not good,' he said. 'She's just depressed all the time. When she isn't crying, she's staring blankly into space. They've prescribed anti-depressants but like they say, doctors always make the worst patients and I don't think she's taking them. She prefers to self medicate with alcohol.'

'I am so sorry, David.'

'All we can do is to take it one day at a time.' He forced a smile. 'Right, final game. And I'm going to stop taking it easy on you.'

25

'There they are,' said Ajazi, nodding over at a white van with the name of a dry cleaners on the side. The van had pulled into the service station and parked next to the petrol pumps. Ajazi was sitting in the rear of Sharpe's grey Skoda, a baseball cap pulled low over his face. Sharpe was in the driving seat and Shepherd was next to him. They were parked in a Tesco car park from where they had a good view of the filling station. They had been there for the best part of six hours. Tuk Marku had told them that they would be there to fill up the van at some point, but didn't know exactly when.

Shepherd had been into the toilet and placed the phone in a Ziploc bag which he had duct-taped to the rear of the toilet bowl in the stall to the left. Then they had waited. And waited. They had moved the car several times, and had been about to move it again when they had seen the van.

A big man in a long brown leather coat climbed out of the driver seat and began filling the tank. A second man got out of the van and jogged over to the toilets. 'That's Tuk,' said Ajazi, but Shepherd had already recognised him. He had never met or spoken to the Albanian undercover agent, but had seen him at a distance in Belgium the night before he had boarded the speedboat. He was wearing the same clothes he'd been wearing in Belgium — a brown leather bomber jacket with a fur collar, black jeans and scruffy Nikes. Marku disappeared into the toilet.

The man in the long coat finished filling the tank and went inside to pay. He came out just as Marku left the toilet and together they walked back to the van.

Shepherd waited until the Albanians had got back into the van and driven away before he got out of the car and walked towards the toilets. There was no one inside and he stepped into the stall on the left and knelt down by the toilet bowl. He reached behind it and felt the Ziploc bag, stuck in place with duct tape. He ripped the bag off the toilet and put it into the pocket of his jacket before heading back to the car.

26

White unlocked the front door. 'I'm home!' he shouted. There was no reply. He closed the door and went through to the kitchen. There was a corkscrew on the kitchen table and the remains of the foil capsule. But no bottle and no glass. White sighed. When she was self-medicating with alcohol, two bottles a day wasn't unusual. 'Rachel, I'm home!' he shouted, but there was only silence.

He took the bag into the hallway and put it into the cupboard under the stairs. At least the corkscrew suggested that she had come downstairs. He opened the door to the sitting room, hoping to see her on the sofa in front of the TV, but the room was empty. He frowned. The garden, maybe. He went back into the kitchen and out of the kitchen door. There was a gazebo at the end of the garden where Rachel sometimes sat and drank when the weather was good, but there was a chill in the air and he wasn't surprised to find the gazebo empty.

He went back into the house, and along the hall to the stairs. 'Rachel, are you up there?' he called. She often fell asleep after her second bottle, but that wasn't usually until midnight. There was no answer.

He headed up the stairs and called her name again. The bedroom door was ajar. He pushed it open. The bed was empty, the duvet on the floor. The door to the ensuite bathroom was closed. White went over to it and knocked. 'Rachel, are you in there?' There was no reply and he knocked again. His stomach was churning. Something was wrong. Something was very wrong. He turned the door handle and pushed but it was bolted. 'Rachel!' He said, louder this time.

There was still no answer but deep down he hadn't expected one. He hit the door with his shoulder but it didn't move. He took a step back and kicked the door just below the handle. The wood splintered and the door flew open. White gasped when he saw his wife's gaping mouth and staring eyes, the cuts in her wrist and the blood that had trickled down over her hand and pooled on the floor tiles. The razor blade she had used was on the side of the bath, next to an open empty bottle of tablets. Sleeping pills. From the look of it she had swallowed all the tablets she had left and then cut her wrists, both of them. Her left arm was hanging over the side of the bath, the other was in the water and had turned it pink.

He walked slowly towards the bath. She was clearly dead and had been for some time. He stood staring down at her, tears filling his eyes. 'Oh, honey . . .' he moaned. He sat down on the toilet and put his head in his hands. His mind began to race with 'if onlys'. If only he hadn't gone to meet Schwartz. If only he'd phoned her to see how she was. If only she had been out of the house, with friends or running an errand. She had seemed fine when he had last seen her. Well, not fine exactly, she hadn't been fine since Hannah and Ella had died. He had thought she was starting to improve, she had even smiled occasionally, but he suspected that had been down to the anti-depressants that the doctor had prescribed. Before the doctor had given her sleeping tablets she had barely closed her eyes at night, she would spend hours just staring up at the ceiling. For the first few days after he had returned

191

to the UK, she had barely left their bedroom, she had spent most of her time curled up with two pullovers, a pink Barbie one that Ella had loved when she was younger, and Hannah's favourite cashmere sweater. White had taken meals up to her, but she barely ate. It was only when the doctor had put her on anti-depressants and sleeping tablets that she had emerged from the bedroom, but even then she had spent most of her time sitting on the sofa, clutching the pullovers and flicking through her photographs on her phone.

He crouched down at the side of the bath and put a hand on her shoulder. She was cold. She'd been dead for some time. Tears welled up in his eyes. 'Oh baby, why? How does this solve anything?' He took out his mobile phone and held it. He knew that he was going to have to call the police eventually, but for the moment he just wanted to sit with her.

27

Shepherd sipped his coffee as he watched Ajazi scribbling on a yellow legal pad. The Albanian had a pair of Bose headphones on and was listening to the latest feed from Tuk Marku's phone. All the conversations were work related, mainly telling Marku where to go and what to do. The phone was presently in a car wash in Ealing, and had been there since the previous night. The car wash was run by Albanians, one of several dozen owned by the Hellbanianz gang through a network of shell companies. It had once been a filling station but the pumps and tanks had been stripped away and half a dozen young Albanians washed cars by hand. Not that they washed many cars, the business wasn't so much about cleaning vehicles as it was about washing money. Drug money was funnelled as cash through the car washes, tax was paid, and the money was in the banking system free and clear. If HMRC had bothered to check, they would have soon realised that the turnover was inflated, but they didn't care as they were getting paid. The NCA had done some investigation into the car washes, but knew that it wasn't the way to bring down the gang. For that they needed evidence of the gang's involvement in people trafficking, drugs or extortion.

There were plenty of conversations about criminal activity — drugs, extortion and people trafficking — but most of the conversations were in slang and nebulous at best. The only work that Marku and the recent arrivals were doing was to wash cars and clean

193

their interiors. What was more helpful was when Marku spoke to the phone, knowing that everything he said would be relayed to Ajazi. On the few occasions he was alone, usually late at night or early in the morning, Marku would whisper to the phone, packing in as much intel as he could. He supplied names, phone numbers when he had them, and details of what the gang was doing. But it was all hearsay, second hand news, and there was no hard intel on Fisnik Haziri, who Marku always referred to as 'Meatball'. Marku hadn't met the man and didn't know where he was.

On the wall was a screen showing a map of London with red dots marking the places recorded by Marku's GPS. It had mainly been at the car wash. Shepherd had decided against mounting surveillance outside the car wash. They knew where Marku was and the phone provided them with all the intel they needed. Parking an Openreach van outside for extended periods was just asking for trouble.

Marku was clearly starting to worry about what the gang had planned for him. Several times hints had been dropped that he would be expected to kill someone, but he didn't know who, or when, or where. It was a test, he'd been told, a test of his loyalty. Ajazi had had a couple of rushed phone conversations with Marku — from call boxes — and Ajazi had stressed that on no account was Marku to carry out a killing, if it reached the point where he thought an assassination was imminent he had to call for an extraction. They had agreed on a rescue phrase — 'I miss Elbasan' — which was the city where Marku had been born. Amar Singh had rigged the phone's computerised monitoring system to sound an alarm if ever that phrase was used and Shepherd, Sharpe and Ajazi would all be notified immediately.

Shepherd's mobile rang. It was Amy, requesting his presence in Giles Pritchard's office. Shepherd patted Ajazi on the shoulder. 'Back in a minute,' he said.

Ajazi nodded and continued to scribble on the pad. Shepherd went out of the office and he headed towards the lifts. His eyes widened when he saw David White walking towards him. White looked uncomfortable, his eyes shifting to the floor as if he was trying to ignore Shepherd.

'David?' said Shepherd.

White looked up and forced a smile. 'Oh, Dan, hi, sorry, I was miles away.'

Shepherd knew that the man was lying, he had seen Shepherd, recognised him, and then looked away. He'd been deliberately trying to avoid Shepherd. 'I'm sorry to hear about your wife, David. So sorry for your loss.'

'Thank you.' He had stopped walking and was shifting uncomfortable from side to side.

'I'm surprised to see you here, I thought you'd have taken some time off.'

'I'd rather be doing something,' said White. He looked at his watch. 'Anyway, sorry, I'm late for a meeting.'

'Sure, yes, I understand. You take care, David.'

White nodded nervously. 'You too. Yes. Take care.' He hurried away, his head down.

Shepherd frowned as he continued walking to the lifts. It was as if White had been embarrassed to see Shepherd and he obviously wanted to keep the conversation as short as possible.

Shepherd went up to Pritchard's floor and Amy

ushered him straight in. Pritchard was standing by the window, jacket off, shirt sleeves rolled up, looking out over the Thames. He turned to look at Shepherd as he walked into the room. 'I thought you needed to know straight away, the Albanian police have found Plauku's family. All dead, and tortured quite horrifically before they were killed.'

'Petrit doesn't know, I just left him downstairs.'

'He'll be told soon enough by his own people, but I thought maybe you could break the news to him. Unless you think he might shoot the messenger.' His lips tightened in a slight smile, 'Not literally, of course.'

'I don't think he'll shoot the messenger, but he might wonder why we knew before he did.'

'Because this is a joint NCA, MI5 and SHISH operation so I'm in constant contact with the other two parties. This news is hot off the presses. It literally broke as I was on the phone to the head of SHISH. It's not as if it was a deliberate attempt to go behind his back.'

'I know that, but perception is everything.'

'So you'd rather that he hears it from his boss?'

'I think it best.'

'Well you know him better than I do, obviously, so I'm happy to give you the benefit of the doubt.'

Shepherd nodded. 'Thank you, I appreciate that,' he said. 'By the way, I just saw David White, I didn't realise he was back in the office.'

'He insisted on coming back. He was told that he could have as much time off as he needed but he told his boss that he was going crazy sitting at home and that he wanted to get back to work.' Pritchard shrugged. 'I guess I understand him. He's lost his wife and his daughters, if he's sitting at home on his own

196

he's going to just wallow in grief. Working might help take his mind off it.'

'I guess we all have our own ways of dealing with loss,' said Shepherd. 'But I can't imagine how he's feeling right now.'

'He seems okay,' said Pritchard. 'But he can't be okay, of course. No one can go through what he's been through and be okay. We've offered him counselling but he says he doesn't need it. His boss is keeping a close eye on him, but so far he really does seem to be fine. Obviously the fact he's on MENAD means that he's part of the fight against Hamas, so maybe that gives him some purpose. Who knows?'

'He seemed a bit on edge when he saw me, but I suppose I bring back bad memories.'

'He owes his life to you,' said Pritchard. 'A lot of the hostages are turning up dead.'

'I just wish I'd been able to save his daughters,' said Shepherd.

'They were killed before you even landed in Israel,' said Pritchard. 'You did everything you could.'

'That doesn't stop me wishing that it had worked out differently,' said Shepherd.

28

White walked along Warwick Avenue and into Rembrandt Gardens, a small patch of parkland that ran alongside the Regent's Canal. Joel Schwartz was already sitting on a wooden bench, looking out over Browning's Pool, the wide expanse of water that formed the junction of Regent's Canal and the Paddington Arm of the Grand Union Canal. A narrowboat was chugging by, a grey haired woman at the tiller, a calico cat sitting on the roof next to a watering can painted in red, green and gold. White sat down. 'I have an address for you,' he said. 'Mohammed Sharif. He is staying in an apartment in Chelsea Harbour.'

'Thank you,' said Schwartz.

'He has a penthouse in Thames Quay. He owns it. He bought it two years ago for just over five million pounds.'

'There is a lot of money in terrorism, my friend. This information, can it be traced back to you?'

White smiled thinly. 'I'm not stupid, Joel. I used a colleague's log on and used a terminal that isn't covered by CCTV.'

'I wouldn't want you to get into trouble, obviously.'

'I'm good. But thank you for your concern.'

'And the other two names?'

'I'm working on it,' said White. 'Look, there's something I want to ask you.'

Schwartz nodded. 'I'm listening.'

'I want to be more involved in this.'

Schwartz frowned. 'In what way?'

'I want to help.'

'You are helping. By giving us the information we need.'

'This bastard planned the attacks that killed my daughters. I want to be the one who pulls the trigger.'

Schwartz stared at White for several seconds before speaking. 'Have you ever killed someone, David?' he asked eventually, his voice a low whisper.

'I've never wanted to. Now I do.'

'Killing is a big thing, David. It's a job best left to professionals.'

'How hard can it be to point a gun and pull the trigger?'

'Not as easy as you seem to think. And it's not just the act, it's dealing with the repercussions. The guilt. PTSD.'

White shook his head. 'I'm guilty now because I didn't protect my daughters. I'm guilty because I didn't prevent my wife from killing herself. Killing Sharif wouldn't lose me a minute's sleep, I promise. In fact I'll feel better because I'll know that I did something to balance the scales. It will help me live with myself. Please, Joel, you have to do this for me. Let me help.'

'If it was up to me, David, I'd say yes. But it isn't. I'm just the middle man here, a conduit. The operation itself will be carried out by a team from Tel Aviv. Professionals. I know how these people operate and they don't work with people they don't know. There's too much at stake.'

'You're saying you don't trust me? After everything I've been through.'

Schwartz patted him on the leg. 'It's not about trust.

Of course we trust you. If I didn't trust you I wouldn't have approached you in the first place. I could get into a lot of trouble for this.'

'Joel, I'm the one putting his life on the line here. If they catch me, they'll throw away the key.'

'They won't catch you, not if you're careful. But if you do get involved at the sharp end of this operation, you do risk exposing yourself. Helping an ally with intel is one thing, carrying out an assassination is a whole different ball game.'

'I'm happy to take that risk.'

'I know you are. And I understand why you want to get more involved. But it's a terrible idea. And as I said, the Mossad hit team won't countenance it.'

'You don't know that for sure until you've asked them.'

'If that is what you want, I'll ask. But I know what they'll say.'

White clenched his fists, then relaxed as he realised that Schwartz was looking at them. 'Let me talk to them,' said White. 'Let me plead my case.'

Schwartz held up his hands. 'They're not going to talk to you, David. Not direct.'

'If it wasn't for me, you wouldn't know where Mohammed Sharif was.'

'True. And we're grateful for that.'

'But not grateful enough to let me be a part of it?'

'David, I keep telling you, you are part of it. A big part. We all have our roles to play and your role is one of the most important.'

'I want to pull the trigger.'

'Most times there isn't a trigger to pull,' said Schwartz. 'They'll make it look like an accident if they can. Or a suicide. They have used bombs in the past. But it's rare for them to resort to a shooting. Too many things can go wrong.'

White sighed. It was clear that Schwartz wasn't going to capitulate. He was talking to a brick wall.

'It's for the best,' said Schwartz. 'You will have your revenge, I promise. The men who planned and funded the October Seven massacres will all be dead soon. You have my word on that.'

White nodded but didn't say anything. If Schwartz wasn't prepared to help him get his revenge up close and personal, he'd find another way.

29

Ajazi's phone buzzed on the table in front of him and he pressed a button to stop the recording and removed his headphones. Shepherd was sitting at the table next to him, reading a translated transcript of conversations that Tuk's phone had overheard the previous day. Most of it was boring chit chat about life back in Albania, though there was some reasonably interesting stuff about forthcoming Premier League matches.

Ajazi put the phone to his ear and had a short conversation in his own language. It was clear from the look on his face that it was bad news, and as soon as he put the phone down he looked across at Shepherd. 'Plauku's family are dead,' he growled.

'I'm sorry.'

Ajazi's eyes narrowed as he stared at Shepherd. 'You knew, didn't you?'

Shepherd looked back, keeping his face impassive as he decided whether or not he should lie. He saw the look of triumph flash across the Albanian's face and realised that lying wasn't an option, not if he wanted to preserve what relationship he had with the man. 'My boss told me, yes.'

'When?'

'Earlier today. I didn't say anything because I figured you needed to hear it from your people and not second hand through me.'

Ajazi nodded slowly. 'Okay,' he said eventually.

'Are we good?'

Ajazi forced a smile. 'Yeah, we're good. You were in a difficult position. I'd probably have done the same.'

'It's a messy business all round,' said Shepherd.

'And getting messier,' said the Albanian. He nodded at his legal pad. 'They've told Tuk that the guy they want him to kill is in Luton. There's an Asian gang there that's been bad-mouthing Fisnik Haziri to the Colombians. The Colombians told Haziri and Hazari wants revenge.'

'When?'

'They haven't told him when exactly,' said Ajazi.

'But it could be short notice, right?'

'They could drive him to Luton at any moment,' said Ajazi. 'Where is Luton?'

'About an hour or an hour and a half or so away,' said Shepherd.

Ajazi sat back in his chair. 'We don't have enough to charge Haziri yet, do we?'

'Not from what I've seen so far,' said Shepherd. 'What about the latest recordings?'

'It's all vague and hearsay, nothing that directly implicates Haziri.'

'Does Tuk want us to pull him out?'

'He's getting twitchy but he wants to continue. He knows that if he leaves now the investigation won't be anywhere near complete. We'll be able to shut down some of Hellbanianz's operations, but not all.'

'What do you think?'

'We've no choice, right? We're in the UK so we have to follow PACE. Which means that under no circumstances can Tuk kill the guy.'

'That's correct. If he does, he'll be charged with murder, no matter what the circumstances.'

'But if they tell him to kill this guy and he refuses,

203

they'll kill him. They'll assume he's a police plant. In fact they'll probably torture him, too. And as strong as Tuk is, everybody talks eventually if they're hurt enough. Everything will fall apart.'

'I'll make sure that he's protected, Petrit. I'll have an armed police unit on standby. We'll look after him.'

'You said that about Plauku, remember? You promised him the earth, and look what happened.'

'That's not fair, we didn't know that Plauku's family was at risk. What about Tuk? Does he have family we need to worry about?'

Ajazi shook his head. 'His parents are long dead, and he never married. No kids that he knows of. He has a brother but he's in the army and I doubt that even the Hellbanianz gang can get him in his barracks.'

'So all we have to do is to protect him, and we can do that. We can pull him out the moment he's told the killing is to go ahead. If nothing else we can do a hard stop on their vehicle on the way to Luton.'

'We need to keep Tuk safe.'

'We will do,' said Shepherd.

30

White needed a gun, a gun that couldn't be traced. Ten minutes prowling through the MI5 database gave him more than a dozen possible sources in London. Despite the fact that guns were illegal in the UK, the capital was awash with them. Every year there were at least a thousand firearms offences committed in the city, but that was the tip of a very large iceberg. Most were in the hands of gang members and were used to settle territorial disputes, but there were dealers who rented weapons as and when they were needed. Criminals who needed a weapon for a specific job could buy what they needed and if the weapon wasn't fired, return it and receive half their money back. Many of the dealers were known to the National Crime Agency, and occasionally one would be busted and sent to prison. But it was hard to catch the dealers in the act, they tended only to deal with people they knew and it could take months to put together a successful prosecution.

There were several possibilities that satisfied the criteria White was looking for. He eventually settled on a man called Perry Smith, a Jamaican gangster who dealt drugs and who sold guns on the side. The NCA had put him under round the clock surveillance for two weeks but while he met dozens of South London villains, the investigators were never able to catch him in the act of selling weapons or drugs. Financial investigators were unable to connect him to any substantial assets, and the decision was taken to stand the investigation down.

White grabbed his coat and headed out of the house. He walked down to Edgware Road and flagged down a black cab who didn't seem happy to be told they were going south of the river.

White had the taxi drop him around the corner from the house where Smith lived. He started walking in the opposite direction, checking for tails. When he was sure he wasn't being followed he turned around and cut through a side street and along to Smith's road. The house was in a terrace, two storeys high and with railings around steps leading to a basement. Most of the houses had been split up into flats but Smith's was in original condition. There were two big men standing outside the front door, one wearing a black Puffa jacket, the other in a long overcoat. They both eyed up White suspiciously as he approached. The man in the Puffa jacket slipped his right hand into his pocket.

'I want to see Perry Smith,' said White.

'He know you?' asked the man in the overcoat. White recognised him from the NCA surveillance photographs. His name was Eddie 'The Hatchet' Newfield, a nasty piece of work who had earned his nickname by savagely beating a rival drug dealer to death with a small axe. Newfield had been arrested but never charged as the few witnesses there were to the murder all developed memory loss shortly afterwards. White didn't recognise Mr Puffa Jacket but he was a type — broad shouldered from steroids rather than exercise, cold eyes and two gold teeth at the front of his mouth.

'He doesn't, but I know him,' said White.

'Mr Smith doesn't do walk-ins,' said Newfield.

'He'll see me, Eddie,' said White. 'How's your boy, by the way? Doing three years in Wandsworth, isn't he?'

Newfield's eyes narrowed. 'What the fuck you talking about?'

'Just asking after Kemar, no need to get shirty.' He reached into his jacket and pulled out a folded sheet of paper. 'Show him this.' Newfield took the paper, opened it and frowned. 'What the fuck is this?'

'It's a surveillance photograph of Perry. I'm sure he'll know when and where it was taken but he'll have a few questions for me. So off you pop.'

Newfield's jaw tightened and he glared at White but White simply stared back at him. 'What are you going to do, Eddie? Shoot me, in the street. Perry is going to want to see that photograph, and then he's going to want to talk to me. And if he ever finds out that you tried to send me away, well, he's not going to be happy.'

Newfield continued to glare at him, then he shrugged, turned around and opened the door. He disappeared inside and closed the door behind him.

'So, have you been working for Perry for long?' White asked Puffa Jacket Man.

The man shrugged. 'Why do you want to know?'

'Just gathering intel.'

'You a cop?'

White shook his head. 'No, not a cop.'

'So why do you want to see Perry? You got beef with him?'

'No, no beef,' said White. 'I've never met the guy, which is why I'm here.' He looked up and down the road. 'Does he have enemies?'

'Everyone has enemies.'

'I suppose they do. But not everyone has two heavies standing guard outside their front door.'

'We're not guards.'

'Well, you sort of are,' said White. 'You're not regular doormen, are you? If you were, you'd have welcomed me with a smile and opened the door for me.'

The man was about to reply but the door opened and Newfield waved at White. 'In,' he said.

'There you go, that wasn't too hard, was it?' said White. He stepped into the hall and Newfield closed the door.

White opened his mouth to speak but the heavy turned him around and kicked his legs apart before running his hands over White, looking for a concealed weapon but not finding one. 'Eddie, if I thought I needed to be armed I would have brought SCO19 with me.' SCO19 was the Metropolitan Police's specialist firearms unit, on call when MI5 needed armed support.

Newfield span White around and sneered at him. 'So you are a cop?'

White shook his head. 'No, I'm not.'

'If I find out that you're a cop, I'll rip your balls off.'

'I'm not, and you won't.'

Newfield continued to sneer at White for a couple of seconds, but when he realised his hard man act was having no effect, he pushed White down the hall. The hall ran the length of the house with a kitchen at the far end, purple doors leading off to the right and a flight of stairs, which had also been painted purple, leading upstairs. Newfield pushed White along the hall to the first room. The walls were a pale purple and there was a large spherical white-paper lampshade

208

hanging from the middle of the ceiling. There were three large sofas around a coffee table that was filled with the remnants of a Chinese takeaway. There was a massive TV screen above the fireplace showing a rap music video with the sound turned off.

Perry Smith was wearing a gold tracksuit and silver Nikes, around his neck was a fist-sized gold medallion and both wrists were festooned with gold chains. He had enough chunky gold rings on his fingers to make a knuckleduster superfluous. He was sprawled on the middle sofa, his legs spread wide. He pointed at the sofa to his left. 'Sit the fuck down.'

White did as he was told. Newfield moved to stand behind White, his massive arms folded across his chest.

Smith was holding the print out in his right hand. 'So what the fuck is this?' he said.

'A surveillance photograph, taken a while back when the National Crime Agency had you under the microscope.'

'For what?'

'Oh come on, Perry. You know for what. For importing drugs, for running county lines into Norfolk and Somerset, and for arms dealing.'

'So you're a bent cop and this is a shakedown?'

White shook his head. 'No, and no. And that photograph is old news. It was taken eighteen months ago and shortly afterwards the NCA closed its investigation on you.'

Smith frowned. 'Why did they do that?'

White smiled thinly. 'Because despite appearances to the contrary, they realised that you're quite smart. Very smart, in fact. You own nothing, pretty much. You have no assets. Your baby mammas are all well

209

set up, and they suspect that you have millions tucked away offshore, but they weren't able to find it. At the same time, you never go near the drugs and you never go near the money. You keep the weapons business at arms length. So that means a successful investigation would requite a hell of a lot of resources and because you have no assets, there'd be no payback.'

'Go me,' said Smith, swinging his feet up on a coffee table.

'Exactly. Go you. And long may your good fortune continue.'

'So who are you, oh bringer of good news?'

'My name's not important.'

'No, but I'd like to know.'

'Call me Gideon, if that makes you feel happier.'

'Are you a Jew?'

White nodded. 'I am, yes.'

Smith rubbed his chin. 'What they did, the Palestinians, that was some mad shit.'

'It was. Mad.'

'How many died?'

'One thousand two hundred, give or take.'

'Fucking idiots, huh?'

'Yeah.'

'But your people are getting their revenge, right? Kicking the shit out of Gaza, right?'

'We are, I suppose. Yes.'

'You've got to do that. You don't have a choice. If someone attacks you, you have to hurt them so badly that they never attack you again. I've had people move against me twice. Nearly killed me the second time. But I made sure that they'd never do it again. You have to stamp on them, hard.'

'I think that's what's happening, yeah.'

'You have to. Those Hamas nutters, if they get the chance they'll do it again. What's it they say? From the river to the sea, right? They want to wipe Israel off the map.'

'That's the aim, yeah.'

Smith looked at White for several seconds, staring at him with unblinking eyes. 'So what is it you want from me, Gideon?'

'Guns,' said White. 'And ammunition.'

'How many guns?'

'Three. Four maybe.'

'And you'll pay me for these guns?'

'I was hoping they'd be a gift.'

Smith grinned. 'Now why the fuck would I be giving you a gift?' He held up the print out. 'Because you told me that the NCA has pulled surveillance on me? Come on Gideon, spell it out for me. You've shown me the carrot, now show me the stick.'

'You're a smart guy. Perry. You can work it out for yourself.'

Smith exhaled slowly. 'I give you the guns or the NCA starts to get busy again. Suddenly I'm not free and clear any more.'

'One email is all it would take. I'm not asking for much, Perry. Just four untraceable guns.'

Smiths eyes hardened. 'So what's to stop me offing you and burying you out in the New Forest?'

'That's a bit drastic. And it would end badly for you.'

'How so?'

'Perry, you don't know who else knows that I'm here.'

Smith shrugged. 'I'm guessing no one. What you're doing smells of lone wolf to me. You're a man on a

211

mission and I think you're flying solo.'

'If I was stupid enough to not tell anyone where I was, don't you think I would have left a thumb drive at home or in the office detailing exactly what I was doing and who I was going to see?'

'That's more likely,' said Smith.

'Then there's my phone.'

'Your phone?'

'Yeah. My phone. It's switched on and it's in my pocket and if I disappear the first thing the cops will do is to check my GPS records and they'll show that I was here in this house. It'll show what time I arrived and what time I left. And then they'll be able to check what other phones were also here. I've no doubt that you use burners a plenty but the cops should be able to tie them to you.'

'Doesn't mean I killed you.'

'No, but it means the cops will be looking at you again and we've already decided that you'd rather avoid that. Perry, all I want is four guns. That's nothing to you, and you know it.'

'What sort of guns do you want?'

'What have you got?'

Smith laughed. 'Plenty of choice. Depends on what you need them for. If you're just going to pop someone, then a Glock would be my weapon of choice. If you don't want to be leaving brass at the scene, a revolver might be better. If you're up against a crowd then an Ingram or an Uzi would fit the bill. Spray and pray. Now if you want to stamp your authority on a situation then you can't do better than a sawn off shotgun.'

'Glocks will be fine.'

'And why would you need four? Man's only got

two hands.'

'Figured that I'd leave them when I'm done. That's not a problem if they're not traceable, right?'

'Waste of a good gun, that. The way I work is, you return a gun unfired I give you back half your money.' He shrugged. 'But as you don't plan on paying me, I guess that's moot.'

'I'll be firing them,' said White. 'And I'd like silencers. One for each gun.'

'Going sneaky beaky, are you? Sure. I can do that.' He looked over at Newfield. 'We can do that, right? Four Glocks, four silencers?'

Newfield nodded. 'Sure.'

'How much ammo do you need?' Smith asked White.

'Just a full magazine in each. What does a Glock hold?'

'Depends on the model. Seventeen or eighteen, as a rule.'

'That'll be fine.'

Smith stared at White again for several seconds, before nodding slowly. 'Okay,' he said. 'Deal. The Hatchett here will take you for a ride and give you what you want. I'd like one more thing from you, though.'

'What would that be?'

'If the NCA does start looking at me again, through their own volition, I'd appreciate a call, just to let me know.'

'I can't do that Perry. That would be . . .' He shrugged, unable to find the words to finish sentence.

'What, illegal? That ship has already sailed, doing what you've done. Blackmailing me and wanting me to give you guns. Once you've taken those guns, the power reverts back to me.'

'So you want to blackmail me, is that it?'

'It's a two-way street, bro.'

This time it was White who stared at Perry without speaking, as he ran through his options. He needed the guns, and even if he backed out now, he'd already crossed a line. What Perry was asking was relatively small in the grand scheme of things, especially considering what White was planning to do. 'Okay, Perry,' he said. 'We have a deal.'

31

'So what are you planning to do with these guns?' asked Newfield, as he accelerated to pass a bus. They were sitting in a black Porsche SUV, heading south.

'Best you don't know,' said White.

'You ever shot someone before?'

'Why do you ask?'

'Because you don't look like you've ever pointed a gun at someone and pulled the trigger.'

'How hard can it be?'

'Oh, bro, it's hard.'

'You've done it?'

'I'm not saying that I have or I haven't, I'm just saying it ain't easy. It's a big thing.'

'I guess.'

'If you're not a cop, what are you? You don't talk like a cop but you know what time it is, that's clear.'

'I'm just a guy that needs some guns, Eddie, can't we just leave it at that?'

'But you've seen my file, haven't you? You knew who I was. You know about my boy.'

'You're known to the police, you know that. You've been in prison three times already.'

'I had a rough childhood. Never knew my dad, mum worked two jobs to keep the family together. Two brothers and me. They're both inside now. I'm guessing you had a different start to your life.'

'You'd be right.'

'Happy families?'

'When I was a kid, sure.'

'And now?'

White swallowed, His mouth had gone suddenly dry. He thought of Rachel and Hannah and Ella and what Hamas had taken from him. Happy families were a thing of the past. 'Now, not so much.'

'Sorry about that,' said Newfield.

'You get the hand you're dealt,' said White. 'Your life is how you play that hand.'

'Ain't that the truth.' Newfield slowed the SUV, then pulled in next to a park. 'See that bench?'

'Sure.'

'Go and wait for me there.'

'Where are you going?'

'Where do you think I'm going? I'm going to get the guns. But what I'm not going to do is to take you to where we keep them. For obvious reasons.'

'I understand.' He put his hand on the door handle. 'How long will you be.'

'It'll take as long as it takes,' said Newfield. 'And the longer you keep talking, the longer it'll take.'

'Got you,' said White. He climbed out and slammed the door. Newfield drove away and White walked across the grass to the bench. He sat down and sighed. Taking a life was a big thing, or at least it was to decent human beings. The animals who had killed his daughters and the hundreds of other youngsters and children hadn't had any such reservations. They had killed with abandon, with glee, many of the fighters were clearly enjoying themselves as they raped and murdered. Taking life was going to be a big thing for White and he wasn't sure how he would deal with the repercussions. But he had every intention of going ahead. He owed it to Rachel and Hannah and Ella to take the lives of the men who had ordered the

216

October Seven attacks. It would be revenge pure and simple. This was one time when White was not prepared to live and let live. Would it be difficult to pull the trigger on an unarmed man? Probably. But when the time came, he was sure that he would be able to do it.

He stretched out his legs and looked up at the sky, clear blue and cloudless. Birds were singing and in the distance, children were laughing. It was just a normal day in London, with people getting on with their lives, raising their families, travelling to and from work, socialising with friends. Regular, normal lives, lives that didn't involve blackmailing drug dealers to hand over illegal weapons. White wasn't happy with the turn his life had taken, but he didn't see that he had a choice. What was the alternative — to pretend that it had never happened, that Hamas terrorists hadn't killed his wife and daughters, that all was well with the world? He gritted his teeth. All was not well with the world. Not with his world, anyway. His life had changed for ever, and there was no going back.

The minutes ticked by. White fought the urge to keep checking his watch. Half an hour crawled by and White began to wonder if Newfield had dumped him. That wouldn't make any sense, of course, because the threat White had made was a real one. It was within his power to get an investigation launched into Perry Smith's activities, and all Smith needed to do was to hand over a few guns. Would White go ahead with his threat if Smith didn't do as he wanted? Probably not. But it would mean he would have to find another source of guns, and that would take time.

White looked to his left and was surprised to see Newfield walking towards him, carrying a black holdall. He stood up but Newfield gestured with his chin for him to sit. White sat back down. Newfield placed the holdall on the seat next to White. 'Wait until I'm well away before you open it, and if I were you I'd wait until I was inside and safe from prying eyes. But it's your call.' He turned to walk back along the path.

'Wait a minute, are you just going to leave me here?' said White.

'You think I want to drive you around with a bag full of firearms?' said Newfield. 'They're your responsibility now, call a cab or get the Tube, or walk for all I care. You've got what you wanted, Perry said I was to give you the gear and that was the end of it. So we're done.'

'I hear you,' said White.

'If I was you, I'd cab it,' said Newfield. 'Guns and public transport aren't a great mix.'

'I'll Uber it,' said White, taking out his phone.

White used the Uber App to arrange a lift as Newfield walked away.

32

Shepherd pushed the door open with his shoulder and carried three mugs of coffee into the room. He placed one in front of Ajazi, who was still listening through his headphones. The Albanian gave Shepherd a thumbs up. Jimmy Sharpe was sitting with his feet up on the neighbouring desk, reading through one of Ajazi's transcripts.

They had placed the whiteboard with the photographs of Fisnik Haziri and the gangsters that Plauku had identified against the far wall. Next to it was another whiteboard on which they had stuck photographs of the names that Marku had been able to provide, including all the men who had been on the speedboat. Ajazi's bosses had emailed over photographs and biographies of all the men that Marku had identified, along with the criminal records. Most of the Albanians had been in the United Kingdom before and several had fled charges of assault, GBH and attempted murder in the past.

Shepherd took his coffee over to the whiteboards. Almost all of the men that Marku had identified could be arrested on the spot and faced long terms behind bars. The problem was that there was still no direct link between the men who had come in on the speedboat, and Fisnik Haziri. The gang boss had done an excellent job of insulating himself from the day to day criminal activities of the gang. In fact they still didn't know where he was, it had been months since he had been seen, and then it was only fleetingly before he

219

had disappeared again.

Sharpe joined Shepherd and nodded at the photograph of Haziri. 'Slippery bugger, isn't he?'

Shepherd nodded. 'The Scarlet bloody Pimpernel. They seek him here, they seek him there . . .'

'They're a whole different breed, the Albanians,' said Sharpe. 'They can be vicious bastards if they have to, but most of the time they use economics to achieve their objectives.'

'How so?' asked Shepherd. He sipped his coffee.

'They always buy from the source, which means they pay bottom dollar. So they buy coke from the Colombian cartels, heroin from the Taliban and cannabis from the Turks. Then they handle the shipping themselves, so that keeps their costs down. There are Albanians right across Europe, in every country. You know the story. When Yugoslavia fell apart and the various countries started kicking the shit of each other, Europe was awash with refugees. Bosnians, Croats, Kosovans, they were given sanctuary right across Europe, including in the UK, and passports were handed out like candy. The Albanians saw an opportunity and literally thousands of them flooded across Europe claiming to be Kosovans. Most of them were taken at face value, especially since so many Kosovans lived in Albania anyway. They reckon that today there are more than fifty thousand Albanians in the UK and thirty thousand Kosovans. But nobody knows for sure.' He shook his head in disgust. 'Border Force has a lot to answer for. Anyway, there are now hundreds of thousand of Albanians living across the EU and while they're not all gangsters a lot of them are, and they cooperate. So you'll have an Albanian working in an Italian port and an Albanian truck driver who takes delivery of a consignment there and drives it to France and an Albanian customs officer in France clears the truck onto a ferry and an Albanian working at Southampton docks lets it through. All working together. That means at the end of the day they can get their drugs into the UK for half the cost of everybody else. And because they're only dealing with their own, it's hard to crack their organisation so they rarely lose a consignment.'

Shepherd nodded. 'That's why Tuk is such a God-send. He's our only hope of bringing down Haziri.'

'And where they're really clever is that they're not greedy. They get their gear into the UK at half price and they pass that saving on to the consumer. They're the Aldi and Lidl of the drugs business. And the Sainsburys and Tescos just can't compete on price. So bit by bit they lose market share to the Albanians. The Albanians don't fight over turf, they just wait for the word to spread that their gear is cheaper and the customers come to them. Now the local dealers aren't happy but they have a choice — walk away or fight for their market share. And as they can't cut their prices they have to literally fight, and that's when the Albanians show their true colours. They're armed and there's a lot of them, and a fair number of them fought in the Balkans so they're not scared of a firefight or two. But the locals know that so generally they just walk away.'

'Sounds like you admire them, Razor.'

Sharpe laughed. 'Not admire, definitely not admire. I've seen what drugs have done to Glasgow, to the whole of Scotland in fact, so drug dealers are scum and that's the end of it. But the Albanians are professional about it, you have to give them that. They're only violent when they're attacked, and you can't say that about the West Indians, the Turks, the Jamaicans, the Hungarians. They go out of their way to cause trouble and don't care if civilians get caught in the crossfire.' He grinned. 'And when Albanians take out their opposition, they're not stupid enough to write a rap song about it.'

'Maybe not, but I've seen my fair share of Albanian gangsters posing with cash and guns on Facebook and Instagram.'

'Just the kids,' said Sharpe. 'The older ones keep a much lower profile.' He gestured at the photograph of Hazri. 'You'll never see the Meatball on social media.'

33

White let himself into his house and carried the bag through to the kitchen. He placed the holdall on the table, then lowered the blinds and switched on the lights. He sat down and unzipped the holdall. There were a number of bubble-wrapped packages inside and he took them from the bag and laid them on the table. Four were clearly the silencers, cylinders about ten inches long. He picked up one of the larger packages and ripped away the bubble wrap. Underneath was an oiled cloth. He peeled away the cloth to reveal the gun. It was a Glock, finished in matte black. It looked new, there were no scratches or blemishes. White had never fired a gun in his life, and knew next to nothing about how to use one. He had read somewhere that Glocks didn't have safeties, and that seemed to be the case, there was no switch to be flicked to get the gun ready to fire. There was a small oblong button set into the butt behind the trigger guard and when he pressed it, the magazine ejected out of the bottom and clattered onto the table. White put down the gun and picked up the magazine. It was fully loaded. He took out the bullets one by one and lined them up on the table. There were fifteen.

White realised he needed a crash course in gun handling so he put down the magazine and spent ten minutes watching YouTube videos on his phone. It seemed simple enough. The Glock didn't need a manual safety switch because it had a special three-part trigger which could not be pulled accidentally

223

and which wouldn't fire if the weapon was dropped. Loading was just a matter of slotting in the magazine and pulling back the slide to push the first bullet into the chamber. All you had to do then was point the gun at the target and pull the trigger. White watched several videos of Glocks being fired and realised that he was going to have to get some practice. He needed to know how it felt when the gun went off, and how it sounded. He had the silencers but he wasn't sure how good a job they would do in cutting down the noise so he couldn't risk firing one in the house or the garden.

He unwrapped the three other guns. Two had the Glock logo on the barrel, along with the number 19 and the word AUSTRIA. Next to AUSTRIA was 9x19. White frowned at the numbers then realised that it meant the type of ammunition the gun used. The other two guns were slightly bigger and had seventeen bullets in their magazines.

Finally he unwrapped the four silencers. They were black, almost two inches in diameter with a screw thread at one end to attach them to the barrels. White screwed one into the barrel of one of the Glock 19s. It made the gun a lot heavier and as he aimed at the clock on the wall his hand began to tremble. He used his left hand to support his right and that made the gun steadier. He slipped his finger onto the trigger. 'Bang, bang,' he whispered.

34

Shepherd got to Thames House at six o'clock in the morning but Ajazi was already at his table with his headphones on. He was wearing the same shirt he'd had on the previous day and he clearly hadn't shaved. 'Didn't you go home last night?' asked Shepherd as he sat down at the adjoining table.

'I'd rather be here than at the safe house listening to your friend whinge and moan. Does he always complain?'

'Jimmy? Yes, about everything.'

'He hates his job, he hates his country, he hates the world. It's bad enough when he's here in the office, I can't face listening to him all night too.'

'That's just his way,' said Shepherd. 'But he's a good cop and his heart is in the right place. How's Tuk?'

'He's been quiet all night,' said Ajazi. 'But there's three of them in the room so he can't talk to us. They were talking until about midnight. They're asleep now.'

'About what?'

'About home, mainly. Gossip. But they keep talking about Luton. Sounds like all three might be going there. Where do we stand if one of them pulls the trigger and Tuk is there? Is he guilty of something then?'

Shepherd shrugged. 'Maybe. It's a grey area. The CPS might see it as conspiracy to murder. It depends.'

'On what?'

'On a lot of things. If he drove the car, for instance.

225

Or was involved in the planning or execution. The thing is, Petrit, we don't want him anywhere near a killing. If it looks as if the murder is going ahead, he needs to tell us and we need to pull him out.'

'This PACE thing makes life difficult,' said Ajazi.

Shepherd grinned. 'You're not the first person in law enforcement to say that,' he said.

35

White thought long and hard about where he should go to fire the guns. He needed to be far enough away from people that they wouldn't hear the shots, because if they did and they called the police, then it would all be over before he had even started. He needed to be somewhere alone, but London was a crowded city, pretty much bursting at the seams. He considered Hyde Park and Regent's Park but dismissed the idea because there were always joggers and dog walkers around. In a perfect world he'd use an abandoned quarry but he doubted there was such a thing in the Greater London area. Perry had joked about burying him in the New Forest but that was a hundred miles away. He was going be using a silencer but he had no idea how loud it would be. He had studied several YouTube videos on the subject and they all stressed that it wasn't like the movies, where assassins fired silenced weapons with just a 'phhht-phhhht' sound.

Eventually he decided on Richmond Park, the 2,500 acre Royal Park he had visited many times with his family, walking with them up King Henry's Mound to see St Paul's Cathedral in the distance and where they had hired bicycles to cycle around the park on the scenic seven-mile long Tamsin Route. The park was policed by the Royal Parks Operational Command Unit of the Metropolitan Force. It sounded impressive but what few officers were in the unit were mostly concerned with handing out fines for littering and dog fouling. The park never closed and White

227

figured that if he got there at dawn there'd be few dog walkers and joggers around.

He arrived at Richmond just after six-thirty in the morning and left his car a short walk away from the Petersham Gate, to the west of the park. The pedestrian gates were open for twenty four hours a day but the vehicle gates were closed at dusk and didn't open until seven thirty. He was wearing a blue Adidas tracksuit and Reebok trainers and carrying a black backpack. He slung the backpack over his shoulders as he walked through the gate, then jogged on to the Tamsin Route, checking to see who else was around. It was too early for most dog walkers and he only saw two joggers, off in the distance. He left the track and headed over to Sidmouth Wood, planted almost two hundred years earlier by the then deputy ranger Viscount Sidmouth. The wood was mainly oak but there were also sycamore, larch, beech and chestnut.

The sun had still to appear over the horizon as he reached the edge of the wood. Dawn was officially just before seven thirty but there was enough light to see by. He had a good look around and this time he saw no one, and he walked across the tree line into the darkness of the woods. To the south of the wood was Oak Lodge, a Georgian building maintained by the National Trust, but nobody lived there and it was only open on Sundays.

White made his way to the middle of the wood, walking softly and listening intently. He reached a small clearing and stopped. His night vision had kicked in and he was able to see fairly clearly. He took off the backpack and unzipped it. He had brought one of the large Glocks and its silencer, and two honeydew melons. He stuck one of the melons in a cleft between a branch and the trunk of a spreading oak and put the other on the grass. He screwed the silencer into the barrel of the gun and pulled the slider back. His heart was pounding and he took several deep breaths to calm himself down. He stood with his feet shoulder width apart and used both hands to aim the gun, his left hand cupped under the right. His hands were shaking, partly from the weight of the gun and the silencer, but mainly because he was so nervous. He lowered the gun and forced himself to relax, breathing slowly and evenly. He smiled, if he was this nervous about shooting melons, how was he going to feel when he was aiming at a living, breathing human being?

He raised the gun again and aimed at the melon in the tree. He took a breath, let half of it out, and squeezed the trigger. All the videos he had watched had been clear on that, the trigger had to be slowly squeezed and not jerked. He increased the pressure, his heart pounding again. Nothing happened and he pulled the trigger harder. There was a loud popping sound, as if a balloon had burst, and the gun jerked in his hand. The empty cartridge tumbled through the air to his right. The melon was untouched and he had no idea where the bullet had gone. He lowered the gun. He doubted that the sound would have carried far, not with so many trees around. But even out in the open, it wouldn't have sounded like a gun, at least not how guns sounded on TV. If he had heard the noise from his neighbour's house, the thought that it might have been a gun wouldn't have occurred to him. That was the good news, but the bad news was that he had missed the target, and that could be fatal if the target was able to fight back.

He was about twenty feet away from the tree, how close did he plan to get to the men he was planning to kill? If he got into the same room as them, he would be a lot closer than twenty feet. He took a couple of steps forward, planted his feet apart and took aim again. This time he was expecting the recoil and the gun didn't jerk as much. There was the same loud pop and this time the bullet clipped the top of the melon. White smiled to himself. A definite improvement. Not that he was planning to go for a head shot. The YouTube videos had been clear on that, the best part of the body to aim for was the chest.

He squeezed the trigger again and the melon exploded, splattering its flesh over the oak tree.

White bent down and picked up the second melon. He stuck it on the tree and walked five paces, about fifteen feet. He took a breath to steady himself, aimed, and fired. The melon burst into a dozen pieces. White lowered the gun. His aim was obviously okay, and he now had a good idea of how much noise the gun made. He put his hand on the silencer to unscrew it and yelped as the hot metal singed his flesh. He grunted at his stupidity. Of course the silencer would be hot after he'd fired three bullets through it. He licked his fingers, then placed the gun on the ground to cool as he looked around for the spent casings. By the time he'd found them and slipped them into his pocket, the silencer had cooled enough for him to unscrew it. He put the gun and silencer into the backpack, zipped it closed and threw it over his shoulder. He stood and listened for a while, then walked back towards the entrance. The sun was just making an appearance as he left the park and headed towards his car.

36

There were four men and a woman in the sixth floor
suite of the Chelsea Harbour Hotel, gathered around
a table on which there were half a dozen surveillance
photographs and a map of the area. The leader of the
group was Gil Stern. He was a few days away from his
sixtieth birthday, but he had no plans to celebrate. His
head was shaved and his right cheek was a mass of scar
tissue from a grenade that had exploded just feet away
from him twenty years earlier. Every time he looked
at a mirror, he knew that he was lucky to be alive.
The group he headed was part of Kidon — Hebrew
for 'tip of the spear' — the department within Mossad that was tasked with assassination of Israel's
enemies. In recent years Kidon had been responsible for targeted killings in Kuala Lumpur, Syria and
the Lebanon but it had gone into overdrive following
the October Seven massacre. Stern's team was one
of five operating around the world all on the same
mission — to exact revenge on the men who had
planned and funded the October Seven attacks.

The single woman in the group was former IDF
soldier Dinah Klein. She was in her late twenties and
had the long legs and killer cheekbones of a catwalk
model. But her attributes were hidden under a black
robe and hajib, and the only makeup she had used
was a touch of eyeliner.

Standing next to her was Nathan Segal, with tanned
skin and black curly hair, his eyes shielded behind
impenetrable Oakley sunglasses. The remaining two

231

men were Micha Abramov and Ben Elon, surveillance experts who often posed as a gay couple, though both were married and the older of the two — Micha — was father to three girls.

'So are we all good?' asked Stern.

They all nodded. They had been over the operation so many times that he didn't expect there to be any questions. Stern looked at his watch. Evening prayers at the West London Islamic Cultural Centre Mosque were due to finish in twenty minutes. Mohammed Sharif walked to the mosque three times a day, and had done for the four days that the Mossad team had been watching him. He went for the early morning Fajr prayers, the mid-day Dhuhr prayers, and finally for the sunset Isha prayers. The walk took him half an hour, and he was accompanied by two bodyguards. Sharif was in his fifties and always wore a traditional Muslim robe and a knitted skull cap. His bodyguards were British Asians usually dressed in leather jackets and jeans. So far as Stern could tell, they weren't armed.

The bodyguards didn't sleep at Sharif's penthouse apartment, they arrived before dawn to walk with him to the mosque, stayed with him all day, and left after delivering him home in the evening.

The apartment was owned by Sharif but they had followed the money trail and had discovered that the five million pounds he had paid came from a shell company in Qatar, a company that was linked to an elderly Qatari prince who was a known supporter of half a dozen Palestinian terror groups including Jund Ansar Allah, Jaljalat and The Popular Resistance Committees.

The sixth member of the team was waiting outside

the mosque. His name was Adam Sharon and he would phone when he saw Sharif leaving.

Stern nodded at Abramov. 'Okay, you and Ben should leave now. Any problems, let me know.'

As Abramov and Elon picked up their backpacks and left, Stern went over to the coffee machine to make his fifth cup of the day.

37

Ajazi raised his hand in the air and clicked his fingers to get Shepherd and Sharpe's attention. 'I'm on the live feed and something's happening,' he said. He stabbed at a button on his keyboard and the audio feed was relayed through a speaker so that they could all hear it, though as the conversation was in Albanian Shepherd and Sharpe couldn't make any sense of it.

'They're in the back room of the car wash, where they wait between jobs,' said Ajazi. 'One of the Meatball's captains has just come in and told a guy called Bleda to go with him. Tuk has asked where they're taking Bleda and the captain — his name is Kristjan Troka, he's there on the board — has told him to mind his own business.'

'Is this a hit?' asked Shepherd.

'Troka just says it's a job and that Bleda is to bring all his stuff with him.'

Sharpe stood up and walked over to the whiteboard to study Bleda's's picture. 'He's a nasty piece of work,' he said, reading the bio underneath the photograph. 'He killed a guy in Norfolk three years ago but fled the country before the cops could arrest him.'

'Yeah, but it wasn't a shooting, was it?' said Shepherd. 'It was an argument outside a pub, Bleda hit the guy and when he went down he cracked his head open on the pavement. So the charge was going to be manslaughter, not murder. The guy's not a professional hitman, so far as we know.'

'Fair point,' said Sharpe.

'Tuk isn't involved in this, is he?' Shepherd asked Ajazi.

Ajazi shook his head. 'He's staying out of it now. What do you think, do we follow them?'

Shepherd looked over at Sharpe. 'What do you think, Razor?'

'We don't have surveillance in place so we'd have to bring in a team and it's hellish short notice. And if Tuk isn't there we won't have any inside track as to what's going on.'

'And if it's a hit?'

Sharpe went over to Ajazi. 'What do you think, Petrit? Is Bleda going to kill someone, to prove himself?'

'Troka just said there was a job for Bleda to do. That's all he said. But he said he was to bring his gear so maybe it's just work. They have plenty of cannabis farms that need looking after. Or they might even be moving him to another car wash. ' He shrugged. 'I don't know. No way of telling.'

'To be honest, I don't think we've got time to put together a surveillance team,' said Sharpe. 'Let's just keep our fingers crossed. And so long as Tuk isn't involved, it's not our problem.'

'I just hope our bosses take the same view,' said Shepherd. His brow furrowed. 'Maybe it's time to get a surveillance team on the car wash.'

'I did a walk through on Google Street View,' said Sharpe. 'There's no office buildings or empty houses where we could put watchers, and there are double yellow lines everywhere. Plus the Albanians are pros, there's a real danger that they'll spot any surveillance. I'd advise against it.'

'I hear you,' said Shepherd. 'Let's stay back for a while longer.'

38

Dinah Klein heard Gil Stern's voice in her left ear, calm and authoritative, a voice that inspired confidence. He was standing at the window of the hotel room from where he had a clear view of the entrance to Sharif's building and the main road that led to Chelsea Harbour. He spoke in Hebrew. Their radios used state of the art encryption but using Hebrew decreased the chances they would be overheard even more. 'Target is approaching the entrance to Chelsea Harbour,' said Stern. 'ETA at the building, three minutes. Ben, are you and Micha, are you in position?'

'Affirmative,' said Elon.

'Are you ready, Dinah?'

'As I'll ever be,' whispered Klein.

'You'll be fine,' said Stern in her ear.

Klein pulled the black niqab across her face. Now only her eyes were uncovered. She was standing at the side of the building with half a dozen large carrier bags at her feet. Chanel. Prada. Louis Vuitton. All the big names.

She saw Sharif in the distance, a mobile phone to his ear and a long chain of Muslim prayer beads hanging from his right hand, flanked by two bodyguards. Sharif was wearing a long grey thobe that almost brushed the ground as he walked, and a white knitted skull cap. There was scarring on the man's left ear, and a hairless patch on his temple above it with more scarring. His bodyguards were wearing almost identical brown leather jackets and tight blue jeans.

They didn't seem particularly alert as they walked with Sharif, and didn't even turn to look when a van drove by. From the look of it they were merely muscle, not properly trained bodyguards.

She timed her walk so that she got to the entrance just as one of the bodyguards had opened the main door for Sharif. The bodyguard still had the door open as Klein hurried up the steps. 'Please, would you be so kind as to keep the door open for me,' she said in Arabic. She was fluent in the language and was always told that she had a Palestinian accent.

The two bodyguards turned to look at her. The taller of the two who was holding the door, nodded. 'My pleasure,' he said, in English. He opened the door wider for her.

She thanked him in Arabic. Sharif had turned at the sound of her voice but he continued to walk to the lift lobby, his sandals scuffing on the marble floor. The bodyguard kept the door open until Sharif reached the lobby and pressed the button to call the lift, then he let go of it and it closed with a loud click behind her.

'Bodyguards now walking away,' said Stern in Klein's ear.

'Lobby is clear,' whispered Klein in Hebrew.

''Ben and Micha, prepare yourselves.'

'Affirmative,' said Elon.

There were two sets of lift doors in the lobby. The ones on the left hissed open. Sharif stepped inside. Klein walked quickly, her heels clicking on the marble floor. When she reached the lift she saw that Sharif was pressing the button to keep the doors open and she thanked him in Arabic. He nodded and stepped back.

She raised her right hand to press the button for her floor, but pretended that the bags were too heavy and she sighed in annoyance.

'Allow me, madam,' said Sharif in Arabic. He stepped forward again. 'What floor?'

'Sixteen, please,' she said. 'Thank you so much. You are a gentleman.'

Sharif pressed the button for the sixteenth floor. 'So you are one floor below me,' he said. 'Which side of the building are you on?'

'I overlook the marina,' she said, demurely averting her eyes. The lift rose smoothly upwards.

'So do I,' he said. 'I wonder if my apartment is directly above yours?'

'If it is, I never hear you,' she said. 'You are as quiet as a mouse.'

Sharif chuckled. 'I am not one for parties. So you live here with your husband?'

Klein shook here head. 'With my sisters. I have no husband.'

'And you are from Palestine?'

'My family lives in Jerusalem.' They passed the tenth floor. 'But my father is Palestinian.'

'Perhaps I know him,' said Sharif.

'Oh, you are from Palestine?'

'Very much so,' said Sharif.

'So you are here on business?'

'Vacation,' said Sharif. 'So your esteemed father, what is his name?'

The lift came to a halt. They had reached the sixteenth floor. There was a slight judder and the doors opened. Abramov and Elon were standing there. They were both wearing black N95 facemasks. Klein took a step forwards, towards them, then feigned confusion. 'I am so sorry,' she said in accented English. She took a step backwards and trod on Sharif's sandalled foot. He yelped and she turned around, brushing his legs with her carrier bags, apologising profusely. She moved so that she was between him and the CCTV camera up in the corner of the lift.

Abramov and Elon stepped into the lift. Klein was talking quickly in Arabic, trying to distract Sharif with her voice, flashing her eyes, cursing her stupidity. As Elon moved in front of Sharif, Klein stepped back, giving him room to manoeuvre. The lift doors closed.

Elon pulled a stun gun from his jacket pocket, pressed the prongs against Sharif's side and pressed the trigger. There was a loud crackle and the man stiffened. Abramov moved in front of Sharif but was careful not to touch him as the electricity coursed through the man's body. The lift rose smoothly to the top floor.

After three seconds, Elon took the stun gun away. Abramov grabbed Sharif around the waist to hold him upright. Elon tucked the stun gun into his jacket pocket and then grabbed Sharif's right arm. As the lift stopped and the doors opened, the two men took an arm each and dragged him out of the lift. Klein followed. They took him along the corridor to his front door. Klein put down her bags and quickly patted down Sharif's robe, found his keys and opened the door. Elon and Abramov took him inside. Klein followed and closed the door.

They were in a hallway that led to a massive double height room with floor to ceiling windows that looked out over the marina and south London beyond. 'Nice view,' said Elon.

'Five million pounds this cost,' said Abramov.

239

'Worth every penny.'

They placed the still unconscious Sharif on the floor, face up. His eyes were closed but his chest was moving. Elon stabbed the stun gun against his chest and gave the man another two second burst.

Klein took off her niqab. She hated having to breathe through the black cloth, hated the confinement. Forcing a woman to cover her face, and her body, was the worst sort of misogynistic control. Most Muslim women had no choice, she knew that. Refusal would result in a beating, or worse.

She knelt down and took a large Louis Vuitton box from one of the carrier bags. She placed it on the floor and opened it. Inside was a bottle of malt whisky, a plastic funnel, and a pair of latex gloves. She put on the gloves and pulled the cork out of the bottle.

Abramov squeezed Sharif's cheeks to open his mouth, and Klein inserted the funnel and slowly poured whisky into it. Sharif's chest heaved but he stayed unconscious as the whisky went down his throat. Elon went over to the sliding window that led on to the penthouse's terrace and opened it. He was also wearing latex gloves now. He went into the kitchen and returned with a large crystal tumbler. He pressed the glass against Sharif's fingers then held it out while Klein poured whisky into it. Elon took the filled tumbler out onto the balcony and placed it on a table.

Klein didn't stop until she had poured almost half the bottle down Sharif's throat, then she took the bottle, pressed Sharif's hand against before taking it out onto the terrace and putting it on the table next to the tumbler.

Sharif was starting to come around, shaking his

head and spluttering.

'We need to move quickly,' said Abramov.

Elon hurried over and the two men dragged the Palestinian to his feet. His eyelids were fluttering now, and he was coughing.

They dragged him through the window and onto the terrace. As they took him over to the edge of the terrace, he began to struggle.

'No, no, no,' he repeated, his words slurring into each other.

'Hush,' said Elon. 'It'll soon be over.'

'Please, no, don't do this,' murmured Sharif.

There was a waist-high railing running around the terrace, on the top of toughened glass panels.

Elon nodded at Abramov and together they hauled the Palestinian on to the railing and then pushed him over. He fell without a sound and a few seconds later they heard the dull wet thud of the body hitting the ground.

They went back into the main room. Klein had already packed the funnel in the box, and put the box back in the carrier bag. She replaced her niqab and stood up, checking her reflection in a mirrored wall.

'We're done here,' said Elon over the radio.

'All clear outside,' said Stern.

Klein took the carrier bags over to the front door. Elon opened it and Klein and Abramov headed to the lift lobby. Elon used a handkerchief to clean the door handles, inside and out, then shut the door and joined Klein and Abramov at the lobby. The lift door opened and they walked in. Elon pressed the button for the ground floor, then he and Klein removed their latex gloves.

'Still all clear outside,' said Stern over the radio. 'A

passerby has seen the body and is on the phone.'

The lift arrived at the ground floor. As soon as the door opened they headed to the entrance.

'On our way out now,' said Elon.

'No police outside, but there are now two passersby with the body. Turn left as you exit, you'll be fine.'

They left the building and walked towards the car. 'You know it's a pity we weren't allowed to shoot him,' said Elon as he pulled open the front passenger door.

'Because then you could say 'I shot the Sharif', is that why?' said Abramov.

'You read my mind,' said Elon with a grin.

Klein shook her head in disgust. 'All this testosterone is making me dizzy,' she said as she got into the back of the car.

'Well done everyone,' said Stern over the radio. 'Good job.'

39

Ibrahim Fayyad's house was in a small village in Hampstead, a few dozen stone buildings scattered around a church, a pub and a village shop that doubled as a post office. White drove by early in the morning, in a ten-year old Ford Fiesta. He had bought the car from a dealer in Croydon for cash, and had left it registered in the previous owner's name. He had insured it online as the police's Automatic Number Plate Recognition System meant that uninsured vehicles were easily spotted and the last thing he needed was to be pulled over while he was carrying a silenced gun and a housebreaking kit.

The house was detached, set in an acre of land, a short walk from the pub. White doubted that Fayyad would use the pub, or the church, and he found the village a strange place for a Hamas official to spend his time. He doubted that Fayyad would have much in common with his neighbours. He spent time on Google Maps, studying the area and doing several virtual walk-bys, getting a feel for the area, but it was only when he drove through the village that he realised the attraction. The house itself wasn't overlooked, and a thick hedge shielded it from prying eyes. There was a large metal gate guarding a short driveway. He could see the upper floors and the roof from the road but that was all. White couldn't see any CCTV cameras.

While the house was in an isolated village, it was less than a forty-five minute drive to Heathrow, and there were sixty trains a day running from nearby Farnham to London.

White had run a Land Registry search on the property and discovered it was owned by a company in Qatar. A check on the MI5 computer showed that the company was a Hamas front, used to transfer large sums of money to various shell companies in the United Kingdom, in the form of dividends.

The Qatar company had purchased the house two years earlier and for a while it had been listed with a local estate agent. The details were still up on the Rightmove website and he was able to examine twenty photographs of the house and the garden.

There was no pavement along the road, so doing a real walk-by was out of the question. He drove slowly by a second time, using his mobile phone to record what he was seeing.

He was hungry and the obvious place to eat would have been the village pub, but he knew that strangers would be remembered, especially in view of what he planned to do. Instead he drove to nearby Farnham and had shepherd's pie and a pot of tea in a cafe off the main road, away from any CCTV cameras. While he waited for his food he replayed the video on the phone. He could just about make out a single car in the driveway, possibly a Lexus. According to the MI5 database, Fayyad's wife and sixteen-year-old daughter were also staying at the house. Both had leave to remain in the country and the girl attended a school in Farnham. It made no sense to White that a known Hamas member and his family were allowed to live in the UK, but then it often seemed that the Home Office and Border Force didn't have the best interests of the country at heart.

In the late afternoon he drove by the house again. There was still only the Lexus in the driveway and no sign of any security. Fayyad was probably assuming that maintaining a low profile was the safest option — CCTV and alarm systems and a security detail would only attract attention in a small village.

White had already decided that the best way in was to cut through the hedge at the rear boundary of the property. The garden bordered farmland which wasn't overlooked and he could park the Fiesta a short walk away on a track that seemed only to be used by farm vehicles. Most farmers downed tools at dusk so he was sure the car wouldn't be seen.

The estate agent photographs showed a sliding glass door that opened from the sitting room onto a terrace. White's housebreaking skills were rudimentary but he knew that most people didn't lock that type of door, but even if it was locked it was generally a simple matter to pry it open with a screwdriver. His fallback position would be to break a glass panel in the kitchen door, and if that failed he had seen an open window at the side of the house that could be reached by climbing a cast iron drain pipe. He had everything he needed in a black backpack, including duct tape, a hammer, a large screwdriver, wire cutters and a set of night vision goggles he had bought online prior to abandoning his house. And the most important items — a Glock and its bulbous silencer.

White stayed in Farnham until the sun went down, then he drove back to the village and parked his Fiesta on the track behind the house. He sat there for almost an hour until it was completely dark, then he climbed out of the car and took the backpack from the boot. He was wearing dark clothing — black jeans and a black hoodie over a black pullover — and black leather gloves. He pulled on the night vision goggles and switched them on. There was a buzzing sound and then he could see everything in a greenish hue.

He walked slowly across the field towards the hedge that surrounded the house. There was only a sliver of moon overhead and clouds obscured most of the stars. He reached the hedge and crouched down. He used the wire cutters to make a hole in the hedge close to the ground. He pushed his backpack through, then crawled after it. There was a gazebo to his right and he headed for it on all fours, dragging the backpack with him.

He sat and watched the house as the minutes ticked by. From his vantage point he could see the terrace, the sliding window, and the sitting room beyond. Fayyad was sitting on a leather sofa, reading a book. He looked exactly as he did in the MI5 photographs White had seen, in his sixties with a greying bushy beard and thick eyebrows and thick lensed glasses perched on his nose. He was wearing Western clothes, a tweed jacket over a plaid shirt. From time to time a woman appeared, in her fifties, wearing a long dress and a headscarf. She placed a mug on a table next to him, which he sipped from as he read his book. At just after ten o'clock Fayyad put down his book, stood up and stretched. The lights in the room went off and a light went on in the next room. The Rightmove listing had floor plans of the house which White had memorised. Fayyad was in the study now. The lights went off upstairs. Presumably the wife and daughter had gone to bed.

White emerged from behind the gazebo and went over to the hedge, keeping parallel to it as he headed towards the house. He went up the steps to the terrace and stood there for several minutes, listening to the sound of his own breathing. He reached for the handle of the sliding door and pushed. It opened with a slight scraping sound. He stopped, listened for a few seconds, and pushed again. He stopped when there was enough room for him to slip through. He stepped inside and took off the night vision goggles. He put them into the backpack and took out the gun and silencer.

He decided to leave the sliding open in case he needed to beat a hasty retreat. He padded over the carpet and put his ear to the door. He heard nothing so eased it open. The hall light was on. To his left was the front door and he caught sight of his reflection in a large gilt mirror on the wall. There were several coats hanging from a rack to the right of the mirror.

Ahead of him were the stairs, leading up to the bedrooms. He headed right and stopped at the study door. He put his ear against the wood. He could hear a voice, a man talking, and he frowned. Was Fayyad with somebody? He listened intently for several seconds and realised it was Fayyad talking in Arabic, probably on the phone. He put his left hand on the door knob but kept his ear pressed against the wood. If Fayyad had gone into the study to make the call, he might well leave the moment he finished. But White couldn't go in until the call was over because whoever Fayyad was talking to might raise the alarm.

Fayyad went quiet. White didn't know if he was using his mobile or a landline. If the latter, then maybe he would hear the click of the receiver being replaced. The silence stretched out. White's hand tensed on the door knob, but then Fayyad spoke again. He was still speaking Arabic. Then White heard him say 'ma'a salama', with peace, a common way of ending a conversation. White turned the knob and pushed the door open. Fayyad was standing by an ornate Louis XIV desk, a mobile phone in his hand. His jaw dropped when he saw White. White waved the gun at him as he closed the door behind him. 'Put the phone on the desk!' he hissed.

Fayyad opened his mouth to protest but White jabbed the gun at his face. 'Do it!'

'Yes, yes, I will,' said Fayyad. He hurriedly put the phone on the desk and then raised his hands in the air. 'If you want money, I have money. Cash. A lot of cash. And my wife has jewellery upstairs. Tell me what you want and you can have it.'

'I want you to stop talking, that's what I want.'

'There is no need for violence, my friend,' said Fayyad.

White sneered at him. 'That's ironic, coming from you,' he said. 'When has Hamas not embraced violence?'

Fayyad's eyes narrowed. 'You're a Jew.'

It was an accusation rather than a question, and White snarled at him. 'No, I'm THE Jew. The Jew who is going to kill you. Now close the curtains. And do it slowly. If I even think you are going for a weapon, I will shoot you.'

'I have no weapons, my friend,' said Fayyad. 'I am unarmed. You are the one with the gun.'

'Close the curtains,' hissed White.

'I will,' said Fayyad. 'You're the boss. You're in charge here.' He walked over to the window and slowly pulled the curtains shut.

'Now move away from the window.'

'Why? Why do I need to move away from the window?' He frowned. 'You are worried that if you shoot me here, the bullet might break the window.'

'Just do as you are told.'

Fayyad put his hands in the air and stepped away from the window. 'There is no need for this, my friend,' he said.

'There is every need. And you are not my friend.'

'And will you be proud of yourself? Shooting an unarmed man. That's the coward's way.'

'It is, isn't it? Only cowards kill the defenceless, don't they?'

'That is what you are, a coward. All Jews are cowards. It's in your DNA.'

White could feel his heart pounding but he kept his voice calm and controlled. 'You sent armed fighters to kill civilians on October Seven. They fired automatic weapons at women and children. So you tell me who the cowards are.'

'We are fighting for our survival. Our children are dying in Gaza. Every day children are dying.'

White shook his head vehemently. 'The people you killed weren't involved in any of that. They were just there to listen to music, to have fun. And you massacred them.'

'I was here when it happened. I can prove that.'

'You flew out of Egypt the day before the attacks. And you talk about cowardice? You're the coward. You couldn't even do your own dirty work. At least I'm prepared to pull the trigger myself.'

'So you are Mossad, and this is your revenge?' Fayyad laughed harshly. 'Killing me will achieve nothing. We will still wipe your race from the face of the earth.' He spat at White's feet. 'You are scum.

Jewish scum.'

'I am not Mossad. I am just a Jew whose family you killed. You call me scum, but that's what you are. You ordered the massacre of hundreds of innocents and you fled here to hide like the coward you are.'

'I am not hiding,' said Fayyad. 'I came to be with my family.'

'And you are lucky to be able to do that,' said White. 'I can never be with my family again. You took them away from me.'

The door opened. 'Baba?' It was the daughter. Long black hair, almond eyes, olive skin, wearing a long white nightdress. She gasped when she saw White. He moved quickly, grabbing her by the arm and pulling her into the room, then kicking the door shut. She ran across the room to her father and hugged him. He put his arms around her and stared at White. 'She is a child. She does not have to see this.'

'How many children did your men kill?'

'You don't understand.'

'Then explain.'

Fayyad continued to stare at him. 'Your people have enslaved the Palestinians. You treat us like animals and keep us caged in Gaza and the West Bank. No matter what we do, no matter how we plead or beg, you show us no mercy. If we do not fight back, Palestinians will be no more.'

'And you fight back by killing women and children.' White's eyes hardened. 'I was there. I saw what they did. I saw the pleasure they took from raping and killing. They were worse than animals.'

'It was a necessary evil,' said Fayyad quietly.

White waved his gun at the girl. 'Does she know who you are?'

'She's my daughter, course she knows.'

'But does she know what you did? Does she know that you ordered the massacre of women and children?'

The girl looked up at Fayyad and spoke to him in Arabic. He replied and stroked her hair, obviously trying to console her. 'You are scaring her,' said Fayyad.

'Do you know how scared my daughters were before they died?' asked White. 'Do you have any idea the terror you put them through? Do you even care?'

'My daughter has nothing to do with this,' whispered Fayyad. 'Whatever it is you are planning to do, she doesn't have to see it.'

The girl spoke to him again in Arabic and Fayyad replied, still stroking her hair. The girl turned to glare at White. 'You filthy fucking Jew!' she shouted. 'Leave my father alone!'

White pulled the trigger without thinking. There was no hesitation, no thought, he just wanted to shut her up. The round smacked into her chest and she slumped to the ground, a red rose spreading across her nightdress. Fayyad wailed and knelt down next to her. Her lips were moving soundlessly and there was panic in her eyes. White took a step back and looked down at her dispassionately. He realised that he felt absolutely nothing. No guilt, no regret, no sympathy. Nothing.

Fayyad was holding her and whispering to her in Arabic as her blood soaked into the carpet. She shivered as pink saliva bubbled between her lips, then her eyes went blank and she went still. Fayyad bent down and kissed her on the cheek, then got to his feet unsteadily. His hands were wet with her blood and he stared at them for several seconds before looking at

White. 'How could you do that?' he whispered. 'How could you kill a child?'

White shrugged. 'I pulled the trigger. The same as your fighters pulled their triggers on October Seven.'

'You killed an innocent child. You will burn in Hell.'

White smiled thinly. 'You forget, Jews do not believe in Heaven or Hell. You might well believe that 72 sloe-eyed virgins are waiting to cater for all your needs when you shuffle off this mortal coil, but I know that no such place exists. All I have is the here and now and killing your daughter is part of the price you have to pay for what you did.'

Fayyad's eyes burned with hatred. 'You can live with yourself? I don't think so.'

'What about you? Your attacks killed almost one and a half thousand people, mainly women and children. Your fighters raped and killed, they beheaded children and babies, and they did it with a smile. How can you live with yourself?' He scowled at Fayyad and aimed the gun at the man's face. 'Not that that's going to be a problem for you.'

'Killing me won't change anything,' said Fayyad quietly.

'It'll make me feel better,' said White. 'It won't bring me any closure but when I think of my wife and daughters at least I'll know that I avenged their deaths. That I meted out punishment where punishment was due.' He sneered at the man. 'If it makes you feel any better, I will grieve for my wife and daughters for the rest of my life. I'm always going to feel the anguish of knowing that they were taken from me, that I'll never see or hear or hug them again. But you, you'll only be grieving for a few more seconds before you join your 72 virgins, so you should be grateful for that.'

Fayyad opened his mouth to speak but White pulled the trigger before he could say anything. There was a loud pop and Fayyad's face imploded. The back of his skull erupted in a shower of blood, bone fragments and brain tissue that splattered across the desk. The fumes immediately stung White's eyes. He pulled the trigger a second time and the round smacked into Fayyad's chest as he fell back. He hit the floor with a dull thud. His right arm flopped out to the side and his hand fell onto his daughter's thigh as if he was reaching out to her in death.

White bent down and placed the gun on the floor, then wiped his eyes with the back of his gloves. The tears were from the fumes and not an emotional reaction, but he hated the sign of weakness. He looked around the room, then went to the doorway and listened, turning his head from side to side. He couldn't hear any sound from upstairs. Had his wife slept through the shots? Or was she already on the phone to the police? Not that it mattered, he would be long gone by the time they arrived.

He took a white surgical mask from his pocket and put it on, then pulled up his hood. He walked down the hallway to the kitchen, and out through the door to the garden. He stood for a few seconds but all he heard was the howling of a dog in the distance. He jogged over to the hedge on the left and kept close to it as he ran to the rear of the garden. He ducked behind the gazebo, crawled through the hole he'd made earlier, and walked across the field to where he'd parked his car. His heart was still pounding fit to burst as he climbed into the driver's seat and started the engine. Schwartz was right, killing was a big thing, and probably best left to professionals. But he was glad that he had killed Fayyad, and he felt no remorse or guilt for shooting the man's daughter. An eye for an eye, a child for a child. Fayyad hadn't given a second thought to ordering the deaths of hundreds of civilians, and he had deserved to die. If monsters like Fayyad truly understood that their evil actions had consequences, maybe they would moderate their actions and step back from the abyss. Perhaps in the last few seconds of his life Fayyad had learned that lesson, but it had been too late.

White's heart rate began to slow as he drove away from the house. He was breathing slowly and evenly. He thought back to the moment when he'd pulled the trigger the first time and killed the girl. He frowned as he realised that he still felt nothing. Absolutely nothing.

40

Dan Shepherd was reading through the latest transcript of the conversation's that Tuk's phone had picked up earlier that day. It wasn't always clear who was talking. Ajazi could recognise when it was Tuk's voice, but often he had to take a guess at who was talking. Ajazi would write the speaker's name with a (P) for possible after it if he wasn't sure. Ajazi was sitting with his headphones on listening to the live feed and making notes, while Sharpe had gone to the canteen for lunch. Most of the chat consisted of the Albanians moaning about their car-washing duties. For a while they discussed where Bleda had gone, but it was all supposition, no one knew for sure. One guy said he had been sent to work on an indoor cannabis farm, another said he was breaking in trafficked girls before they were set to work in brothels, another said that he was now one of the Meatball's personal bodyguards. The rumour mill was in full swing. Tuk would ask if any of the men knew for sure, but they all had to admit that they didn't.

Shepherd's mobile rang. He looked at the screen. It was Giles Pritchard's secretary. 'Yes, Amy.'

'Mr Pritchard would like to see you at the Tamesis Dock.'

'No problem, Amy. What time?'

'As soon as you can, Dan. He's there now.'

'I'll get right over,' said Shepherd, and he ended the call. Tamesis Dock was a pub that had been converted from a 1930s Dutch barge. It was moored

255

between Lambeth and Vauxhall Bridge, sometimes floating on the Thames and sometimes resting on the river bed. It was a buzzing night-time live jazz venue and packed with brunch-eating hipsters at the week-end, but Shepherd knew that Pritchard was there because Tamesis Dock was midway between Thames House in Millbank and the SIS Building at Vauxhall Cross, making it the perfect place for off-the-books meetings between operatives from the two agencies.

Shepherd caught a black cab and it dropped him close to the garish red and yellow barge. The deck was lined with trestle tables overlooking the Houses of Parliament, the London Eye and Battersea Power Station. As Shepherd walked to the gangplank, he saw Pritchard sitting at one of the tables, and he wasn't surprised to see his companion — Julian Penniston-Hill, the head of MI6. Two men in dark overcoats were sitting at a table by the gangplank. They had the look of bodyguards and they casually looked over at Shepherd as they nibbled on crisps. Shepherd didn't recognise the men but assumed they were Penniston-Hill's minders.

He walked across the deck to Pritchard's table. There were two plates of fish and chips on the table, and a half finished bottle of white wine. Pritchard nodded at Shepherd and put down his knife and fork. 'Grab a pew, Dan,' he said. 'Julian and I are grabbing a quick bite, do you want to join us?'

Shepherd shook his head. 'No thanks. I'm a big fan of the fish and chips here, but I had a sandwich at my desk. I could do with a coffee, though.'

'Coffee it is,' said Pritchard, and he waved over a waitress.

'Regular coffee, with a splash of milk,' Shepherd

said to her.

The waitress flashed him a beaming smile. 'Americano?' she said in an Australian accent.

'Sure, so long as it's coffee with a splash of milk, I'll be happy whatever it's called,' said Shepherd.

'Good to see you again, Dan,' said Penniston-Hill as the waitress walked away. He was wearing a dark blue suit, a crisp pink shirt and an MCC tie.

'How's the Albanian investigation going?' asked Pritchard.

'Slowly but surely,' said Shepherd. He doubted that the Albanians were the reason he had been summoned, but was equally sure that Pritchard would get to the point sooner rather than later. He wasn't one for small talk. 'We're getting all our ducks in a row, it's just that there are a lot of ducks.'

'You might have to take a back seat on that investigation for a while,' said Pritchard. 'Something has come up.' He nodded at Penniston-Hill. 'I'll let Julian give you the details as the intel came from Six.' He picked up his knife and fork and tucked into his fish and chips.

Penniston-Hill looked over at Shepherd. 'You remember David White, the MI5 analyst you rescued from Hamas?' He smiled thinly. 'Stupid question,' he said. 'Your trick memory means you never forget anything, right?' He didn't wait for Shepherd to respond and carried on talking. 'The thing is, Mr White has gone rogue, in a big way. He has killed a senior member of Hamas here in the UK, and killed his daughter. We're not a hundred per cent sure that the daughter wasn't collateral damage but the early indications are that she was deliberately shot.'

'I haven't seen anything on the TV or in the papers.'

'And hopefully you won't,' said Penniston-Hill. 'We've managed to keep it under wraps so far.'

'Who was he?'

'Ibrahim Fayyad. He was one of the organisers of the October Seven attacks. He flew out of Egypt the day before the attacks started.'

Shepherd frowned. 'I'm sorry? A Hamas terrorist was allowed into the country? Why wasn't he stopped?'

'You'd have to address that question to Border Force,' said Penniston-Hill. He put down his knife and fork and took three photographs from his inside pocket. He passed one to Shepherd. A Palestinian man in his sixties, balding with a bushy beard stared at the camera through thick-lensed spectacles. 'This is Fayyad.' He forced a smile. 'I suppose I should say was, this was Fayyad.' He passed over a second photograph, this man a decade younger with a hooked nose and piercing brown eyes. There was scarring on the man's left ear, and hairless patch on temple above it with more scarring. 'On the same plane was this man, Mohammed Sharif. Another Hamas official, also believed to have been involved in the planning of the October Seven attacks.'

'Now this I did read about,' said Shepherd. 'He fell out of a window, didn't he? From his apartment in Chelsea Harbour?'

'Indeed,' said Penniston-Hill.

'The papers said there were no suspicious circumstances.'

'And there weren't,' said Penniston-Hill.

'There was a suggestion that he was drunk.'

'Sharif was a devout Muslim, he never touched alcohol.'

'So this Sharif was also killed by David White, is

that what you're saying?'

Penniston-Hill shook his head. 'Oh no, David White did most definitely not kill Sharif.'

'You seem very sure of that,' said Shepherd. Pritchard continued to tuck into his fish and chips, but Shepherd saw a flicker of amusement in the man's eyes and he realised he was on to something. 'So who did kill Sharif, if it wasn't an accident?'

Penniston-Hill flashed Pritchard a look, but the MI5 director was concentrating on his food. Penniston-Hill sighed. 'We believe that Mossad was behind Sharif's death.'

'Believe, or know for a fact?' said Shepherd. 'If you are so sure it wasn't White, you must know for some certainty that it was the Israelis.'

'Yes, right, fine,' said Penniston-Hill. 'In the interests of transparency I can tell you, in complete confidence, that it was Mossad who assassinated Sharif.'

'In retaliation for the October attacks?'

'Indeed. But that isn't what we're here to talk about.' He passed Shepherd a third photograph, this one of a man in his forties, with slicked back glistening black hair, thick eyebrows and a strong jaw, a black and white keffiyeh scarf around his neck. 'A third member of Hamas was on the plane from Egypt. Ahmed Abu-Rous. He travelled with his wife and young son and they are presently in the Midlands. We believe that David White intends to kill him.'

Shepherd frowned. 'How do you know that Mossad aren't the ones who want Abu-Rous dead? If you're so sure that they killed Sharif, presumably they'll also be after Abu-Rous.'

'The issue here is David White,' said Penniston-Hill. 'We need to stop his killing rampage.'

'To clear the way for Mossad, you mean?' said Shepherd.

'I really am not prepared to be questioned like this,' said Penniston-Hill archly.

Pritchard put down his knife and fork. 'Julian, Dan's SAS background means that he is used to briefings where the aim is to reach a consensus, and it's considered perfectly acceptable to question anything and everything. Chinese parliament they call it, though that's probably a politically incorrect term these days.'

'I don't see how we can possibly operate under a system where every decision we make is questioned.'

'Absolutely, there are times when we just need people to follow orders and carry out instructions. But I think we can agree that this is a special case. And so far as Dan goes, I have always found that honesty is the best policy.'

Penniston-Hill picked up his glass and took several gulps of wine.

'Perhaps as White is our man, I could take it from here?' said Pritchard.

'Go ahead,' said Penniston-Hill. He picked up his knife and fork and savagely stabbed a chip.

Pritchard smiled at Shepherd. 'You know that David White's two daughters died in the Hamas attacks, but what you probably don't know is that his wife recently committed suicide. She had been depressed following the death of her children and had been on medication, but she took her own life which we believe triggered White into taking his current course of action. Mossad knew that the three Hamas officials had flown to the UK, and they asked White to help them track them down.'

'Why didn't Mossad ask officially? Hamas is a

260

proscribed terrorist organisation. I don't have to tell you that membership and expressing support for Hamas is an illegal act in the UK, punishable by up to 14 years in prison. In fact they should never have been allowed in the country in the first place.'

'Well, as Julian said, you would have to take that up with Border Force. And we have to deal with the way the world is, not the way we'd like it to be. What I can tell you is that Number Ten made it clear that we are not to help the Israelis carry out assassinations on British soil. It's bad enough that the Russians seem to think they have carte blanche to kill their enemies here, but we can't be seen to be helping the Israelis to do the same.'

'So they asked White for help in tracking the men down?'

'Exactly. He gave them details of where to find Sharif. And he said that he wanted to play a more active role.'

'To kill him, you mean?'

Pritchard nodded. 'Mossad said no, they wanted to use professionals. Which is when White went rogue and killed Fayyad and his daughter. We are fairly sure he will now go after the third man on the plane, Abu-Rous.'

'So it was Mossad who told you what White is doing?' said Shepherd. 'They don't want him queering their pitch.'

'They're professionals, Dan. Sharif's death can be explained away as an accident, Fayyad and his daughter were shot to death in their house.'

'So if White was better at covering his tracks, you'd let him get on with it?'

Pritchard waved his knife. 'There's a thin line

261

between valid questioning and insubordination, Dan,' he said coldly. 'Be careful you don't cross it.'

'I just don't like the fact that Mossad clearly wanted White to spy for them, and now they're throwing him under the bus. If we stop White, that doesn't save Abu-Rous, does it? The Israelis will still want him dead.'

'We'll be doing everything we can to keep Abu-Rous alive,' said Penniston-Hill.

'Why are we suddenly so keen to be protecting terrorists?' asked Shepherd. 'Is this coming from Number Ten?'

'What David White doesn't know, what nobody knows, is that Ahmed Abu-Rous is one of our assets,' said Penniston-Hill.

Shepherd frowned. 'How can that be? You said he was a high-ranking Hamas official. That he planned the October Seven attacks. Now you're saying he's an MI6 agent?'

'Those facts are not mutually exclusive,' said Penniston-Hill.

'Twelve hundred civilians died in those attacks. If he was working for you, why didn't he tip you off?'

'Our relationship with Abu-Rous is complicated.'

'I'll say. You let him into the country after he organised the massacre of civilians. And now you want to protect him from Mossad's retribution?'

Penniston-Hill looked over at Pritchard, who shrugged. 'I'd say that Dan has a point,' said Pritchard.

'Dan doesn't have the full picture,' said Penniston-Hill. He put down his knife and fork and took another drink of wine. 'Abu-Rous was educated in this country, at the London School Of Economics, no less. While there he struck up a relationship with one of our

262

people, a relationship which has stood the test of time. He made it clear from the start that he would never betray the secrets of Hamas, or do anything that he saw as being detrimental to the Palestinian people. At least those Palestinians who support Hamas. But he has been a valuable source of intel about other Palestinian terror groups, including the Palestine Liberation Front, Palestine Islamic Jihad, the Popular Front For The Liberation, the Democratic For The Liberation of Palestine, and the Abu Nidal Organisation.'

'So basically he was using you to bring down his rivals,' said Shepherd.

Penniston-Hill ignored the jibe. 'And he has provided a great deal of information about Hezbollah, information which over the years has saved thousands of lives.'

Shepherd nodded but didn't say anything. Hezbollah was Iran's terror proxy in the south of Lebanon, a group who wanted nothing less than the elimination of Israel. While most of its activities were in the Middle East, the terror group was also active across Europe and Africa, carrying out bombings and assassinations. Shepherd could see how a man like Abu-Rous would be a useful asset, but how could that possibly excuse his involvement in the October Seven attacks? He knew there was no point in raising the matter with the MI6 chief, who was already clearly annoyed at Shepherd's questioning.

'Abu-Rous is presently in his house outside Birmingham with his family and I need you to oversee his security,' said Pritchard. 'You know White so hopefully you have some insight into how he operates.'

'As White knows where Abu-Rous is, why not move

him to a safe house?'

Pritchard wrinkled his nose. 'I thought of that, obviously. But if we do, and White realises that we've moved Abu-Rous, he'll know we're on to him. At the moment he might assume that we don't know what's going on and that he has a clear run.'

'And if Abu-Rous is out of reach, he might start selecting other targets?'

'Exactly. At least if he goes for Abu-Rous, we can be prepared.'

'So Abu-Rous is the bait in a trap.'

'I wouldn't describe him as bait,' sighed Penniston-Hill.

'But that's the situation, isn't it? This is more about stopping White than it is about protecting Abu-Rous. That's a fact.'

'That's your interpretation of the situation, but that's not the way we see it,' said Pritchard. 'We can do both.' He smiled. 'You can do both.'

Shepherd nodded. 'This might sound obvious, but has anyone tried to contact White, to explain that Abu-Rous is an agent?'

'He's gone dark,' said Pritchard. 'He hasn't been home for several days, he has dumped his phones, he hasn't used any of his credit or debit cards, he has cut all contact with friends and colleagues. And even if we were to contact him, I doubt he'd be persuaded to stop.'

Shepherd nodded thoughtfully. 'And what happens to him, if we do catch him?'

'What do you mean?' asked Pritchard.

'I mean a great deal of effort has gone into keeping this under wraps, but that all falls apart if he appears in court.'

'We're hoping that won't happen, obviously,' said Penniston-Hill.

'So what do you want to happen?'

'I'm assuming that when we eventually do find White, he will be armed and unwilling to surrender,' said Penniston-Hill. He shrugged. 'That can only end one way, obviously.'

'You want him dead.'

'I don't want him dead. That's not what I'm saying. But I think that is probably how this will end.'

'And what about the Israelis? How are they going to feel if White dies as a result of them telling you that he was Fayyad's killer?'

'We can cross that bridge if and when we get to it,' said Penniston-Hill.

Shepherd looked over at Pritchard. 'So when do you want me on Abu-Rous's security detail?'

Pritchard looked at his watch. 'I suggest you arrange to hand over your Albanian case and then head up to Birmingham this afternoon.'

Shepherd nodded. The waitress returned with his coffee. He looked up at her and smiled. 'Can I take that to go, please?' he asked.

41

David White wasn't a fan of Birmingham. It was supposedly England's second city but in terms of importance he always ranked Manchester higher. He had visited both cities several times and always found Manchester more welcoming. It was possibly because one third of Birmingham's population was Muslim, and more than half of them were of Pakistani origin. It wasn't a city where Jews felt welcome, which is why they accounted for less than one per cent of the city and numbers were decreasing every year. Parts of the city could well have been Karachi, with women in full burkhas, men in traditional Muslim dress, and signs everywhere in Arabic and Urdu and he kept driving by walls plastered with posters supporting Palestine. There were more than two hundred mosques in the city and White's work as an analyst had taught him that dozens of them were hotbeds of radicalism. London was still the epicentre of the country's terrorism problem, but Birmingham was a close second.

Abu-Rous owned a house in Edgbaston, a wealthy suburb southwest of Birmingham city centre. There were tree-lined roads lined with large detached houses, parks, a golf course, Edgbaston Stadium, home of Warwickshire Country Cricket Club, and Birmingham Botanical gardens. Abu-Rous had purchased the house five years earlier, that much was on the Land Registry database, but there were no estate agents details on Rightmove. White had driven past several times but there was a high wall around the house and behind it a towering Leylandii hedge, so he couldn't see much in the way of detail. There was a CCTV camera covering the front gate.

The house was detached with large chimneys that gave it the look of an oceangoing liner, but he couldn't see if anyone was at home or what if any security there was.

White drove back to the city and parked in the Bull Ring shopping centre carpark. He went into the shopping centre and devoured a cream cheese bagel and a coffee while he read through that day's *Times* on his iPad. There was no mention of the death of Fayyad and his daughter. He was fairly sure that Fayyad's wife had been upstairs which meant she would almost certainly have discovered the bodies later that night and called the police. The fact that there was nothing in the paper suggested that MI5 had invoked a Defence and Security Media Advisory Notice, an official request to news editors not to publish or broadcast items on specified subjects for reasons of national security.

There had been no such restriction on the death of Mohammed Sharif, who had fallen from the terrace of his Chelsea Harbour penthouse, allegedly with copious amounts of Scotch whisky in his system. White had smiled at that. It was a typical Mossad move, to take out an enemy and besmirch his reputation at the same time. The fact that MI5 hadn't served a DSMA notice on Sharif's death suggested they didn't realise it was an assassination. But following Fayyad's death, they would have put two and two together. If White was lucky, his bosses would assume that Mossad was responsible for both killings.

The problem was that MI5's investigators would

almost certainly start looking for connections between the two men, and it wouldn't take them long to discover that they were both on the same flight out of Egypt the day before the October Seven massacres. And if they then checked the plane's manifest, they would see that Ahmed Abu-Rous was also on board. Once they realised that Abu-Rous was a target, they would have two choices — beef up his security or whisk him away to a safe house.

After he had finished his bagel, White wandered around the shopping centre in search of a technology store and found one on the third floor, its window full of state of the art drones. He had the shop assistant — a young bearded man with an almost impenetrable accent explain the various functions of the different models and White ended up buying one for close to a thousand pounds, along with three spare batteries. He paid in cash.

42

Shepherd took the stairs to Pritchard's office. Amy Miller smiled when she saw him and waved at his door. 'He says you're to go straight in,' she said.

Shepherd thanked her and pushed open the door. Pritchard was sitting at his desk, his face close to one of his computer terminals. His tie was at half mast and his suit jacket was hanging on the back of his chair. He sat back and nodded at the two chairs opposite his desk. Shepherd sat down. The fact that he was on one of the wooden chairs and not on the sofa by the window meant that he wouldn't be in the office for long. 'So, are you all set?' Pritchard asked.

'I've briefed Chris Adkins, he's been on the Albanian investigation from Day One, so he knows what's what. He's already met Petrit. And Jimmy Sharpe of the NCA will have a chat with him tonight.'

Pritchard raised an eyebrow. 'I thought Sharpe had retired.'

'The NCA doesn't want to let him go,' said Shepherd.

'Is he as politically incorrect as he always was?'

Shepherd grinned. 'He's a bit better, having done the full range of diversity courses on offer. But he's old school, that's for sure.'

'Well to be fair, Dan, you're old school too. But you've learned how to not offend people.'

Shepherd shrugged. It wasn't his place to be defending Razor, the world had changed and while his friend was trying to change with it, some of his opinions did clash with the more woke members of staff.

'Bloody good copper, though,' said Pritchard. 'He's been on some very successful undercover operations with you over the years.'

Shepherd nodded. 'His age is an advantage when it comes to being undercover,' he said. 'Most villains assume he's too old to be police.' He grinned. 'I'm probably getting to that stage myself.'

'You've a fair few years ahead of you yet, Dan,' said Pritchard. There was a plastic bottle of Evian water on his desk and he took a drink. The fact that Shepherd hadn't been offered water or a coffee also suggested that Pritchard wasn't planning to have him in the office for long. 'So, Mr Abu-Rous and his family are at home as we speak. They have an MI6 minder looking after him at the moment, his name is Howard Boylan.' He passed a piece of paper across the desk. 'That's Boylan's mobile number. He can brief you on the drive up. There is a team of four CTSFOs already there. I'll leave it up to you as to how you use them.'

The Counter Terrorist Specialist Firearms Officers were the highest standard of armed police in the UK. They were part of the Metropolitan Police Service but had jurisdiction across the country. The vast majority of firearms officers in the Met went through their entire careers without firing a shot in anger, but the CTSFOs were much more like the SAS trained to kill and sent into situations where killing was often the only option. CTSFOs often worked undercover, and all at some point underwent training with the SAS at the Stirling Lines barracks.

'What have they been told?' asked Shepherd.

'That Mr Abu-Rous is a high value target and that

he is to be protected at all costs.'

'And David White's involvement.'

'I'll leave that up to you.'

Shepherd pulled a face. 'From what Penniston-Hill was saying, he wants them to slot White.'

'Slot? That's a horrible word.'

'Slot. Eliminate. Terminate. Kill. The end result is the same. One dead MI5 analyst.'

'An analyst who has gone rogue and is committing murder.'

'Who is doing exactly what Mossad is doing,' said Shepherd. 'Except those guys will probably end up with medals while all White will get is a bullet.' He shrugged. 'I wouldn't want to see him dead. Especially after all the trouble it took to get him out of Gaza.'

'No one is saying that you have to kill him, Dan. That's not how we work. You know that.'

'Then somebody needs to tell the head of MI6 that.'

'I think what Julian meant was that if David White does show up with a gun and there is a chance that Mr Abu-Rous would be shot, then our people must do what is necessary to stop him.'

'Neutralise the threat?'

'Exactly. And if you can do that without killing him, all the better.'

Shepherd sighed. He didn't believe what Pritchard was telling him. There was no way that White could be allowed to stand trial, not in open court anyway. And even if his trial was kept behind closed doors, there were plenty of investigative journalists around capable of sniffing out the story. If what White had done ever became public knowledge, Pritchard's job would be on the line. 'This whole thing is such a mess,' he said.

'Most of what we do is messy,' said Pritchard.

'I still don't understand what Hamas thought they would gain by attacking Israel the way they did,' said Shepherd. 'And how could their intelligence services not have seen it coming?'

'I am told that they did know,' said Pritchard. 'I heard that a warning came out of Egypt that the Gaza situation was about to explode. I can only suppose that the warning was ignored. Soldiers on the ground, close to Gaza, had been warning about suspicious activity for weeks before the attacks. Hamas fighters were seen near the fence, near border posts, and there were reports about high-ranking Hamas officials being seen, again close to the fence. But the reports never went up the chain of command.'

'Why was that?'

'The feeling among the officers was that Hamas didn't have the balls or the equipment to fight a full war, they were being worn down by the blockade and Israeli bombing, and we were using aid to control them. The consensus was that Hamas was no longer a military threat, apart from their rocket attacks.' He shrugged. 'Hindsight is a wonderful thing.'

'You can say that again. But I'm surprised that heads haven't rolled over the whole affair.'

Pritchard shrugged. 'Maybe they have and they just haven't been made public. But with hindsight it's clear that Hamas had joined with at least five other Palestinian terror groups to plan the October Seven attacks. It turns out from 2020 onwards they were carrying out joint drills close to the border and posting them on social media.'

Shepherd frowned. 'That's ridiculous.'

'Ridiculous but true,' said Pritchard. 'Analysis of the footage posted shows fighters from Ali Mustafa Brigades, Palestinian Islamic Jihad, the Mujahideen Brigades, Al-Quasim units and Al-Aqsa Martyrs Brigades. It defies belief that the Israeli intelligence agencies didn't know what was going on under their noses. I've seen the footage and you can clearly see them rehearsing hostage-taking, raiding compounds and breaching the border. Hamas had actually set up training grounds in Gaza strip and ran exercises where they were obviously practising attacking IDF positions and tanks. I've put out a few feelers trying to work out what was going on and the response I keep getting is that they knew Hamas were up to something but they didn't know what.'

'Do you believe that?'

Pritchard shrugged wearily. 'I don't know what to believe. If it's true, then somebody was asleep on the job. Will heads roll? I doubt it. They rarely do. All we can do is to deal with things the way they are, not the way we want them to be.' He looked at his watch, his not-so-subtle way of telling Shepherd that the meeting was over.

Shepherd stood up. 'What about White? What's being done to find him?'

'We haven't gone public, obviously. And we haven't passed his details on to the police. But GCHQ is looking for him electronically. And we have a team keeping watch on his house just in case he's stupid enough to go back.'

'When he was looking at the databases for intel on the three Hamas chiefs who flew out from Egypt, did he check any other names?'

'We're not sure. It looks as if he was using other

273

officers' logons to carry out his searches. We've got an IT team working on it.'

Shepherd nodded. 'Because if he is hell bent on revenge, he might not stop with the three. There are plenty of other Hamas sympathisers in the UK.'

'I hear you, Dan. We're on it.' He leaned forward and peered at the screen on his left, leaving Shepherd in no doubt that his time was up.

43

White spent an hour and a half on Edgbaston golf course practising flying the drone. It was pretty much idiot proof. Its onboard GPS meant that a simple press of a button would make it return to its starting point. Pressing another button put the drone into a static hover, all the time sending a live video feed to his mobile phone, which was clipped to the controller. The battery was good for almost thirty minutes, though the salesman had said that it was best to get the drone back after about twenty, just to be on the safe side.

He had four batteries and after he had drained them all he sat in the car and recharged them. He was starting to get hungry again so he drove five minutes to a McDonald's and had two cheeseburgers washed down with coffee as he studied Google Maps on his iPad. He did a virtual walk by of the house but there wasn't much to see. The satellite view showed the house and the extensive gardens behind it. The gardens backed on to another house and there were houses either side. The resolution wasn't good enough to see if there were CCTV cameras covering the house.

Once the four batteries were fully charged he drove to the Worcester and Birmingham canal which cut diagonally through Edgbaston. The house was a hundred yards away but he didn't want to get any closer. He hadn't seen any security in the road when he had driven by, but that didn't mean there weren't people stationed outside the house or looking through the windows.

He climbed out of the car, clipped his phone into the controller and activated the drone. He pressed a button to put it into a vertical climb that took the drone a hundred feet into the air. He checked the camera view, then sent the drone towards the house. After thirty seconds he put the drone in a hover again as he got his bearings, then took it up another hundred feet. He sent it forward again, watching the ground move slowly by on his phone.

After another thirty seconds, the house came into view. He put the drone in a hover and moved the camera to get a better view of the front of the house. There were four vehicles parked there. The overhead view prevented him from seeing what makes the cars were.

He took the drone down to a hundred feet and moved it away from the house. One of the cars was a black Range Rover, a vehicle favoured by gangsters and CTSFOs. Next to it was a Mercedes coupe, possible Mrs Abu-Rous's, and a BMW 7 Series which White knew was registered in the name of a company controlled by Mr Abu-Rous. The fourth car was a grey Ford Puma.

He changed the camera angle and checked the vehicles in the street outside the house, but wasn't able to discern if any of them had watchers in them.

He realised that twenty minutes had passed so he pressed the button to get the drone to return to him.

44

Pritchard looked up from his twin screens as Amy ushered Donna Walsh into his office. Walsh headed up MI5's London surveillance operations and was worked off her feet but he had added to her crippling workload by asking her to check on David White. The fewer people that knew White had gone rogue, the better. 'Donna, would you like a coffee?' asked Pritchard as he stood up and walked around his desk.

'I'm well over my caffeine allocation today,' she said. She looked frazzled. Her dark-framed glasses were pushed up on her chestnut hair and she had rolled up the sleeves of her shirt. She turned and smiled at Amy. 'Do you have any of that camomile tea?'

'I do,' said Amy.

'It's so calming, and at the moment I need calming.'

'I'll have some too, Amy, please,' said Pritchard, waving Walsh to the sofa by the window.

They sat down as Amy left the office. 'I'm sorry about dumping this on you, Donna, I know how busy you are,' said Pritchard.

'Not a problem, Giles,' she said. 'I know how sensitive it is.' She was holding a manila folder and she opened it and fanned out half a dozen printouts. 'Okay, so David has two phones that we know about, one for work and one for personal use. Both have been dark for three days. GPS coordinates show that he was at home the last time they were on. His car is parked outside his house. None of his debit and credit cards

277

have been used for the past three days. So either he's incapacitated or he's hiding.'

'I think we can assume the latter,' said Pritchard.

'Prior to him going dark, he withdrew large amounts of cash from several bank accounts. Twenty thousand pounds in total. Obviously, we're keeping a watch on his accounts but he's flush with cash at the moment so I'm not holding out much hope. We've run him through facial recognition and he hasn't been seen on any government or council CCTV cameras, but he'll know to avoid them.'

'He's desk bound most of the time these days but he has been used on active operations in the past and his operational training is up to date,' said Pritchard. 'He knows the drill.'

Walsh nodded. 'We've run a full analysis of his phone records. Clean as a whistle, but as you said, he knows the drill. We've run an analysis on all the phones that have regularly pinged the cellphone tower nearest his house and there's no evidence of him using a burner phone. But again, he'd know not to use it at home.' She smiled. 'We did however find two drug dealers in the same road, one of whom is involved in the importation of a sizeable amount of ketamine, so it's an ill wind, as they say. I've passed the details over to NCA.'

'Do we know what vehicle he's using?'

Walsh shook her head. 'His Tesla is parked outside his house. We've checked with all the major rental companies but drawn a blank. I'm guessing he's bought something second hand and paid cash.'

'What about CCTV footage around Fayyad's house on the night he was killed?'

'Nothing definite,' said Walsh. 'Several possibilities

but none where we can say it's definitely him. We're following up as best we can but I think we're chasing shadows.'

'The gun?'

'Bog standard Glock, originally sold at a gun fair in Miami three years ago. We suspect it was smuggled into the country. No fingerprints on it, the suppressor or the ammunition. The suppressor was home made but of high quality and it doesn't match anything we've seen before so the assumption is that it's also from the US.'

'The fact that David left it at the scene suggests he knows there's nothing about the gun that could point to him.'

Walsh nodded. 'Agreed. If he was caught with it in his possession then it'd be game over, but once he was away from the scene there's no way of linking it to him.'

Pritchard nodded thoughtfully. 'It's all very well thought out, that's for sure. Which suggests that it wasn't a one-off, he's planning to do it again. Did you find any evidence of him looking at Fayyad and the other two names on our databases?'

'Not at first. There didn't seem to be any record of him looking at Fayyad. But then of course he would know that any searches would leave an electronic trail so we went about it in reverse — checking who had looked at Fayyad and checking CCTV to see who was at the terminal at the time. Over the past month, prior to his death, Fayyad was the subject of just five searches, mainly from MENAD officers, but not David. In four of those cases we were able to see that the officer at the terminal matched the log in but in the fifth it was David. The previous user hadn't

279

logged off and you can see him slipping in before the automatic log off occurred.'

'Naughty, naughty,' said Pritchard.

'Exactly, that's a sackable offence, obviously.'

Pritchard smiled ruefully. 'That's the least of his transgressions,' he said. 'So David was able to access all Fayyad's details?'

'Everything, including his address, phone numbers and bank accounts. He spent close to half an hour accessing databases across the system. He also did a thorough search for Mohammed Sharif and Ahmed Abu-Rous and obtained all their details.'

'And when was this?'

'A week before Fayyad was killed.'

'And did he search for anyone else other than those three names?'

'Not this time. But this is where it gets difficult, Giles. It's perfectly possible that David did this on other occasions, but finding out when is going to be time consuming. We'd have to work backwards, clocking each time a Hamas official or supporter was searched for, then checking CCTV to see if the person doing the searching was actually logged in. Hundreds of instances, each one of which will need checking. I can't possibly do it all myself. Not in any sensible timeframe, obviously.'

'I hear you,' said Pritchard. 'We need to know who else David has been looking at, so you can bring in another pair of eyes. Obviously, they need to be sworn to secrecy, the fewer people who know what David is up to, the better.'

The door opened and Amy brought in a tray with two cups of camomile tea and a plate of Hobnobs, which she placed on the table in front of them.

'That's a nice surprise,' said Pritchard, nodding at the biscuits.

'You've barely eaten all day,' said Amy. 'We need to keep your blood sugar up.'

Walsh waited until Amy had left the room before continuing. 'Another pair of eyes isn't going to do it, Giles. Not if you want to cover every single Hamas member and supporter. MENAD alone carried out more than four hundred searches last month on Hamas contacts. It will take a couple of minutes to get a date and time on the search, then a couple more to check the CCTV. From my experience, four minutes is pushing it. But even four minutes times two hundred is one thousand six hundred minutes which is twenty six hours. And no one can work at that pace all day.'

'So how many pairs of eyes do you need?'

'The clock is ticking, right? You want the intel today, I assume.'

'The sooner the better.'

'I can stay on it, but my backlog is getting longer by the minute. But even with me on the case I think I'll need at least three more officers. Ideally four. But again, that's just to check the MENAD searches. But David could have used pretty much any of the terminals in Thames House and if we open it up to the whole of MI5 . . .' She shrugged. 'It's a major operation.'

Pritchard nodded. 'Let's start with MENAD. And bring on three other officers.' He sighed. 'I'd hoped to keep this between the two of us,' he said.

'I'll choose people who don't know David personally. I also thought I would use officers in the vetting department. They're used to investigating our own.'

281

'That would work,' said Pritchard. 'Do you want me to come up with names?'

She handed him a sheet of paper with three names on it. Pritchard studied it and nodded. 'Good choices.' He gave the paper back to her. 'You knew I'd agree to three officers,' he said.

'I guessed.'

He grinned. 'Good guess. And what about David's contacts over the past few months, since he returned from Israel?'

'Everything on his work phone checks out,' said Walsh, sliding the sheet of paper back into her file. 'His personal phone is also clean, but I would expect nothing else, as I said he would know to use a burner phone and encrypted message apps like Signal and Telegram. There was something interesting though. He recently struck up a relationship with a press officer at the Israeli Embassy. He has registered him as a contact and they've been playing badminton at a club in Maida Vale.'

'Would that by any chance be a Mr Joel Schwartz?'

'I thought you might know him,' said Walsh.

'I do indeed,' said Pritchard. He smiled. 'Very naughty of you to save the best news until last, Donna.'

'I thought it might cheer you up,' said Walsh, gathering up her papers.

'It did,' said Pritchard. 'Thank you.'

45

The M40 was clear but even so it took Shepherd almost three hours to drive from London to Edgbaston in his BMW X5 SUV. As he passed by Oxford he phoned Howard Boylan on hands free. Boylan had a slight Geordie accent that suggested he hadn't been home for a few years, and he had the clipped tones that suggested he'd been in the military. He confirmed that Abu-Rous and his family were in the house and that the CTSFOs had arrived just before dawn.

'The principal is not a happy bunny,' said Boylan. 'Says if his family are in danger in the UK then he wants to leave.'

'What have you told him about the nature of the threat?'

'My boss says I'm not to discuss that with the principal. But he obviously assumes it's Israeli intelligence, or 'dirty fucking Jews' as he insists on calling them.'

'Just hang tight,' said Shepherd. 'I'll talk to him when I get there. But on no account he is to leave the house.'

'Understood,' said Boylan.

Shepherd ended the call.

He phoned Boylan again as he drove down the road towards Abu-Rous's house and the gate was rattling back as he arrived. There were four vehicles parked in the driveway, including a CTSFO Range Rover. Shepherd tutted under his breath. If David White were to see the vehicle, he'd know that the police were there.

He parked next to the Mercedes and climbed out. It was a big house, red brick with a double height entrance. Thick ivy covered most of the left side of the house and there was a twin garage, also covered with ivy. He looked back at the gate, which had closed behind him. The gate was a good ten feet tall, as was the wall that surrounded the garden, and extra cover was provided by a line of towering Leylandii conifers.

As he walked towards the house, the front door was opened by a man in a grey suit, presumably Howard Boylan. Shepherd nodded and said hello. He didn't see the small drone, hovering a hundred feet in the air above the house, videoing his every move.

46

White stared at his phone screen, watching the man walk away from the white BMW SUV. He had taken the drone down to a hundred feet to get a better look at the visitor. He frowned as he recognised the man as Dan Shepherd. It was only when White was back in Thames House that he had learned that Dan Shepherd was pretty much a living legend, former SAS, a former cop, a former SOCA officer, and now one of MI5's top operators. It couldn't have been a coincidence that Shepherd had been sent to protect Abu-Rous. It almost certainly meant that they knew that White had killed Fayyad. White grimaced. His years as an MI5 analyst had taught him that coincidences did happen but that they were rare. Most things happened for a reason. Cause and effect. MI5 knew that White was on a killing spree and so they had put Shepherd on the case because of their history.

But how did they know that White intended to kill Abu-Rous? White had gone to a lot of trouble to cover his tracks. There was no way that White could have been identified as the killer from the crime scene. He had left nothing behind that would point to him as the killer, and he had been careful to avoid witnesses and CCTV as he went to and from Fayyad's house.

His frown deepened. Could it be a coincidence that they had sent Shepherd? Assuming they knew about Fayyad and his daughter, with Mohammed Sharif also dead it wouldn't take much for them to realise that the third Hamas official on the plane out

285

of Egypt was also at risk. So it would make sense for MI5 to put measures in place to protect Abu-Rous. But did it make sense to send Shepherd? Was he a random choice? If it wasn't random then it could only be because they knew that White was planning to kill Abu-Rous. And that brought him back to how, how could they possibly know that he had killed Fayyad?

He saw movement in the bedroom window at the far right of the house. He caught a glimpse of a bald man peering down at the parked cars and then the curtains were drawn.

The only reason they would be protecting Abu-Rous would be because they knew that Fayyad and Sharif were dead. And, coincidence notwithstanding, they had sent Shepherd because they knew that White was involved. The only person who knew with any certainty that White had killed Fayyad and his daughter would be Joel Schwartz from the Israeli Embassy. He must have realised that White had kept the intel on Fayyad and Abu-Rous to himself. Fayyad's death would have confirmed that. How would Mossad react to the discovery that White was killing their targets? Would they see him as a distraction and want him out of the way? So what would their options be? Mossad wasn't averse to killing its enemies, but White, despite his transgressions, was still a serving MI5 officer and he doubted that even Mossad would be prepared to cross that line. And even if they did decide to kill him, they'd have to find him first and they didn't have the resources to do that.

He took another drink of water as his mind raced. So, Mossad couldn't kill him, either for practical or ethical reasons, so what other options did they have?

Realisation dawned and he smiled thinly. They could betray him. They could tell MI5 what White was doing and leave them to clean up the mess. Maybe they had even blamed him for Sharif's death. He wouldn't put it past them. Mossad had no reservations about getting their hands dirty, and were happy enough to bend the truth if it achieved their objectives.

He tapped the water bottle on his leg as he considered his options. MI5 knew what he was doing and had sent Shepherd to stop him. Maybe even kill him. There was no way that MI5 would allow White to appear in open court, not with everything he knew about the organisation. White didn't just know where the bodies were buried, he knew who had put them there and why. There was no way that they would allow him to go public. So Shepherd wasn't just there to protect Abu-Rous. He was there to kill White.

47

Howard Boylan closed the front door, then shook hands with Shepherd. He was in his early thirties with receding blond hair and square framed glasses. His eyes were a pale green and there was a faint smell of smoke about him. His teeth were slightly yellow and there were nicotine stains on the first two fingers of his right hand, so he was definitely a smoker. 'Good to meet you,' said Boylan. 'I've heard a lot about you.'

'That's not good, considering the business we're in,' said Shepherd.

'Nothing confidential, obviously,' said Boylan. 'Just that you've had some awesome successes in your career.'

'I've been busy, that's for sure,' said Shepherd. He looked around. 'Where are the CTSFOs?'

'Upstairs. Mr Abu-Rous said he didn't want them upsetting his son.'

Shepherd shook his head. 'They're no good upstairs, are they?'

'He was insistent. And I didn't want to put pressure on him. If he decides to put his family in the car and drive to the airport, how are we going to stop him? He's not under arrest.'

'I hear you,' said Shepherd. 'Has he threatened to do that?'

'He says if his life is in danger, he'd be better off in Qatar. He's well in with some prince there and he says he'll get all the protection he needs.'

'Where is he?'

'The kitchen. His wife and son are with him. The wife is also not happy at us being in her home.'

'What have you told him about the situation?'

' I was told to convey only the bare minimum, that we have received credible intelligence that there was a threat against him and his family.'

'So you haven't mentioned Mossad or David White?'

'I was told not to.' He grinned. 'To be honest, I was told just to babysit him until you got here.'

'So you know nothing about Abu-Rous's background?'

'Just that he's with Hamas.'

Shepherd wrinkled his nose. The fact that Boylan didn't know that Abu-Rous was an MI6 asset suggested he was well down the totem pole. But it made sense to keep that information confined to as few people as possible. 'Right, can you introduce me? Use the name Derek Simpson.'

'No problem. I'm using Jake Walker. Not that he ever calls me by name.'

It was standard procedure not to use real names when dealing with anyone outside the intelligence agencies, unless there was a good reason for it.

Boylan took Shepherd down the hall and opened the door to the kitchen. It was large enough to do justice to a bustling restaurant, with a six burner oven that didn't look as though it had ever been used, a massive twin-door American-style fridge, huge swathes of marble countertops and a large marble-topped island with a double sink set into it. There was no sign of Abu-Rous and his family and Shepherd frowned. Boylan gestured at a sliding door that led to a large conservatory, full of green plants and wicker furniture. 'Through there,' he said.

Shepherd's frown deepened. A glass-sided conservatory was one of the last places you should put a family at risk of assassination, especially when there was no security in the garden.

Abu-Rous was bending over a book with his son next to him. The boy was five or six years old. His wife was sitting in a wicker armchair, staring at the screen of her phone. Abu-Rous looked up as Boylan and Shepherd stepped into the conservatory. 'Mr Abu-Rous, can I introduce you to Derek Simpson. He'll be in charge of security from here on in.'

Abu-Rous was in his late forties, and looked pretty much the same as he was in the photograph that Pritchard had shown him. His slicked back black hair glistened, his thick eyebrows were knitted into a frown and his jaw jutted up aggressively. He was wearing denim jeans and a white linen shirt, open to reveal matted chest hair. 'You are a policeman?' he snapped.

'No, Sir. I'm with the Home Office.'

Abu-Rous laughed. 'You're a spy. I can always tell a spy.'

'I'm here to assuage any concerns you might have, and to make sure that you and your family are safe,' said Shepherd.

'Just admit that you're a spy.'

'Mr Abu-Rous, I'm a security specialist, that's why I've been sent here. Now, can I have a word with you? In private.'

'We can talk in the garden.'

'That's not a good idea, Sir,' said Shepherd. 'In fact, you and your family should stay away from the windows.'

'You want us to hide in the dark, is that it? As if we

290

were frightened animals.'

'Is the glass bullet-proof, Sir?' asked Shepherd.

'Of course not,' snapped Abu-Rous.

'Then you need to stay to stay away from the windows.'

'You think they would send a sniper?'

'It's just better to be safe than sorry.' He gestured at the door to the kitchen. 'Perhaps we could talk in the kitchen.'

Abu-Rous ruffled his son's hair and spoke to him in Arabic. The boy giggled and nodded, then sat back on the sofa and began reading his book. Abu-Rous stood up. His wife looked up from her screen and he said something to her in Arabic and she shrugged and went back to her phone.

Abu-Rous walked into the kitchen and over to the fridge. He opened it and took out a bottle of VOSS water, then sat on a stool at the kitchen island. 'This can not continue,' he said.

'What can't continue?' asked Shepherd.

'This invasion of my privacy. This is my home and you have invaded it. You know there are armed police upstairs?'

'They're of no use to you up there, Sir. Your life is in danger and they are here to protect you.'

Abu-Rous gestured at Boylan with his bottle. 'That's what he keeps saying, but he won't give me any details. For all I know, you're just trying to scare me.'

Shepherd sat down on a stool on the opposite side of the island. 'No one is trying to scare you, Sir. There is a very real threat against you. You flew out of Egypt the day before the October Seven massacre, correct?'

'I think you'll find that hundreds of people left

Egypt on October Six.'

'Yes, but not all of them were Hamas officials. Not like Mohammed Sharif, Ibrahim Fayyad, and yourself. You planned the attacks, you put everything together, and then you flew to England before the shit hit the fan.'

'I had nothing to do with the October Seven attacks.'

'Well, I'm not here to argue about that,' said Shepherd.

Abu-Rous leaned forward and lowered his voice to a whisper. 'I work for MI6. I have helped this country, more than you know.'

'Which is why we are so keen to protect you, Sir. I am tasked with doing whatever is necessary to keep you from harm. Your two comrades — Mohammed Sharif and Ibrahim Fayyad — are both dead.'

'Mohammed fell from his apartment,' said Abu-Rous.

'He was helped in that fall, we believe by Mossad.'

Abu-Rous's eyes widened. 'That is not possible.'

'If you know anything about Mossad, you'll know it is very possible,' said Shepherd. He stood up and walked around the island to stand close to the Palestinian. 'And then there is Ibrahim Fayyad, He is also now dead, along with his daughter.'

Abu-Rous shook his head vehemently. 'No. You are lying.'

'Why would I lie about something like that. He was shot. So was his daughter.'

'And you say Mossad did this?'

Shepherd kept his gaze steady. He had worked undercover enough to know how to lie convincingly. There was no way he could tell Abu-Rous that a rogue MI5 officer was on a killing spree, so he had to stick to the Mossad story. 'You must have known that this would happen,' he said. 'The Israelis are out for revenge, big time. The same as they were after the Black September terrorists killed their athletes at the West German Olympics.'

Abu-Rous's hand began to tremble and he put down his water bottle. 'They killed Ibrahim's daughter?'

Shepherd nodded. 'They did.'

'They are animals,' said Abu-Rous.

Shepherd didn't want to get into a discussion about who the animals were in this situation. Yes, David White had crossed a line when he had shot Fayyad and his daughter, but Shepherd could empathise with him. His daughters were brutally slain by Hamas fighters and he had lost his wife not long after. A loss like that could push anyone over the edge. 'So you understand why we need to protect you, at least until we can track down this Mossad hit squad?'

'You are looking for them?'

'Of course we are looking for them. This is England, we don't allow assassination teams to go around killing people. But until we find them, we need to make sure that you stay safe.'

Abu-Rous's hand had stopped trembling and he picked up his bottle of water again. The door to the kitchen flew open and Boylan yelped like a startled puppy. Abu-Rous flinched and the bottle fell from his hands. The little boy burst into the room, a bundle of energy.

Shepherd leaned forward and his hand shot out and he caught the bottle before it smashed onto the tiled floor.

Abu-Rous shouted at the boy in Arabic and he took a step back, tears welling up in his eyes.

'It's all right, Sir, no damage done,' said Shepherd, putting the bottle on the island.

'He must learn not to intrude on adults like that,' said Abu-Rous. He frowned at the bottle, then looked at Shepherd. 'You have very quick reactions.'

'It was an easy catch.'

'I don't think so.'

Shepherd bent down and smiled at the boy. 'My name is Derek,' he said, 'What's your name?'

The boy was still close to tears. He looked at his father as if asking for permission to speak. Abu-Rous nodded and the boy looked back at Shepherd. 'My name is Idris,' he said.

'That's a great name,' said Shepherd. 'Have you heard of the actor Idris Elba? He's one of my favourite actors.'

'We don't allow Idris to watch Western television or movies,' said Abu-Rous.

'Ah, okay,' said Shepherd. He smiled at the boy. 'So, me and some of my friends are going to be here to take care of your daddy for a while. We'll try to keep out of your way but don't worry if you see us moving around.'

'Is my baba in trouble?'

'No, your baba isn't in any trouble,' said Shepherd. 'We're just here to make his life a little easier, that's all.'

Abu-Rous spoke to his son in Arabic again and the boy hurried out of the kitchen. 'You have children?' asked Abu-Rous.

'A son, but he's a lot older than Idris.'

Abu-Rous nodded. 'Nothing must befall my family,'

he said. 'I don't know what I would do if anything happened to them.'

Shepherd's lips tightened. David White had probably felt exactly the same, but there was no way he could tell Abu-Rous that.

48

White accelerated as he joined the motorway. He was taking the M6 heading south, and then the M1 into London. He had thought long and hard about what he should do, but truthfully it had been an easy decision. The black Range Rover was almost certainly a CTSFO vehicle, though the vehicle was also favoured by the SAS. He doubted that it belonged to Abu-Rous, the large BMW was more more his style. CTSFO or SAS, either way they would be carrying guns and know how to use them. If White went up against trained professional killers, it would only end one way, and he wasn't prepared to die just then. He had work to do.

He slowed to keep the Ford Fiesta below the speed limit. There were speed cameras all the way to London and he needed to stay below the radar. Literally and figuratively.

White wanted to kill Abu-Rous, he wanted it so bad that he had to fight the urge to throw caution to the wind and just go in, guns blazing. His heart began to pound so he pushed the thought from his mind and took deep breaths. Abu-Rous could wait. White had other targets. Plenty of other targets. At some point Dan Shepherd and his armed colleagues would be withdrawn, and when that happened, White would be back.

49

Shepherd looked around the bedroom, smiling and nodding. Facing him were three men and one woman, all of them trained to kill. They were seasoned CTS-FOs, hard as nails and twice as sharp, the best of the Met's firearms officers, and they carried themselves accordingly, meeting his gaze with chins jutted up, shoulders back. Shepherd knew two of them by name as he had trained with them at Stirling Lines. Gerry Owen was the most senior of the group, a sergeant with more than fifteen years experience as an armed officer. Owen was one of the officers who shot dead three terrorists in the summer of 2017 after they had run over pedestrians on London Bridge, then attacked Saturday night revellers with knives. Eight people were killed and 48 injured before armed officers confronted the gang in Borough Market. The ring-leader, Khuram Butt, and his accomplices, Rachid Redouane and Youssef Zaghba, all died within seconds as the armed police fired a total of 46 rounds. Although the men were only carrying knives, they were all wearing what looked like explosive belts, so a court ruled that the killings were justified. The joke among the armed officers later was that there was so much lead in the terrorists that they had to be moved with fork lift trucks.

Shepherd had met Owen at Stirling Lines, and been impressed by the officer's drive and commitment. Many armed officers began to wind down when they reached their forties but Owen was like the Energiser

Bunny, he just kept on going.

Nick Brett was the other officer he had met before, running him and his CTSFO colleagues through various training scenarios in the SAS's Killing House. He was a serious, no-nonsense officer though unlike Owen he had never killed anyone.

The male officer that Shepherd hadn't crossed paths with was Simon Wilsher, the youngest member of the team. He was leaning against the wall, his arms folded, chewing gum. He was wearing a black bomber jacket and black jeans and had a cheap Casio watch on his left wrist. Shepherd had smiled when he first noticed the timepiece — a Casio F91W. It was one of the world's most common watches — three million a year had been sold since the Nineties — and it was especially popular with terrorists who liked to use it as a timer on improvised explosive devices. It was regularly found on the wrists of al-Qaeda and ISIS fighters. At some point Shepherd was going to ask Wilsher if he was wearing the watch ironically, but now wasn't the time.

The one female member of the team was Rebecca Reilly, petite with short blonde hair and a sprinkling of freckles over a snub nose. She was wearing a black reefer jacket with the collar up, tight jeans and black Nikes. Like the men, she had a Glock in an underarm holster.

'Right guys,' said Shepherd. He nodded at Reilly. 'And girl. Lady. Sorry.'

'I think of myself as one of the guys, Sir' said Reilly with a grin.

'Good to know,' said Shepherd. 'And it's Dan. Or Spider. I don't have a rank. So, as you already know, we're here to protect one Ahmed Abu-Rous. He's

298

downstairs with his wife and son. So far as the radio is concerned, Abu-Rous is Papa One, Mrs Abu-Rous is Papa Two and the boy is Papa Three. I'm Charlie One, Gerry is Charlie Two, Simon is Charlie Three, Nick is Charlie Four, and last but not least Rebecca is Charlie Five. I'm going to suggest you do eight hour shifts with shifts starting every four hours. So eight hours on, eight hours off, eight hours on. Effectively that means sixteen hour days and I apologise for that, but on the plus side the Met has approved overtime, for a week anyway.'

Brett grinned. 'That's my new kitchen paid for,' he said.

'Every cloud,' said Shepherd. 'Now when you're off duty, you stay in this room and use the bathroom next door. The protection is covert, no outside patrols and we keep away from the windows. Mr Abu-Rous knows that he is to stay inside, and the same goes for his wife and son. The son won't be going to school, anything they need will have to be delivered.'

'So we can't leave the house?' asked Reilly.

'I'm afraid not,' said Shepherd. 'If this was just about scaring the killer off, we'd put a couple of uniforms on the door. This is about catching him in the act.' He reached inside his pocket and pulled out half a dozen head and shoulder shots of White. He handed them out. 'This is the man we think is trying to kill Abu-Rous. His name is David White, and for your ears only he is an analyst on MI5's Middle East and North Africa desk. Also for your ears only, his two daughters were killed in the Hamas attacks of October Seven. His wife recently killed herself, which we believe was the trigger for his actions. White has already killed an associate of Abu-Rous's, and the

299

man's teenage daughter. For him it's personal. He blames these men for the death of his family and is out for revenge. We need to catch him in the act, not scare him off.'

'I heard on the grapevine that Abu-Rous is in Hamas,' said Reilly. 'Is that right?'

'It's true, yes. So was the man that White has already killed. Just so you know, both men helped plan the attacks in Israel.'

Brett held up a hand. 'Wait, what, so we're here to protect a terrorist? Is that what you're saying?'

'I know it sounds topsy turvy but murder is murder, and whatever his motive, David White has killed two people already and plans to kill Mr Abu-Rous and possibly his family.'

'Yeah, but Spider, if members of my family were killed in those attacks I'd be the one hunting them down,' said Brett.

The others nodded in agreement. These were not officers who were trained to turn the other cheek.

'I think we can all empathise with Mr White after what he went through, but that doesn't excuse murder,' said Shepherd.

'Why isn't this Abu-Rous under arrest?' asked Wilsher. 'Hamas is a proscribed terrorist organisation, membership alone is a criminal offence.'

'I hear you,' said Shepherd, holding up his hands. 'All I can tell you is that it's complicated.' He knew that was weak, but he couldn't tell the CTSFOs that Abu-Rous was an MI6 asset. That information had to be restricted to as few people as possible.

'This sucks,' said Owen. 'We're protecting a terrorist, but who was protecting White's daughters when they needed taking care of? They died and we're now being told to protect the man who killed them.'

'Abu-Rous didn't personally kill anyone,' said Shepherd. 'And at the moment he's not a threat to anyone. We've been tasked to keep him alive, and I know you guys are all professionals and will do that to the best of your ability.'

'Spider, if White does turn up with a gun, what are we supposed to do?' asked Reilly quietly.

'You know the drill,' said Shepherd. 'You neutralise the threat.'

'So this is a shoot to kill operation?' asked Wilsher.

'Not unless that is your only option,' said Shepherd. 'I fully empathise with White, he's just a regular guy who has been pushed too far. There but for the grace of God etc etc. So if possible, let's try to stop him without violence. But bear in mind that he has already killed a teenage girl for no other reason than that she was Fayyad's daughter. If he gets one of you in his sights, I don't think he will hesitate to pull the trigger. And your safety is paramount, okay?'

He was faced with a wall of nodding heads, but he could tell from their eyes that they weren't convinced.

50

It had been a year or two since Giles Pritchard had phoned Joel Schwartz so he wasn't sure that the number still worked, but Schwartz answered on the third ring. 'Giles, long time no hear,' he said. 'How can I be of help?'

'What makes you think I need help, Joel?'

Schwarz laughed. It was a strange laugh, the sound always reminded Pritchard of a barking fox. 'Let's be honest, Giles, you only ever call me when you want something.'

'You know me so well,' said Pritchard. 'Something has come up and I'd like a face to face, if you're up for it.'

'Sure,' said Schwartz. 'Official or off the books?

'Oh, no need to make it official yet, I'd just like a chat.'

'We could play squash? It's been ages since we had a game.'

'My knee's playing up at the moment. The doc says I shouldn't put it under any strain. Plus I'd prefer that it was sooner rather than later.'

'How soon?'

'Are you free now?' asked Pritchard.

Schwartz didn't seem perturbed by the request. 'Hyde Park? The bandstand?'

The Israeli Embassy was in South Kensington, close to Kensington High Street, a short walk from Hyde Park. It meant that Pritchard would need to take a cab, but that wasn't a problem 'Perfect,' he said. 'Can we say half an hour?'

'It sounds urgent.'

'No, it's just that I have back to back meetings later this afternoon. Rush, rush, rush.'

'See you in half an hour, then.'

Schwartz was on the embassy staff list as a Public Affairs Manager but in reality he was Mossad's official representative in London. He was generally desk bound and not involved in active operations, but he was the only man permitted to talk to the Press about the organisation's activities, usually off the record.

Schwartz was sitting on a bench overlooking the bandstand when Pritchard arrived, wrapped up in a dark overcoat and sipping a Costa coffee. The wind was tugging at his comb-over. There was another cup on the bench. 'Double shot cappuccino, no sugar,' said Schwartz.

'Brilliant, thank you,' said Pritchard. He sat down and picked up the cup.

Schwartz gestured at the octagonal bandstand. 'One of the oldest bandstands in Britain,' he said. 'It's been there since 1886.'

'Is that a fact?' Pritchard sipped his coffee.

'Prior to that it was in Kensington Gardens. I'm not sure why they moved it. I do know they used to hold concerts in it three times a week. Not so much these days.' He shrugged and sipped his coffee. 'So, what's so urgent, Giles?'

'Oh, I think you know, Joel. And I have to say I'm disappointed in you. I thought we were friends.'

'We are. Of course we are.'

'And yet it seems that you have been running one of my analysts as a double agent.'

Schwartz laughed his strange laugh and waved

a hand. 'That's not what happened at all.' He was smiling but his eyes were ice cold, he was clearly calculating how much trouble he might be in.

'Really? He wasn't passing you information on Hamas officials in the UK?'

'We're allies, Giles. Allies share intelligence, don't they?'

'Of course they do. But the information wasn't shared, it was stolen.'

'Because we were told that the information would not be made available to us. Our prime minister was told by Number Ten that intel on the three Hamas officials who flew in from Egypt on October Six would not be forthcoming.'

'Because the UK couldn't be seen to be cooperating with an assassination operation, obviously.'

'Well, you say 'obviously'. I think we take the same view that George W Bush took after 9-11 — you're either with us or against us. And the fact that your government refused to help us was more a reflection of a growing anti-Semitic sentiment in the UK, as demonstrated by the anti-Israel demonstrations we keep seeing.'

'But the end result was that you coerced one of our analysts to become a double agent.'

'There wasn't much in the way of coercion needed, not after what happened to his family.'

Pritchard sipped his coffee. 'But he wasn't satisfied with just feeding you with information, was he? He wanted more?'

'It became personal for him, and that never ends well.'

'That's down to you, isn't it? You created a monster.'

Schwartz pulled a face. 'I think perhaps we under-estimated his depth of feeling.'

'His whole family had been taken away from him. He was in a mess, emotionally. And once you approached him, the floodgates opened. Now he's on a rampage and we have to stop him. And by we I mean MI5.'

'What is it you want, Giles? An apology? You think I need to apologise for loving my country.'

Pritchard shook his head. 'I don't want an apology, that doesn't help us.'

'So what, then?'

'I want to understand what has happened. And I want to resolve this without killing David, because as things stand, that's where we're heading. Was it you who went to MI6 and told them what David had done?'

'No. Definitely not.'

'But you know who did?'

'This conversation is the first I've heard of this.'

Pritchard looked Schwartz in the eyes, trying to work out if he was telling the truth or not. 'But you knew that David had killed Fayyad, and his daughter.'

Schwartz wrinkled his nose and nodded. 'I had been told that, yes.'

'Which means that you are in contact with the assassination team, because we have kept Fayyad's death under wraps. Seems to me that you're being used, Joel. You're getting the mushroom treatment?'

'Keeping me in the dark and feeding me bullshit?' Schwartz shrugged. 'You might be right.'

'David was your man, you were running him. Yet they went behind your back and betrayed him, knowing that there is a good chance he'll end up dead.'

Schwartz's eyes narrowed. 'You're not trying to

turn me are you, Giles? Because you'd be wasting your time. My first loyalty is to my country. Always has been and always will be.'

'I wouldn't insult you by trying to turn you, Joel,' said Pritchard. 'If I was, I'd be warning you that under the 2023 National Security Act, the offence of obtaining or disclosing protected information is now punishable with a maximum sentence of life imprisonment.' He smiled thinly. 'I just need your help, that's all. As a friend.'

'What sort of help?'

'First, are you still in contact with David?'

Schwartz shook his head. 'He hasn't replied to my last few messages.'

'His regular phone or a burner?'

'We didn't use burner phones. We played badminton and he had registered me as a contact. Everything was above board.'

'With me you played squash.'

Schwartz grinned. 'I play a lot of games.'

'Yes, you do. A man of many talents. Obviously if he does get in touch, I'd like you to let me know.'

'I will.'

'And I have another favour to ask.'

'Ask away.'

'I need you to tell the Mossad hit team to stand down.'

'For how long?'

'For the foreseeable future. At least until we have resolved the David White matter.'

'I'm not sure they'll listen to me, Giles.'

'Fayyad's death has changed everything. If any more Hamas people are killed, no matter the circumstances, red flags are going to be raised. They need to down tools.'

'I can ask, but I can't guarantee they'll agree.'

'Then you need to explain how important this is. We can't have them muddying the waters. We need to have all our attention fixed on David. This is important, Joel.'

'I understand.'

Pritchard nodded. 'Good. And one final thing. Did you ask David to check up on any other names for you?'

'Just the three who flew in from Egypt. Mohammed Sharif, Ahmed Abu-Rous and Ibrahim Fayyad. Why do you ask?'

'I just wondered how many Hamas officials and supporters he was looking at.'

'We only gave him the three names.'

'Were you planning to run more names by him?'

Schwartz shifted uncomfortably on the bench. 'I suppose so.'

'So this hit team would be ongoing?

'I am not party to their mission parameters,' said Schwartz. 'I was just told to make contact with David and assess how receptive he would be to helping us.'

'And he was very receptive?'

'Initially he was hesitant, but his mood changed after his wife's suicide.'

'Which is hardly surprising. He was in a very vulnerable place and you took advantage of that.'

'I did what I had to do, Giles. I could hardly refuse.'

'And did David give you intel on all three names?'

Schwarz shook his head. 'Just Sharif. He said it was difficult because MI5 does not trust its own people.'

'But clearly he had Fayyad's details.'

'Clearly. Though I suppose he could have got them

307

after he gave me the intel on Sharif and I made it clear he couldn't have an operational role.'

Pritchard smiled and nodded. Donna Walsh had already ascertained that White had done a search for the three names at the same time, so White had clearly been playing his cards close to his chest. Presumably he had given Sharif's details to Schwartz to feel him out, and once he realised that he wasn't going to be allowed to take part in the actual killings he had kept the rest of the intel to himself. 'And just to confirm, you didn't give him any other names to check?'

'I swear,' said Schwartz.

'Okay. I'll have to take your word on that, though God help you if I find out that you've lied to me. And I need you to get the Mossad team to step down. We can probably keep a lid on the two deaths that have happened, but if there are any more it's bound to get into the public domain.'

'And that wouldn't be good for you, Giles, would it?'

'Or you, Joel. I can see two stellar careers coming to an abrupt end.'

Schwartz smiled thinly. 'I will speak to them, as a matter of urgency.'

Pritchard sipped his coffee. 'Thank you.'

51

Edgware Road, the bustling thoroughfare that ran between Marble Arch and the Marylebone flyover had many nicknames — Little Cairo, Little Beirut or Little Arabia were just a few. Anti-terrorist police referred to the street in more colourful terms, not the least because millions of pounds every year went through its currency exchange shops, helping to fund terrorist organisations around the world. For many years the capital's most secure anti-terrorist police station — Paddington Green had been located at the flyover end of the road. The station was used as an interrogation centre for prisoners suspected of terrorism and in the basement were sixteen special cells and a separate custody suite. Famous residents included members of the IRA, British Asians released from Guantanamo Bay, and the infamous July 2005 London bombers. Not the July 5 bombers because they all killed themselves attacking the London Tube system, but the wannabes who tried to replicate the attacks two weeks later but had allowed their explosives to deteriorate to the point where their rucksack bombs didn't go off. There was a lot of black humour among the anti-terrorist police that day.

The station was closed for good in 2018, and demolished to make way for a development of almost eight hundred homes, shops, cafes and community spaces. But while the police station had long gone, Edgware Road continued to be a hub for the capital's Arab Muslim community, and both sides of the road were packed with Middle Eastern restaurants, cafes and shops. As White walked south along the road towards Marble Arch he heard languages from all over the Middle East, but mainly Arabic. Bearded men sat at outdoor tables smoking hookah pipes and drinking coffee, usually with at least one mobile phone in front of them. Women in full burkhas walked by, usually with a child in a pushchair, often in groups, blocking the pavement as if it was their right of way. White kept his head down, avoiding eye contact. London generally no longer felt welcoming to Jews, but Edgware Road was the epicentre of Muslim hatred. When White had returned to London after he had been rescued, he learnt that following the Hamas attacks on Israel, cars drove up and down the road, sounding their horns and waving Palestinian flags, celebrating the massacre.

There were dozens of currency exchange outlets along the road, often combined with a shop selling cheap electrical goods or tacky souvenirs. The currency exchanges were legitimate licensed businesses, but it was rare to see a tourist exchanging a wad of dollars or Euros for British pounds. Most of the exchanges were there to carry out hawala transactions, the money transfer service used by terrorists and criminals around the world, but primarily in Asia.

Hawala was based on trust, and honour, and the end result was transferring money around the world without actually moving it. A client would hand cash to a hawala broker — or hawaladar — in his own country, to be transferred to another client in a different country. The hawaladar then called another hawaladar in the recipient's city and told him how much money was to be paid, and gives him a password that had to be used to collect the money. The money would be handed over and both hawaladars entered the transaction into their books. At some point the books would be balanced, which is where the trust came in.

White had a hoodie pulled low over his face, and was wearing sunglasses and a medical face mask. It wasn't much of a disguise and he was fairly sure that facial recognition would pick him up some point, no matter how he turned his face away from the plethora of CCTV cameras that covered the road. He was fairly sure that MI5 already knew what he was doing, all that mattered was that he didn't get caught in the act.

His backpack was slung over his left shoulder. Inside was one of his Glocks, the silencer already attached. It was a Glock 19 with fifteen rounds in the magazine. Fifteen would be more than enough, he had planned an assassination, not a gunfight.

He slowed as he approached the souvenir shop that housed Mohammed Sanawer's currency exchange. He had walked past it the previous night after it had closed, to familiarise himself with the layout. The wall to the left was lined with t-shirts and sweatshirts, in the middle of the shop were three lines of wheeled suitcases, mainly with London scenes printed on the side, and to the right were racks of cheap souvenirs including, pens, key rings, shopping bags and snow globes. The currency exchange was at the far end of the shop and to the right of it was the shop's cash register. There were no CCTV cameras in the shop, Sanawer was a man who valued his privacy and the privacy of his clients.

Mohammed Sanawer was a Palestinian who had

moved to the UK following the Gaza War which took place over the winter of 2008. The Israelis referred to the conflict as Operation Cast Lead, while the Palestinians called it the Gaza Massacre. More than twelve hundred Palestinians were killed in the conflict, including Sanawer's parents, two brothers and three of his children. After the ceasefire, Sanawer had managed to get to London with two of his wives and six of his children, where he had been granted asylum, the right to remain, and eventually British citizenship. He had brought a third wife and their two children over in 2013 and another four children were born in the UK. His three wives lived in separate houses in West London, along with the twelve children that Sanawer had fathered. Only the sons were allowed to help run the business. His daughters, once they reached eighteen, were married off to Palestinians, all of whom were active members of Hamas. MI5 had blocked four of the grooms from setting foot in the country, but two had been allowed in.

Hamas supporters were frequent visitors to the currency exchange, but as all transfers were cash-based and always took place behind the closed door. MI5 had never had enough evidence to close the operation down.

White stopped at the entrance to the shop and adjusted his backpack as he looked around. The only customers were two Canadian tourists, their country's red maple leaf proudly displayed on the rucksacks, looking through the t-shirt display. White walked by them to the back of the shop. There was an Arab man in his twenties sitting behind the shop cash register, his head bent over his mobile phone. It wasn't one of Sanawer's sons or any of the relatives that had appeared in MI5's surveillance photographs.

White walked up to the currency exchange. Behind the glass partition was another Arab man, sitting on a stool reading an Arabic newspaper. White recognised him as one of Sanawer's sons. Muhmad Sanawer, thought by MI5 to be a Hamas fundraiser and financier though their suspicions had never been proved. The fact that Sanawer only used his sons to help him run the business meant that it had been impossible to get anyone close to the heart of the operation. Muhmad looked up from his newspaper as White approached.

'I have some money I want to send to Egypt,' said White.

Muhmad spoke to him in Arabic but White shrugged. 'Sorry mate, I don't speak Arabic. I was born here. But I need to send this to Cairo, for my family.' He pulled a thick wad of fifty pound notes from his jacket pocket. Actually there were only half a dozen genuine notes, the rest was blank paper, but the man wouldn't be able to tell that. White gestured at the door which had two signs on it, one saying 'STAFF ONLY', the other in Arabic. 'Can I go through? Mr Sanawer knows me.' He waved the money again.

White knew from the MI5 file that the hawala business was conducted behind the door, and that Sanawer was usually accompanied by at least one of his five sons. The man nodded and gestured at the door. White shoved the notes back in his pocket and pushed the door open. The office beyond was windowless, about twelve feet square with three desks, each with two computers. Against the wall to the right

313

was a huge safe with a chrome wheel and a keypad. The safe was open and White saw stacks of banknotes and piles of manila files. High on one wall was a TV screen showing the Al-Jazeera news channel with the sound muted.

Sanawer was sitting by the desk next to the safe on a high-backed leather executive chair. He was in his seventies with a neatly trimmed grey beard and gold-framed spectacles. He had a woven skull cap on his head and a chain of Muslim prayer beads in his right hand. Sitting at the desk opposite him was his oldest son, 48-year-old Nabil. Nabil was wearing a brightly coloured Versace shirt and tight blue Versace jeans. He had a Patek Philippe watch on his left wrist and White was reasonably sure it was the genuine article.

White let the door close behind him. 'I have some money I need to send to Cairo,' he said, swinging his backpack off his shoulder.

Sanawer waved his left hand impatiently. White smiled and put his backpack on the unoccupied desk and unzipped it. He had his back to Sanawer but Nabil could see what he was doing.

He pulled out the gun and slipped his finger over the trigger. Nabil threw up his hands and opened his mouth to speak but before he could say anything, White pulled the trigger twice. It was difficult to see the blood against the garish shirt but Nabil fell back, the life fading from his eyes.

White turned the gun on Sanawer who was star-ing at his dying son with a look of horror in his eyes. 'From here I will go to kill your three wives, and your children,' hissed White. 'And as each of them dies I will tell them that they are dying because of you.'

'Who are y-y-you?' stammered Sanawer.

314

'Just a Jew,' said White. 'Just one of the dirty Jews that you would happily wipe from the surface of the earth.'

He walked over to the door that led to the currency exchange booth and pulled it open. Muhmad was twisting around on his stool, the newspaper on his lap. White shot him in the chest, twice, then stepped aside so that Sanawer could see his son die.

As Muhmad slid off his stool and fell to the ground, White closed the door and aimed his gun at Sanawer. 'Two down, ten to go,' said White.

Sanawer was shaking his head in shocked disbelief, unable to comprehend what he was seeing.

'Look at me,' said White.

Sanawer turned his head slowly. Tears were running down his cheeks into his beard. 'G-g-god will p-p-punish you for this,' he said.

'I can look God in the eye and justify what I've done,' said White. 'I don't think you will ever be able to do the same. Go to hell.' He pulled the trigger and the bullet ripped through Sanawer's throat. Blood spurted down his robe and over the desk as he slumped back in his chair. White stood and watched him die. He wasn't planning on killing Sanawer's wives, he just wanted him to die in anguish. The fact that he believed it was punishment enough. Sanawer glared at White with hatred for several seconds as blood continue to gush from his throat, then his chest heaved one final time, and he went still. White hurried over to the open safe, grabbed handfuls of banknotes, and shoved them into his backpack. He slung the backpack over his shoulder and pulled open the door. The man sitting at the cash register was holding his phone to his ear as he stared at Nabil's

315

body in the currency exchange booth. White pointed the gun at him. 'Give me the phone,' he said, holding out his left hand.

The man did as he was told. White glanced at the screen. He had been calling 999 but the call hadn't been answered. The days of a 999 emergency call being answered immediately were long gone. White dropped it on to the floor and stamped on it, hard.

'How do you know Sanawer?' he asked the man. 'Is he your father? Your uncle?'

The man's mouth worked soundlessly, his eyes wide and fearful.

White pointed the gun at the man's face. 'Who is he to you?'

The man shook his head. 'Nothing. I just work here. He's my boss. That's all.' He had a strong Essex accent. 'To be honest, mate, him and his family are right pricks.'

White stared at the man for several seconds, then decided that the man was telling the truth. He nodded curtly and walked away. The Canadian tourists had gone and there were two women in headscarves standing by the display of London t-shirts, hugging each other for comfort. White waved the gun at them and they screamed in terror. 'Shalom, ladies,' he said. 'Shalom.' He shoved the gun into his backpack and walked out of the shop. No one outside the shop appeared to have heard the shots and no one gave him a second look as he walked quickly back down the road towards the former Paddington Green police station.

52

Pritchard shook his head as he watched the video. It showed CCTV footage from a Westminster Council camera on Edgware Road, not far from the shop where White had shot dead Muhmad Sanawer and his two sons. A man was walking away from the shop, his head down, the hoodie, sunglasses and face mask concealing his face. 'This is a mess, Donna,' he said. Even though his face was hidden, it was clearly White. 'He's on a spree now.'

'Well, yes, you could say that,' said Walsh. She was standing behind him, looking over his shoulder at the terminal that was showing the video. 'But he only killed Sanawer and his sons who are all Hamas fundraisers. He didn't kill a member of staff and he walked by two Muslim women who were in the shop at the time.'

Pritchard wrinkled his nose. 'That doesn't make it any better,' he said.

'Agreed, but David isn't a random spree killer. He's not even targeting Muslims, he is very specific who about his targets are. Money is constantly moving from London to Gaza through Sanawer's shop, so there's a very good chance that he helped finance the October Seven attacks. If he was in a true anti-Muslim rampage, he could easily have shot the women in the shop. In fact he said 'Shalom' to them as he walked by.'

'Shalom?'

'Hebrew for peace. He was probably being ironic,

317

but he could just as easily have shot them. The fact that he didn't, and didn't shoot the shop assistant, suggests that he is targeting his attacks.'

Pritchard sat back in his chair. Walsh walked around his desk and stood facing him, waiting to see what he wanted to do. News of the killings had already been broadcast on TV and radio and the internet was buzzing with it. There were hundreds of videos of the outside of the shop, cordoned off with blue and white police tape as white-overalled CSOs moved back and forth from their vans. 'Is anyone saying it's racial yet?'

'The police have done as we asked and put out a line saying that it was an armed robbery.'

'Let's hope that sticks,' he said. 'How far were you able to track White?'

'Down Edgware Road to Harrow Road, then along Harrow Road to the canal. Head down all the way so we don't have his face. We lost him at the canal.'

Pritchard nodded. 'He lives in St John's Wood, that whole area is his stamping ground. He'll know where all the cameras are.'

'He didn't go home, we have someone outside keeping watch.'

'Oh, I don't think for one moment he'll go home, he's far too savvy for that. But he'll know where to leave a vehicle where it can't be caught on CCTV. And he took the gun with him this time?'

Walsh nodded. 'The shop assistant said he put it into his backpack as he left the shop.'

'He knows we're on to him,' said Pritchard. 'So it no longer matters if he's apprehended with a gun or not.' He leaned forward, rested his elbows on the desk and steepled his fingers against his chin. 'So how does he know, that's the question?'

'He must have known it would always be a matter of time before we would ID him.'

'Yes, but why now? Why so soon? He killed Fayyad and his daughter but we kept a lid on that. His name hasn't been given to the Press. Why would he think that we'd ID'd him after one killing? The only way we know he killed Fayyad is because Mossad told us. And he couldn't have foreseen that, could he? And having killed Fayyad, why didn't he target Abu-Rous? He got all Abu-Rous's details from the MI5 database at the same time that he was looking at Sharif and Fayyad. He gave Sharif's details to the Israelis, he killed Fayyad, so why didn't he try to kill Abu-Rous? Instead of going for the third Hamas guy who was on the plane out of Egypt, he targets a man who hasn't been out of the country for two years at least.'

'Presumably he targeted Sanawer because he helped finance the October Seven attacks.'

Pritchard waggled his head from side to side. 'Yes, I get that. I can see how David would think that Sanawer was a valid target. But he had the intel on Abu-Rous all ready to go. Why not follow through on that?'

'Because as you say, he knew we are on to him. So he goes for a target that he assumes we won't know about.'

'That's how I read it, yes.' Pritchard sat back in his chair. 'I suppose someone here might have tipped him off. A friend, maybe.'

'A Jewish friend?'

Pritchard scowled. 'I don't want to go there, Donna. I really don't. There's no place for a religious witch hunt here. And if Mossad did have another agent in place in Thames House, they wouldn't want him warning David. They're the ones who betrayed him in the first place.' He frowned. 'What if he had already targeted Abu-Rous but knew that we were protecting him? He could have seen the CTSFOs go in to the house. Or Shepherd. He knows Shepherd. If he knew that Abu-Rous was being protected, he might well pull back and choose another target.' He nodded. 'That makes sense.' He looked up at Walsh. 'So we need to find out who else David has been looking at. If he got sight of Sanawer's file there are bound to be others over the past few weeks, and we can assume that he was pulling his trick of using someone else's log in.'

'I'll get the guys on it straight away,' said Walsh. 'What about Dan?'

'Let me talk to him. If David has switched targets, he might be better placed in London.'

53

White parked his Ford Fiesta and walked to Limehouse Basin. The marina was two miles east of London Bridge and home to more than a hundred boats. He took his bag from the boot and carried it down to the jetties. Most of the boats were moored all year round and were connected to the marina's electricity and water supply. White was staying on a forty foot narrowboat called *Over The Hull*. It was dark green with a gold trim, and though it was more than twenty years old it had been well cared for and was in good condition.

He had spent his first few nights away from home staying in cheap hotels in Bayswater, and while they had accepted cash he figured it was only a matter of time before MI5 started checking hotels and guest houses across the city so he decided to look for something more secure. Limehouse Basin was a good choice, it was close to Central London and there were always boats to rent. Some owners had switched to Airbnb but many preferred to take cash in hand to avoid paying tax on the income.

He had wandered around the jetties until he had spotted *Over The Hull*. There had been a sign in the window saying that the boat was for rent, and he had called the phone number. The owner lived on a second, larger, boat moored a short walk away. He was in his late seventies or early eighties but trim and fit with a full head of white hair that merged into a close cropped beard. He'd introduced himself as Bill. White said that he needed somewhere to stay for a week or so and was happy to pay cash in advance. Bill's only concern was whether White intended to take the boat on a trip but White assured him he wasn't going anywhere. Bill was curious about why White needed a place to stay and White told him that his wife had died and he couldn't face being in his house, there were just too many memories. The lie was close enough to the truth that tears had welled up in White's eyes, and Bill had actually stepped forward and hugged him, promising him that he could stay on the boat as long as he wanted.

White had handed Bill a wad of fifty pound notes, Bill gave him a key, and the deal was done. Bill had spent a few minutes showing White how to use the shower and toilet. There was a microwave and an electric oven. There were four solar panels on the roof of the boat but power came from an electric socket on the dock and water was piped in. 'I'm just down there aways,' Bill had said, pointing down the dock. 'Any problems, give me a call or walk down. My boat's the *Narrow Escape*.'

White looked around as he headed for the boat. He wasn't expecting trouble, but he could never let his guard down. He had his hoodie up and he turned his face away from the CCTV cameras that he passed. He climbed on to the stern and unlocked the door that led down into the saloon. He took a final look around before heading down and closing the door behind him.

The boat was compact but had everything he needed. The saloon had a dinette with two wooden benches facing each other across a wooden table. Bill had said it could be folded into a double berth if needed. Next to the saloon was the galley, with a fridge, a twin hotplate, an oven and microwave.

Beyond the galley was a shower room with a WC and a tiny washbasin, and in the prow was the bedroom, with a double bed and a built-in wardrobe. White put what few clothes he had in the wardrobe, then sat down at the dinette. He realised that anyone walking by could see in so he pulled the curtain closed. He took out his iPad and switched it on, then called up the photographs he'd taken in Thames House.

Two dozen men featured in the files he'd photographed, all of them Palestinians. All had been investigated by MI5 at some point, and while the investigators had no doubt that they had been funding or supporting Hamas, there was never enough evidence to secure a conviction. Of the twelve, seven had British citizenship, three had the right to remain in the country, and two had asylum claims pending. Two of the men lived in Glasgow with their families, three were in Manchester, and the rest lived in and around London.

White concentrated on the London targets, seven in all. Most of them were aged fifty and above, but two were in their twenties. One had served two years in prison for an arson attack on a synagogue in East London. Raed Jabari had thrown a petrol bomb at the door and only the quick action of a security guard had prevented the building going up in flames. There were more than a hundred worshippers in the synagogue at the time, but no one was injured. Jabari was caught on CCTV and when police searched his house they found Hamas literature in his bedroom and terrorism material on his computer. Despite all the evidence, Jabari was only sentenced to four years in prison, of which he actually only served two. White shook his head in disbelief. Two years behind bars for a racist attack that could have killed God knows how many people. There was something very wrong with the British justice system.

If anything Jabari became even more radicalised in prison and on release he set up an anti-Semetic website, promoting acts of aggression against Jews around the world, Jabari went into overdrive after the October Seven attacks, posting videos of the Hamas fighters killing civilians and praising their heroism. When Jewish women in London began putting up posters calling for the release of the hostages being held by Hamas, Jabari filmed himself ripping the posters down and spitting at them.

White's heart pounded as he read through Jabari's file. He was angry at the man, but he was just as angry at the British Establishment for not punishing Jabari severely enough. Two years in prison for setting fire to a synagogue was an insult. The website he had set up was blatantly anti-Semetic and promoted terrorism and acts of violence, and he had racially abused a Jewish woman on camera as he pulled down her posters. The police had stood by and done nothing. But if someone was even slightly critical of Islam on social media, they risked the police turning up on their doorstep and charging them with hate crimes. The police were scared of the Muslim community and treated them with kid gloves. The Jewish community adopted a much lower profile and weren't known for their violence and disregard for the country's laws and customs, so they were treated with indifference if not outright contempt.

White sat back and took deep breaths to calm

himself down. If the Establishment didn't want to punish Jabari, then White would. He would do what needed to be done.

54

Shepherd's mobile rang and he pulled it from his pocket. It was Giles Pritchard, calling him direct. He winced. A direct call from the MI5 director was almost never good news. He was in the kitchen with Boylan, who was waiting for confirmation that he could leave the house and head back to the office. Boylan had made coffee but it was weak and insipid and Shepherd wasn't enjoying it. He was hungry, too, and Abu-Rous hadn't offered them food. The fridge was packed with cold meats, cheese and various pastries, and there was a large bowl of fruit on the island but Shepherd didn't want to antagonise Abu-Rous by taking so much as an apple without permission. He held up the phone. 'I've got to take this,' he said. He went into the hall and along to a music room with a baby grand piano and a Bang and Olufsen sound system before taking the call.

'Dan, we have a problem,' said Pritchard.

Shepherd didn't bother feigning surprise, he just said 'Okay.'

'David White has just killed three more Palestinians in London. A currency exchange in Edgware Road. He shot Mohammed Sanawer and two of his sons. He left behind a witness so we're sure it's him.'

'Sanawer is a major Hamas fundraiser, right? He gives speeches at mosques all over London, he's been on our watch list for years.'

'Oh, he's a thorn in our side, no question of that. And every operation we have ever launched against him has got nowhere. But that's no excuse for killing him, obviously.'

'So David must have gathered intel on Sanawer,' said Shepherd. 'Why didn't we know that?'

'The name would have come up all the time at MANAD. Sanawer and his sons are frequent visitors to Palestine. But Donna is checking log in records as we speak. If he did look specifically at Sanawer, there's a good chance he dipped into other files at the same time. But the big question is why he didn't go after Abu-Rous? He had Abu-Rous's details, and he had no qualms about taking out Fayyad.'

'He might have taken a look at the house and seen the CTSFO vehicle,' said Shepherd. 'A black Range Rover with tinted windows was parked outside for all to see. I had it moved into the garage, but it was there for most of the morning.'

'How did that happen?'

'Because the MI6 guy they sent is as much use as a chocolate teapot,' said Shepherd. 'He had the CTSFOs upstairs because he didn't want to upset Abu-Rous and he was allowing the family to sit in the conservatory in full view of the garden. We were lucky that David didn't make a move because he'd probably have gotten away with it.'

'But you have a lid on it now?'

'We're good. But Abu-Rous isn't happy. He keeps making noises about flying to Qatar.'

'He needs to know that he's very much on Mossad's shit list and they'll have no problem getting to him in Qatar.'

'I made that clear to him.'

'But he doesn't know about David?'

'No. Neither does the chocolate teapot, apparently.

But I had to brief the CTSFOs. They need to know who they're up against. So what do you think, that David has discounted Abu-Rous as a target and has moved on?'

'That's supposition, and we both know how suppositions can lead to problems.'

'Can we at least prove that David came to Edgbaston?'

'I don't see how, not at the moment anyway. He's using burner phones and we don't know what vehicle he's using. Presumably he bought a second hand car for cash.'

'He's going to run out of cash eventually.'

'We think he took money from the currency exchange. We're saying that it was a robbery, and according to the surviving brothers there's close to twenty five thousand pounds missing.'

'So no one realises that this was a revenge killing?'

'The one witness said he thought the killer was Egyptian. Must have been something that David said, but yes, they don't know that the Sanawers were killed because of their Palestine connection. What do you think, Dan? Do you think David has just put Abu-Rous on the back burner or has he given up for good?'

'I'm not sure I know him well enough to make that call,' said Shepherd. 'I only met him twice — out in Gaza and once in Thames House.'

'True, but you're good at reading people. I've met him a few times but only as his boss's boss so he was on his best behaviour.'

Shepherd thought for several seconds. 'He blames Hamas for the loss of his family, so he sees anyone connected to Hamas as a valid target. But the three men who flew out of Egypt, he knows that they planned or funded the massacre. He's so full of hatred for them that he killed Fayyad's daughter. That more than anything shows how unbalanced he has become. That's true hatred, and it's not something he'll be able to control, which means that he won't be able to walk away from Abu-Rous. He'll be back. Unfinished business.'

'That sounds about right,' said Pritchard. 'So are you okay to stay there?'

'Unless you find a way of tracking him, then I think it's best,' said Shepherd. 'What about the CTSFOs?'

'We can leave them in place for a few days at least,' said Pritchard. 'I'll let you know if that changes.'

Pritchard ended the call and Shepherd put the phone away. As he left the room, he saw Abu-Rous coming down the stairs. 'Is everything okay?' Abu-Rous asked.

'I was just checking in with the office,' said Shepherd. 'I wanted to ask you about catering arrangements for the security team. They're going to need feeding, plus they tend to drink a lot of coffee and tea. Are you okay with them using the kitchen?'

'Can't they bring in food from the outside?'

'Well, in theory, yes. But every time a delivery driver turned up we'd be in full security mode. Every visitor to the house is a potential threat.'

Abu-Rous forced a smile. 'My wife will not be happy to have strangers using her kitchen.'

'We'll keep it to a minimum, Mr Abu-Rous. I promise.'

He nodded. 'Very well. I will explain the situation to my wife.' He looked at his watch. 'How long do you think this will go on for?'

'That's an impossible question to answer. Until

there is no longer a threat to you and your family.'

'So the police are hunting this Mossad team?'

'Not the police, no. Publicity would be counter-productive. So it will be MI5 which is doing the hunting.'

Abu-Rous grinned. 'I knew you were a spy.'

Shepherd held up a hand. 'I'm just here to supervise your security,' he said.

'So you've done this before? Protected people?'

'Several times.'

'And how does it usually work out?'

Shepherd smiled. 'I haven't had any complaints.'

Abu-Rous looked at him with unsmiling eyes. 'Well you wouldn't, not if the people you were trying to help ended up dead.'

'They didn't,' said Shepherd. 'You have my word on that.'

55

White drank from his bottle of water as he stared through the windscreen. He was dressed all in black and his backpack was in the footwell of the passenger seat. The Fiesta was parked down the road from where Raed Jabari lived with his parents, in a three bedroom semi-detached house. The front garden had been paved over and there were two cars parked there, a white Prius and a red Toyota Yaris. He had watched Raed Jabari and his father return home at just after seven thirty. They came from the direction of the West London Islamic Centre, which was Ealing's main mosque. They went inside and the light went on in the front room and then the flickering light on the curtains suggested they were watching television. The television and light went off at eleven o'clock and lights went on in the upstairs bedroom.

White had checked the electoral register and there were only three people living in the house — Raed Jabari, his father Bashir Jabari and his older brother, Jemal. There was no mention of a woman, so Bashir Jabari's wife had either died or left. Bashir Jabari was a GP, currently under suspension for being a member of the Hizb ut-Tahrir terrorist group, and for posting anti-Semetic comments on his Facebook page. Jemal was an Uber driver who, like his brother, had been on MI5's watch list ever since he was a teenager. The police had always suspected that Jemal was also involved in the arson attack on the synagogue but Raed had always insisted that he acted alone, and accepting his guilty plea was the easy option. Both the brothers had been arrested as teenagers after assaulting a young Muslim girl who had been seen out with a white boyfriend. The girl's brother had recruited Jemal and Raed and several others to give her and the boyfriend a beating. The boy had run away when he saw the gang approaching, and they had laid into the girl. Jemal and Raed had pulled out knives and slashed the girl across her face and arms. The attack took place in front of dozens of witnesses in Ealing Broadway shopping centre, but by the time the police mounted an investigation all the witnesses had incurred memory loss and the girl was nowhere to be found. Relatives said she had gone to Pakistan to marry her childhood sweetheart. She was never seen again and Jemal and Raed were never charged with the attack.

By midnight, the house was in darkness. During all the time he had been sitting outside the house, White had not seen a single police officer. The days of constables patrolling a beat were long gone, now they travelled in vans or cars and only arrived when summoned.

He left it until two o'clock in the morning before driving around the corner and parking a hundred yards away from the house. He pulled his backpack out of the footwell and got out of the car.

He walked back to the house, keeping a watchful eye out for other pedestrians, but he was alone on the street. He turned into the driveway and walked between the Prius and the Yaris and down the side of the house. There were glass panels in the kitchen door. Breaking them would risk waking up the occupants so he walked back to the front of the house. He took off his backpack and opened it. Inside were two squeezy bottles that had contained washing up liquid. He had emptied the bottles, washed and dried them, then filled them with petrol syphoned from his car. He took out one of the bottles, opened the cap and stuck it through the letter box. In less than a minute he had emptied all the petrol into the hall. The vapour stung his eyes and he blinked away tears. He put the bottle back into his backpack, took a quick look around to reassure himself that no one was walking by, then took a box of matches from his pocket. He lit one and pushed it through the letter box. Almost immediately he heard the 'whoosh' of the petrol igniting.

He walked quickly back around the side of the house, taking the second bottle out of his backpack. He used his elbow to smash one of the glass panels in the kitchen door, then quickly squirted the petrol across the kitchen floor and over the kitchen cabinets that were in range. Again the vapour made his eyes water. He emptied the bottle, lit a match and flicked it through the broken window. The petrol ignited immediately and he took a step back. The flames engulfed the kitchen cabinets and the room quickly filled with black smoke.

The nearest fire station was in Uxbridge Road, only a few minutes away with the blues and twos on, but a few minutes were all that he needed. The smoke would spread quickly, and providing the men didn't wake up, they would die in their sleep. If they did wake up, the only way out would be down the stairs, which would take them directly into the path of the flames, or to jump out of the windows. White took his gun from the backpack. If they did manage to jump and escape the flames, he'd be waiting for them.

56

Shepherd's phone rang. It was Pritchard. He sighed and took the call, knowing that it almost certainly wasn't going to be good news. 'David White has killed again,' said Pritchard. 'A father and two sons in Ealing, all on our watch list. He set fire to their house. They died before the fire brigade got there.'

'That's not good.'

'It gets worse,' said Pritchard. 'We've found the Thames House log on he used to get Sanawer's details. We don't have CCTV but it's definitely him. He was on for almost an hour during which time he looked at more than two dozen files, including the files on the family in Ealing.'

'So we know who else he's targeting?'

'We know the two dozen files he looked at, but we've no way of knowing which of them he's going to go after. Some of the files were of men in prison, a couple have left the country. Looks like he was fishing for targets.'

'That's a lot of files,' said Shepherd. 'How did he get the information out of Thames House? I'm assuming his memory isn't as good as mine, and the terminals don't have USB sockets.'

'We saw him taking screenshots with an iPad. Easy enough to do. The question is, what do we do about Abu-Rous?'

'What do you want to do?' asked Shepherd.

'It's a tough call. We've got potentially two dozen or so potential targets now, and most of them are in

London. I don't see how we can justify keeping four CTSFOs in Birmingham on the off chance he decides to leave the capital.'

'David is going to want to kill Abu-Rous, there's no doubt about that. Sooner or later he'll be back.'

'I hear you, Dan. But he's in London now, that's where we have the best chance of apprehending him.'

'That might be his plan all along,' said Shepherd.

'What do you mean?'

'If he did realise we were guarding Abu-Rous, he might think that attacking targets in London might persuade us that we were wasting our time. He's worked for MI5 long enough to know how we operate.'

'But how will he know if we've dropped Abu-Rous's protection?'

'He won't. He'll have to come back to check. We need to know what vehicle he's using. Or get a fix on one of his burner phones.'

'As you said, he knows how we operate. He'll be switching phones constantly and the car will be well hidden.'

'Any CCTV around the house he torched?'

'A few council cameras on the roads. We're checking but it'll be a needle in a haystack. Look, Dan, the thing is we know for sure who his possible targets are in London. This is where we need the CTSFOs, not twiddling their thumbs in Birmingham.'

'You want to pull them out?'

'I don't see that I've got a choice. When Abu-Rous was in the firing line it made sense to have enhanced protection, but now he's one of two dozen or so targets.'

Shepherd sighed. 'The difference is that Abu-Rous

is an MI6 asset. There's a duty of care, right?'

'There is. But that duty falls on MI6. I'll talk to Julian Penniston-Hill.'

'That won't do any good if he sends the chocolate teapot back.'

'I'll tell him that.'

'What about me?' asked Shepherd.

'What about you?'

'Are you calling me back to London?'

Pritchard sighed. 'I respect your instincts, Dan. You know I do. So if you think you should stay, then by all means stay. I'll leave it to you.'

'I'll stay, for a day or two anyway.'

'Not a problem,' said Pritchard. 'Stay safe.'

Pritchard ended the call and Shepherd went in search of Gerry Owen. He found him in the kitchen, frying bacon at the stove. 'Just making bacon butties for the guys,' he said. 'Fancy one?'

'Sure,' said Shepherd. Tesco had delivered a week's worth of food the previous evening. Wilsher had done the cooking and produced a very agreeable chicken curry.

'Red sauce or brown?' asked Owen.

'Ah, the eternal question,' said Shepherd. 'I've seen squaddies come to blows over this. But me, I always go with HP.'

'Food of the Gods,' said Owen. 'You made the right call.' He used his spatula to lift out two pieces of fried bacon and put them on a slice of white bread, then went back to the frying pan and dropped in two more slices.

The kitchen door opened and Mrs Abu-Rous appeared, her face contorted with rage. 'What are you doing?' she screamed.

336

Owen took a step back from the stove, the frying pan in his hand, stunned by her ferocity. 'Cooking breakfast,' he said.

She pointed at the frying pan. 'How dare you bring that into my house!' she screamed. 'Shame on you!'

Owen looked down at the bacon, frowning in confusion.

'How dare you! Have you no shame?'

'Mrs Abu-Rous, we meant no disrespect,' said Shepherd. 'We're just feeding our people, that's all!'

'You pollute my kitchen and my house with your filth!' she screamed.

The door opened again. It was Abu-Rous, wearing a gold and red dressing gown over black silk pyjamas. He spoke to his wife in Arabic and she replied, speaking quickly and animatedly with a lot of hand waving.

Owen looked over at Shepherd, still frowning in confusion. 'What the fuck?' he mouthed.

Abu-Rous replied to his wife but whatever he said failed to mollify her and she stormed out of the kitchen, tossing her hair and continuing to rant and rave.

Abu-Rous glared at Shepherd. 'What were you thinking?' he said, and followed his wife out.

Owen grinned at Shepherd. 'I guess she's not a fan of bacon butties, red sauce or brown,' he said.

'I didn't expect her to kick off like that,' said Shepherd. 'The family seems Westernised, it's not as if she wears a burkha or even a headscarf.'

Owen held up the frying pan. 'What do I do with this? She doesn't expect me to throw it away, does she?'

'Just finish up and give the guys their sandwiches,' said Shepherd. 'But make sure that Mrs Abu-Rous

337

doesn't see you. And give the place a good clean.'

Shepherd went through to the hall. Mrs Abu-Rous was heading up the stairs, muttering darkly. Her husband was watching her, his face set like stone.

'I'm so sorry,' said Shepherd. 'I guess we didn't think.'

Abu-Rous turned to look at him. 'No, you didn't. My wife is distraught, as you can see.'

'We'll clean the kitchen from top to bottom, it'll be as if we were never here.'

Abu-Rous shook his head. 'That won't be enough for my wife, unfortunately,' she said. 'She is insisting on the kitchen being replaced. The whole thing. Every cupboard. Every work surface. Every appliance.'

Shepherd frowned. That seemed an over reaction to a few slices of bacon, but he knew better than to say that to Abu-Rous. 'As I said, we'll give it a good clean and I'll throw away any pork products.'

'That will be too little, too late. My wife wants you all out of the house, now.'

'Well she's going to get her wish,' said Shepherd. 'My boss has already said he's recalling the armed police to London.'

Abu-Rous frowned. 'Why? Have they caught the assassins?'

'No, but intel suggests that you are no longer a primary target.'

'You have a spy inside Mossad?'

'I have no idea, all I know is that you are no longer being classed as in immediate danger so the team will be withdrawn. I'll stay, though.'

'Why? If I'm in no danger, why do you have to stay?'

'Because I don't think you should be without protection,' said Shepherd.

'So you disagree with your boss?'

'Disagree is a bit strong,' said Shepherd. 'He's happy for me to stay here for a while longer. Until I'm sure that you and your family are safe.'

'My wife thinks we should go to Qatar. We have friends there.'

'That would be your call, of course,' said Shepherd. 'But Mossad operate around the world. If they want you dead, geography won't be an issue.'

'But I am no longer a primary target, you said?'

'You're not a primary target, but that doesn't mean you've been dropped from their hit list. Three Palestinians were killed in an arson attack in London last night, and my boss takes the view that there will be more attacks in London.'

'And Mossad, if they come for me, they will also target my wife and son?'

'Fayyad's daughter was killed,' said Shepherd, avoiding the question.

'I need to guarantee the safety of my family,' said Abu-Rous. He rubbed the back of his neck. 'I think perhaps they should go and stay in Qatar.'

'That would be your call, Sir.'

'But what do you think? You're the so-called expert.'

Shepherd didn't react to the insult as he considered what to say. David White wanted Abu-Rous dead, that was without doubt. When White had killed Fayyad, he had also shot Fayyad's daughter. But it was almost certainly a case of wrong place, wrong time. If she hadn't been in the house, would White have sought her out? Probably not. 'I think you're probably right, Sir. You're the target, not your wife and son.'

'I'll talk to her,' said Abu-Rous. 'Can you help me

get them to the airport?'

Shepherd nodded. 'Sure, I can do that.'

57

White was sitting in the dinette, the curtains drawn and the light on. He had a soldering iron plugged into one of the galley's electric sockets. He had opened up the Nokia mobile phone to expose the circuit board and was in the process of attaching wires to it. The Nokia 105 was a cheap phone with a very long battery life — up to 22 days in standby mode. It didn't run apps or have a camera, but it was the most popular phone for setting off IEDs, in the Middle East and around the world. White had come across details of many different types of IEDs in his role as a MENAD analyst, but the simplest was using a Nokia 105 to detonate a triacetone triperoxide mixture.

TATP was the explosive that homegrown UK terrorist Richard Reid tried to detonate in his shoe on a flight from Paris to Miami. He'd tried to set off the shoe bomb with a match and failed, and had received three life sentences plus 110 years with no chance of parole, for his trouble. TATP was usually very easy to detonate — a flame would do it, even hitting it with a hammer could set it off. Reid was overpowered by passengers before he managed to detonate the TATP in his shoe, but it had been close.

TATP — also known as the Mother Of Satan — was often used by suicide bombers in Israel, and had been used in the 2017 Manchester Concert bombing and the attempted bombing of a London Tube train at Parsons Green four months later. Terrorists loved it because it was so effective and relatively easy to prepare. When detonated, a few ounces of TATP would produce hundreds of litres of gas in a fraction of a second creating a deadly explosion.

Preparation involved three simple ingredients easily obtained from chemists, hardware stores and make up shops — hydrogen peroxide, acetone, and a strong acid, either sulphuric or hydrochloric. The mixing and crystallisation could be done pretty much anywhere, and while the narrowboat was cramped, there was enough space for White to work. He had made the explosive at night, with the windows open but the curtains drawn. The preparation involved mixing the acetone with the hydrogen peroxide, then adding the acid while stirring. Adding iced water then precipitated the TATP, which was then washed and dried. Over the course of the night he had made half a pound of the explosive, which was sealed in a Tupperware container in the fridge.

White finished his soldering. He checked the circuit then used his burner phone to dial the number of the Nokia. The Nokia vibrated, then half a second later a small bulb in the circuit switched on. White smiled. Perfect. The bulb was from a string of Christmas lights. When the glass was removed from the bulb by gently breaking it, the glowing filament would be more than enough to detonate the explosive. He began gathering up the waste materials and unused chemicals and put them in a black rubbish bag, He planned to dispose of it far from the marina, but first he needed to sleep. He was exhausted and the fumes had given him a splitting headache.

58

Shepherd walked in to the kitchen. Owen was sitting at the island and nursing a cup of coffee. His Glock was on the counter in front of him, next to the remains of his bacon sandwich.

'All good?' asked Shepherd.

Owen nodded. He gestured over at the counter by the fridge. 'Your bacon butty is there, with HP sauce.'

'Mrs Abu-Rous is livid, still.'

Owen shrugged. 'We're here to protect her and her family and she gives me shit about what I want for breakfast?'

'It's not halal.'

'Of course it's not halal, it's bacon. It's her religion, not mine.'

Shepherd fetched his sandwich and sat down on a stool opposite Owen. He bit into it. It did taste good and he couldn't help smiling.

Owen laughed. 'See?'

Shepherd chewed and swallowed. 'I'm a big fan of the bacon butty, but you can understand how it might offend her.' He forced a smile. 'Anyway, it's all going to be moot soon, Mr Abu-Rous is sending her and the kid to Qatar.'

'Because of the bacon?'

'Because I explained to him that they're going to be pulling you sooner rather than later.'

'Why's that?'

'My boss reckons White has earmarked targets in London.'

'So the pressure is off Abu-Rous?'

'My boss says yes, but I'm not sure. I'm going to stay here for a while.'

Owen frowned. 'Why are you so keen to protect him? He's a fucking terrorist. You saw what Hamas did in Israel. Fucking animals.'

Shepherd smiled thinly. There was no way he could tell Owen that Abu-Rous was an MI6 asset. He wasn't sure that it even made a difference — Abu-Rous wasn't helping MI6 out of altruism, he was doing it to further his own ends. And Shepherd didn't believe him when he claimed to have had nothing to do with the October Seven attacks. He had left Egypt with Mohammed Sharif and Ibrahim Fayyad the day before the massacres, that can't have been a coincidence. Shepherd didn't really care whether Abu-Rous lived or died, as Owen had said, he was a terrorist, even if he was cooperating with MI6. But Shepherd did care about David White, and he wanted to do whatever he could to keep the man alive. 'I do worry about the wife and son,' said Shepherd, which was partly true. 'They haven't done anything, they don't deserve to be caught in the crossfire.'

'I didn't realise you were such a softy.' Owen sipped his coffee.

'Only where civilians are concerned,' said Shepherd. 'I've got a son, I wouldn't want him in harm's way because of something I did.' He leaned forward. 'The thing is, when you guys pull out, I don't have a gun.'

Owen put down his mug. 'Well that's because MI5 officers aren't licensed to carry firearms. That's why you call us in.'

'But if you're not here, I'll need a weapon.'

Owen sat back shaking his head. 'I can't give you my gun, Spider.'

'I'm not asking for your sidearm. But you have a gun safe in the Range Rover. What do you have in there?'

'Spider, listen to yourself. I can't go handing out guns.'

'You won't be handing it out to just anyone, Gerry. It's me.'

'I know it's you. But reverse it, back when you were still in the SAS. Would you have given a weapon to someone outside the regiment?'

Shepherd shrugged. 'It would depend on the circumstances.'

'Okay. But what would have happened to your career if it had become common knowledge?'

'That won't happen in this case,' said Shepherd. 'The gun won't leave the house. It's just insurance.'

'Spider, I can't. I just can't. I'd lose my job, my pension, everything.'

Shepherd sighed. 'Okay. Yes, you're right. But what if my boss gives the okay?'

'Your boss would have to talk to my boss, and my boss would have to give the okay. That's the only way I could give you a gun. Sorry.'

Shepherd forced a smile, 'I'll get on it.'

59

David White parked and climbed out of his car. It had taken him almost three hours to drive to Edgbaston. He had made a conscious effort to drive smoothly, the TATP bomb was in the boot and the explosive was unstable at the best of times. He looked around. There was a woman walking her dog in the distance but she was heading away from him. He took out the drone, slotted in a fresh battery, and launched it.

He took the drone up to two hundred feet, then did a slow 360 to get his bearings before heading to the Abu-Rous house. He put the drone in a hover above the front driveway. The Range Rover had gone, as had the white BMW that Dan Shepherd had arrived in. The only vehicles there were the Series Seven BMW and the Mercedes. Had Shepherd and the CTSFOs gone? He had hoped that by carrying out a couple of high profile assassinations in London he would make them think he wasn't after Abu-Rous, but he hadn't expected his ruse to be accepted so quickly.

He took the drone over the garden and aimed the camera at the conservatory windows but couldn't see anyone there. Then he took the drone around the perimeter but there was no sign of any guards.

His plan was to leave the bomb on the front doorstep and ring the bell. He had taped several hundred nails and bolts to act as shrapnel, then wrapped it in bubble wrap and placed it inside a Fortnum & Mason hamper with Abu-Rous's name and address on a label. As an added twist, he had also put the number of the bomb's trigger phone on the label. Hopefully it would be Abu-Rous who answered the doorbell and picked up the box, in which case it would be game over, but if the wife answered, he would wait until she had carried it inside. If Dan Shepherd was still there he probably wouldn't be caught unawares, but if he took it inside then White could detonate it and take out most of the ground floor.

He kept the drone above the house for twenty minutes, then brought it back to the car. He sat by the canal and ate a couple of cheese sandwiches that he'd bought from a motorway service station on the drive up. He considered his options. If the CTSFOs had definitely pulled out, he'd give the bomb a go. If not, he'd take it back to London and use it against one of his targets there. The clock was literally ticking — TATP had a very short shelf life, more so when it wasn't being kept in a fridge.

60

Shepherd was making himself a coffee when Gerry Owen came in from the hall. He had his own gun in a holster on his thigh, but he was holding another Glock in a nylon underarm holster. Owen placed it on the island and gave Shepherd a mock bow. 'Your wish is my command, oh master,' he said.

Shepherd grinned and picked up the gun. 'Your boss okayed it?'

'He wasn't happy, but yes. 'Fucking spooks shouldn't be allowed anywhere near firearms' was the gist of it. But apparently Giles Pritchard said you could be trusted.'

'Well that was nice of him.'

Shepherd checked the action of the Glock, then ejected the magazine. It was a Glock 17 and the magazine held 17 rounds.

'I can give you another magazine if you need it,' said Owen.

Shepherd slotted the magazine back into the Glock and took off his jacket. 'I'm not planning on any shoot-outs,' he said.

'That's good to know.'

Shepherd hung his jacket on one of the stools, then slipped on the holster. It fitted just fine and didn't need adjusting. He slid the Glock into the holster and put his jacket back on, then practised reaching for the weapon a few times.

'My boss also said we're pulling out today. They're taking the view that Abu-Rous is no longer a priority.'

348

'Yeah, I figured that was going to happen.'

'Sorry to leave you in the lurch and all.'

'Nah, it doesn't make sense having the four of you here when it's only a maybe,' said Shepherd. 'When will you be going?'

'After lunch, probably. I'll get the guys to start packing their stuff.'

The door opened again. This time it was Abu-Rous. His face was a blank mask. 'So, my wife and son are booked on a flight on a 2pm flight from Birmingham. Qatar Airways, direct to Doha.'

'And you're staying?' said Shepherd.

'As you said, it's better that we're apart until this unpleasantness is resolved.' He looked at his watch. 'We can leave here at midday, that'll give us plenty of time.'

Shepherd nodded. The airport was just thirty minutes from the house. He looked at Owen. 'How about you give us an escort, then once we've got to the airport you can head back to London?'

'That works for me.'

'So they have decided I don't need police protection?' asked Abu-Rous.

'We have other priorities,' said Owen. 'But if anything changes, we'll be right back.'

'We'll use my car to get you to the airport,' said Shepherd.

Abu-Rous shook his head. 'No, I'll drive. We'll take the BMW.'

'I'll need to be with you, Sir.'

Abu-Rous sighed. 'Fine. But please do not speak or do anything to upset my wife. She really is at the end of her tether.'

'I'll be as quiet as a mouse.'

61

David White launched the drone and let it soar upwards until it was two hundred feet above the ground, did a slow circuit of the immediate area, then pushed the joystick to send it towards Abu-Rous's house. He frowned when he saw the black Range Rover was back in the driveway.

He put the drone in a hover and put it in a slow turn. A man and a woman came out of the house carrying holdalls and got into the Range Rover. White stared at the screen. Were they leaving? The garage door was open. Presumably the vehicle had been there all the time. Another man appeared out of the front door, carrying a suitcase. White moved the drone to the side to get a better look. It was Dan Shepherd, he realised. Shepherd took the suitcase to the rear of the BMW and opened the boot.

They were leaving. But going where? Was Shepherd moving the family to a safe house? White wouldn't be able to follow them with the drone, the battery would only last thirty minutes or so at best. He'd have to follow them in the car.

Another man came out of the house, pulling a wheeled suitcase after him. He dragged the case over to the BMW, then went over to the Range Rover and climbed into the driving seat. He had a gun holstered on his thigh.

White wanted to take the drone lower but he knew that to do so would run the risk of it being spotted.

Abu-Rous appeared from the doorway, holding his

son's hand. His son was dragging a small wheeled carry-on bag. Behind them was Mrs Abu-Rous, wearing a black burkha and dark glasses. She also had a small wheeled suitcase, and a Chanel handbag.

Shepherd opened the rear passenger door for her and she climbed in. Shepherd slotted the suitcases in to the back of the BMW while Abu-Rous helped his son into the back of the vehicle.

A big man with a gun strapped to his thigh came out of the house carrying a large black kitbag and got into the Range Rover.

If they were heading to a safe house, they weren't taking much luggage. Could they be leaving the country? The fact that they were leaving in Abu-Rous's BMW suggested not. But if they were flying out, which airport would they use? Birmingham Airport was a half hour drive, Manchester Airport was ninety minutes away and in just two hours they could be at Heathrow. He pressed the button to recall the drone. He was going to have to follow them.

62

Abu-Rous got into the driver's seat and started the BMW as Shepherd walked over to the Range Rover. Owen wound the window down. 'Parting is such sweet sorrow,' said the CTSFO with a grin.

'I'll miss having you guys around, farting and belching,' said Shepherd.

'Hey, we're all house trained,' said Reilly in the front passenger seat. She winked at Shepherd.

'How do you want to play this, Spider?' asked Owen.

'He wants to drive them there, check them in and see them off, then we'll drive back here,' said Shepherd. 'I think all you need do is to follow us to the airport, make sure we get there in one piece and that no one is following us.'

'Sure, we can do that.' He threw Shepherd a mock salute. 'It's been a pleasure.'

Shepherd grinned and went back to the BMW. He climbed into the front passenger seat. 'All good,' he said.

Abu-Rous nodded and pressed a key fob. The gate rattled open and they drove through to the road. The Range Rover followed. Abu-Rous pressed the key fob again and the gate closed.

They drove to the M42. The quickest route was a loop that took them north east and then down to the airport on the M6. Abu-Rous was a sloppy driver, switching lanes without indicating, braking sharply when misjudging the speed of the vehicles in front of him, and rarely if ever checking his rear view mirror.

The boy was playing a shooting game on his phone, and Mrs Abu-Rous kept snapping at him in Arabic, presumably to tell him to turn the volume down.

Shepherd kept looking in the side mirror to check on the Range Rover. On the drive to the motorway, Owen had stayed close, never further than half a dozen car lengths back. Once on the motorway he stayed further back, obviously looking for any vehicles that were tailing the BMW. So far as Shepherd could tell, no one was following them.

Abu-Rous undertook a removal van on the left, accelerating and muttering darkly in Arabic. He was truly an appalling driver and often Shepherd's right foot would twitch in anticipation of hitting a brake that he didn't have.

The Range Rover overtook the van on the right, its indicator on. Shepherd could imagine what Owen was saying to his colleagues. The way Abu-Rous was driving, they were currently more at risk from dying in a car crash than they were of being killed by an assassin.

They reached the airport after thirty minutes, by which time Shepherd's nerves were frazzled and his right leg was aching. They were heading towards the short term car park when Shepherd's phone buzzed. He took it out of his pocket. It was Owen. 'Are you okay for us to leave you here, Spider? I'm getting my chain yanked. You were all clear on the way here.'

'No problem, Gerry, thanks for everything.'

'Hope it works out. Stay safe.'

The line went dead and Shepherd put his phone away. He looked in the side mirror and watched as the Range Rover turned off the road and headed for the exit. Abu-Rous drove into the multi-storey car park, narrowly missing scraping the offside wing against a concrete pillar. He found a parking space on the third floor, but even with the BMW's rear view camera it took him four attempts to fit the car in.

Shepherd climbed out and looked around. The terminal was only a minute or so walk away. Abu-Rous popped the boot open and Shepherd took out the suitcases. Mrs Abu-Rous got out of the car and waved for her son to follow her, chiding him in Arabic.

Abu-Rous took the two carry-on cases and hurried after his wife and son, leaving the two larger cases with Shepherd. 'I'll get these then, shall I?' Shepherd muttered. He closed the boot, grabbed the handles of the wheeled cases and followed the family to the terminal.

63

White watched Shepherd head out of the car park, pulling two large suitcases behind him. He smiled to himself at the breach of bodyguarding protocol. Bodyguards shouldn't be carrying parcels or pulling suitcases, they were supposed to have their hands free at all times so that they could react to any threats. But Abu-Rous was clearly a man who was used to people carrying out tasks for him, he had walked away without a backward look. Mrs Abu-Rous was clearly unhappy, her face was set in stone and her eyes hidden behind dark glasses.

David White had parked his Fiesta on the other side of the multi-storey, next to a white van that provided plenty of cover. Following the BMW had been relatively easy. He had arrived outside the house just as it and the Range Rover were heading down the road. The Range Rover was clearly there to provide protection so he didn't have to stay close to the BMW, all he had to do was to keep the black Range Rover in sight and it was hard to miss.

First they had headed north, which meant that London or Heathrow wasn't an option. He figured they were heading for a safe house in the north, or Manchester Airport, but then they had taken the M6 west which mean that Birmingham Airport was more likely.

Once it was clear that the airport was their destination, White was able to move closer to the Range Rover as most of the traffic was now heading that way.

When the Range Rover turned off the road, White accelerated in time to see the BMW turn into the multi-storey car park and he had followed it up to the third floor.

White knew that Qatar Airways had a direct flight to Doha once a day and they had arrived at the airport with plenty of time to check in for that flight. The big question was, who was flying out? The son had his own case, so he was clearly going. White doubted that the son would go anywhere without his mother. But what about Abu-Rous? Was he leaving the country? White rubbed his chin thoughtfully. If he was leaving, he would probably have left the BMW in a long term car park. Unless of course Shepherd was planning to drive the car back to Edgbaston. But Shepherd hadn't driven to the airport, that had been Abu-Rous, and White hadn't seen Abu-Rous give the keys to Shepherd. The balance of probabilities was that Abu-Rous was there to see his family off, and that he'd be back to the car once he'd checked them in and seen them off.

White went over to his car and opened the rear door to look at the Fortnum & Mason hamper. It would be too big to push under the BMW, but if he removed the bubble-wrapped bomb, there'd be more than enough room. He looked at his watch. He had plenty of time.

64

Shepherd kept away from the first class check-in desk as Mrs Abu-Rous and her son checked in for their flight to Doha. Abu-Rous had their passports and he handed them over, then waved for a Qatar Airways employee to load the cases onto the scales. Shepherd's eyes were constantly moving, checking out potential threats, even though he was fairly sure that David White wouldn't try anything in an airport terminal. Two armed police officers, dressed in black with baseball caps, were standing at the entrance, their SIG Sauer MCXs across their chests.

Once Mrs Abu-Rous and her son had their boarding passes, Abu-Rous walked with them to airport security, pulling their carry-on cases. Mrs Abu-Rous was still clearly unhappy, her jaw tight and her lips clamped together. Abu-Rous picked up his son and kissed him on the cheek. The boy was tearful, not wanting to leave his father, but his mother grabbed him by the hand and pulled him away. She grabbed her case, made sure that her son had his, then nodded curtly at Abu-Rous, turned on her heels and walked into the security area with the boy.

Abu-Rous stood and watched until they had passed from view, then he walked over to Shepherd. 'At least they're out of harm's way now,' said Abu-Rous.

'Will someone be meeting them in Doha?'

Abu-Rous nodded. 'We have good friends there.'

'I bet you have,' thought Shepherd, but he didn't

357

say it out loud. Qatar liked to portray itself as a peace-maker in Middle Eastern conflicts, but in reality the Muslim state was a key financial supporter and ally of Hamas, transferring hundreds of millions of dollars to the terrorist organisation every year. Three top Hamas leaders lived openly in Qatar, and according to the New York Post, Ismail Haniyeh, Moussa Abu Marzuk and Khaleed Mashal controlled a fortune of more than ten billion dollars which they spent lavishly in the emirate's hotels and restaurants, flying everywhere by private jet. The behaviour was obscene considering that most of the Palestinians they were supposed to represent lived in abject poverty.

'Do you think they'll be safe?' asked Abu-Rous.

'I don't think Mossad makes a habit of killing women and children,' said Shepherd pointedly.

Abu-Rous's eyes narrowed. 'What are you insinuating?' he hissed.

'Me?' said Shepherd. 'Nothing.'

'I know what you're implying. You're implying that Hamas does kill women and children and the Jews don't.'

'I said Mossad,' said Shepherd. 'And you're not a mind reader, with the greatest of respect you don't know what I'm thinking.'

'They are Jews,' said Abu-Rous contemptuously. 'And do you know how many women and children the Jews have killed in the occupied territories? From malnutrition and lack of health care and Israeli army attacks?' He sneered at Shepherd and shook his head dismissively. 'You have no idea what you're talking about.'

'I didn't say anything, Sir,' said Shepherd. 'You were asking if your wife and son would be safe, and I said yes, they probably will be now that they are away from you.'

Abu-Rous shook his head again. 'You were being judgmental without knowing the facts. Every day newborn babies die in the Palestinian Territories from diarrhoea, hypothermia, dehydration and infections that would normally be treatable. Unemployment is at sixty per cent, there is a shortage of basic necessities such as food, fuel and medicine. Electricity and water supplies are sporadic at best, and when the Israeli military attacks Gaza, they kill women and children as often as they kill Hamas fighters.'

'And this justifies the October Seven massacres, does it?'

'Of course not. That's not what I'm saying. Look, I was against the attacks, right from the start, and I said so even though it put my life at risk. I told them, nothing good would come of attacking civilians. But nobody listened to me.'

'But you're still a part of the organisation.'

Abu-Rous sneered at Shepherd. 'Have you any idea what would happen to me if I tried to leave? You don't walk away from Hamas, not if you want to live. The best I could do was to point out how disastrous it would be to attack the Supernova festival and the kibbutzes. It was obvious that the Jews would respond with violence, and the US and Europe would be behind them. Plus we would be putting ourselves personally at risk. It was clear to me how Mossad would respond.'

'So why didn't they listen to you?'

'The ones in favour said that the Muslim world would unite behind us, and that together we would drive the Jews from our lands. But how was that going to work? Would Iran send in troops? Of course not.

359

They use Hamas to fight a proxy war with Israel, they don't want to dirty their hands. In fact Iran wants the Jews to attack Hamas in retaliation because that will turn the rest of the Arab world against them. Iran was enraged when the United Arab Emirates normalised relations with Israel, following Egypt and Jordan. Then Morocco agreed to establish full diplomatic and trade relations with Israel, and approved direct flights between the two countries. But when Saudi Arabia started talking about normalising relations, that was the straw that broke the camel's back. Iran wanted to put a stop to that, and what better way than getting the Jews to invade Gaza and kill Palestinian civilians?' He sneered again and shook his head. 'Why am I telling you this? You don't care how my people have suffered.'

'I care,' said Shepherd. 'But what Hamas did on October Seven was unforgivable.'

'You think I don't know that? Look, I did what I could to dissuade them, but there were bigger forces at work here. Russian money was pouring in to help fund the attacks because Putin was looking to distract the world from what was happening in Ukraine. America's military-industrial complex was rubbing its hands together with glee at the prospects for their arms businesses.'

'Are you saying the Americans knew that the attacks were going to happen?'

Abu-Rous looked around as if he feared being overheard. 'Everybody knew,' he said. 'Can't you see that? All those people, all that equipment, all the training and rehearsal that was necessary. There is more surveillance in Gaza than almost anywhere else in the world, how could all that preparation have possibly

360

gone unnoticed?' He shook his head again. 'I played a very small role in the attacks and that role was to speak against them, and yet I'm the one whose life is on the line.'

'Life isn't fair at the best of times,' said Shepherd.

Abu-Rous's eyes narrowed. 'You think this is funny?'

'No, but I find it bizarre that you expect fairness in the world. If you did try to stop the attacks, why not let the Israelis know?'

'You think I have a direct line to Mossad?'

'No, but I'm told that you have helped our security services in the past. If Mossad was aware of that, they might call off their dogs.'

'Yes, and if Hamas were to find out, I would be dead within days.'

Shepherd nodded. Abu-Rous was right. The fewer people who knew that he was an MI6 asset, the better. And the one thing that Shepherd couldn't tell Abu-Rous was that the threat to his life wasn't from Mossad, but from David White, a lone wolf killer out for revenge.

Abu-Rous looked at his watch. 'I am wasting my time here,' he said, and began walking to the car park. Shepherd hurried after him, looking around for potential threats and seeing none.

The two men walked into the car park. Abu-Rous had his key fob in his hand and he clicked it to unlock the BMW. Shepherd walked around the rear of the car as Abu-Rous pulled opened the driver's door. Abu-Rous climbed in as Shepherd put out his hand to open the passenger door. Which is when the car exploded in a ball of light and heat and noise, blowing Shepherd into the air and sending him crashing on to the bonnet of the vehicle behind him.

361

65

David White stood open mouthed as he surveyed the damage that his bomb had caused. The BMW was a ball of flame and he could just about make out the charred body of Abu-Rous in the front seat. Dan Shepherd had been blown off his feet, smashed into the car behind him and rolled on to the floor, out of sight. Car alarms were blaring out all around him. White didn't know if Shepherd was alive or dead, and he couldn't stay around to find out. He hadn't wanted to kill Shepherd and had detonated the bomb the moment that Abu-Rous was sitting in the driving seat. Most of the pressure wave and shrapnel would have gone straight up into the car, so hopefully Shepherd had escaped the worst effects of the blast.

White climbed into his Fiesta, started the engine and drove slowly out of the car park. In the distance he heard the sound of sirens. By the time they reached the car park he would be on his way back to Birmingham. His heart was pounding as the adrenaline coursed through his system. Abu-Rous was dead, but White figured the man had gotten off lightly. Death would have been close to instantaneous. There would have been none of the fear and terror that his daughters had gone through before they died, or the grief and sadness that his wife had suffered. But dead was dead and Abu-Rous had deserved his fate. Maybe he was already in heaven, being tended to by his seventy two sloe-eyed virgins, but somehow White doubted it.

He drove along the airport road, heading towards the A45. Killing Abu-Rous at the airport had been a spontaneous decision, one that had worked well but which had put White at risk. The authorities would be sure to check CCTV at the airport, and it wouldn't take them long to identify the Ford Fiesta. Once they realised that he had detonated the bomb by phone they would start checking mobile phone activity in the area. White knew from experience that checking phone activity took time, every police force in the country made demands on the phone companies, and even though the security services usually had priority, there were only so many checks that could be done in a day. But first things first, he had to get rid of the car.

66

Shepherd was sitting up in bed when Giles Pritchard arrived. He had been taken to Birmingham City Hospital in an ambulance with full on blues and twos, and taken straight into Accident & Emergency where a nurse had used a pair of shears to cut away his bloodstained jeans. In fact most of the damage was superficial. Several pieces of shrapnel had torn into his legs below the knee, but the cuts weren't deep. The pressure wave had lifted him into the air and smashed him into the car behind him but no bones had been broken, though his back and legs were badly bruised.

Shepherd had been unconscious when the paramedics loaded him into the ambulance, but he started to come around as they arrived at the hospital. That had been three hours earlier and his ears were still ringing. He had been lucky. After a doctor had sewn up the wounds on his legs, they had taken him for a chest X-ray and an MRI scan of his head, but his lungs were fine and there were no signs of a brain bleed. In fact if it wasn't for the fact that he didn't have any clothes, he'd have checked himself out earlier.

'I come bearing gifts,' said Pritchard, handing Shepherd a bulging carrier bag. Pritchard ran the curtain around the bed while Shepherd emptied the bag. There was a Wrangler denim shirt, blue jeans, socks and underwear. He held up the shirt. 'You thought you'd go for the cowboy look?' he said.

'It was all a bit of a rush, I didn't have time to go the made-to-measure route,' he said. 'Besides, as soon as we get you back to London you can change.'

Shepherd shrugged off his hospital robe and pulled on the underwear and socks. Pritchard gestured at the dozen or so plasters on Shepherd's legs. 'Are you okay?'

'I'm fine,' said Shepherd. 'Plenty of stitches and I'll have a few permanent scars to add to the collection, but yeah, it could have been a lot worse.'

'Your guardian angel was watching over you.'

'Yeah, maybe,' said Shepherd, ripping the price tag off the shirt and pulling it on. 'I think David was in the car park when the bomb went off,' he said.

'How so?'

'Abu-Rous used the key fob to open the car but he didn't get the chance to start the engine. So the bomb wasn't detonated by the engine starting. He had just got into the driver's seat when it went off, so it could have been a pressure trigger, but the car was outside his house all the time we were there so I don't see that David could have got to it. So David must have set the bomb off when he saw Abu-Rous sitting in it, which means either a control wire or a phone detonator. I can't see that he'd risk running a wire along the ground because it'd be easy to spot, so I'm guessing he used a phone.'

'So we need to check what phones were used in the car park just before the bomb went off?'

Shepherd finished fastening his shirt buttons and pulled on the jeans. 'Exactly. And he must have used a vehicle, he won't have carried the bomb in by hand. We need to check CCTV footage of all the vehicles that entered the car park after Abu-Rous's BMW.'

'I'll get right on to it. Do you want a lift back to London?'

'I'll go and pick up my car, it's still at Edgbaston.' He pulled a face. 'I can't, can I? It's behind a locked gate and the key was in the BMW.'

'I'll get people out to retrieve your car and you can come back with me,' said Pritchard. 'You realise that David could easily have killed you, too?'

Shepherd frowned. 'I'm supposed to be grateful?'

'Of course not. I'm just pointing out that if he did have sight of the car, he'd have known that you were still outside. He could just as easily have waited until you were both in the car with the doors closed. The outcome would have been very different, obviously.'

Shepherd forced a smile. 'I'll be sure to thank him if I ever get the chance.'

67

David White parked the white Prius and climbed out. He had left the Ford Fiesta in a supermarket car park on the outskirts of Birmingham, and bought the ten-year-old Prius from a dealer under a railway arch not far from Birmingham New Street station. The dealer had asked for identification but hadn't been perturbed that White wasn't able to supply any, he just wrote down the fake name and address that White gave him and pocketed the cash without issuing him with a receipt. Birmingham had the highest percentage of untaxed and uninsured vehicles in the country and there was a thriving second hand car market where cash was king.

White looked around the marina, but didn't see any obvious surveillance activity. Not that he actually expected to spot any watchers, surveillance was one of the many things that MI5 was expert at. If there were watchers around, he'd never spot them. He opened the rear door and took out the bag containing his drone and spare batteries, and a carrier bag full of food that he'd picked up at a service station on his way into London.

He walked along the jetty to the *Over The Hull*. He had left a matchstick wedged in between the frame and the door that led to the saloon and it was still there so he knew that no one had been on board in his absence.

He went down the steps, stripped off his clothes and shaved and showered, before pulling on a clean polo shirt and fresh jeans. He made himself a mug of coffee and microwaved a beef lasagna, which he ate at the dinette table. He had the television on, and as he tucked in to his lasagna the news started and the top item was the explosion at Birmingham Airport. There was no mention of the car being a BMW or that Ahmed Abu-Rous was the victim. In fact there was very little information, just that police were investigating the aftermath of an explosion in which one man had died. There were shots of the car park surrounded by blue and white police tape, and forensic teams moving in, dressed from head to toe in white. There was no mention either of Dan Shepherd, which was to be expected. Dead or alive, MI5 would have made sure that his involvement wasn't made public.

The next story was about ongoing street demonstrations calling for a ceasefire in Gaza. Hundreds of thousands of pro-Palestinian demonstrators had already marched through the streets of London, and a major rally was planned for the weekend. The police had stood back during previous demonstrations, ignoring the protesters calling for death to Jews and an end to Israel. A common phrase chanted and written on posters was 'from the river to the sea, Palestine will be free'. The police were taking the view that the phrase was merely a description of the area that made up Palestine, between the River Jordan and the Mediterranean Sea. But White, like most Jews, knew exactly what was meant by it. Hamas had used it in its 2017 charter, calling for the dismantling of Israel and the extermination or removal of the Jewish population. It was a call for genocide.

Another often heard chant was 'Globalize the intifada'. The slogan had been used at anti-Israel

368

demonstrations for years, referencing violence against civilians to achieve political aims. The police either didn't know or didn't care what the chant referred to, but White knew that it was a call for indiscriminate violence against Jews and Jewish institutions around the world.

White felt his heart pounding in his chest. Hundreds of thousands protested against Israel defending itself, but how many had taken to the streets to protest against the murder of fourteen hundred innocent civilians by the Hamas terrorists?

A clip of a bearded Muslim cleric addressing a crowd flashed onto the screen. White recognised him from the files he'd photographed in Thames House. Imam Salim Dabush was a regular feature at anti-Israel demonstrations, and had been on MI5's watch list for almost ten years, suspected of sending young British Muslims out to training camps in Pakistan. Dabush was in his seventies, with white hair and a bushy grey beard, his eyes hidden behind dark glasses. He was never seen without a white knitted skullcap and favoured long loose-fitting grey thobe robes, covering his body from his neck to his ankles.

The clip showed Dabush baying at a crowd in Arabic, calling for the death of all Jews, in Israel and around the world. White shook his head in disbelief. The editor of the programme clearly hadn't bothered to get a translation of what the cleric was saying.

The clip of Dabush was replaced by a photograph of another imam, younger and wearing a suit, who would also be addressing the demonstrations at the weekend. Nasim Halawah was an imam at the Al Manaar mosque in West London, which had long been a breeding ground for home-grown terrorists,

369

including three of the men who had gone on to become the infamous Beatles, torturing and killing hostages in Syria. The failed 21/7 bombers had also been regulars at the mosque. Halawah had been one of the first to slam Israel for its attacks on Hamas, claiming that the Israelis were killing women and children, razing homes and businesses to the ground, and were intent on destroying the Palestinian people. Halawah never once mentioned what had provoked the attack and never expressed any sympathy for the victims of the Hamas massacre. Halawah was also in the files on White's iPad. He was a fundraiser for Hamas and had funnelled millions of pounds to the terrorist organisation, much of it raised through collections at the country's mosques. Halawah would travel the country accompanied by two burly bodyguards, giving passionate speeches behind closed doors, after which the bodyguards would walk around with plastic buckets collecting donations, making it clear that they expected notes and not coins. Halawah had been questioned about his fund raising several times by anti-terrorist police, but had always managed to produce receipts that showed it had gone to Muslim charities.

The picture of Halawah was replaced with a map of London, showing the routes of the weekend's demonstrations. White smiled grimly as he stared at the screen. At least he knew exactly where Dabush and Halawah would be that weekend. He could kill two birds with one stone.

68

Shepherd stared out of the side window as Pritchard continued his conversation on his mobile. They were sitting in the back of a black Lexus, heading down the M1 towards London. Pritchard finished his conversation but kept his phone in his hand. 'Preliminary reports suggest that it was a TATP bomb with ironmongery for shrapnel. No signs of a wire and it was on the ground when it went off, so you're probably right about it being phone detonated. We're getting phone mast data as we speak.'

'TATP is easy enough to manufacture, but it's hellishly unstable,' said Shepherd.

'I think we can assume that David knows what he's doing,' said Pritchard.

'It's a big step, though, isn't it? To go from guns to car bombs.'

'He's hell bent on getting his revenge, I don't think he's too concerned about the methods he's using. I do wonder how he knew that Abu-Rous was at the airport.'

'He must have followed us,' said Shepherd. 'He must have been watching the house.'

'You didn't see him?' He pulled a face. 'Sorry, stupid question.'

'The thing is, the CTSFOs gave us an escort to the airport. They were behind us. So David could have kept them in sight knowing that we were in convoy. By the time the CTSFOs peeled off, we were at the airport. Spotting surveillance isn't their forte, so they might have missed him.'

'We're going to be checking CCTV coverage of the parking garage, once we've ID'd his vehicle we can run it through ANPR and see where he went. Ditto with his burner phone. Presumably he'll have dumped it after the explosion, but we'll be able to see which towers he pinged off prior to that.'

'And what potential targets?'

'We still have two dozen that we know he looked at in addition to the three who flew out of Egypt. One of them was Mohammed Sanawer, who was killed in the Edgware Road money exchange so that leaves eleven. Two are in Glasgow, three are in Manchester and the rest are in London.'

'Do we warn them?'

'We're getting the police to inform them that there's the possibility of a threat, but we don't have the resources to offer them all protection. And for all we know there could be others that David checked up on that we don't know about.'

'So what's the plan?'

'We ID his phone and his car, and we see where he was prior to the car bomb.'

'He's not stupid, he'll have dumped both and he'll have changed locations.'

'True. But hopefully it'll give us an insight into what he's planning to do next.'

Shepherd nodded and stared out of the window. White had stayed one step ahead of them from the start, and it didn't feel as though they were any closer to apprehending him. Finding out where he had been was all well and good, but to have any hope of catching him they needed to know where he was going to strike next.

69

David White woke at dawn. He made himself scrambled eggs and coffee and then headed out to buy what he needed to make his second batch of TATP. The ingredients were simple to buy but this time he needed larger quantities so he spread the purchases out across more than a dozen shops in and around London. He bought two pay-as-you-go phones and four SIM cards and a Puffa jacket one size too big for him and picked up several bags of ice from a corner shop near the marina.

It took him the best part of four hours to buy everything he needed, then he drove back to the marina. He parked the Prius and carried all his purchases on to the *Over The Hull*, taking a long look around before opening the door and heading down into the saloon.

He already had everything else he needed — Christmas tree lights, duct tape, and the soldering iron. He closed all the curtains but kept the windows open to let the fumes out. He took a deep breath and exhaled slowly. It was going to be a long day.

70

Shepherd arrived at Thames House just after nine o'clock in the morning and went straight up to Donna Walsh's office. She wasn't there but her PA told him she was in an operations room down the corridor. Shepherd had ditched the Wrangler shirt and jeans and was wearing a grey suit with a white shirt and dark blue tie. When he pushed open the door to the operations room, he saw that Walsh was more casually dressed in a long white linen shirt over baggy blue jeans and vibrant green Crocs.

There were six pods in the room. Four were occupied by three young women and a man who was wearing a similar suit to Shepherd's. Each pod had a keyboard and three screens. The man and one of the women were watching CCTV footage, the two other women were talking quietly into their headsets.

Walsh had her mobile phone to her ear but she ended the call as soon as she saw Shepherd and hurried over to him. She hugged him tightly. 'You had a narrow escape,' she said. 'Please don't do that again. The first reports we got was that there were two fatalities. My heart was in my mouth.'

'I was lucky,' said Shepherd.

She gave him a final hug and then released him.

'Any joy with David White's car?' asked Shepherd.

'It's been a nightmare,' said Walsh. 'The airport carpark uses its own system and there's no facility to download footage to our computers. We can get footage from the departure and arrivals area of the terminal directly, and we have access to the cameras covering the drop-off areas, but the carparks are part of a separate system. By the time we realised that, their office was shut for the night and their IT people were unavailable. We had a guy there first thing and they gave him the footage on a portable hard disk. He's in our Birmingham office now and we're trying to get a feed fixed up. If that doesn't work we'll have to bike the disk down. It's as if we're still in the last century.'

'And what about tracking the mobile phones in the area of the car park when the bomb went off?'

'Again, it's in hand. But you know as well as I do how problematical it is dealing with the mobile phone companies. We should go to the top of the list, but they don't work nights.'

'He'll almost certainly have dumped the burner phone and the one he used in the bomb will obviously have been destroyed. But at some point he must have tested the system by calling the bomb phone from his burner phone and there'll be a record of that. And hopefully that will give us his location at the time.'

'As I said, we're on it and we're flagged as a priority.'

One of the female officers held up her hand. 'Donna, we have lift off,' she said.

'Finally,' said Walsh. She pointed at a bank of four large screens on one wall. 'Put the feed through one of the big screens, Jessica.'

Jessica tapped on her screen and the top left screen flickered into life. There were sixteen CCTV views, laid out on a grid.

'Please tell me that you can isolate individual feeds,' said Walsh.

Jessica pulled a face as her fingers played across the

375

keyboard, then she shook her head. 'It's just the one file,' she said.

'That doesn't make any sense at all,' said Walsh. 'Call Tommy in Birmingham and explain what's happened. See if he can fix it and if not then get our IT boys on it.' She shrugged at him. 'You can see what we're up against,' she said. 'It's as if the whole world is conspiring against us.'

Shepherd walked over to look at the screen. The individual images were labelled with the time and number of the car park, followed by an individual letter, A, B, C or D. There were three multi-storey car parks, 1, 2, and 3. Car Park 4 was a surface car park. Shepherd pointed at the screen. 'We were parked in number one,' he said. 'All these cameras are outside, were there no cameras inside?'

'We're told not,' said Walsh.

Shepherd stepped closer to the monitor and looked at the four feeds from Car Park 1. Two showed the registration plates of cars arriving at the two entrances. A third showed the rear plates of cars leaving, and the fourth was pointed down the walkway that led from the car park to the terminal. Across the bottom of each feed was a date and time. They were the same on every feed — just before noon the previous day. 'Can we run ahead to about ninety minutes before the bomb went off?' he asked.

'Is that doable, Jessica?' asked Walsh.

'I think so,' said Jessica. 'But it'll be all the feeds.'

'That's okay,' said Shepherd.

Jessica tapped on her keyboard and the image on the large monitor jumped ahead. Shepherd concentrated on the two monitors showing the licence plates of vehicles entering the car park. 'Is there any way of speeding it up?' asked Shepherd.

'I don't think so,' said Jessica.

Another of the women raised a hand. 'IT are on the way,' she said.

'They'll probably just tell us to switch it off and on again,' said Walsh. 'That seems to be their cure for everything.'

The seconds ticked by. The two feeds only showed the registration numbers, there was no way of identifying the drivers. After ten minutes of staring at the screens, Shepherd spotted the BMW. 'There we are,' he said. 'That's us.' He looked over at Walsh. 'So, we can assume that David followed us into the car park,' he said. 'So he must be in one of the cars next in.'

'Well, yes, but that's an assumption, of course,' said Walsh. 'He might have driven in behind you and followed you up. But it's just as possible that he went in some time later and walked around until he found the BMW.'

Shepherd nodded. 'You're right, of course. Except that I doubt he would be on foot carrying a bomb.'

'If we focus on the first few cars then we might miss him. Better to check them all out. The plan is to make a list of all the vehicles that entered after the BMW and contact the registered keepers. Hopefully we'll have spoken to them all by the end of the day and once we've ruled out the genuine owners we'll be left with White's vehicle.'

The BMW went through and another vehicle took its place. From the look of the grille it was probably a Jaguar. A Nissan approached the second camera. All Shepherd could see was the front of the car and the registration plate. His eidetic memory kicked in — he was sure he had never seen either number before. Though if David had kept his distance during the drive to the airport, there would have been almost no chance of Shepherd spotting him.

The Jaguar went through and was replaced by an SUV, Shepherd couldn't tell what make it was. He looked over at Jessica, who was scribbling in a notebook, presumably making a note of the registration numbers. He grunted in frustration. There was no short cut, they would just have to keep contacting the registered owners until they found the vehicle that David had acquired.

'We'll get there eventually,' said Walsh. 'You know what they say, a watched kettle never boils.'

'Are you telling me to get out of your kitchen?' Shepherd asked.

She smiled. 'As soon as we know anything, I'll call you.'

71

David White stood up and stretched. Every muscle ached and the fumes had given him a blinding headache. All the windows were open but he had to keep the curtains drawn and the hatch closed, so there wasn't much in the way of ventilation. He had been mixing the chemicals in batches, each batch producing three or four ounces of TATP. The white crystals went into Tupperware containers, which he was storing in the small fridge. So far he had filled four of the Tupperware containers and he hoped to fill another two before he ran out of precursor chemicals.

He wanted a cup of tea but the galley was thick with fumes and he couldn't risk lighting a burner. He had taken a bottle of Evian water out of the fridge to make room for the Tupperware containers. He unscrewed the top and drank from the bottle. His head was throbbing and he decided he needed some fresh air.

He climbed the steps and pushed open the hatch. He stepped on to the rear deck and looked around. He didn't see anyone nearby but almost all the boats in the marina were liveaboards and people were always walking along the jetties. He stretched his arms in the air, then bent down and touched his toes. He really wanted to go for a walk but if he did and he bumped into someone there was a good chance they'd smell the fumes.

He stood up again, put his hands on his head and twisted from side to side, loosening up his spine.

An elderly man emerged from a narrowboat along the jetty, with a small Jack Russell on a lead. He started walking towards the *Over The Hull*. White pulled open the hatch and went down the stairs, closing it behind him.

72

Shepherd's phone rang. It was Donna Walsh. 'Hi Donna,' he said. He was sitting in the canteen with a half-eaten plate of fish and chips in front of him.

'We've nailed his phone,' said Walsh.

'I'll be right there,' said Shepherd. He grabbed a chip, popped it into his mouth and washed it down with the last of his coffee before heading down the stairs to the operations room.

Walsh was looking up at one of the large screens showing a map of the lower half of the UK, from Manchester down to the south coast. There were hundreds of red dots on the map, mainly around London and Birmingham. Shepherd joined her. He looked at the clusters of dots around the two cities and nodded. 'Well that's pretty conclusive, isn't it?'

She pointed at the M1 motorway leading out of London. 'He pinged towers all the way up Edgbaston, then hung around Abu-Rous's house and then came back to London. He went up again the day of the explosion and immediately after that the phone went dark.'

'Any calls or messages?'

'Just internet use. He used the phone as a personal hotspot and then did various DuckDuckGo searches.'

Shepherd nodded. DuckDuckGo was an American search engine that offered extra privacy protection for people browsing the internet, allowing them to search anonymously.

'We can see what he was looking at?' said Shepherd.

'Unfortunately not, but he spent hours and hours on it so I doubt he was looking for advice on Bitcoin.' She pointed at Birmingham on the map. 'So, the phone was pinging a phone mast not far from Abu-Rous's house.'

'What time?'

Walsh picked up a clipboard. 'He arrived in Birmingham at just after eleven o'clock. He spent an hour in Birmingham city centre and then ninety minutes at Edgbaston golf course.'

'Seriously?'

'The tower data doesn't lie.'

'But he's not a golfer, is he?'

'Maybe he wanted some fresh air. Anyway, not long after that he was in the vicinity of Abu-Rous's house.'

'What time?'

'From about 2pm until almost 5pm.'

Shepherd nodded. 'I got there about three thirty. If he was watching the house, he'd have seen me arrive.' He tutted. 'That's why he pulled out. He saw me and knew that we were protecting Abu-Rous. So he headed back to London and petrol bombed Bashir Jabari's house and shot Mohammed Sanawer and his sons in their currency exchange as a way of dragging attention away from Birmingham.'

Walsh nodded and pointed at the monitor. 'Then he heads back to Edgbaston just in time to see you leaving for the airport. At this point he must already have the bomb prepared so he puts it under Abu-Rous's car and detonates it when he sees Abu-Rous getting into it. You, unfortunately, were collateral damage.'

'And when he was in London, do we know where he was staying?'

382

Walsh smiled. 'We do. Limehouse Basin. And he was there the first time he used the burner phone to call the bomb phone. And it's where he was most nights, usually searching on his iPad.'

'So he's on a boat?'

'That's another assumption, Dan. There are hundreds of boats there, but there are also a number of apartment blocks overlooking the marina that would ping off the same mast. But yes, if you were looking for a place to hide below the radar, a boat would fit the bill.'

73

The black Range Rover pulled up next to Shepherd's BMW SUV. There was definitely something intimidating about the Range Rover and its tinted windows, which is presumably why the CTSFOs favoured it. But it certainly didn't blend into the background. Gerry Owen was driving and he raised his hand in greeting. Shepherd waved back. Nick Brett was in the front passenger seat. Rebecca Reilly climbed out of the rear on one side and Simon Wilsher the other.

Owen switched off the engine and he and Brett got out and looked around as Shepherd walked over. They couldn't see the marina from where they were but they could see the modern apartment blocks that bordered the area. Limehouse Basin was a historic dock area that had undergone significant redevelopment. It was built in the early nineteenth century when it served as a crucial junction for goods transported along the River Thames and the Regent's Canal. Now it was a thriving marina, surrounded by modern residential developments and office buildings, with a waterside promenade lined with cafes and restaurants.

'You don't look bad for someone who was blown up by a car bomb,' said Reilly. She was wearing her reefer jacket and a black beanie hat.

'I was lucky,' said Shepherd.

'It was just Abu-Rous who bought it, right?' said Wilsher.

'Yeah, the wife and son were on the way to the

plane. It was just me and him. He got into the car and I didn't which is why I'm still alive and he's not.'

'Even so, there doesn't seem too much damage,' said Brett.

Shepherd held out his arms to the side and grinned. 'A few scratches on my legs, but yeah. I got off lightly.'

'Where did he get the explosives from?' asked Owen.

'He's made TATP. And a lot of it.'

'That's not good news, is it?' said Owen. 'Does that mean he might set off a bomb again?'

'I'm afraid so,' said Shepherd.

'Because that changes things, obviously.'

'I hear you,' said Shepherd. 'Right, you're probably wondering why I called you here. David White used a burner mobile phone to detonate the bomb that killed Mr Abu-Rous. Prior to the explosion in Birmingham, that phone was observed in this area, often overnight, so we have reason to believe that David is staying on one of the boats here. It's also possible that he's staying in one of the apartments overlooking the marina, so we need to keep this as low profile as possible. The phone went dark after the explosion, so we don't know for sure if he's still here, but we need to proceed as if he was which means no police markings and no visible weaponry. Softy, softly.'

He handed out photographs of White. 'I suggest we split up and take different sections to see if anyone recalls seeing him. No police radios, you can hear them a mile away, I'm going to suggest we set up a WhatsApp group and text each other. Does that work for everyone?'

The four CTSFOs nodded and took out their phones. They exchanged numbers and Shepherd set

385

up a WhatsApp group. He had just finished when his phone rang. It was Donna Walsh. 'We've ID'd the car that David used,' she said. 'A Ford Fiesta. It used to belong to a teacher in Clapham and she sold it on eBay, for cash.'

'David bought it on eBay?'

'No, we've spoken to the woman and it was a dealer, from the sound of it. Paid her with a wad of fifty pound notes and said he'd handle the paperwork with DVLA. He obviously didn't, just sold it on for cash again, presumably to David.'

'And ANPR?'

'Lots of hits. All over London, then on the motorway to Birmingham, then back to London, and finally back to Birmingham. Several hits in and around Egbaston. He was seen in Birmingham after the explosion, but nothing since then. He's possibly dumped it and bought another vehicle. We're looking for the Fiesta but I don't see how we can ID the vehicle he's using now.'

'And was it spotted near Limehouse Marina?'

'It was, several times.'

'That's great, Donna, good work, thanks.'

'Are you there now?'

'We are.'

'Please be careful, Dan. Even cats only have nine lives.'

'I'm in good company, Donna, I'll be fine.'

He ended the call and put the phone away. 'I've just had confirmation that a vehicle belonging to David White was seen in this area prior to the explosion in Birmingham,' he said. He took the CTSFOs to the edge of the carpark so that they had a view of the entire marina. There were four jetties facing them, each with up to thirty boats, and across the marina was a fifth with another sixteen vessels, mainly narrowboats. In all there were close to a hundred and twenty boats there. 'Gerry, why don't you take the jetty on the far side, then left to right on the nearest four jetties we can go Rebecca, Nick, Simon and me. Everyone okay with that?'

They all nodded.

'If anyone does spot him, pull back and communicate on the WhatsApp group. No going in solo, he is definitely armed and he could well have explosives.'

The team nodded again, then they made their way towards the marina. They reached the main jetty and Reilly went left. Brett, Wilsher and Shepherd split up and headed for their respective jetties.

There were four boats to the left of the jetty at the far end and beyond them were boats left and right, moored stern to stern with a pontoon running between them. The four boats on the left were all quite small, no more than thirty feet. Their bows were pointing towards the second jetty, where Wilsher had just climbed aboard a gleaming white cruiser to speak to a woman in a fluorescent green windbreaker.

The first boat on Shepherd's left was also a cruiser, about twenty feet long with the name — *Tax Deductible* — painted across the bow. A balding man in a bright blue anorak was sitting on one of two chairs, reading a copy of *The Times* with his feet propped up on a canvas stool. 'How are you doing?' asked Shepherd.

'How does it look like I'm doing?' growled the man in a West Country accent.

'Looks like you're at peace with the world,' said Shepherd.

387

'I'm like the swan,' said the man. 'Calm as you like on the surface, but pedalling like fuck under the water.'

Shepherd chuckled and held out the photograph. 'You haven't seen this guy have you?'

The man reached out a hand and Shepherd leaned over to give the photograph to him. The man bit down on his lower lip as he studied the picture. 'You a debt collector?'

'No, I'm just looking for him. He went missing a week or so ago and someone said they'd seen him around the marina.'

The man shook his head and handed the photograph back to Shepherd. 'Doesn't ring a bell. But I tend to keep to myself.'

'Thanks anyway,' said Shepherd.

He headed towards the second boat, another cruiser, this one about five feet longer than the *Tax Deductible*. 'There's no one on board,' called the man.

Shepherd walked back. 'Are you sure?'

'Of course I'm sure,' snapped the man. 'What, do you think I'm senile?'

'I'm sorry, no. Of course you're sure.'

'The owner is a banker with HSBC. He's hardly ever here and if he is it'll be at the weekend to take some of his banker mates out on the Thames. Banker being Cockney rhyming slang, of course.'

'Does he ever rent it out?'

'Lucas? No, he's richer than God, and there's no way he'd let a stranger on his precious boat.'

'Thanks,' said Shepherd, 'much appreciated.'

The man waved him away without looking up from his newspaper.

Shepherd walked to the third boat. It was a Dutch

388

barge with a blue hull and a red wheelhouse that was full of potted plants. Shepherd had never owned a boat but knew that the etiquette was not to step on board until invited. It was the same in prisons — you weren't supposed to enter another man's cell unless you were given permission. There was no one in the wheelhouse, but as he moved along the side of the boat he saw movement through one of the windows. He tapped on it and a woman slid it open. 'Can I help you?' she said in a brittle tone that suggested that helping him was the last thing she wanted to do.

'I'm sorry to bother you, but have you seen this man?' He passed the photograph through the window. 'He's my brother in law, my wife is worried sick and we were told he might be staying at the marina.'

The woman screwed up her face as she studied the photograph, then she shook her head, handed it back without a word, then slid the window shut and lowered the blind.

The fourth boat looked like an old tug, with a black hull, a white wheelhouse and bright red railings around the deck. There was a young man in the wheelhouse, sitting on a stool and nodding his head to the music he was listening to through headphones. There was the sickly sweet smell of cannabis wafting off the boat and as Shepherd watched the man put a large joint to his mouth and took a deep drag. Shepherd waved to get the man's attention. The man grinned, put down the joint and put the headphones around his neck. He slid off the stool and opened the wheelhouse door.

'What's up, man?' he said as he stepped out on to the deck

'Have you seen this guy around? My brother in law,

he's gone AWOL.'

The man held the photograph in front of his face and blinked as he tried to focus. He squinted at the photograph and then held it at arm's length. 'Yeah, maybe,' he said.

'Maybe?'

The man wrinkled his nose. 'I think I saw him carrying a hamper.'

'A hamper?'

'Yeah, Fortnum & Mason.' He looked at Shepherd, still blinking his eyes. 'Would that be him?'

'When was this?'

'Yesterday. Or the day before.'

'Where exactly did you see him?'

The man passed the picture back to Shepherd. 'On the jetty.'

'Coming from where, do you know?'

'I don't . . .' He shrugged. 'I might have been a bit high at the time.'

'How sure are you that it was him? On a scale of one to ten?'

The man waggled his head. 'Eight. Nine.' He frowned. 'Eight and a half, maybe.'

'Okay, thanks,' said Shepherd.

The man smiled, went back into the wheelhouse and shut the door.

Shepherd walked along to the next boat. It was long, more than seventy feet, and the roof was dotted with solar panels, potted plants, and a battered old bicycle. A white haired man in blue dungarees was cleaning the side of the boat with a brush and a bucket of soapy water. 'Nice day for it,' said Shepherd.

'It is indeed,' said the man, in a deep, resonating

voice that reminded Shepherd of the actor Brian Blessed. He put down the brush and turned to look at Shepherd, smiling amiably. He was probably over eighty but he looked as fit as the proverbial butcher's dog.

'Have you by any chance seen this man around?' asked Shepherd, holding out the photograph.

The man looked at it and it was clear from the look on his face that he recognised White. He narrowed his eyes as he looked at Shepherd. 'What's this in connection with?'

'We just need to know where he is. What's your name, Sir?'

'My name's Bill, not that that's any of your business. Are you with the police?'

'Yes, I am.'

'Then you won't mind showing me your warrant card.'

Shepherd smiled thinly. 'I said I was with the police, not that I'm a police officer.' He took out his phone. 'But give me a moment and I'll get an officer with a warrant card.'

He opened WhatsApp and typed in his location followed by ASAP.

'So, Bill, you do recognise him, don't you?'

'Let's wait until I've seen a warrant card,' said Bill, getting back to his cleaning.

Rebecca Reilly was the first to arrive. 'You've found him?' she asked.

'Possibly,' said Shepherd. 'Would you mind showing Bill here your warrant card.'

'Of course.' Reilly reached inside her jacket and took out a black wallet with a Met crest on it. She flipped it open so that Bill could see the warrant card, but his eyes were fixed on the Glock in her underarm holster.

'Is that real?' he asked.

Reilly laughed. 'I bloody well hope so,' she said, putting the wallet back in her pocket.

'So, have you seen that man or not?' asked Shepherd.

'I have. His name's David. He's renting my other boat. *Over The Hull.*' He pointed down the jetty. 'Eight boats down. The green forty footer.'

'Is he there now?' asked Shepherd.

'I assume so, but the curtains are always drawn so it's hard to tell.'

'Bill, could we possibly take this inside? We'd like to talk to you in private.'

'I don't see why not,' said Bill, picking up his bucket and brush. 'I'm due a brew.'

He climbed on to the rear deck, placed the bucket and brush next to the tiller, and went down the steps to the saloon. Shepherd and Reilly followed him. There was a small sofa against one wall and a wicker chair with a union jack cushion on it. 'Grab a pew,' said Bill as he walked along to the galley and filled a kettle with water from the tap. Like the cushion, the kettle was also painted in union jack colours.

Shepherd sat down on the wicker chair and Reilly took the sofa. Bill lit a burner and put the kettle on the flame.

'So how long has David been on your other boat?' asked Shepherd.

'About a week.'

'Did you ask for ID?'

Bill's eyes narrowed again. 'Are you with the revenue or the police?'

Shepherd shook his head. 'I don't care about the financial side of the deal,' he said.

'What's he done?'

'We're not sure,' said Shepherd. 'At this stage we just want to talk to him.'

'You send armed police for a chat, do you?' said Bill. 'Please, don't try to kid a kidder.'

Before Shepherd could reply, there was a shout from outside.

'Permission to come aboard!' It was Gerry Owen.

'Come on in, Gerry!' called Shepherd.

'Belay that order!' said Bill. 'Only the captain gives permission to come aboard. You're a guest, it's not your call.'

'Bill, you're right, and I apologise,' said Shepherd. 'I just didn't want him to be standing outside longer than necessary.'

'Permission granted!' shouted Bill in his deep, booming voice.

Owen appeared in the doorway and came slowly down the stairs. 'Oh, I like this,' he said. 'This is one hell of a nice boat.'

'This is Bill, the owner,' said Shepherd. 'He's rented another boat to David. Further down the jetty.'

'Is he there now?'

'We don't know, possibly,' said Shepherd.

Owen sat down next to Reilly and looked around. 'My parents live on a narrowboat, much like this,' he said. 'They sold everything, bought a narrowboat and they just potter around the country. No permanent mooring, they just go where the whim takes them. *Narrow Escape*, they called it.'

'I used to take her out and about, but not so much these days,' said Bill. 'So who wants sugar?'

Owen raised a hand. 'Three please.'

Reilly and Shepherd shook their heads.

Shepherd's phone buzzed. It was Nick Brett. 'I'M OUTSIDE.'

'Bill, we have another arrival,' said Shepherd. 'If you could do the honours.'

Bill grinned. 'Come aboard!' he boomed.

The boat rocked as Brett climbed onto the rear deck. 'How do you like your tea?' asked Bill.

'One sugar, splash of milk,' said Brett. He looked around and when he realised there was nowhere to sit, so he leaned against the wall and folded his arms. By the time the tea was ready, Wilsher had arrived. He sat on the steps as Bill handed mugs of steaming tea around. 'So, Bill, now we're all here, tell us about the boat that David's on. The *Over The Hull*.'

'It's a forty footer, similar layout to this but only the one cabin.'

'How many ways in?' asked Owen.

'There's a hatch at the stern, similar to what I have here. Then the cabin has double doors that lead on to the bow.'

'Are they open?'

'Possibly not,' said Bill. 'I usually keep them locked, but I don't know about David.'

'How sturdy are they?' asked Brett. 'I'm guessing that a good kick will open them, right?'

'You're not going to damage my boat, are you?' asked Bill, clearly worried by the idea.

'Not unless we have to,' said Owen.

'You do realise that I have a key, don't you?'

'Well I do now,' said Owen. 'That'll make our life easier.'

'And I don't want to be digging bullets out of the

woodwork,' said Bill. 'Look, you want to know if David is there or not, why don't I just walk up and announce myself? I can say I want to talk to him about the rent. It's due tomorrow so he should be expecting me.'

Shepherd looked over at Owen, who nodded. 'Works for me,' he said. 'So long as we keep out of the way. Close enough to move in if we have to, but not so close that he'll spot us.'

'I'm not happy about putting you in harm's way, Bill,' said Shepherd.

'You said you only want to talk to him,' said Bill.

'We do, but we don't know how he's going to react.'

'What has he done?'

Shepherd forced a smile. He didn't take pleasure in lying to Bill, but he couldn't tell him the truth, that David White was on a killing rampage that had already taken nine lives. 'He's just a person of interest,' he said.

'He seems like a nice guy. Just having a tough time with the death of his wife.'

'He said that?'

Bill nodded. 'He said she'd passed away and he couldn't face staying in the house, that there were too many memories.' He frowned and scratched his beard. 'Was that a lie?'

'No, that's true, his wife died. And it affected him a lot, which is why we're not sure what his state of mind is right now.'

'Well his state of mind isn't going to be helped by you guys going in waving guns around, is it?'

'Fair point,' said Shepherd. 'Okay then, will you come with us? You can call out and ask to go aboard, if he is there you pull back and we'll move in.'

They drained their mugs and handed them to Bill,

395

who piled them in the sink.

'David knows me, so I'll have to stay back,' said Shepherd. 'Rebecca, why don't you walk with Bill. Nick, you go first and walk past, then stop. Fake a phone call or something. Gerry and Simon, you can be walking together, chatting away. Time it so you are near the stern while Bill is calling out. From then on we play it by ear. Okay?'

The four CTSFOs nodded. 'Sounds like a plan,' said Wilsher.

'Just bear in mind that he's now using explosives,' said Shepherd. 'For all we know, he could have the boat rigged to explode. So stay sharp.'

74

White checked the circuit for the tenth time. He couldn't afford to make a mistake, he would only get one chance. He was using Christmas lights to detonate the explosive again, but this time there would be ten lights, each embedded in a separate lump of the TATP. Each block of explosive would have its individual bulb, the glass broken so that the glowing filament would cause the detonation. Once he had broken the bulbs and inserted them into the explosive, he would cover each block with nuts and bolts and nails and then wrap them with duct tape.

It was the switch that had taken the most thought. Usually a switch worked by completing a circuit, you flicked the switch and the current started to flow. And if the current was running to a bulb embedded in TATP, then you had an explosion. White wanted his switch to work in the opposite way — he wanted detonation to occur when the pressure was removed. The technical term was a dead man's switch, often used in industry on heavy machinery to ensure that the machinery would stop working if the operator was disabled for any reason. There were plenty of commercial dead man's switches available, but they weren't the sort of thing you could buy from a local hardware store, so White had improvised, using his soldering iron, a hand grip exerciser and some wire. So long as the handle was compressed, the circuit was dead. But when the handle was released, the spring forced two contacts together and the circuit was live.

There was also a simple on-off switch in the circuit. It was important to get the sequence right to avoid accidental detonation. The handle had to be squeezed to disconnect the circuit. Then the on-off switch had to be turned on. At that point the only thing stopping the circuit from being completed was the pressure on the hand exerciser. Releasing the pressure would complete the circuit and detonate the bomb.

During his time on MENAD, he read several reports of wannabe suicide bombers meeting an untimely end by getting the sequence wrong, Darwinian selection at work. White was determined that he wouldn't make a mistake, hence his constant checking of the circuit.

He held the exerciser in his left hand and compressed it. He had weakened the spring so it took a minimum of pressure because he had no way of knowing how long it would have to be in his hand.

The lights stayed off. He smiled. So far so good. He used his right hand to flick the on-off switch to the on position. The lights stayed off. He slowly released the pressure on the hand exerciser and as the spring clicked back, the lights went on. White sat back and smiled. Bang. Job done.

75

Shepherd stood on the jetty at the rear of Bill's boat. The *Over The Hull* was far enough away that he couldn't be seen by anyone on board. Nick Brett was walking along the jetty, holding his phone to his ear and muttering into it. The mobile phone was a God-send to surveillance operations. In the old days a watcher would need to carry a newspaper or a book to blend in, but the arrival of mobile phones meant that a watcher could sit on a bench or stand on a corner for hours without looking out of place. Brett was just a guy on his phone, nothing to see here, folks.

Shepherd nodded at Reilly. 'Okay,' he said. 'Break a leg.'

Reilly laughed and looped her arm through Bill's.

He was momentarily confused by the gesture but then he beamed with pleasure. 'I can't tell you how long it's been since I had a pretty girl on my arm,' he said. There was a spring in his step as they walked towards the *Over The Hull*.

Brett had drawn level with the boat now, walking slowly and talking animatedly into his phone. His eyes were taking in everything, the drawn curtains, the closed hatch, the absence of any signs of life.

He walked by the bow, checking it out with a side-long glance, then he tapped on the screen. Shepherd's phone vibrated. It was a WhatsApp message from Brett. 'I DON'T SEE ANYONE.'

Owen and Wilsher looked over his shoulder. 'Doesn't mean he's not there,' said Owen. He clapped

Wilsher on the back. 'Okay, let's go.'

The two men started walking along the jetty.

Reilly and Bill had reached the stern. Reilly took her arm from his and took a step to the side, giving herself room to pull out her gun if necessary.

'David, it's Bill! Permission to come aboard.' Bill's booming voice echoed around the marina.

Owen and Wilsher were about fifty feet away from them, walking slowly and pretending to be deep in conversation.

Brett had stopped, with his phone pressed to his ear, about thirty feet ahead of the boat.

'David, are you there?' Bill shouted. 'Permission to come aboard.'

When there was no reply, Bill handed his keys to Reilly. 'I'm coming aboard, David!' he shouted, then Reilly shooed him away and stepped on to the rear deck.

Shepherd began walking down the jetty, his right hand reaching inside his jacket.

Reilly was by the hatch now, inserting the key.

Brett put his phone away and began walking quickly to the bow, reaching for his gun.

Owen stepped onto the rear of the boat. He already had his gun out, pointing upwards. Wilsher followed him.

Reilly had unlocked the door and she stepped back, reaching for her gun.

Time slowed for Shepherd as it always did when the bullets were about to fly.

He saw Brett stepping on to the bow, his gun aimed at the front hatch.

Reilly had her gun out now and her mouth was set tight, her lips forming a straight line, a slight frown on her face.

Owen pulled the hatch open. Wilsher was just behind him, his gun pointing at the floor, finger not yet on the trigger.

Bill was backing away from the boat, his hands waving around as if he was swatting flies.

Shepherd reached Bill and he put a hand on his shoulder. Bill flinched and ducked away. 'It's okay Bill, just stay well back,' said Shepherd, then he stepped around him and started jogging towards the stern.

Brett was on the bow now, his gun in both hands, covering the front of the boat.

Owen was heading down the hatch, into the saloon.

Wilsher had his finger on the trigger of his Glock, but the barrel was pointed upwards.

Reilly had her left hand on Wilsher's shoulder, ready to follow him inside.

Owen was through the hatch now. Shepherd heard him shout 'Armed Police!'

Wilsher was inside too. 'Armed Police!' he shouted.

Shepherd tensed, expecting shots to be fired, or worse, but the seconds ticked by in silence.

'Clear!' shouted Owen eventually.

Reilly headed down the steps, though she had taken her finger off the trigger.

Shepherd followed her, his gun at his side.

Owen was standing at the doorway to the bedroom, sticking his Glock back into its holster.

Shepherd caught a glimpse of Brett on the bow, still standing with his legs apart, his gun in both hands.

Wilsher was by the toilet, and Reilly was in the galley.

'He's not here,' said Owen.

Shepherd sniffed. The air was thick with the scent

of nail polish remover. 'Smell that?' he said.

Owen nodded. 'Acetone.'

'Acetone?' repeated Reilly. 'What's that when it's at home?'

'One of the ingredients of TATP explosive,' said Shepherd. 'He was building a bomb here.'

Wilsher pulled a large black rubbish bag out of the bathroom. 'A big one, too, looking at all the crap he's left behind.'

76

White went over to the window and looked down at the street below. He was in a cheap hotel in Bayswater, close to Queensway Tube station and just a short walk from Hyde Park. The Indian guy on reception had wanted to see ID and a credit card, but White had told him that he had been robbed at knifepoint the previous day and his wallet had been taken. The Indian had nodded sympathetically and agreed to take cash, a hundred and twenty pounds for the night, with another two hundred pounds as a deposit.

White had asked to see the room before he handed over the cash, not because he cared if the sheets were clean or how the bathroom smelt, he wanted to know if there was a fridge in the room and how big it was. There was a fridge, and it was more than big enough to hold the six Tupperware containers filled with TATP.

He had left the Prius in an underground car park behind the tube station. It had cost thirty four pounds a day and he had paid for five days. He had no intention of ever collecting the car but if it was parked underground it couldn't be spotted by one of the many mobile ANPR vehicles that prowled the city.

He figured they would find the *Over The Hull* eventually, either by tracking his Ford Fiesta or using mobile phone mast tracking. He'd had to stay on the boat to manufacture the TATP because the fumes would be too noticeable in the hotel, but as soon as he'd finished he had packed everything into his Prius and driven to central London.

He locked the door and went downstairs. The Indian receptionist looked up from a medical book and smiled. 'Is the room okay, Mr Williams?' he asked.

'It's perfect,' said White. 'I'm just going to get some food. I can eat in my room, can't I?'

'Of course you can,' said the receptionist.

'I won't be long,' said White. He stepped out of the front door and looked right and left. Bayswater was one of the most cosmopolitan areas of the city, with residents coming from all over the world, augmented by tourists flocking to the area's cheap hotels. It was the perfect place to hide, though White wouldn't have to hide for long.

77

Giles Pritchard sat back in his chair and rubbed his chin. He had rolled his shirtsleeves up and his club tie was loose around his neck. Shepherd was sitting on one of the two wooden chairs facing Pritchard's desk. 'How big a bomb, do you think?' asked Pritchard.

'Going by the containers he left behind, there could be as much as a couple of pounds of TATP. Enough to blow up a small building.'

Pritchard winced. 'It was bad enough when he was shooting people, but he's gone from that to petrol bombs to a car bomb and God only knows what he's got in mind now.'

'We know he's out for revenge, he's not attacking at random. Everyone he's killed so far has been targeted.'

'He nearly killed you. And you saved his life.'

'He could have killed me, easily. But he didn't. Abu-Rous was the target, I was collateral damage, yes, but he detonated the bomb before I got into the car.'

'The shrapnel could have killed anyone in the area, Dan, you can't defend the man.'

'I'm not defending him, I'm just pointing out that he's been very selective about his targets, nothing has changed on that front.'

'I don't see that he can be selective with two pounds of high explosive. That sounds to me as if he's targeting a mosque.'

Shepherd shook his head. 'This isn't about Muslims, he's not attacking people because of their

405

religion, he's killing people that he blames for the death of his family.'

'He's changed, though. You have to see that. When he embarked on this revenge mission, it was personal, he used a gun and he got up close. Now he's using petrol bombs and car bombs. The danger is that he's evolving and now sees Muslims everywhere as the enemy.'

'I really don't see any evidence of that,' said Shepherd. 'Yes, his methods are changing but his targets are all specific. He did kill Fayyad's daughter, and she wasn't a specific target, but after what happened to his own daughters, I do see the logic of him killing her.' He forced a smile. 'Logic is the wrong word, obviously. He's clearly unbalanced and logic no longer applies. But in terms of what he's doing, there is a twisted logic to it.'

'So far.'

'Yes, so far. But everyone he has targeted was someone he researched on the MI5 database. To date he hasn't strayed from that.'

'So you think he'll continue to target people he researched?'

'I do. And we know who they are. We need to focus our attention on the names that he was looking at.'

Pritchard nodded and bent over his keyboard. He tapped away, then peered at the screen on his left.

'Leaving aside the three men who flew in from Egypt, in all White looked at the files of twenty four men, all connected in some way to the October Seven Hamas attacks. Of those twenty four, six are now dead.'

'So who is left?'

Pritchard read through the names. Shepherd listened. His memory was able to provide him with a picture and biography of most of the names on the list. 'Two of these names are addressing the pro-Palestinian March in London tomorrow,' said Shepherd once Pritchard had finished.

'Really?'

Shepherd nodded. 'Salim Dabush. He's an imam and been on our watchlists for years. And Nasim Halawah is an imam at the Al Manaar mosque in West London.'

'Yes, Halawah I've heard of. David would have seen all the intel on him and it's pretty damning.'

'Dabush is just as bad,' said Shepherd.

'How do you know they'll be addressing the march?'

'It was on the news. BBC. It'd be a perfect opportunity for David to cross two names off his list. Can we call off the march?'

'Even if we could, we couldn't,' said Pritchard. 'This is not a group that follows the rule of law, it'll go ahead, banned or not. But the Government won't want to be seen banning a public protest.'

Shepherd flashed a wry smile. 'They're more likely to go down on one knee, aren't they?'

'The government is in an impossible situation,' said Pritchard coldly. 'A rock and hard place.'

'It just feels to me like they're playing favourites at the moment. Certain groups get to break the law with impunity. I know if I was Jewish I'd feel threatened by these protests. And where were the protests against what Hamas did?'

'Ours not to reason why, Dan. You know that. Our priority is to protect the general public, no matter their race or religion. And frankly, this isn't a discussion we need to have. The answer to your question is no, we can't ban the march. But we do know that two of David's targets will be there, which gives us an edge.'

'Just so long as you see the irony in all the resources we are putting in to protecting men who arranged the massacre of more than a thousand innocent civilians.'

'I do. But I have to deal with the way the world is, not the way I'd like it to be.'

'So what will you do? Warn the two imams to stay away from the march?'

'We can do that, but again, they're not the type to listen to us. They'll assume we just don't want them addressing the crowds.'

'Even if you tell them there's a credible threat to their lives?'

'We can tell them there is a threat, but we can't divulge any of the details. Both of them will have a direct line to Hamas. And if we don't give them any specifics, they're unlikely to follow our advice.'

'So we do what, say nothing and let them go ahead and address the march?'

'Do you have a better idea?'

'With the greatest of respect, I'm not the one who's paid to have better ideas. I'm paid to carry out orders.'

'And you do a great job. Which is why you'll be running security at the march tomorrow.'

'So we use them as bait?' asked Shepherd. 'That's the plan?'

'Not bait, no. Not exactly. But if you're right and David will try to kill them tomorrow, it gives us a fighting change of stopping him.'

'Define stopping,' said Shepherd.

Pritchard stood up, walked around his desk and went over to the window. He stood looking out, rubbing the back of his neck. 'David White has crossed a line, and I don't see that he can come back. Do you?'

'You don't want him on trial, is that it?'

Pritchard turned to look at him. 'There would be repercussions if it became public knowledge that an MI5 officer was killing Muslims.'

'He isn't killing Muslims, he's killing terrorists, the very same terrorists who are responsible for the death of his family.'

'That's how we see it, yes. But the UK's four million or so Muslims might think otherwise.'

'And you're scared that they might take to the streets?' Shepherd laughed harshly. 'That ship has sailed, hasn't it?'

'It's about maintaining balance, Dan. That's what we do, We maintain the status quo.'

'I've got to say this, just so there's no misunderstanding,' said Shepherd. 'If I come face to face with David, I'm not sure that I'd be able to pull the trigger.'

'I understand that. It would be your call.'

'Just so you know.'

'I hear you. But tell me this. What if by shooting him you avert an explosion in which people might die?'

'I'll cross that bridge when I come to it,' said Shepherd.

'I hope you make the right decision.'

Shepherd flashed him a tight smile. 'So do I.'

409

78

David White walked past a group of Japanese tourists who were photographing one of the lions at the base of Nelson's Column, chattering away in their own language. He was wearing his oversized Puffa jacket and had the hood up. It had always been one of his favourite places in London. When he was a child his father had brought him on Sunday to feed the pigeons. Back then vendors had sold bird seed in small plastic cups and he would stand with his arms outstretched, a cup in either hand, covered with pigeons trying to get the food. It was the Mayor Ken Livingstone who banned the feeding of the pigeons in 2003, claiming that they caused too much damage. Anyone who tried to feed the birds now faced prosecution and a fine. Thirteen years later Livingstone's career ended in disgrace when he was forced to resign from the Labour Party over allegations of anti-Semitism following public comments he made about Hitler and Zionism. He always denied that what was said was anti-Semetic but went out of his way to apologise to the Jewish community for any offence he had caused.

The thousands of men and women who would be crowding into Trafalgar Square on Saturday wouldn't be apologising to the Jewish Community, far from it. Their demonstrations only served to show the hatred and contempt they had for Jews around the world. The politicians made no attempt to ban the anti-Israel marches, the police stood by while anti-Semetic chants echoed around the streets, and the media seemed to have forgotten that 1,200 innocent civilians had been massacred in Israel. Now it was all about calling for a ceasefire, as if it was Israel that was somehow at fault.

A Japanese girl appeared in front of him, holding her phone. 'Please take picture,' she said, gesturing at her friends who had gathered together at the base of the lion. One of them, a young man in a Pokemon hoodie, had climbed on to the back of the lion and was holding his arms up. White nodded. 'Sure,' he said.

The girl thanked him and hurried over to stand among her friends. 'Say cheese!' He shouted, then realised they probably had no idea what that meant. He took several pictures and a short video panning from them to the column, then walked over and gave her back the phone. She thanked him profusely and they all bowed.

'Free Palestine! Free Palestine!'

White turned to look in the direction of the shouts. A group of young men in black and white keffiyeh scarfs were standing by a long table from which hung a banner proclaiming 'Stop The Israeli Attacks!' Two young women in black headscarves were handing out leaflets to passersby.

'Sign the petition now!' screamed one of the men, waving a clipboard. 'Get the Jews out of Gaza! Stop them killing innocent children!'

White flashed back to the men with guns at the Supernova festival, screaming their hatred and firing their guns, and for a couple of seconds he struggled to breathe, as if there were metal bands around his chest. He took several slow deep breaths to calm himself down. Innocent children? What about his children?

What about them? Did they care about the children that Hamas had murdered? He gritted his teeth. Part of him wanted to go over and confront them, to tell them just how wrong they were, but he knew it would be a pointless exercise. There was nothing he could say that would change their views or how they felt.

'From the river to the sea, Palestine will be free!' chanted one of the men. His friends joined in and soon the chant echoed around the square. Nobody tried to stop them, nobody objected to what they were doing. In fact some of the passers-by were joining in, as if it was a football chant and not a call for the death of Jews.

White turned and walked away. Tomorrow would be soon enough for them to feel his wrath, and share his grief. Let them have their chants and their leaflets and their petition and to hell with them.

79

The Lexus dropped Pritchard and Shepherd outside a four storey building at 109 Lambeth Road. The three numbers were posted in huge white letters to the left of the building, close to the south bank of the River Thames and better known as the Lambeth Central Communications Command Centre. It was only a fifteen minute walk from Thames House but Pritchard had a full diary and so had taken the car.

They were expected and a uniformed Superintendent was waiting for them in reception. He was an Asian in his early fifties, slightly overweight with skin the colour of burnished mahogany. He introduced himself as Superintendent Mo Kamran and offered his hand to Pritchard first. They shook, and Pritchard introduced Shepherd. 'Pleasure,' said the superintendent, shaking Shepherd's hand.

He took them down a flight of stairs to the special operations room, which occupied the entire basement of the building. He opened a door for them and stepped to the side to let them go in first. The special operations room was half the size of a football field with no windows, illuminated by banks of fluorescent lights and filled with dozens of pod-like workstations, several of which were occupied by shirt-sleeved police officers, their triple screens filled with data and CCTV feeds. There were white supporting pillars a metre or so in diameter spaced around the room, and a dozen or so whiteboards on stands.

'Have either of you been in an SOR before?' asked

413

the Superintendent.

Both men shook their heads.

'I'll give you the tour then,' he said. 'This is GT Ops, the call sign for the Lambeth command centre. There are three of these command centres in London, the other two are in Bow and Hendon. Every day, between them, they handle six thousand emergency and fifteen thousand non-emergency calls. They're also used to provide specialist communications for major incidents, with experts from the police, Fire Brigade, Ambulance and any other of the emergency services that might be needed. On our left is the Gold Commander's suite, where you'll usually find me, and next to it is the Silver Command suite where the various commanding officers hold their own briefings.'

He pointed at the far end of the room where there were four pods, each pod consisting of three desks pushed in to a triangle, with identical high-backed black ergonomic chairs.

'The pod on the left is manned by the Diplomatic Protection Group pod and next to it is the pod used by SCO19.'

The DPG pod was empty but a uniformed officer was sitting at one of the SCO19 desks.

'This is Inspector Marty Windle, he'll be in charge of armed response on the day' said the superintendent, taking them over to the desk. The inspector stood up and shook hands with them. 'Giles and Dan,' said the superintendent by way of introduction. 'They're with Five.'

The inspector's jaw clenched but he continued to smile. Generally police officers had a low opinion of the intelligence agencies and this was reflected in a general reluctance to work with them. Unlike police officers who always had to identify themselves and had to follow the rules of the 1984 Police and Criminal Evidence Act, MI5 officers tended to work in the shadows and often appeared to play by their own rules.

The superintendent pointed at the pod in the middle of the group. 'This will be manned by the Pan London support staff, who will handle outgoing calls to the various units around the capital, and we have other pods for the London Ambulance Service and the Fire Brigade. Over there, by the door, is the pod where supervisors look after the support staff and next to it is the General Policing Command pod which will be staffed by a chief inspector and an inspector.'

He waved his arm around the room. 'As you can see there are dozens of other pods and we can staff them with whatever resources the Gold Commander — i.e. my good self — considers necessary.'

'And when will you be up and running for the Palestinian march?' asked Pritchard.

'The march is scheduled to start at noon, but we'll be here from six o'clock,' said the superintendent. He took them to a large screen on the wall which was showing a map of the city. He pointed at the middle of the screen. 'Most of the protesters will gather at Tube Stations at Oxford Circus, Regent's Park, Great Portland Street and Bond Street, we're expecting crowds to start gathering from nine o'clock onwards. From there they will walk to the BBC HQ in Portland Place. There'll be a protest there at the BBC's coverage of the attacks on Gaza and the police will be monitoring any speeches made for anti-Semetic comments.'

'The whole march is anti-Semetic,' said Shepherd.

'That's sort of the point of it, right?'

Pritchard flashed Shepherd a warning look. 'And who will be addressing the protesters at that point?'

'That we don't know,' said the superintendent. 'They haven't given us a play list and I suppose a lot depends on who turns up. Anyway, from Portland Place the march will move to Trafalgar Square where there will be more speeches, after which the march will hopefully disperse peacefully with people leaving via St. James' Park, Embankment, and Charing Cross stations.'

'And how many protesters are we expecting?' asked Pritchard.

'The organisers say two hundred thousand but they always hype their figures. They said the last march was two hundred thousand strong but our estimate was considerably less than half of that.'

'And what policing will there be?'

'We'll have as many boots on the ground as possible, and we'll have TSG units near by in case of any trouble.'

The Territorial Support Group specialised in public order policing, usually cruising around London in marked Sprinter vans, using the call sign prefix Uniform with a sergeant, seven constables and a driver on board.

'But the last few marches have passed off without incident so we're not expecting trouble,' the superintendent added.

'So how many boots on the ground?' asked Shepherd.

'A thousand officers, give or take,' said the superintendent. He smiled. 'So two thousand boots.'

'CTSFOs?' asked Shepherd.

'Not in plainclothes,' said the superintendent. 'They tend not to blend in on demonstrations like this, and if they're spotted carrying a weapon there could be a backlash. We'll have uniformed CTSFOs nearby but parked up away from the main route, ready to move in if necessary. But things would have to be pretty bad for us to send them in.'

'Just to let you know, Dan will be there, and he'll be armed, but discreetly. And he'll have four CTSFOs with him. They'll be in radio contact with each other but is there a way of also patching them into comms here?'

The superintendent nodded. 'Absolutely,' he said. 'They can have my Gold Commander feed, which will have everything I say but that might prove to be sensory overload. It might be better to have a feed from Marty, he can pass on anything that might be useful to your team. Also it means you and your team will keep Marty in the loop.'

'Perfect,' said Pritchard, and Shepherd nodded in agreement.

'What about snipers?' asked Shepherd.

'We'll have CTSFO snipers up high covering the route but again maintaining a low profile,' said the superintendent.

'They'll need to be briefed that I'll be among the crowds with four CTSFOs,' said Shepherd.

The superintendent nodded. 'I'll make sure that's done.'

'And what rules are being applied to the protesters?' asked Pritchard.

'The same as for previous marches,' said the superintendent. 'We've made it clear that we won't tolerate any hate crimes during the march. Expressing support for Palestinians is fine but praising Hamas in any form is not. And officers will intervene if protesters use the word 'jihad' in chants, even though there is some dispute as to what the word means.'

'I think everyone knows exactly what it means,' said Shepherd, and he received another frosty look from Pritchard for his trouble.

'We'll have one helicopter overhead and another on standby,' said the superintendent.

'Mounted police?' asked Shepherd.

'There are cultural considerations when it comes to using horses in situations like this,' said the superintendent. 'The same with dogs. But there have been relatively few problems with previous marches. Far more incidents occur at the Notting Hill Carnival every year.'

'Well it looks as if you've got all bases covered,' said Pritchard.

Superintendent Kamran smiled. 'Well as our American cousins say, this isn't my first rodeo,' he said. 'So can you tell me the specific nature of the threat you're worried about?'

'He's a lone wolf with a grudge against all things Hamas,' said Pritchard. 'He has guns, we know that, and we suspect that he has access to explosives.'

The superintendent's jaw dropped. 'Who is he?'

'His identity isn't the issue,' said Pritchard. 'We can supply you with pictures but they mustn't leave this room. We will have our own small team of plainclothes CTSFOs in place, and they will be looking for him. I hear what you say about the dangers if they get spotted, but they're pros, they know what they're doing. Dan here has met the man so he'll be there, too.'

'If shots are fired, it'll possibly cause a stampede,'

said the superintendent.

'Any weapons used will be silenced,' said Pritchard.

Shepherd resisted the urge to correct his boss — guns were never silenced, they were suppressed, and the bulbous cylinder screwed into the barrel was a suppressor, not a silencer.

'And you said he might have access to explosives?' said the superintendent.

'It's possible. But the intel suggests that he has two specific targets in mind — the imams Salim Dabush and Nasim Halawah. We don't think there's a threat to the protesters in general.'

The superintendent frowned. 'Bombs aren't generally known for their surgical precision,' he said.

'Well hopefully we'll intercept him before that becomes an issue,' said Pritchard. 'And on that score, what sort of CCTV monitoring will you have?'

'Full real time access to all Government and council CCTV cameras, plus a live feed from the helicopter.'

'What about super recognisers?' asked Pritchard.

'We usually have one or two just keeping an eye out for known major criminals or people on our most wanted, but in view of the fact that you have a specific suspect, I'll talk to my boss and see how many more we can draft in.'

Super recognisers had the ability to recognise and recall faces at a level much higher than most people. It appeared to be a gift of genetics, an ability that occurred in less than one per cent of the population. it wasn't a skill that could be acquired by practice, you were either born with the ability or you weren't. A super recogniser could memorise and recall thousands of faces, often having seen them only once. They were used in police control rooms to spot prolific offenders or to target gang crime at events such as the Notting Hill Carnival. They were used to identify ticket touts at football matches and spot known drug dealers and pickpockets at pop concerts and music festivals. The super recognisers were drafted in after the Grenfell tower block fire to weed out fake compensation claims. They viewed thousands of hours of CCTV footage from around the block and were eventually able to confirm that seventeen people who claimed to be resident there were lying.

Shepherd had the same skill, he never forgot a face once he'd seen it, and was able to pick out people in crowds and at a distance. But his memory skills went way beyond just being able to memorise faces, Shepherd pretty much remembered everything he had ever seen or heard.

'That would be useful,' said Pritchard. 'As many as you can get, obviously. If we can spot our man before he gets anywhere near his targets, we all come out of this smelling of roses.'

80

White lay on his bed, staring up at the ceiling. He was wearing just a t-shirt and shorts. The shirt had belonged to Hannah. It was a Fallout Boy shirt, one of her favourite bands. He'd bought it for her one night after they'd seen the band at the O2 in Greenwich. He had found it in the laundry basket in the bathroom and it still had her scent.

Going to concerts together was something he'd always enjoyed, not so much for the songs but because she took such pleasure from live music. Her eyes would flash and first chance she got she would be on her feet dancing. That was the main reason he had allowed her and Ella to persuade him to take them to the Supernova festival. He just wanted to spend time with them and build memories, so that in the future they'd look back and remember what a great dad he was. He bit down on his lower lip. What was it they said? People plan and God laughs? Now the only one who had the memories was White, and the memories brought tears to his eyes and made him want to die. He understood why Rachel had taken her own life. It was simply too painful to live with the memories, knowing how the girls had died. Tears welled up in his eyes. He missed them so much. He missed Hannah and he missed Ella and he missed Rachel so badly that it was like a punch to the solar plexus every time he thought about them.

Did the men who went on the rampage that day realise the heartbreak and sadness their actions would cause? Did they have any idea how many lives they would take that day, but also how many lives they would destroy afterwards? One thousand two hundred men, women and children were murdered, but how many more friends and relatives would be left to grieve? How could anyone behave that cruelly and still consider themselves human?

Tears ran down his cheeks and soaked into the pillow.

His religion said that revenge was wrong, that vengeance belonged to God, only God was entitled to punish those who did wrong. But White wasn't prepared to wait until God decided to punish the men responsible for tearing his family apart. Mossad were happy enough to take revenge, and so was White. He'd do what he had to do, and then he would join Hannah, Ella and Rachel, and he'd do it free of guilt or remorse.

He closed his eyes, but knew that there was almost no chance of sleeping that night. He tried to fill his mind with thoughts of happy times, the moments when he had been with his family and enjoying life, but time and time again the images of Hamas fighters raping and killing took over, screaming allegiance to their God as they fired their guns.

81

Shepherd was in the CTSFO's East London base at Leman Street at just before seven o'clock in the morning. He parked in a side road a short walk away and headed up the stairs to the main entrance. There were no police markings on the six-storey concrete buildings, in fact there were no signs at all indicating its function, but it was where the SCO19 armed police were based in the east of the city, and where they kept their weapons. It was also a CTSFO base, with a firing range and a gym. Everything an armed police officer needed to keep himself — or herself — in peak condition.

Shepherd pressed a button on an unmarked intercom. After a few seconds he heard a gruff 'yeah?'

'It's Dan,' he said.

'On my way down,' said the voice, which Shepherd recognised as Gerry Owen. A minute passed and then Owen appeared on the other side of the glass door. He was wearing a waxed cotton jacket and a black and white scarf loosely knotted around his neck. He opened the door and grinned when he saw Shepherd looking at the scarf. 'Thought it might help me blend,' he said.

'Good idea,' said Shepherd. He was also casually dressed in a leather flight jacket with a sheepskin collar and jeans. He'd chosen the jacket because it zipped up meaning he could get to his Glock without having to fumble with buttons.

Owen closed the door and took Shepherd up to

423

a room where the three other members of the team were waiting, drinking coffee and munching on bacon rolls. They were all dressed casually with black and white scarves around their necks. There was a plate of bacon rolls on a table and Shepherd took one. 'Right, just so you know, we think White has two targets in mind, two imams who will be addressing today's meeting at some point. With just two targets, it would make sense for him to use a gun. But he's used petrol bombs and a car bomb, so all bets are off.'

'You've still got the Glock I gave you?' asked Owen.

Shepherd nodded and patted the bulge under his left armpit. 'But we need to use suppressors, just in case we have to shoot among the crowd. We don't want to start a panic.'

'We've got suppressors,' said Owen.

'And did you get comms fixed up?'

Owen turned his head to show Shepherd the earpiece in his left ear. 'We'll get a feed from GT Ops closer to the time. I've got a receiver and earpiece for you. We'll hear Marty Windle and be able to talk to each other.'

Shepherd frowned. 'The earpieces are a bit of a giveaway, aren't they?'

Owen grinned and pulled a blue wool beanie hat from his pocket with a flourish. He pulled it on so that it covered both ears. Shepherd nodded. 'That works.'

Owen gestured at a table where there were several wool hats. 'Help yourself.'

'So what's the plan today?' asked Reilly.

'We follow the march, basically,' said Shepherd, picking up one of the beanie hats. 'It's due to start at the BBC building in Portland Place. We blend as much as we can and we keep an eye out for David

White. There will be a team of super recognisers at GT Ops who will be watching the CCTV feeds looking for White, and if they spot him, Inspector Windle will inform us. As I said, the two men that White is targeting are imams who will be addressing the demonstrators at some point. We don't have a schedule so we'll have to play it by ear.' He reached into his jacket and brought out eight photographs, four of Salim Dabush and four of Nasim Halawah. 'These are the men he is targeting. So when they do eventually appear, you'll need to get close.' He handed the photographs around and the four CTSFOs studied them.

Shepherd's phone rang. It was Jimmy Sharpe. 'What's up, Razor?' Shepherd asked, walking away from the CTSFOs.

'Tuk has just been told that he's being taken to Luton.'

'When?'

'Now. We heard it through his phone. They've told him to leave his stuff and that he'll be back later tonight or tomorrow. They've not said for sure what he's doing, but it sure smells like a hit.'

'Has he used his get-out phrase?'

'No. Petrit reckons that Tuk wants to be a hundred per cent sure before he calls us in. The problem is, once he's on the move it's going to be that much harder to pull him out.'

'I hear you,' said Shepherd. 'How are you fixed up with armed response?'

'They wouldn't give us our own unit, but I've got a number I can call that they assure me will get an ARV out to us within minutes. But I'm not sure how good that promise will be if we're up in Luton. Plus, chances are that it won't be an unmarked vehicle, it'll be a BMW with all the trimmings so they'll see us coming.'

'What does Petrit think?'

'He thinks we should pull Tuk out now. He was pretty shaken up by what happened to Plauku and I don't think he wants another death on his hands.'

'And evidence wise, what do we have?'

'It's vague, Spider. Nothing that will link this to the Meatball. I'm afraid.'

'So what do you want?'

'I think we can let it run, for a while longer. But we need an undercover firearms team.' Sharpe cursed. 'Sorry, Spider, Petrit says they've just told Tuk that the car will be there in half an hour. We're going to have to go.'

'You're geared up for following Tuk's phone?'

'Yeah, your pal Amar Singh gave us a tablet that shows the GPS position, so we can follow them no problem. Petrit and I will go in my car and we can probably pull in Chris Adkins. He said I was to call him as soon as we had anything, but obviously I called you first.'

'Okay, you and Petrit follow them up to Luton. Tell Chris what's happening but make it clear he doesn't need to get involved. Also tell him that I'll check in with Giles Pritchard once I'm mobile. I'll get a CTSFO team and join you.'

'As easy as that?'

Shepherd turned to look at Gerry Owen and his team. 'Yeah, mate, as easy as that.'

82

'They're leaving the car wash,' said Ajazi, looking at
the tablet in his lap. The tablet showed the location of
Marku's phone. It was moving slowly along the road,
away from the car wash.

'What are they saying?' asked Sharpe, who was
driving the Skoda, powering along the central lane of
the M1.

Ajazi had an earphone in which allowed him to listen to the audio feed from the phone. 'They've got a
gun.'

''What sort of gun?'

'They haven't said. One of the gang has it. Tuk
asked for it but they said they won't be giving it to
him until they arrive in Luton.'

'Have they said who the intended victim is?'

'Not by name but they've given Tuk a photograph.
Tuk asked who the guy was but they said he didn't
need to know, they'd be taking him to a corner shop
and all he had to do was to walk into the shop and
shoot the guy.'

Sharpe used hands free to call Dan Shepherd. 'Dan,
it's me. They have a gun in the vehicle.'

'What sort of vehicle is it?'

'We don't know for sure, we're not there yet. All we
have is the GPS locator.'

'Well that's not good.'

'Tuk did ask why he had to get into the back of the
van, so we know that much. Where are you?'

'East London,. Heading for the M1. I'm in my

427

BMW but I'm with a CTSFO vehicle so they're using blues and twos, it won't take us long to reach you. Just keep me informed as to your position.'

83

The Range Rover was in the outside lane of the M1, its siren wailing and blue lights flashing from behind the front grille. Traffic wasn't heavy but what vehicles there were all moved out of the way. Shepherd was tucked in behind the Range Rover in his BMW. He had his amber hazard warning flashers on. They were approaching Watford, about midway between London and Luton.

Shepherd had his mobile phone on a dashboard mounting and the speaker on. His Met earpiece was in place and he'd covered it with a black wool beanie.

'Spider, we have the vehicle in sight,' said Sharpe over the phone. 'It's a van. A blue Ford Transit with the name of the car wash on the side.' He read out the registration number and it went straight into Shepherd's memory.

'Gerry, did you get that?' asked Shepherd.

'Got it,' said Owen in Shepherd's ear.

'We're dropping back now,' said Sharpe. 'We're just coming up to the A414 junction to Hemel Hempstead.'

'We're about three miles behind you, Razor,' said Shepherd.

The Range Rover killed its siren and lights. Shepherd switched off his hazard lights and both vehicles slowed to the speed limit. There was no point in letting the Albanians know they were coming.

84

Giles Pritchard sipped his tea as he looked at the screens on the wall of the Gold Commander's suite. He had decided to spend the day at the Lambeth command centre, knowing that he wouldn't able to relax if he stayed at home. He had made it clear to Superintendent Kamran that he was only there as an observer and wouldn't be concerning himself with operational matters. The screens were showing CCTV footage around several West End Tube stations. Crowds were already starting to gather, with protesters carrying pro-Palestinian placards and displaying the Palestinian flag on their clothes and bags. No trouble had been reported and none was expected. There had been next to no violence at previous demonstrations, mainly because there had been no opposition to the marchers and the police had treated the protesters with kid gloves.

Pritchard's mobile rang. The caller was withholding their number but he took the call anyway. It was Joel Schwartz. 'Sorry to bother you on a Saturday, Giles, but this is urgent.'

'Not a problem, I'm working.'

'The Trafalgar Square march?'

'Indeed.'

'You should just ban it and have done with it.'

'You know that MI5 doesn't have anything to do with banning demonstrations, Joel. Decisions like that are taken at a much higher pay grade than mine.'

'But you're worried that David White might be

planning to disrupt the march?'

'I'm just an observer,' said Pritchard. 'The police are looking after crowd control.'

'But you'll have your own people in place, presumably?'

Pritchard chuckled softly. 'I'm hardly likely to discuss operational matters with you, am I?'

'Can we meet, Giles?'

'Not really, I'm in Lambeth at the moment.'

'With Six?'

'I really can't disclose my location.'

'So not Ceauşescu Towers?'

Ceauşescu Towers was one of many nicknames for the MI6 Building at Vauxhall Cross. Pritchard had also heard it described as Legoland, Babylon-on-Thames, the Ziggurat, and the Vauxhall Trollop.

'What is so urgent, Joel?'

'I really don't want to tell you over the phone, it has to be face to face.'

Pritchard looked at the clock on the wall. It was only eight o'clock and the march wasn't due to start until midday. 'Do you know Archbishop's Park?'

'Of course. It was opened to the public in 1901. Before that it was part of the grounds of Lambeth Palace. Hence the name.'

'You're very well informed,' said Pritchard.

'I spend a lot of time in parks,' said Schwartz. 'When can I see you? The sooner the better.'

'And you can't tell me what it's about?'

'I'm sorry. Not over the phone. But you will want to hear what I have to say, trust me.'

'I'm not sure that I do, Joel. But I'll see you in the park in half an hour.'

431

85

David White woke up and blinked several times before he realised where he was. The cheap hotel in Bayswater. He was surprised that he had slept but slept he had, for almost six hours. He sat up. Today was the day. His last day on earth. His last day of suffering. He had one final thing to do and then he would be at peace.

He padded to the tiny shower room that smelled of mould. He shaved, then showered, then dried himself on a towel that he had brought from his house. It was a Peppa Pig towel that Ella had used when she was a toddler. She had grown out of it but it had remained in the airing cupboard, neither he nor Rachel could bring themselves to throw it away.

He pulled on clean underwear and socks, then put on the Fallout Boy shirt. He wanted Hannah's scent next to his skin. He put a denim shirt over the top of the t-shirt and slowly fastened the buttons as he ran through everything that he needed to do. He pulled on his jeans and trainers, then spread a copy of *The Guardian* on the bed. He retrieved the Christmas lights circuit and a pair of pliers from his bag, then carefully and methodically began breaking the glass bulbs.

86

As he drove on to the M1 Shepherd called Giles
Pritchard on hands-free and explained what had happened to Tuk Marku. 'Luton?' said Pritchard. 'Where
in Luton?'

'We don't know, it's going to be a hard stop as soon
as they leave the motorway. Marku has now used his
rescue phrase twice already, he's desperate for us to
pull him out. If we don't he's either going to have to
kill their target or be killed himself.'

'You need to be back in London before midday,
you know that?'

'We will be.'

'I mean it, Dan. I understand how concerned you
are about Marku, but he's just one man. Hundreds
are at risk if David White does have a bomb.'

'We'll be back in a couple of hours. Three at the
most. Gerry Owen is liaising with the Luton cops
to take the gang members into custody and Jimmy
Sharpe and Petrit will whisk Marku away. The
CTSFOs and I will head straight back to London.
Gerry has also arranged for an ARV to be on standby
at the Luton exit, plus an ambulance.'

'What about the gang members? You're bringing
them to London?'

'We think it's better to do the first interrogation in
Luton. Once Jimmy and Petrit have got Marku to a
safe place, they can question the gang members and
see if any of them can be turned. There's a gun possession charge but there's also a very strong possibility

of getting them all on conspiracy to murder. If we can turn just one of them, we should be able to get him to phone Fisnik Haziri, maybe even fake some pictures of the job done and hand those over. But even a phone call to Haziri confirming that the job is done might be enough to nail him on conspiracy charges. We're going to have to play it by ear, obviously.'

'Just make sure you and the CTSFOs are back in London for the march.'

'We'll be there.'

'Don't let me down, Dan.'

'I won't. Any news on David?'

'Some news, yes. But not what we were expecting. Are you alone?'

'I am. Yes.'

'You will not believe what I am about to tell you.'

87

White poured the brightly coloured bits of broken glass into the toilet and flushed them away, then went back to the bed. He checked again that the main switch was in the off position. That was the crucial part of the circuit. So long as it was in the off position, nothing could happen. He hadn't added the trigger to the circuit, that was one of the last things to be done.

He went over to the small fridge and took out the six Tupperware containers. Between them they contained almost two kilograms of explosive. More than enough.

He took a roll of duct tape from his bag, and four plastic boxes of nuts, bolts, and screws. The explosive was deadly enough, but the ironmongery would turn into deadly shrapnel when the bomb went off, ripping through flesh and bone. All he had to do was to get close to the imams Salim Dabush and Nasim Halawah. Basic physics would do the rest.

435

88

Shepherd saw Sharpe's grey Skoda ahead of him and he slowed and moved over to the inside lane. He was now ahead of the black Range Rover. He called Sharpe on his mobile, hands free. 'Okay, I'm behind you, Razor. You have eyes on?'

'The van is about a hundred yards ahead of us,' said Sharpe.

'We'll do a hard stop as soon as he's off the motorway,' said Shepherd. 'I've got the CTSFOs on the radio. You're hearing this, Gerry?'

'Loud and clear,' said Owen in Shepherd's earpiece.

'Right, for the purposes of identification, Razor's Skoda is Alpha, my BMW is Bravo and the Range Rover is Charlie. The target van is Tango. Once we are about to leave the motorway, Alpha will overtake Tango. Bravo will move up close behind Tango. Alpha will announce the hard stop and brake. Bravo will come in close behind and lock Tango in place. Charlie will come in on the right alongside Tango. You guys pile out, shock and awe, should be over in seconds. All good?'

'Roger that,' said Owen.

'No problem,' said Sharpe.

'We know they have at least one gun on board Tango, but they're not expecting trouble,' said Shepherd. 'Tango has no side or rear windows but the rear doors shouldn't be locked so we need to get them open as soon as possible.'

'I'll take the rear door, with Rebecca,' said Owen.

436

'Nick and Simon will secure the front.'

'I'll provide cover at the rear,' said Shepherd.

They passed a sign that said the Luton turn off was just a mile ahead. Shepherd checked his mirror. The Range Rover was coming up behind him.

They were travelling at almost seventy miles an hour so the turn off was less than a minute away. Time started to crawl by and Shepherd became hyper aware of his surroundings. The sky overhead was clear blue. He could see the individual blades of grass on the verge to his left. He could feel the air from the vents, brushing against his skin. The hardness of the steering wheel on his fingers. The seat pressing into his back. The pressure of his foot on the accelerator. All his senses were in overdrive, the result of the adrenaline coursing through his system, the body's way of dealing with fright, fight and flight. Except this time fright and flight weren't options.

He saw the turn off ahead of them. He took out his gun and placed it on the front passenger seat.

'Alpha overtaking Tango now,' said Sharpe over the phone.

'Alpha overtaking Tango now,' repeated Shepherd to make sure that Owen heard it over the radio.

Shepherd saw the Skoda's right indicator start flashing, then the car pulled out and accelerated past the blue Transit van.

Shepherd pressed his foot on the accelerator. 'Bravo closing up on Tango.'

The Range Rover kept pace with him as he accelerated towards the van, which now had its left indicator on.

The Skoda was now indicating left and moving towards the slip road. Shepherd could imagine the van driver cursing, wondering what the Skoda was playing at. He'd find out soon enough.

'Alpha leaving the motorway,' said Sharpe. 'Tango is following.'

'Bravo now leaving the motorway,' said Shepherd, flipping his turn indicator on and still accelerating.

'Charlie now leaving the motorway,' said Owen in Shepherd's earpiece.

They were all driving along the ramp now, curving to the left.

'Hard stop in five, four, three, two, one,' said Sharpe, then he slammed on the brakes. The Transit van braked too but the driver's reactions were slow and he shunted into the back of the Skoda.

Shepherd came up behind the van close enough to stop it from reversing but leaving enough space for the rear doors to be opened.

The Range Rover shot by Shepherd's BMW and then braked hard, the tyres squealing on the tarmac. The doors flew open and the CTSFOs piled out, moving quickly and decisively, the result of hundreds of hours of training.

Shepherd grabbed his gun, stepped out of the BMW and took aim at the rear doors.

Brett and Wilshire had their Sig Sauer SG516s up against their shoulders, aiming at the driver and the front passenger. Brett stayed where he was as Wilsher moved around the front of the van. They were all wearing black baseball caps with POLICE on the front.

'Armed police, hands in the air!' shouted Brett.

Owen and Reilly rushed to the rear doors. Reilly pulled open the right hand door and Owen stepped forward, his carbine at the ready. 'Armed police, hands in the air!' he yelled.

Reilly had her gun up now. 'Armed police, stay where you are!' she shouted.

There were four men in the back of the van, all in a state of shock. They raised their hands, eyes and mouths wide open.

'Out of the van and lie down on the floor!' shouted Owen.

Sharpe and Ajazi, were out of the Skoda now. Ajazi walked to the back of the van and shouted at the men in Albanian.

One by one they jumped down from the back of the van and lay on the ground, arms outstretched.

Ajazi continued to shout at them in their own language.

Shepherd moved forward, covering the men with his Glock.

Owen was on his radio now, calling in the Bedfordshire Police ARV and van.

The driver and front seat passenger climbed out and lay face down on the ground. They began talking to each other in Albanian and Brett shouted at them to shut up.

Reilly let her carbine hang on its sling and she pulled half a dozen white zip ties from her pocket. She used them to bind the wrists of the Albanians. Brett did the same to the Albanians at the front of the van.

A grey BMW X5 pulled up, tyres squealing and three armed cops piled out, guns at the ready. They fanned out, guns pointed at the prostate Albanians.

'Gun!' shouted Reilly. She pulled a Glock from the waistband of one of the Albanians and handed it to one of the Bedfordshire armed cops.

Ajazi went over to Marku and dragged him to his feet. He and Sharpe took him over to the Skoda and put him into the back seat.

A Mercedes Sprinter police van arrived and uniformed Bedfordshire cops put the Albanians in the back. Less than ten minutes after Sharpe had jammed on his brakes, the slip road was clear and Shepherd and the CTSFOs were heading back to London.

440

89

The woman said that she was a BBC journalist, and she was in full flow, poring scorn on her employers for not doing enough to decry the actions of the IDF in Gaza. 'Women and children are dying, homes are being razed to the ground, hospitals are being destroyed!' she shouted. 'The BBC watches genocide taking place and does nothing to stop it. Shame on them! Shame on them!' The crowd bayed its approval.

The woman was in her late twenties, wearing a black jihab over a dark suit. She was standing outside the entrance to Broadcasting House — home to the BBC — in Portland Square, flanked by four young men with black and white scarves around their necks. Behind them was a line of more than a dozen men and women wearing Muslim clothes and holding aloft placards calling for Palestine to be freed. She spoke accentless English and White figured she had probably been born in the UK, but as she ranted he heard nothing but contempt for the UK, its government, its institutions and its people, a contempt that was echoed by the tens of thousands of people around him. The more she spoke the less he recognised the country that she was describing, but she had the support of the protesters and before long the street was echoing with a chant of 'Free Palestine, Free Palestine.'

There was no sign of the imams Salim Dabush and Nasim Halawah. The main speeches were going to be at Trafalgar Square, a thirty minute walk away so White was expecting them to be there. By then the crowds would have swollen to more than a hundred thousand protesters, but White had no interest in them. He only cared about Dabush and Halawah.

90

Shepherd arrived back in London as the protesters began to move from Portland Place, heading south to Trafalgar Square, where a podium surrounded by Palestinian flags had already been erected with a sound system including half a dozen six feet high loudspeakers. He drove to Charing Cross Police Station, followed by Gerry Owen and the CTSFOs in the black Range Rover. As he and the CTSFOs drove through the entrance to the underground car park at the rear of the building, crowds were already gathering amid chants of 'Free Palestine' and 'Globalize the intifada'.

By the time Shepherd and the CTSFOs left the car park, Trafalgar Square was bursting at the seams with protesters, a sea of black and white scarfs, Palestinian flags and placards, most of which appeared to have been professionally printed.

There were police officers around the square, marked by their fluorescent jackets, but they stood in groups and seemed reluctant to interact with the demonstrators. It was a marked contrast to the way they dealt with football supporters, where the Met thought nothing of using horses, dogs and the threat of batons and arrest to control unruly fans. The fact that the Met had been drastically reducing its standards to hit its diversity targets was clearly demonstrated by the number of short, overweight and out of condition constables in ill-fitting fluorescent jackets. Shepherd doubted that many of them would be able to chase down and apprehend a criminal, but as beat cops were a thing of the past in most boroughs, it probably wasn't an issue. They appeared to be there as observers rather than to police the demonstration.

The CTSFOs spread out and moved into the crowd. They all had beanie hats covering their radio earpieces and black and white scarfs tied loosely around their necks.

Shepherd headed towards the podium at the north of the square.

The square was home to Britain's smallest police station. It was at the south-east corner of the square, built in 1926 to hold a single police officer or two prisoners. Back in the day it had a direct phone line to Scotland Yard and a constable could survey the square through a set of narrow windows. Whenever the phone was picked up, an ornamental light at the top of the box would start to flash, summoning nearby constables. These days Westminster City Council used the box to store cleaning equipment and the police kept the square under observation through a plethora of CCTV cameras. When needed they would arrive in Mercedes Sprinter vans with their radios and body cameras rather than on foot and blowing their whistles.

Super recognisers back at GP Ops in Lambeth would be studying the protesters on the CCTV feeds, but so far none of them had identified David White. It was hardly surprising as many of the protesters had covered their faces, either with covid masks or keffiyeh scarves.

A man with a microphone appeared on the podium and a cheer went up. He began thanking everyone for turning up, telling that it was vital that they kept up the pressure on the British Government, that only sanctions and threats would make the Israeli government pull their troops out of Gaza. 'Children are dying every day. Women are dying, mothers are dying. We are witnessing a genocide of the Palestinian people. We want the troops out of Gaza now.'

He began a chant of 'Free Palestine!' that was quickly taken up by the demonstrators.

Shepherd moved through the crowd, his eyes scanning the faces around him. There were placards everywhere calling for Israel to pull out of Gaza, people with their faces painted in the colours of the Palestinian flag, and several banners celebrating the Hamas attacks. A group of women had photographs of paragliders stuck to their backs, a clear reference to the armed paragliders that had flown over the border into Israel.

There were plenty of uniformed police around, but they were huddled together in groups on the periphery of the demonstrations, avoiding eye contact with the protesters.

Shepherd had his hands in his pockets and his beanie hat pulled down over his radio earpiece. He could hear Marty Windle checking in with the various ARVs in the area. The demonstration had been peaceful so far and there had been no arrests. And still the super recognisers hadn't had a single positive sighting.

The crowd had stopped chanting now and a second man had appeared on the podium, an elderly bearded man that Shepherd recognised as a Labour MP. The man punched his fist in the air and started a chant of 'Free Palestine, Israelis Out!' that was soon taken up by the crowd. People began punching the air in time with the MP. Shepherd looked around. He saw a man in a black Puffa jacket with the hood up who wasn't punching the air and Shepherd moved towards him. From the back the man looked to be the size and the build of David White, but the bulky coat made it difficult to be sure.

Shepherd's hand moved towards the zip of his jacket. He was six feet away from the man when Nasim Halawah appeared on the podium and the crowd erupted in cheers. The imam raised his hands in the air and shouted 'Allahu Akbar!' He was wearing a dark blue suit and gleaming black shoes and looked more like a used car salesman than a religious figure.

The crowd echoed the phrase, so loud that Shepherd felt his spine tingle.

He saw the man in the Puffa jacket stiffen. Shepherd moved to the side. It was White. He had a covid mask covering his nose and mouth but it was definitely him. He was probably flashing back to Israel when the Hamas fighters had wreaked havoc screeching that God was great.

The imam was yelling again. 'Free Palestine! Free Palestine!' he shouted, walking back and forth like a rapper winding up his audience. The protesters screamed the phrase back at him. Allahu Akbar! God is great!

Shepherd drew level with White. 'David?' said Shepherd.

White jerked as if he had been stung. He took a step back. Then his left hand emerged from the pocket of his Puffa jacket. He was holding what looked like a hand exerciser and there were wires running from it. 'Don't come near me, Dan,' he said.

'Is that live?' asked Shepherd.

White opened his jacket just enough for him to be able to see the packs of explosive around his waist. There were half a dozen packages that Shepherd could see, each with wires running to it. There was a small switch on White's belt and he flicked it with his thumb. 'It is now,' said White. He moved his hand so that his jacket closed. 'Go away, Dan. Go away now.'

'You don't have to do this, David.'

'Yes I do.' The hand with the trigger disappeared into the pocket of his jacket.

Nick Brett appeared at Spider's shoulder. His hand was inside his jacket but he hadn't pulled out his gun. Shepherd held up a hand. 'It's okay, Nick, we're just talking here.'

Brett nodded but kept his hand inside his jacket.

'You won't just kill Nasim Halawah and Salim Dabush,' Shepherd said to White. 'A lot of people will die, David, and they don't deserve it.'

'Listen to them, Dan. Listen to the hatred. Can't you hear it?'

The crowds were shouting now. 'Free Palestine! End the genocide now!' But Shepherd could hear other shouts too, abuse that was anti-Semetic and hateful. The imam was revelling in it, winding the crowd up.

'I hear it, David. But they're just words.'

'Sticks and stones, is that what you mean? You don't understand the hatred they have for me and my people.'

A second man appeared on the podium, wearing a long robe and blue skull cap. It was imam Salim Dabush. White looked over at the podium. 'You need to go, Dan. This is going to happen whether or not you're here. I'd rather you weren't.'

'You could have killed me at Birmingham Airport but you didn't.'

'I'm sorry about that. Are you okay?'

His concern seemed genuine, which was bizarre considering the situation they were in. 'A few scratches,' said Shepherd. 'It could have been a lot worse, obviously.'

'Please go, Dan. My hand's getting tired.' He turned and took a step towards the podium. Nasim Hala-wah was addressing the crowd now, cursing Israeli soldiers for killing women and children, describing Jews as heartless killers, animals who wouldn't stop until every Muslim had been driven from the Palestinian lands. The Jews needed to be stopped, the man shouted. Stopped by any means necessary. His words were greeted with whoops and cheers.

'I need you to look at me, David!' Shepherd shouted over the noise of the baying crowd. 'Look at me and listen to me.'

'You need to go now, Dan. I don't want to hurt you, but I have to do this.'

Brett moved around so that he was side on to White. White glared at him. 'Stop moving.'

'It's okay, Nick,' said Shepherd. 'David and I are just talking. We can work this out.' He looked back at White. 'You don't have to do this, David, because Hannah isn't dead. Hannah is alive.'

White frowned and turned to look at him. 'What?'

'Hannah is alive. Hamas have her as a hostage.'

White shook his head. 'No, that's impossible. I saw her die.'

'I don't know what you saw, but Hannah is alive. Hamas released six hostages yesterday and during

448

the debriefing they were shown photographs of missing people. Two of the hostages identified Hannah, by name. They saw her and spoke to her. There is no doubt, David. It's her and she is alive.'

White shook his head again.

'I swear to you, it's the truth,' said Shepherd. 'And if everything goes to plan, she'll be released soon. The Israelis are negotiating for the release of the remaining hostages, they've started talking and the Israelis are prepared to make concessions. But you have to stop this now.'

'It's too late, Dan. What's done is done.'

'It's not too late. You can stop this now. We can take you into custody and as soon as Hannah is freed we can arrange for you to meet her.'

White looked around. 'My life is over. After what I've done . . .'

'You're in deep shit, David, there's no denying that. But your life is far from over. A lot of people will understand why you did what you did. After what happened to you and your family, there'll be empathy. And whatever happens in the future, Hannah will need her father. If you die here today, then she'll have lost everything. You are all the family she has left, David. You know what it feels like to have your family taken away from you. Do you want her to go through that?'

White bit down on his lower lip.

Around them the crowds were shouting 'From the river to the sea, Palestine will be free!' — oblivious to the danger in their midst.

'She needs you, David. Hannah needs her father. If you do this now, how is she going to feel? She'll be all alone in the world. Who else is going to help her

449

put her life together? It has to be you. There is no one else.'

White took the trigger from his pocket, frowning as if he was seeing it for the first time. Brett started to pull his gun from its holster and Shepherd caught a glimpse of the butt. 'Nick, no!' said Shepherd. He held his hands up, fingers splayed. 'It's okay.' He looked at White again 'You can stand down, David,' he said, quietly.

'It's too late.'

'It's never too late. You have something to look forward to, David. You can watch your daughter grow into a woman, maybe see her have children. You could become a grandfather. You need to be in their life, too. You need to explain about what happened, not just let them read about it on the internet.'

White looked back at Shepherd. 'Are you lying to me, Dan?'

'Absolutely not.'

'Cross your heart?'

Shepherd couldn't tell if the man was being serious, but decided to give him the benefit of the doubt. He made the sign of the cross on his heart. 'I swear.'

White forced a smile but he was close to tears. 'I'll trust you,' he said.

Shepherd heard running footsteps off to his left.

White reached down to the vest with his right hand. He stuck out his thumb and smiled at Shepherd. 'Okay,' he said.

'Armed police!' shouted Reilly over Shepherd's left shoulder. 'Put your hands in the air!'

White used his thumb to flick the switch.

Reilly fired twice, in quick succession. The first bullet hit White in the chest, the second in the head.

He fell backwards and hit the ground, hard. People began screaming in panic, pushing to get away.

Shepherd looked over at Reilly. 'Rebecca, what have you done?' he said.

'He was about to detonate the bomb!'

Shepherd shook his head. 'He was deactivating it.'

Reilly's eyes widened and she began to tremble as she stared at White's body. Blood was pooling on the flagstones around him. People were screaming in terror and running in all directions. Shepherd put his hand on her shoulder. 'We have to go,' he said. Owen and Wilsher ran up, guns drawn.

'What happened?' asked Owen. He scowled and swore under his breath as Shepherd filled him in.

91

Paramedics arrived within minutes of the shooting. They were still working on White as they loaded him into an ambulance and sped away, blue lights flashing and siren wailing. Shepherd and Brett whisked Reilly out of the square and in to the Charing Cross Police Station car park.

Reilly was shaking as she sat in the back of the Range Rover. A good stiff drink might have gone some way to calming her down, but that wasn't an option, she would have to be interviewed under caution within the hour by members of the Metropolitan Police's Directorate of Professional Standards.

Gerry Owen had stayed to deal with the uniformed cops who had run towards the sound of the shots. Owen had removed his beanie, whipped out a police baseball cap from his pocket and put it on, then raised his hands above his head. Wilsher and Brett had done the same. Through his earpiece, Shepherd could hear Marty Windle summoning armed response vehicles to the square. The podium was empty now, the speakers had all been rushed out of the square.

Brett had taken Reilly's Glock from her and put it in the Range Rover's gun safe. Having fired her weapon, Reilly would now be treated as guilty until proved innocent. An armed police officer had no special legal status when they fired their weapon and were subject to criminal law and the law of self defence. Under the law they were legally responsible for every shot they fired, and for a shot to be legal the officer had to prove that that they were acting in the defence of themselves or others and that their actions were proportionate and reasonable. Shepherd was sure that Reilly would be okay — section three of the 1967 Criminal Law Act made the law clear — 'A person may use such force as is reasonable in the prevention of crime.' Reilly believed that White was about to detonate his bomb and that lives would have been lost, so she hadn't committed an offence. But she was going to have to live with the fact that she had killed a man who was in the process of surrendering.

Shepherd sat next to her in the back of the Range Rover. She was slouched in her seat staring out of the window and sniffing. 'I'm fucked,' she said.

'No, you're not.'

'He wasn't going to detonate the bomb.'

'You didn't know that.'

'If I'd just waited . . .' She wiped her nose with the back of her hand.

'You saw him with his hand on a switch,' said Shepherd. 'So far as you knew, that would have detonated the bomb. That's all you have to say, Rebecca.'

She turned to look at him, her eyes filled with tears. 'But I know the truth, don't I?'

'Only with hindsight. Only because I told you. At the time, in the moment, you did the right thing.'

She shook her head. 'I didn't. You know I didn't.'

'Based on the knowledge you had and based on what you saw, you did exactly what I would have done in the same position.'

She frowned. 'Really?'

Shepherd looked her in the eyes. 'Really.' It wasn't a lie. She hadn't been talking to White, she hadn't heard the conversation prior to him reaching for the switch.

In a perfect world she might have trusted Shepherd and followed his lead, but the world wasn't perfect and Reilly had had less than a second to process what she was seeing and take the action that she deemed appropriate. It was hard to fault her, and Shepherd was confident that after Professional Standards had investigated it would be declared a valid and justified shooting. Reilly wouldn't face charges, there'd be no stain on her record, but Shepherd doubted that she would ever be the same again. Taking a life was never easy, no matter what the justification.

92

THREE WEEKS LATER

Shepherd finished his third circuit of Battersea Park. He glanced at his watch. The third circuit had been his fastest. He was wearing a grey sweatshirt and a black tracksuit. As usual he was wearing boots for his run. In the real world you never had chance to change into shorts and trainers before giving chase so it made sense to run as much as possible in regular footwear. He slowed and decided to head for home. As he jogged along the path he saw a face he recognised ahead of him. Joel Schwartz was a small man, barely five feet six, with pointed features and a thin black comb-over that did little to conceal his bald patch. He was wearing a shabby brown raincoat with the collar turned up, and as Shepherd got close he held up a hand to stop him.'Mr Shepherd, can I have a word?' he said.

Shepherd stopped and began jogging slowly on the spot. 'Sure.'

'My name is Joel Schwartz . . .'

'I know who you are, Joel. I've seen your file.'

Schwartz nodded and smiled. 'Ah, then it's true about your magical memory,' he said. 'You never forget a face, right?'

'How can I help you, Joel?'

Schwartz reached inside his coat and took out a small manila envelope. 'This is a token of my country's appreciation for the help you have given.'

Shepherd stopped jogging. 'Help, what help?' He looked around. Schwartz was still holding out the envelope and it would be a perfect photo opportunity, a chance to snap a picture of Shepherd accepting a bribe from a foreign power.

'This isn't a set up, Mr Shepherd. It's a genuine thank you from a grateful nation which doesn't have too many friends at the moment.'

'I can't take your money, you must know that.'

Schwartz smiled. 'It's not money, Mr Shepherd.' He waved at a nearby bench. 'Why don't we sit?'

Shepherd looked around but he didn't see anyone with a camera nearby. 'Okay. You've piqued my curiosity,' he said.

The two men walked over to the bench and sat down. Schwartz still had the envelope in his hand and again he held it out to Shepherd. Shepherd shook his head. 'I was always taught never to accept gifts from strangers,' he said. 'Especially from strangers who work for Mossad.'

'I work for the Israeli Embassy, Mr Shepherd.'

'I've seen your file, Joel. I know exactly who you work for.'

Schwartz gave him a small bow. 'I shall not argue the point, we can simply agree to disagree,' he said. 'But please, this is for you. From a grateful ally.'

'Grateful for what?'

Schwartz smiled. 'Remember the little girl you rescued in Gaza?'

'There were several.'

'This one was called Naomi. Her parents were killed and she was taken hostage. You got her out.'

Shepherd nodded. 'Yes. Naomi. Is she okay?'

'She is fit and well, but obviously still traumatised.

456

She is with her grandparents now.'

'That's good. She went through a lot.'

'Her grandfather is number two at the Israeli Ministry of Defence,' said Schwartz. 'His daughter and her husband were murdered, as you say, and he is now taking care of her. He wants to thank you and this is a token of that gratitude.' He pushed the envelope towards Shepherd.

Shepherd shook his head again. 'I didn't read about her family connections,' he said.

'You will have read very little about her,' said Schwartz. 'Her identity is being kept under wraps. For obvious reasons.'

Shepherd shook his head. 'Secret bloody squirrel.'

'It can be tiring, can't it, keeping so many secrets?' He held out the envelope again. 'Please, take this. And accept it with our thanks.'

'I didn't do anything,' said Shepherd. 'If anything it was another of the hostages that helped her.'

'David White?'

'Exactly.' Shepherd frowned as he stared at Schwartz for several seconds. 'You know about White.' It was a statement, not a question.

'That is another reason for our desire to reward you,' said Schwartz. 'You could have killed David White, you could have shot him in Trafalgar Square, but you chose not to. You tried to negotiate with him, and you succeeded. You persuaded him not to detonate the bomb. You saved a lot of lives that day.'

'He still died, Joel.'

A slight smile flashed across Schwartz's face. 'Or did he?'

Shepherd wrinkled his nose. 'Of course he did. What a stupid thing to say. I was there. I saw him die.'

'You saw him being shot, Mr Shepherd. There's a difference. If it had been you who had fired the shots, yes, David White would almost certainly be dead. But you didn't fire the shots, it was an armed police officer and she was under a lot of pressure.'

'She hit him twice. A double tap.'

'Indeed. One shot in the shoulder and another to the head. But neither were fatal. Life changing, but not fatal.'

Shepherd frowned. 'What are you saying?'

'I'm saying that David White was shot but his injuries were not fatal. He was taken straight to hospital and the doctors managed to save his life. Your bosses decided to pretend that he was dead, because that meant there wouldn't be a trial. We all know how damaging it would be to put him in the witness box. The story is being given to the Press that it was a crazed lone wolf with right-wing connections and mental health issues and that said lone wolf is now dead.'

Shepherd leaned towards him. 'You're telling me that David White is alive?'

'He was flown out of the UK yesterday and is now in Israel. In a hospital in Tel Aviv to be precise. We hope to reunite him with his daughter soon. His recovery will take time, but he is in good hands. And MI5 knows that its secrets are safe with us.'

'Who else knows about this? Does Giles Pritchard know?'

'That's not for me to say.'

Shepherd's eyes hardened. 'Don't mess me around, Joel. Does Pritchard know?'

Schwartz looked around as if he feared being overheard. 'He does. But he's one of a very small number of people who are privy to the knowledge. This was

458

all done at the very highest level.' He held out the envelope again. 'We owe you a debt of gratitude, Mr Shepherd. So please accept this.'

Shepherd took the envelope and weighed it in his hand. If it did contain cash, there wasn't much of it. He opened the flap and slid out the contents. It was a navy blue passport. On the front cover was the Israeli national emblem — a seven stick candelabra flanked by olive branches — with the words 'מדינת ישראל' and 'STATE OF ISRAEL' in Hebrew and English. Shepherd frowned as he opened the passport. It contained his photograph, date and place of birth, and his signature. His frown deepened. The signature looked genuine, but of course it couldn't possibly be.

'What is this?' he asked.

'You know what it is,' said Schwartz.

'It's a passport. In my name.'

'Oh, it's more than that, Mr Shepherd. It's citizenship. You are now an Israeli citizen and entitled to all the benefits that go with citizenship. Should you ever need a home or a refuge in the future, you have it. Israel will be that home. And Israel never extradites its citizens to another country, unlike the United Kingdom, which will happily send its people to be tried in other jurisdictions. You can trust Israel, Mr Shepherd, in a way that you can no longer trust your own country.' He stood up. 'And with that, I shall bid you good day.'

Shepherd held out the passport. 'I can't accept this.'

'Yes you can, Mr Shepherd. Whether you choose to accept it is of course up to you. But it is a genuine gesture of thanks and respect, one which we hope you will accept in the spirit it was given.' He nodded and turned and walked away.

459

Shepherd watched him go. Eventually he looked down at the passport, trying to work out what he should do with it. Keep it or throw it away? He stood up and started walking back to his building. This needed some thought.

Other titles published by Ulverscroft:

CLEAN KILL

Stephen Leather

Terrorists have shot down a British helicopter in West Africa and taken the crew hostage. Their lives are on the line and the British government is refusing to negotiate. The pilot is Liam Shepherd, and only his father — Dan 'Spider' Shepherd of MI5 — can help.

Shepherd and an SAS team fly out to the badlands of Mali to rescue the kidnapped Brits.

But the mission takes Shepherd away from an investigation in a high security prison that is about to explode into violence. Hundreds of lives are at risk, and Shepherd is running out of time . . .